CHAP-BOOKS
OF THE EIGHTEENTH
CENTURY

JOHN ASHTON, b. 1834, ed.

CHAP-BOOKS
OF THE EIGHTEENTH
CENTURY

NEW FOREWORD BY
VICTOR NEUBURG

AUGUSTUS M. KELLEY, PUBLISHERS
NEW YORK 1970

First published in 1882. This edition published in the U.S.A.
in 1970 by Augustus M. Kelley, 1140 Broadway, New York,
N.Y. 10001.
Foreword © Victor Neuburg, 1970.
L.C.C. card no. 70-111202
SBN 678 08011 9

Reproduced and Printed in Great Britain by
Redwood Press Limited,
Trowbridge & London.

FOREWORD

The chapbook world is still to a very large extent unexplored. "I hope", wrote John Ashton in his Introduction in 1882, "I have succeeded in producing a book which is at once both amusing and instructive, besides having rescued these almost forgotten booklets from the limbo into which they were fast descending." The motives implied in amusement and instruction were those we should expect to find in the late Victorian age. It was a period characterized by a great love for antiquarianism, when besides Ashton's many books, Sabine Baring Gould, P.H. Ditchfield, John Timbs and others were writing; and not only were the energies of nineteenth century antiquarians devoted to folklore of all kinds, but the history of individual parishes, of inn signs and a host of other subjects, were also chronicled with a bewildering amount of detail.

It would be easy to deprecate all this activity. There is perhaps a tendency to dismiss much of this work as pleasant enough, but of little real value to the scholar; but such a view would be an over-simplification. The great merit of antiquarians like those I have mentioned is that they sank shafts into a number of important fields of enquiry, and have preserved facts and attitudes which, if it had not been for their industry, would never have survived at all. If their methods were crude and their presentation of material less precise than it ought to have been, there remains none the less much that is of value to us. Paradoxically, this very lack of precision has made its contribution. Because so little discrimination was shown, because so many examples were included, we are left with a vast amount of source material to which it becomes possible to address questions which are significant for contemporary historians.

This was the achievement of the nineteenth century antiquaries: they have bequeathed to us a priceless mass of information which is the raw material of social history. The debt in this respect that we owe to them has hardly been acknowledged, and in the present climate of computerised research it is unlikely to be. So much of the fragmentary and scattered knowledge of past social life to be found in their books is of unequal value; indeed, much of it is scarcely fact at all, but rather an indication of attitudes and values shedding an oblique light upon patterns of behaviour and the assumptions by which men lived their lives in the past. This is all an important part of what Edward Thompson has called "the mental universe of the village", and this is emphatically not a theme which lends itself to statistical analysis. We can aim to understand the world of feeling in this context, rather than to assess it; and having stated this in general terms, let me relate it to chapbooks.

These little books more than any other evidence we have open a window on the world of the eighteenth century poor. In chapbooks we find the tales which enthralled them, the ballads which had been passed on from one generation to another, and a good deal of the lore of the weather and of primitive medicine which was part of the background which they took for granted. It is hard to envisage a more important source for the history of popular culture.

The term "popular culture", however, has connotations other than those which are connected somewhat loosely with traditional tales, ballads, folklore and so on. The eighteenth century was a crucial period in its development, for not only did its closing decades bear decisive witness to some of the more striking evidences of industrialism, but this was also the century in which the traditional culture of England's peasantry was challenged by the new way of life which industrialism brought and also by the enormous spread of printing and of the education which enabled the poor—at least a large number of them—to cope more or less adequately with the printed word. The means by which they were enabled to do this were the charity schools and dame schools where—in the case of the latter institutions, for a trifling fee—the elements of reading, and sometimes writing, were taught.

The textbooks which were used offer striking evidence about the teaching of reading. In the first place, there were a surprisingly large number of different ones, and some of these went through a succession of editions, testifying not only to their popularity but also to how widespread instruction in reading was. Moreover, the authors of several of these textbooks were closely connected with charity schools. Thomas Dyche taught in one. His *A Guide to the English Tongue in Two Parts* was first published in 1709, and was still being reprinted more than one hundred years later. Thomas Dilworth's *New Guide to the English Tongue* enjoyed a similar popularity. So too did *The English Instructor* by Henry Dixon, who taught in charity schools in London and Bath. Francis Fox was Vicar of Reading, and his *An Introduction to Spelling and Reading* was originally written for the charity school in the town, but in fact it turned out to be a best selling textbook, and many editions of it were published. *A New Grammar* by Anne Slack (née Fisher) first appeared in Newcastle in 1750, and it ran through edition after edition for more than fifty years. These were the best known textbooks. Others could be added to the list, but it is enough in the present context simply to draw attention to the amount of material which was available, and to argue from this that the teaching of reading was very far from being uncommon.

How is the effectiveness of this educational endeavour to be measured? Or to put the question in another way: to what extent was the ability to read a common achievement amongst the poor of the eighteenth century? Attempts have recently been made to suggest that literacy in pre-industrial England can be estimated by counting the signatures in parish registers of bridegrooms who could sign their names. This seems to me to be an entirely misleading procedure. In the first place, contemporary writers on popular education made a clear distinction between the arts of reading and of writing; in the second, it must be remembered that within the context of the eighteenth century the need to be able to write would have arisen rarely, if ever, for the poor, while appeals to them through the printed word in the form of tracts were not uncommon even from the early years of the century.

The existence of a widely diffused popular literature suggests strongly that commercial printers, no less than philanthropists, made certain assumptions about the ability of poor men and women to read. The mere presence of books may indicate nothing more than a commercial or a pious endeavour based upon fundamental misconceptions about society. An *increase* in the number of books available, on the other hand, points unmistakably to the existence of more and more readers; and it can be demonstrated that there was such an increase throughout the eighteenth century, during a time when the number of printers and publishers engaged in the chapbook trade, in both London and the provinces, also increased very considerably. It is this fact which provides the most valuable clue we have to the extent of reading amongst the poor at this time.

John Ashton did not, of course, have anything to say about significances of this kind which we can now attach to chapbooks; but because, with religious and admonitory tracts, they formed virtually the only reading matter for the poor, and because he made so many of them available for study, he has shown us their richness as a source for educational and social history. As examples of popular taste, they are superb. The vigorous woodcuts, and the prose which rarely matches their liveliness, offers a unique view of the imaginative world of lowly men and women during the eighteenth century. Here are the heroes and legends of a lost antiquity, the lore and superstitions of the past, together with scraps of history and occasional versions of popular novels. This is very much a "people's literature", with its roots firmly in the life of those who read and enjoyed it.

The tone of the eighteenth century chapbook was emphatically unsophisticated, and there are few, if any, social or political overtones to be found. Even *The History of the Royal Martyr King Charles the First* (p.398) or *England's Black Tribunal; Being the Characters of King Charles the First, and the Nobility that Suffer'd for him* (p.403) perpetuate conventional attitudes to the Civil War and emphasise the drama of the King's execution; and neither is sufficiently of interest to Ashton for him to quote from it in extenso. If, then, we seek recognisable or even rudimentary political attitudes in chapbooks, we shall do so in vain. There is no hint in them of either political or religious awareness except in the most trivialised and romantic accounts of Queen Elizabeth's love for the Earl of Essex (p.396), or *The Story of King Edward III and the Countess of Salisbury* (p.390). And precisely because so much of their subject matter is trivial, chapbooks are interesting. So often triviality reflects accurately the accepted modes and assumptions in society, and it is this shifting, imprecise and largely undocumented area of human activity that is most difficult for the historian to reconstruct.

What chapbooks can show us, then, is the kind of popular literature which informed some part of the inner world of working men and women. The unsophisticated nature of such a popular literature was almost entirely a result of its development from the ballads, romances and lore of the Middle Ages, and does not therefore imply a conscious rejection of critical and social themes. With its absence of controversy and lack of even the most rudimentary radical attitudes, the eighteenth century chapbook stands in sharp distinction to the street ballad of the nineteenth century city, which did exhibit political and religious points of view in a way that was both sophisticated and often complex.

The difference between these two worlds is immense; and it is, I think, not too fanciful to suggest that the chapbook provided the means by which men and women who had achieved a bare literacy, in the sense that they could read a page of print, were enabled to make the cultural leap into the industrial world of the nineteenth century. Without the eighteenth century chapbook opportunities for reading would have been very much more restricted, and thus might this skill have withered amongst those whose poverty precluded the purchase of any literature other than these little books available so cheaply, and designed so specifically to appeal to them. As it was, the skill developed; and as the nineteenth century dawned the mere fact that they were able to read political pamphlets meant that politics at working class level were not simply a matter of a demagogue haranguing a mob. Radicals were able to disseminate their ideas through the medium of the printed word, with every hope of reaching a large number of readers. Had this not been so, the history of the working class might have been very different, and their politics might have remained at the primitive level of riot and disturbances. Clearly, other factors were at work here: differing economic and social pressures were influential in making the working class, but the factor of literacy was an important one.

These are historical questions of which John Ashton was unaware, and one suspects that he would have had little understanding of them, and even less sympathy. We may, however, salute him as a pioneer who made available for study a whole range of material. If he was regardless of its social and political implications, this fact does not in any way invalidate our debt to him, nor make his achievement any less praise-worthy.

Victor E. Neuberg.

A CHAPMAN.

From "The Cries and Habits of the City of London," by M. Lauron, 1709.

CHAP-BOOKS

OF

THE EIGHTEENTH CENTURY

WITH

FACSIMILES, NOTES, AND INTRODUCTION

BY

JOHN ASHTON

London

CHATTO AND WINDUS, PICCADILLY

1882

INTRODUCTION.

ALTHOUGH these Chap-books are very curious, and on many accounts interesting, no attempt has yet been made to place them before the public in a collected form, accompanied by the characteristic engravings, without which they would lose much of their value. They are the relics of a happily past age, one which can never return, and we, in this our day of cheap, plentiful, and good literature, can hardly conceive a time when in the major part of this country, and to the larger portion of its population, these little Chap-books were nearly the only mental pabulum offered. Away from the towns, newspapers were rare indeed, and not worth much when obtainable—poor little flimsy sheets such as nowadays we should not dream of either reading or publishing, with very little news in them, and that consisting principally of war items, and foreign news, whilst these latter books were carried in the packs of the pedlars, or Chapmen, to every village, and to every home.

Previous to the eighteenth century, these men generally carried ballads, as is so well exemplified in the " Winter's Tale," in Shakespeare's inimitable conception, Autolycus. The servant (Act iv. sc. 3) well describes his stock : " He hath songs, for man, or woman, of all sizes ; no milliner can so fit his customers with gloves. He has the prettiest love songs for maids ; so without bawdry, which is strange ; with such delicate burdens of ' dildos' and 'fadings :' 'jump her' and 'thump her ;'" and where some stretch-mouthed rascal would, as it were, mean mischief, and break a foul gap into the matter, he makes the maid to answer, ' Whoop, do me no harm, good man ;' puts him off, slights him, with ' Whoop, do me no.

harm, good man.'" And Autolycus, himself, hardly exaggerates
the style of his wares, judging by those which have come down
to us, when he praises the ballads : " How a usurer's wife was
brought to bed of twenty money-bags at a burden ; and how
she longed to eat adders' heads, and toads carbonadoed ; " and
" of a fish, that appeared upon the coast, on Wednesday the
fourscore of April, forty thousand fathom above water, and
sung this ballad against the hard hearts of maids ; " for the
wonders of both ballads, and early Chap-books, are manifold,
and bear strange testimony to the ignorance, and credulity, of
their purchasers. These ballads and Chap-books have, luckily
for us, been preserved by collectors, and although they are
scarce, are accessible to readers in that national blessing, the
British Museum. There the Roxburghe, Luttrell, Bagford, and
other collections of black-letter ballads are easily obtainable
for purposes of study, and, although the Chap-books, to the
uninitiated (owing to the difficulties of the Catalogue), are not
quite so easy of access, yet there they exist, and are a splendid
series—it is impossible to say a complete one, because some
are unique, and are in private hands, but so large, especially
from the middle to the close of the last century, as to be
virtually so.

I have confined my self entirely to the books of the last
century, as, previous to it, there were few, and almost all black-
letter tracts have been published or noted ; and, after it, the
books in circulation were chiefly very inferior reprints of those
already published. As they are mostly undated, I have found
some difficulty in attributing dates to them, as the guides,
such as type, wood engravings, etc., are here fallacious, many—
with the exception of Dicey's series—having been printed with
old type, and any wood block being used, if at all resembling
the subject. I have not taken any dated in the Museum
Catalogue as being of this present century, even though internal
evidence showed they were earlier. The Museum dates are
admittedly fallacious and merely approximate, and nearly all
are queried. For instance, nearly the whole of the beautiful
Aldermary Churchyard (first) editions are put down as

1750 ?—a manifest impossibility, for there could not have been such an eruption of one class of publication from one firm in one year—and another is dated 1700 ?, although the book from which it is taken was not published until 1703. Still, as a line must be drawn somewhere, I have accepted these quasi dates, although such acceptation has somewhat narrowed my scheme, and deprived the reader of some entertainment, and I have published nothing which is not described in the Museum Catalogue as being between the years 1700 and 1800.

In fact, the Chap-book proper did not exist before the former date, unless the Civil War and political tracts can be so termed. Doubtless these were hawked by the pedlars, but they were not these pennyworths, suitable to everybody's taste, and within the reach of anybody's purse, owing to their extremely low price, which must, or ought to have, extracted every available copper in the village, when the Chapman opened his budget of brand-new books.

In the seventeenth, and during the first quarter of the eighteenth century, the popular books were generally in 8vo form, *i.e.* they consisted of a sheet of paper folded in eight, and making a book of sixteen pages ; but during the other seventy-five years they were almost invariably 12mo, *i.e.* a sheet folded into twelve, and making twenty-four pages. After 1800 they rapidly declined. The type and wood blocks were getting worn out, and never seem to have been renewed ; publishers got less scrupulous, and used any wood blocks without reference to the letter-press, until, after Grub Street authors had worked their wicked will upon them, Catnach buried them in a dishonoured grave.

But while they were in their prime, they mark an epoch in the literary history of our nation, quite as much as the higher types of literature do, and they help us to gauge the intellectual capacity of the lower and lower middle classes of the last century.

The Chapman *proper*, too, is a thing of the past, although we still have hawkers, and the travelling "credit drapers," or "tallymen," yet penetrate every village ; but the Chapman, as described by Cotsgrave in his "Dictionarie of the French and English Tongues" (London, 1611), no longer exists. He is there faithfully portrayed under the heading "BissoÜART, m. A paultrie Pedlar, who in a long packe or maund (which he carries for the most part open, and (hanging from his necke) before him) hath Almanacks, Bookes of News, or other trifling ware to sell."

Shakespeare uses the word in a somewhat different sense, making him more of a general dealer, as in "Love's Labour's Lost," Act ii. sc. 1 :

> "*Princess of France.* Beauty is bought by judgment of the eye,
> Not uttered by base sale of Chapmen's tongues."

And in "Troilus and Cressida," Act iv. sc. 1 :

> "*Paris.* Fair Diomed, you do as Chapmen do,
> Dispraise the thing that you desire to buy."

Unlike his modern congener, the colporteur, the Chapman's life seems to have been an exceptionally hard one, especially if we can trust a description, professedly by one of the fraternity, in "The History of John Cheap the Chapman," a Chap-book published early in the present century. He appears, on his own confession, to have been as much of a rogue as he well could be with impunity and without absolutely transgressing the law, and, as his character was well known, very few roofs would shelter him, and he had to sleep in barns, or even with the pigs. He had to take out a licence, and was classed in old bye-laws and proclamations as "Hawkers, Vendors, Pedlars, petty Chapmen, *and unruly people.*" In more modern times the literary Mercury dropped the somewhat besmirched title of Chapmen, and was euphoniously designated the "Travelling," "Flying," or "Running Stationer."

Little could he have dreamed that his little penny books would ever have become scarce, and prized by book collectors, and fetch high prices whenever the rare occasion happened that they were exposed for sale. I have taken out the prices paid in 1845 and 1847 for nine volumes of them, bought at as many different sales. These nine volumes contain ninety-nine Chap-books, and the price paid for them all was £24 13s. 6d., or an average of five shillings each—surely not a bad increment in a hundred years on the outlay of a penny; but then, these volumes were bought very cheaply, as some of their delighted purchasers record.

The principal factory for them, and from which certainly nine-tenths of them emanated, was No. 4, Aldermary Church-yard, afterwards removed to Bow Churchyard, close by. The names of the proprietors were William and Cluer Dicey—afterwards C. Dicey only—and they seem to have come from North-ampton, as, in "Hippolito and Dorinda," 1720, the firm is described as "Raikes and Dicey, Northampton;" and this con-nection was not allowed to lapse, for we see, nearly half a century later, that "The Conquest of France" was "printed and sold by C. Dicey in Bow Church Yard : sold also at his Warehouse in Northampton."

From Dicey's house came nearly all the original Chap-books, and I have appended as perfect a list as I can make, amounting to over 120, of their publications. Unscrupulous booksellers, however, generally pirated them very soon after issue, especially at Newcastle, where certainly the next largest trade was done in this class of books. The Newcastle editions are rougher in every way, in engravings, type, and paper, than the very well got up little books of Dicey's, but I have fre-quently taken them in preference, because of the superior quaintness of the engravings.

After the commencement of the present century reading became more popular, and the following, which are only the names of *a few* places where Chap-books were published, show the great and widely spread interest taken in their production :—Edinburgh, Glasgow, Paisley, Kilmarnock, Penrith, Stirling, Falkirk, Dublin, York, Stokesley, Warrington, Liverpool, Ban-bury, Aylesbury, Durham, Dumfries, Birmingham, Wolver-hampton, Coventry, Whitehaven, Carlisle, Worcester, Cirencester, etc., etc. And they flourished, for they formed nearly the sole literature of the poor, until the *Penny Magazine* and Chambers's penny Tracts and Miscellanies gave them their deathblow, and relegated them to the book-shelves of collectors.

That these histories were known and prized in Queen Anne's time, is evidenced by the following quotation from the *Weekly Comedy*, January 22, 1708 :—" I'll give him Ten of the largest Folio Books in my Study, Letter'd on the Back, and bound in *Calves Skin*. He shall have some of those that are the most scarce and rare among the Learned, and therefore may be of greater use to so *Voluminous* an *Author;* there is '*Tom Thumb*' with *Annotations* and *Critical Remarks*, two volumes in folio. The ' *Comical Life and Tragical Death of the Old Woman that was Hang'd for Drowning herself in* Ratcliffe High-Way :' One large Volume, it being the 20th Edition, with many new Additions and Observations. '*Jack and the Gyants ;*' formerly Printed in a small Octavo, but now Improv'd to three Folio Volumes by that Elaborate Editor, *Forestus, Ignotus Nicholaus Ignoramus Sampsonius ;* then there is ' *The King and the Cobler*,' a Noble piece of Antiquity, and fill'd with many Pleasant Modern Intrigues fit to divert the most Curious."

And Steele, writing in the *Tatler*, No. 95, as Isaac Bickerstaff, and speaking of his godson, a little boy of eight years of age, says, " I found he had very much turned his studies, for about twelve months past, into the lives and adventures of Don Bellianis of Greece, Guy of Warwick, The Seven Champions, and other historians of that age. . . . He would tell you the mismanagements of John Hickerthrift, find fault with the passionate temper in Bevis of Southampton and loved St. George for being Champion of England."

As before said, their great variety adapted them for every purchaser, and they may be roughly classed under the following heads :—Religious, Diabolical, Supernatural, Superstitious, Romantic, Humorous, Legendary, Historical, Biographical, and Criminal, besides those which cannot fairly be put in any of the above categories ; and under this classification and in this sequence I have taken them. The Religious, strictly so called, are the fewest, the subjects, such as " Dr. Faustus," etc., connected with his Satanic Majesty being more exciting, and probably paying better; whilst the Supernatural, such as "The Duke of Buckingham's Father's Ghost," "The Guildford Ghost," etc., trading upon man's credulity and his love of the marvellous, afford a far larger assortment. About the same amount of popularity may be given to the Superstitious Chapbooks—those relating to fortune telling and the interpretation of Dreams and Moles, etc. But they were nothing like the favourites those of the Romantic School were. These dear old romances, handed down from the days when printing was not—some, like "Jack the Giant Killer," of Norse extraction; others, like "Tom Hickathrift," "Guy of Warwick," "Bevis of Hampton," etc., records of the doughty deeds of local champions; and others, again, "Reynard the Fox," "Valentine and Orson," and "Fortunatus," of foreign birth— hit the popular taste, and many were the editions of them. Naturally, however, the Humorous stories were the prime favourites. The Jest-books, pure and simple, are, from their extremely coarse witticisms, utterly incapable of being reproduced for general reading nowadays, and the whole of them are more or less highly spiced; but even here were shades of humour to suit all classes, from the solemn foolery of the "Wise Men of Gotham," or the "World turned upside down," to the rollicking fun of "Tom Tram," "The Fryer and the Boy," or "Jack Horner." In reading these books we must not, however, look upon them from our present point of view. Whether men and women are better now than they used to be, is a moot point, but things used to be spoken of openly, which are now never whispered, and no harm was done, nor offence taken; so the broad humour of the jest-books was, after all, only exuberant fun, and many of the *bonnes histoires* are extremely laughable, though to our own thinking equally indelicate. The old legends still held sway, and I have given four—"Adam Bell," "Robin Hood," "The Blind Beggar of Bethnal Green," and "The Children in the Wood"—all of them remarkable for their illustrations. History has a wide range from "Fair Rosamond," to "The Royal Martyr," Charles I., whilst, naturally, such books as "Robinson Crusoe," "George

Barnwell," and a host of criminal literature found ready purchasers.

I have not included Calendars, and I have purposely avoided Garlands, or Collections of ballads, which equally come under the category of Chap-books. I should have liked to have noticed more of them, but the exigencies of publishing have prevented it ; still, those I have taken seem to me to be the best fitted for the purpose I had in view, which was to give a fairly representative list : and I hope I have succeeded in producing a book at once both amusing and instructive, besides having rescued these almost forgotten booklets from the limbo into which they were fast descending.

CONTENTS.

	PAGE
The History of Joseph and his Brethren	I
The Holy Disciple	25
The Wandering Jew	28
The Gospel of Nicodemus	30
The Unhappy Birth, Wicked Life, and Miserable Death of that Vile Traytor and Apostle Judas Iscariot	32
A Terrible and Seasonable Warning to Young Men	33
The Kentish Miracle	34
The Witch of the Woodlands	35
The History of Dr. John Faustus	38
The History of the Learned Friar Bacon	53
A Timely Warning to Rash and Disobedient Children	56
Bateman's Tragedy	57
The Miracle of Miracles	60
A Wonderful and Strange Relation of a Sailor	61
The Children's Example	62
A New Prophesy	64
God's Just Judgment on Blasphemers	65
A Dreadful Warning to all Wicked and Forsworn Sinners ...	66
A Full and True Relation of one Mr. Rich Langly, a Glazier ...	67
A Full, True and Particular Account of the Ghost or Apparition of the Late Duke of Buckingham's Father	68
The Portsmouth Ghost	70
The Guilford Ghost	72
The Wonder of Wonders	74
Dreams and Moles	78
The Old Egyptian Fortune-Teller's Last Legacy	79

PAGE

A New Fortune Book 83
The History of Mother Bunch of the West 84
The History of Mother Shipton 88
Nixon's Cheshire Prophecy 92
Reynard the Fox 95
Valentine and Orson 109
Fortunatus 124
Guy, Earl of Warwick 138
The History of the Life and Death of that Noble Knight Sir Bevis of
    Southampton 156
The Life and Death of St. George 163
Patient Grissel 171
The Pleasant and Delightful History of Jack and the Giants ... 184
A Pleasant and Delightful History of Thomas Hickathrift ... 192
Tom Thumb 206
The Shoemaker's Glory 222
The Famous History of the Valiant London Prentice 227
The Lover's Quarrel 230
The History of the King and the Cobler 233
The Friar and Boy 237
The Pleasant History of Jack Horner 245
The Mad Pranks of Tom Tram 248
The Birth, Life, and Death of John Franks 253
Simple Simon's Misfortunes 258
The History of Tom Long the Carrier 263
The World turned Upside Down 265
A Strange and Wonderful Relation of the Old Woman who was
    Drowned at Ratcliffe Highway 273
The Wise Men of Gotham 275
Joe Miller's Jests 288
A Whetstone for Dull Wits 295
The True Trial of Understanding 304
The Whole Trial and Indictment of Sir John Barleycorn, Knt. 314
Long Meg of Westminster 323
Merry Frolicks 337
The Life and Death of Sheffery Morgan 341
The Welch Traveller 344

Contents.

PAGE

Joaks upon Joaks 349

The History of Adam Bell, Clim of the Clough, and William of Cloudeslie 353

A True Tale of Robin Hood 356

The History of the Blind Begger of Bednal Green 360

The History of the Two Children in the Wood 369

The History of Sir Richard Whittington 376

The History of Wat Tyler and Jack Straw 382

The History of Jack of Newbury 384

The Life and Death of Fair Rosamond 387

The Story of King Edward III. and the Countess of Salisbury 390

The Conquest of France 392

The History of Jane Shore 393

The History of the Most Renowned Queen Elizabeth and her Great Favourite the Earl of Essex 396

The History of the Royal Martyr 398

England's Black Tribunal 403

The Foreign Travels of Sir John Mandeville 405

The Surprizing Life and Most Strange Adventures of Robinson Crusoe 417

A Brief Relation of the Adventures of M. Bamfyeld Moore Carew 423

The Fortunes and Misfortunes of Moll Flanders 427

Youth's Warning-piece 429

The Merry Life and Mad Exploits of Capt. James Hind 433

The History of John Gregg 437

The Bloody Tragedy 439

The Unfortunate Family 440

The Horrors of Jealousie 441

The Constant, but Unhappy Lovers 442

A Looking Glass for Swearers, etc. 443

Farther, and More Terrible Warnings from God 444

The Constant Couple 446

The Distressed Child in the Wood 447

The Lawyer's Doom 448

The Whole Life and Adventures of Miss Davis 449

The Life and Death of Christian Bowman 453

The Drunkard's Legacy 455

PAGE

Good News for England 458

A Dialogue between a Blind Man and Death 459

The Devil upon Two Sticks 461

Æsop's Fables 463

A Choice Collection of Cookery Receipts 472

The Pleasant History of Taffy's Progress to London 475

The Whole Life, Character, and Conversation of that Foolish
Creature called Granny 478

A York Dialogue between Ned and Harry 479

The French King's Wedding 481

Appendix 483

CHAP-BOOKS

OF

THE EIGHTEENTH CENTURY

THE HISTORY OF
JOSEPH AND HIS BRETHREN.

THE first printed metrical history of this Biblical episode is the book printed by Wynkyn de Worde, a book of fourteen leaves, and entitled "Thystorie of Jacob and his twelue Sones. Emprȳted at Lōdon in Fletestrete at the sygne of the Sonne by Wynkyn de Worde" (no date). It is chiefly remarkable in connection with this book, as mentioning Chapmen.

> "Now leaue we of them & speak we of the Chapman
> That passed ouer the sea into Egipt land.
> But truely ere that he thether came
> The wind stiffly against them did stand;
> And yet at the last an hauen they fand.
> The Chapman led Joseph with a rope in the streat
> Him for to bye came many a Lord great."

A metrical edition is still used in the performance of a sort of miracle play, entitled "Joseph and his Brothers. A Biblical Drama or Mystery Play." 1864. London and Derby.

The action of this piece is reported to be somewhat ludicrous, the performers being in their everyday dress, or, rather, in their Sunday attire.   There is no scenery, and very little life or motion in connection with the dialogue, the quality of which may be judged by the following specimen :—

> " (*Joseph, weeping, offers Benjamin his goblet.*)
>
> Here, my son,
> Drink from my Cup ; the sentiment shall be
> ' Health and long life to your aged father.'
> (*Benjamin drinks.*)
> Now sing me one of your Hebrew Songs
> To any National Air ; for we in Egypt
> Know little of the music of Chanaan.
>
> *Benjamin.* If such be your wish, I'll sing the song
> I often sing to soothe my father's breast
> When he is sad with memory of the past.
>
> (*He sings.*) Air, ' *Phillis is my only joy,*' etc. :—
>
> > Joseph was my favourite boy,
> > Rachel's firstborn Son and pride :
> > His father's hope, his father's joy,
> > Begotten in life's eventide," etc.

THE HISTORY

OF

Joseph and his Brethren,

WITH

Jacob's Journey into Egypt,

AND

HIS DEATH AND FUNERAL.

ILLUSTRATED WITH TWELVE CUTS.

JOSEPH BROUGHT BEFORE PHAROAH.

PRINTED AND SOLD IN ALDERMARY CHURCH YARD,
BOW LANE, LONDON.

THE HISTORY OF

JOSEPH AND HIS BRETHREN.

JACOB'S LOVE TO JOSEPH, WITH JOSEPH'S FIRST DREAM.

In Canaan's fruitful land there liv'd of late,
Old Isaac's heir blest with a vast estate ;
Near Hebron Jacob sourjourned all alone,
A stranger in the land that was his own :
Dear to his God, for humbly he ador'd him,
As Isaac did, and Abraham before him.
And as he was of worldly wealth possest,
So with twelve sons the good old man was blest,
Amongst all whom none his affections won,
So much as Joseph, Rachel's first-born son,
He in his bosom lay, still next his heart,
And with his Joseph would by no means part :
He was the lad on whom he most did doat,
And gave to him a many colour'd coat.
This made his bretheren at young Joseph grudge,
And thought their father loved him too much.
At Jacob's love their hatred did encrease,
That they could hardly speak to him in peace.
But Joseph, (in whose heart the filial fear
Of his Creator early did appear)
Not being conscious to himself at all,
He had done ought to move his brethren's gall,
Did unto them a dream of his relate, ⎫
Which (tho' it did increase his bretheren's hate, ⎬
Did plainly shew forth Joseph's future state ⎭
This is the dream, said Joseph, I did see :
The Corn was reap'd, and binding sheaves are we,

When my sheaf only was on a sudden found,
Both to arise and stand upon the ground.

Then yours arose, which round about were laid, ⎫
And unto mine a low obeisance made,   ⎬
Is this your dream, his brethren said?   ⎭
Can your ambitious thoughts become so vain,
To think that you shall o'er your brethren reign?
Or that we unto you shall tribute pay,
And at your feet our servile necks should lay?
Believe us brother, this youll never see,
But your aspiring will your ruin be.
Thus Joseph's bretheren talk'd, and if before
They hated him, they did it now much more;
The father lov'd him, and the lad they thought,
Took more upon him, than indeed he ought.
But they who judge a matter e'er the time,
Are oftentimes involved in a crime:
'Tis therefore best for us to wait and see
What the issue of mysterious things will be;
For those that judge by meer imagination,
Will find things contrary to their expectation.

JOSEPH'S SECOND DREAM.

How bold is innocence ! how fix'd it grows !
It fears no seeming friends nor real foes.
'Tis conscious of no guilt, nor base designs,
And therefore forms no plots nor countermines :
But in the paths of virtue walks on still,
And as it does none, so it fears no ill.

Just so it was with Joseph : lately he
Had dream'd a dream, and was so very free,
He to his bretheren did the dream reveal,
At which their hatred scarce they could conceal.
But Joseph not intending any ill,
Dream'd on again, and told his bretheren still.

Methought as on my slumb'ring bed I lay,
I saw a glorious light more bright than day :
The sun and moon, those glorious lamps of heaven,
With glittering stars in number seven,
Came all to me, on purpose to adore me,
And every one of them bow'd down before me :
And each one when they had thus obedience made,
Withdrew, nor for each other longer staid.

When Joseph thus his last dream had related,
Then he was by his bretheren much more hated.

This dream young Joseph to his father told,
Who when he heard it, thinking him too bold,
Rebuk'd him thus : What dream is this I hear?
You are infatuated, child I fear,
Must I, your mother, and your bretheren too,
Become your slaves and bow down to you.
 Thus Jacob chid him, for at present he,
Saw not so far into futurity :
Yet he did wonder how things might succeed,
And what for Joseph providence decreed,
For well he thought those dreams wa'nt sent in vain
Yet knew not how he should these dreams explain.
For those things oft are hid from human eyes,
Which are by him that rules above the skies
Firmly decreed ; which when they come to know,
The beauty of the work will plainly shew,
And all those bretheren which now Joseph hate,
Shall then bow down to his superior fate :
Old Jacob therefore, just to make a shew,
As if he was displeased with Joseph too,
Thus seem'd to chide young Joseph, but indeed
To his strange dreams he gave no little heed ;
Tho' how to interpret them he could not tell,
Yet in the meanwhile he observ'd them well.
 How great's the difference 'twixt a father's love,
And brethren's hatred may be seen above.
They hate their brother for his dreams, but he,⎞
Observes his words, and willing is to see   ⎟
What the event in future times may be.   ⎠

JOSEPH PUT INTO A PIT BY HIS BRETHEREN.

When envy in the heart of man does reign,
To stifle its effects proves oft in vain.
Like fire conceal'd, which none at first did know,
It soon breaks out and breeds a world of woe :

Young Joseph this by sad experience knew,
And his brethren's envy made him find it true :

For they, as in the sequel we shall see,
Resolv'd upon poor Joseph's tragedy ;
That they together at his dream might mock,
Which they almost effected, when their flock
In Sechem's fruitful field they fed, for there
Was Joseph sent to see how they did fare :
Joseph his father readily obeys,
And on the pleasing message goes his ways.
Far off they know, and Joseph's coming note,
For he had on his many colour'd coat ;
Which did their causeless anger set on fire,
And they against Joseph presently conspire :
Lo yonder doth the dreamer come they cry,
Now lets agree and act this tragedy.
And when we've slain him in some digged pit
Let's throw his carcase, and then cover it,
And if our father ask for him, we'll say,
We fear he's kill'd by some wild beast of prey.
This Reuben heard, who was to save him bent, ⎫
And therefore said, (their purpose to prevent,) ⎬
To shed his blood I'll ne'er give my consent ; ⎭
But into some deep pit him let us throw,
And what we've done there's none will know.

This Reuben said his life for to defend,
Till he could home unto his father send.
To Reuben's proposition they agree,
And what came of it we shall quickly see.
Joseph by this time to his brethren got,
And now affliction was to be his lot;
They told him all his dreams would prove a lye,
For in a pit he now should starve and die.
Joseph for his life did now entreat and pray, ⎫
But to his tears and prayers they answered Nay, ⎬
And from him first his coat they took away. ⎭
Then into an empty pit they did him throw, ⎫
And there left Joseph almost drown'd in woe, ⎬
While they to eating and to drinking go. ⎭

    See here the vile effects of causeless rage,
    In what black crimes does it oftimes engage.
    Nearest relations ! setting bretheren on
    To work their brother's dire destruction.
    But now poor Joseph in the pit doth lie,
    'Twill be his bretheren's turn to weep and cry.

JOSEPH SOLD INTO EGYPT.

As Joseph in the Pit condemn'd to die,
So did his grandfather on the altar lie,

The wood was laid, a sacrificing knife,
Was lifted up to take poor Isaac's life.
But heaven that ne'er design'd the lad should die,
Stopt the bold hand, and shew'd a lamb just by,
Thus in like manner did the all-wise decree,
His brethrens plots should disappointed be :
For while within the Pit poor Joseph lay,
And they set down to eat and drink and play,
And with rejoicing revel out the day :
Some Ishmaelitish merchants strait drew near,
Who to the land of Egypt journeying were,
To sell some balm and myrrh, and spices there.
This had on Judah no impressions made,
And therefore to his bretheren thus he said,
Come Sirs, to kill young Joseph is not good,
What profit will it be to spill his blood?
How are we sure his death we shall conceal?
The birds of air this murder will reveal.
Come let's to Egypt sell him for a slave,
And we for him some money sure may have ;
So from his blood our hands shall be clear,
And we for him have no cause for fear.
To this advice they presently agreed,
And Joseph from the Pit was drawn with speed :
For twenty pieces they their brother sell
To the Ishmaelites, and thought their bargain well.
And thus they to their brother bid adieu,
For he was quickly carried out of view.
Reuben this time was absent, and not told
That Joseph was took out of the pit and sold,
He therefore to the pit return'd, that he
Might sit his father's Joy at liberty.
But when, alas ! he found he was not there,
He was so overcome with black despair,
To rend his garments he could not forbear ;
Then going to his bretheren thus said he,
Poor Joseph's out, and whither shall I flee?

But they, not so concern'd, still kill'd a goat,
And in its blood they dipt poor Joseph's coat,
And that they all suspicion might prevent,
It by a stranger to their father sent,
Saying, We've found, and brought this coat to know
Whether 'tis thy son Joseph's coat or no.
This brought sad floods of tears from Jacob's eyes,
Ah! 'tis my son's, my Joseph's coat he cries:
Ah! woe is me, thus wretched and forlorn,
For my poor Joseph is in pieces torn:
His sons and daughters comfort him in vain,
He can't but mourn while he thinks Joseph slain,
And yet those sons won't fetch him back again.

JOSEPH AND HIS MISTRESS.

How much for Joseph's loss old Jacob griev'd,
It was not now his time to be reliev'd:
And therefore let's to Egypt turn our thought,
Where we shall find young Joseph sold and bought,
By Potiphar a Captain of the Guard;
Sudden the change, but yet I can't say hard;
For Joseph mercy in this change did spy,
And thought it better than i' th' pit to lie;
And well might Joseph be therewith content,
For God was with him where so 'er he went;

And tho' he did him with afflictions try,
He gave him favour in his master's eye,
For he each work he undertook did bless,
And crown'd his blessing with a good success.
So that his master then him steward made,
And Joseph's orders were by all obey'd :
In which such diligence and care he took,
His master needed after nothing look.
But his estate poor Joseph long can't hold,
His Mistress love so hot, made his master's cold,
For Joseph was so comely, young and wise,
His mistress on him cast her lustful eyes ;
Joseph perceiv'd it, yet no notice took,
Nor scarcely on her did he dare to look.
This vex't her so, she could no more forbear,
But unto Joseph did the same declare ;
Joseph with grief the unwelcome tidings heard,
But he his course by heavens directions steer'd.
And therefore to his mistress thus did say,
O mistress I must herein disobey ;
My master has committed all to me,
That is within his house, save only thee :
And if I such a wickedness should do,
I should offend my God and master too ;
And justly should I forfeit my own life,
To wrong my master's bed, debauch his wife.
But tho' he thus had given her denial,
She was resolv'd to make a further trial,
She saw he minded not whate'er she said,
And therefore now another plot she laid.
Joseph one day some business had to do,
When none was in the house beside them two,
When casting off all shame, and growing bold,
Of Joseph's upper garment she takes hold ;
Now Joseph you shall lie with me, said she,
For there is none in the house but you and me ;
But while she held his cloak to make him stay,

He left it with her, and made haste away ;
On this her lust to anger turns, and she,
Cries out help ! help ! Joseph will ravish me,
Whose raging lust I hardly could withstand !
But fled, and left his garment in my hand.

JOSEPH CAST INTO THE DUNGEON.

Poor Joseph's innocence was no defence,
Against this brazen strumpet's impudence,
She first accus'd, and that she might prevail,
She to her husband thus then told her tale.
Hast thou this servant hither brought that he
Might make a mock upon my chastity ?
What tho' he's one come from the Hebrew Stock,
Shall he thus at my virtue make a mock ?
For if I once should yield to throw't away
On such a wretch.—O think what you would say?
And yet he sought to do't this very day.
But when he did this steady virtue find,
Then fled, and left his garment here behind.
No wonder if this story so well told
Stirr'd up his wrath, and made his love turn cold ;
He strait believ'd all that his wife had said,
And Joseph was unheard in prison laid.

Joseph must now again live underground,
And in a dungeon have his virtue crown'd,
But tho' in prison cast and bound in chains,
His God is with him, and his friend remains ;
So here he with the gaoler favour finds,
That whatsoe'er he does he never minds :
The Gaoler knew his God was with him still,
And therefore lets him do whate'er he will.
King Pharoah's butler and his baker too
Under their Princes great displeasure grew
And therefore both of them were put in ward,
As prisoners to the captain of the guard
Where Joseph lay ; to whom they did declare,
Their case, he serving them whilst they were there.
    One night, a several dream to each befel,
But what it signify'd they could not tell.
Joseph perceiving they were very sad,
Demanded both the Dreams that they had had,
On which they each their dream to Joseph told,
Who strait the meaning of it did unfold.
The butler in three days restor'd shall be,   ⎫
The baker should be hang'd upon a tree,   ⎬
But when this comes to pass remember me,   ⎭
Said he to the Butler, for here I am thrown,
And charg'd with crimes that are to me unknown,
In three days time (such was their different case)
The Baker hang'd, the Butler gains his place ;
And he again held Pharoh's cup in his hand,
And stood before him as he us'd to stand.
And yet for all that he to Joseph said,
Joseph in prison two years longer staid,
In all which time he ne'er of Joseph thought,
Tho' he his help so earnestly besought.
    So in affliction promises we make,
    But when that's o'er forget whate'er we speak.

JOSEPH'S ADVANCEMENT.

MORE than two years Joseph in prison lay,
Yet had no prospect of the happy day
Of his release; nor any means could see,
By which he could be set at liberty;
But God who sent him thither to be try'd,
In his due time his mercy magnify'd.

For as King Pharaoh lay upon his bed,
He had strange things which troubled his head,
He saw seven well fed kine rise out of Neal,
And seven lean ones eat them in a meal.
Again he saw seven ears of corn that stood
Upon one stalk, and were both rank and good:
Yet these were eaten up as the kine before,
By seven ears very lean and poor.
What this imported Pharoah fain would know,
But none there were that could the meaning show.
This to the Butler's mind poor Joseph brought,
Who till this day of him had never thought.
Great Prince! I call to mind my faults this day,
And well remember when in gaol I lay,
I and the Baker each our dreams did tell,
Which a young Hebrew slave expounded well:

I was advanc'd and executed he,
Both which the Hebrew servant said should be.
Go, said the King, and bring him hither strait,
I for his coming with impatience wait.
Joseph was put in hastily no doubt,
And now more hastily was he brought out.
His prison garment now aside was laid,
And being shav'd was with new cloaths array'd;
To Pharaoh being brought, canst thou, said he,
The dream I've dream'd expound me?
'Tis not me, great Sir, Joseph reply'd,
To say that I could do't were too much pride,
And so 'twould be for any that doth live,
But God to Pharaoh will an answer give.
Then Pharaoh did at large his dreams relate,
And Joseph shew'd him Egypt's future fate.
Seven years of plenty should to Egypt come,
In which they scarce could get their harvests in.
Which by seven years of dearth eat up should be;
As were the fair kine by the lean he see.
For FAMINE Sir, said he, provide therefore,
And in the years of PLENTY lay up store.

    What Joseph said, seem'd good in Pharoh's eyes,
Who did esteem him of all men most wise:
Since God, said Pharoah has shewn this to thee,
Thou shalt thro' all the land be next to me.
Then made him second in his chariot ride,
And bow the knee before him all men cry'd.

JOSEPH'S BRETHEREN COME INTO EGYPT TO BUY CORN.

Now Joseph's Lord of Egypt, all things there
Are by the King committed to his care:
The plenteous years come on as Joseph told,
The earth produces more than barns can hold:
New store-houses were in each city made,
Where all the corn about it up was laid,

Till he had gotten such a numerous store,
That it was vain to count it any more.

But famine does to plenty next succeed,
And in all lands but Egypt there was need;
For they neglecting to lay up such store,
Had spent their Stock, and soon became so poor,
That in the land of Egypt there was bread,
By fame's loud trump, thro' every land was spread.
Old Jacob heard it, and to his sons thus said,
Why look you thus, as if you was afraid?
There's Corn in Egypt, therefore go and try,
That we may eat and live, not starve and die.
Joseph's ten bretheren straitway thither went,
Their corn in Canaan being almost spent.
This Joseph knew, for him they came before,
As being Lord of all the Egyptian store;
And as they came to him did each one bow,
But little thought he'd been the Dreamer now.
From whence came you? said Joseph as they stood,
My Lord say they from Canaan to buy food.
I don't believe it, said Joseph very high,
I rather think you came the land to spy,
That you abroad its nakedness may tell,
Come, come, I know your purpose very well;

Let not, say they, my Lord, his servants blame,
For only to buy food thy servants came.
Said Joseph sternly, Tell me not those lies,
For by the life of Pharaoh ye are spies.
We are twelve bretheren, sir, they then reply'd,
Sons of one man, of whom one long since dy'd:
And with our father we the youngest left,
So that he might not be of him bereft.
Hereby said Joseph 'twill be prov'd I trow,
Whether what I have said be true or now.
Your younger brother fetch, make no replies,
For if you don't, by Pharoah's life ye are spies.
On this they unto prison all were brought,
Where how they us'd their brother oft they thought.
When they in prison three days time had staid,
He sent for them and this proposal made,
They to their father should the corn convey,
And Simeon should with him a prisoner stay;
Until they brought their youngest brother there,
Which should to him their innocence declare.
This they agreed to, and were sent away,
Whilst Simeon did behind in prison stay.

BENJAMIN BROUGHT TO JOSEPH.

OLD Jacob's sons came back to him, report,
How they were us'd at the Egyptian court:
Taken for spies, and Simeon left behind,
Till Benjamin shall make the man more kind.
This news old Jacob griev'd unto the heart,
Who by no means with Benjamin would part;
But when the want of corn did pinch them sore,
And they were urg'd to go again for more;
They told their father they were fully bent,
To go no more except their brother went.
Then take your brother and arise and go,
Said good old Jacob, and the man will show

You favour, that you may all safe return,
And I no more my children's loss may mourn.

Then taking money and rich presents too,
To Joseph they their younger brother shew.
Then he his steward straitway did enjoin
To bring those men to his house with him to dine.
When Joseph came, he kindly to them spake,
When they to him did low obeysance make,
He ask'd their welfare, and desir'd to tell
Whether their father was alive and well.
They answer'd Yea, he did in health remain,
And to the ground bow'd down their heads again.
Then Benjamin he by the hand did take,
And said, Is this the youth of whom ye spake,
Then God be gracious unto thee my son,
To whom he said; which when as soon as done,
Into his chamber strait he went to weep,
For he his countenance could hardly keep.
Then coming out, and sitting down to meet,
He made his brethren all sit down to eat:
He sent to éach a mess of what was best,
But Benjamin's was larger than the rest.
Then what he further did design to do,
He call'd his servant, and to him did shew;

Put in each sack as much corn as they'll hold,
And in the mouth of each return his gold,
And see that you take my silver cup,
And in the sack of the youngest put it up.
The steward fill'd the sack as he was bid,
And in the mouth of each their money hid.
Then on the morrow morning merry hearted
With this their good success they all departed ;
But Joseph's steward quickly spoil'd their laughter,
Who by his master's orders strait went after,
And to the eleven brethren thus he spake,
Is this the return you to my master make ?
Could you not be contented with the wine,
But steal the Cup in which he does divine ?
This is unkind. And therefore I must say
You've acted very foolishly to day.

JOSEPH MAKES HIMSELF KNOWN TO HIS BRETHEREN.

THE steward's words put them into a fright,
They wonder'd at his speech, as well they might
Why does my Lord this charge against us bring ;
For God forbid we e'er should do this thing :
The money that within our sacks we found,
We brought from Canaan ; then what ground

Have you to think, or to suppose that we
Of such a crime as this should guilty be.
With whatsoever man this cup is found,
Both let him die, and we'll be also bound
As slaves unto my Lord.   Let it so be,
Reply'd the steward, we shall quickly see
Whether it is so or not; then down they took*
And when the steward he had search'd them round,
Within the sack of Benjamin the cup was found.
To Joseph therefore they straitway repair,
To whom he said as soon as they came there,
How durst you take this silver cup of mine
Did you not think that I could well divine?
To whom Judah said, My Lord we've nought to say
But at your feet as slaves ourselves we lay.
No, no, said Joseph, there's for that no ground,
He is my slave with whom the cup is found.
Then Judah unto Joseph drew more near,
And said, O let my Lord and Master hear :
If we without the lad should back return,
Our father would for ever grieve and mourn,
And his grey hairs with sorrows we should bring
Unto the grave, if we should do this thing ;
For when your servants father would at home
Have kept the lad, I begg'd that he might come,
And said, If I return him not to thee,
Then let the blame for ever lay on me.
Now therefore let him back return again,
And in his stead thy servant will remain,
And how shall I that piercing sight endure,
Which will I know my father's death procure.
This speech of Judah touch'd good Joseph so,
That he bid all his servants out to go.
He and his brethren being all alone,
He unto them himself did thus make known.

* Here seems a line missing.

I am Joseph :—Is my father alive?
But to return an answer none did strive;
For at his presence they were troubled all,
Which made him thus unto his brethren call,
I am your brother Joseph, him whom ye
To Egypt sold; but do not troubled be;
For what you did heaven did before decree.
Then he his brother Benjamin did kiss,
Wept on his neck, and so did he on his,
Then kist his bretheren, wept on them likewise,
So that among them there were no dry eyes.

JOSEPH SENDS FOR HIS FATHER WHO COMES TO EGYPT.

THEN Joseph to his bretheren thus did say,
Unto my father pray make haste away,
Take food and waggons here, and do not stay,
They went, and Jacob's spirits did revive,
To hear his dearest Joseph was alive,
It is enough, then did old Jacob cry,
I'll go and see my Joseph e'er I die;
And he had reason for resolving so,
For God appear'd to him and bid him go.
Then into Egypt Jacob went with speed,
Both he, his wives, his sons, and all their seed.

And being for the land of Goshen bent,
Joseph himself before him did present.
Great was their Joy they on that meeting shew'd,
And each the others cheeks with tears bedew'd.
Then Joseph did his aged father bring
Into the royal presence of the King,
Whom Jacob blest, and Pharaoh lik'd him well,
And bid him in the land of Goshen dwell.

JACOB'S DEATH AND BURIAL.

JACOB now having finished his last stage,
And come to the end of earthly pilgrimage.
Was visited by his son Joseph, who
Brought with him Ephraim and Manassah too.
When Jacob saw them, who are these said he?
The sons said Joseph, God has given me
Then Jacob blest them both, and his sons did call,
To shew to each what should to them befal.
Then giving orders unto Joseph where
He would be buried, left to him that care;
Then yielded up the ghost upon his bed
And to his people he was gathered.
Then Joseph for his burial did provide,
And with a numerous retinue did ride,

Of his own children and Egyptians too,
That their respect to Joseph might shew,
And with a mighty mourning did inter
Old Jacob in his fathers sepulchre.

FINIS.

THE HOLY DISCIPLE;

OR, THE

History of Joseph of Arimathea.

Wherein is contained a true Account of his Birth; his Parents; his
Country; his Education; his Piety; and his begging of Pontius Pilate the
Body of our blessed Saviour, after his Crucifixion, which he buried in a
new Sepulchre of his own. Also the Occasion of his coming to England,
where he first preached the Gospel at Glastenbury, in Somersetshire, where
is still growing that noted White Thorn which buds every Christmas day in
the morning, blossoms at Noon, and fades at Night, on the Place where he
pitched his Staff in the Ground. With a full Relation of his Death and
Burial.

TO WHICH IS ADED,

*MEDITATIONS on the BIRTH, LIFE, DEATH, and
RESURRECTION of our LORD and SAVIOUR
JESUS CHRIST.*

NEWCASTLE: PRINTED IN THIS PRESENT YEAR.

THE HOLY DISCIPLE;

OR, THE

HISTORY OF JOSEPH OF ARIMATHEA.

THE text of this book is simply an amplification of the title-page, which is sufficient for its purpose in this work. The legend of his planting his staff, which produced the famous Glastonbury Thorn, is very popular and widespread. The writer remembers in the winter of 1879, when living in Herefordshire, on Old Christmas Day (Twelfth Day), people coming from some distance to see one of these trees blossom at noon. Unfortunately they were disappointed. Loudon, in his "Arboretum Britannicum," v. 2, p. 833, says, " *Cratægus præcox,* the *early* flowering, or Glastonbury, *Thorn,* comes into leaf in January or February, and sometimes even in autumn; so that occasionally, in mild seasons, it may be in flower on Christmas Day. According to Withering, writing about fifty years ago, this tree does not grow within the ruins of Glastonbury Abbey, but stands in a lane beyond the churchyard, and appears to be a very old tree. An old woman of ninety never remembered it otherwise than it now appears. This tree is probably now dead; but one said to be a descendant of the tree which, according to the Romish legend, formed the staff of Joseph of Arimathea, is still existing within the precincts of the ancient abbey of Glastonbury. It is not of great age, and may probably have sprung from the root of the original tree, or from a truncheon of it; but it maintains the habit of flowering in the winter, which the legend attributes to its supposed parent. A correspondent (Mr. Callow) sent us on December 1, 1833, a specimen, gathered on that day, from the tree at Glastonbury, in full blossom, having on it also ripe fruit; observing that the tree blossoms again in the month of May following, and that it is from these later flowers that the fruit is produced. Mr. Baxter, curator of the Botanic Garden at Oxford, also sent us a specimen of the Glastonbury Thorn, gathered in that garden on Christmas Day, 1834, with fully expanded flowers and ripe fruit on the same branch. Seeds of this variety are said to produce only the common hawthorn; but we have no doubt that among a number of seedlings there would, as in similar cases, be found several plants having a tendency to the same habits as the parent. With regard to the legend, there is nothing miraculous in the circumstances of a staff, supposing it to have been of hawthorn, having, when stuck in the ground, taken root and become a tree; as it is well known that the hawthorn grows from stakes and truncheons. The miracle of Joseph of Arimathea is nothing compared with that of Mr. John Wallis, timber surveyor of Chelsea, author of 'Dendrology,' who exhibited to the Horticultural and Linnæan Societies, in 1834, a branch of hawthorn, which, he said, had hung for several years in a hedge among other trees; and, though without any root, or even touching the earth, had produced, every year, leaves, flowers, and fruit!"

Of St. Joseph himself, Alban Butler gives a very meagre account, not even mentioning his death or place of burial; so that, outside Glastonbury, we may infer he had small reputation. We must not, however, forget that he is supposed to have brought the Holy Grail into England.

Wynkyn de Worde printed a book called "The Life of Joseph of Armathy," and Pynson printed two—one "De Sancto Joseph ab Arimathia," 1516, and "The Lyfe of Joseph of Arimathia," 1520.

THE
WANDERING JEW;

OR, THE

SHOEMAKER OF JERUSALEM.

Who lived when our Lord and Saviour
JESUS CHRIST was Crucified,

And by Him Appointed to Wander until He comes again.

With his Travels, Method of Living, and a
Discourse with some Clergymen about
the End of the World.

PRINTED AND SOLD IN ALDERMARY CHURCH-YARD,
BOW LANE, LONDON.

THE WANDERING JEW.

THIS version is but a catchpenny, and principally consists of a fanciful dialogue between the Wandering Jew and a clergyman. This famous myth seems to have had its origin in the Gospel of St. John (xxi. 22), which, although it does not refer to him, evidently was the source of the idea of his tarrying on earth until the second coming of our Saviour. The legend is common to several countries in Europe, and we, in these latter days, are familiar with it in Dr. Croly's " Salathiel," "St. Leon," " Le Juif Errant," and "The Undying One." It is certain it was in existence before the thirteenth century, for it is given in Roger of Wendover, 1228, as being known ; for an Armenian archbishop, who was then in England, declared that he knew him. His name is generally received as Cartaphilus, but he was known, in different countries and ages, also as Ahasuerus, Josephus, and Isaac Lakedion. The usual legend is that he was Pontius Pilate's porter, and when they were dragging Jesus out of the door of the judgment-hall, he struck him on the back with his fist, saying, " Go faster, Jesus, go faster : why dost thou linger ? " Upon which Jesus looked at him with a frown, and said, " I, indeed, am going ; but thou shalt tarry till I come." He was afterwards converted and baptized by the name of Joseph. He is believed every hundred years to have an illness, ending in a trance, from which he awakes restored to the age he was at our Saviour's Crucifixion. Many impostors in various countries have personated him.

THE

GOSPEL OF

NICODEMUS.

In thirteen Chapters.

1. Jesus Accused of the Jews before Pilate.

2. Some of them spake for him.

3. Pilate takes Counsel of Ancient Lawyers, etc.

4. Nicodemus speaks to Pilate for Jesus.

5. Certain Jews shew Pilate the Miracles which Christ had done to some of them.

6. Pilate commands that no villains should put him to his Passion, but only Knights.

7. Centurio tells Pilate of the Wonders that were done at Christ's Passion ; and of the fine Cloth of Syndonia.

8. The Jews conspire against Nicodemus and Joseph.

9. One of the Knights that kept the Sepulchre of our Lord, came and told the Master of the Law, that our Lord was gone into Gallilee.

10. Three men who came from Gallilee to Jerusalem say they saw Jesus alive.

11. The Jews chuse eight men who were Joseph's friends, to desire him to come to them.

12. Joseph tells of divers dead Men risen, especially of Simon's two sons, Garius and Levicius.

13. Nicodemus and Joseph tell Pilate all that those two Men had said ; and how Pilate treated with the Princes of the Law.

NEWCASTLE : PRINTED IN THIS PRESENT YEAR.

THIS is a translation by John Warren, priest, of this apocryphal Gospel, of which the frontispiece is a summary, and varies very little from that given by Hone, who, in his prefatory notice says, "Although this Gospel is, by some among the learned, supposed to have been really written by Nicodemus, who became a disciple of Jesus Christ, and conversed with him; others conjecture it was a forgery towards the close of the third century, by some zealous believer, who, observing that there had been appeals made by the Christians of the former Age, to the Acts of Pilate, but that such Acts could not be produced, imagined it would be of service to Christianity to fabricate and publish this Gospel; as it would both confirm the Christians under persecution, and convince the Heathens of the truth of the Christian religion. . . . Whether it be canonical or not, it is of very great antiquity, and is appealed to by several of the ancient Christians."

Wynkyn de Worde published several editions of it—in 1509, 1511, 1512, 1518, 1532—and his headings of the chapters differ very slightly from those already given.

The unhappy Birth, wicked Life, and miserable Death of that vile Traytor and Apostle

JUDAS ISCARIOT,

Who, for Thirty Pieces of Silver betrayed his Lord and Master

JESUS CHRIST.

SHEWING

1. His Mother's Dream after Conception, the Manner of his Birth; and the evident Marks of his future shame.

2. How his Parents, inclosing him in a little chest, threw him into the Sea, where he was found by a King on the Coast of Iscariot, who called him by that Name.

3. His advancement to be the King's Privy Counsellor; and how he unfortunately killed the King's Son.

4. He flies to Joppa; and unknowingly, slew his own Father, for which he was obliged to abscond a Second Time.

5. Returning a Year after, he married his own Mother, who knew him to be her own Child, by the particular marks he had, and by his own Declaration.

6. And lastly, seeming to repent of his wicked Life, he followed our Blessed Saviour, and became one of his Apostles; But after betrayed him into the Hands of the Chief Priests for Thirty Pieces of Silver, and then miserably hanged himself, whose Bowels dropt out of his Belly.

TO WHICH IS ADDED,

A Short RELATION of the Sufferings of Our

BLESSED REDEEMER,

Also the Life and miserable Death of

PONTIUS PILATE,

Who condemn'd the Lord of Life to Death.

Being collected from the Writings of Josephus Sozomenus, and other Ecclesiastical Historians.

DURHAM: PRINTED AND SOLD BY ISAAC LANE.

A Terrible and seasonable Warning to young Men.

Being a very particular and True Relation of one *Abraham Joiner* a young Man about 17 or 18 Years of Age, living in *Shakesby's* Walks in *Shadwell*, being a Ballast Man by Profession, who on *Saturday* Night last pick'd up a leud Woman, and spent what Money he had about him in Treating her, saying afterwards, if she wou'd have any more he must go to the Devil for it, and slipping out of her Company, he went to the *Cock* and *Lyon* in *King Street*, the Devil appear'd to him, and gave him a Pistole, telling him *he shou'd never want for Money*, appointing to meet him the next Night at the *World's End* at Stepney ; Also how his Brother perswaded him to throw the Money away, which he did ; but was suddenly taken in a very strange manner ; so that they were fain to send for the Reverend Mr. Constable and other Ministers to pray with him ; he appearing now to be very Penitent ; with an Account of the Prayers and Expressions he makes use of under his Affliction, and the prayers that were made for him to free him from this violent Temptation.

The Truth of which is sufficiently attested in the Neighbourhood, he lying now at his mother's house, etc.

LONDON : PRINTED FOR J. DUTTON, NEAR FLEET STREET.

THE

KENTISH MIRACLE

𝔒𝔯, 𝔞 𝔖𝔢𝔞𝔰𝔬𝔫𝔞𝔟𝔩𝔢 𝔚𝔞𝔯𝔫𝔦𝔫𝔤 𝔱𝔬 𝔞𝔩𝔩 𝔖𝔦𝔫𝔫𝔢𝔯𝔰

SHEWN IN

The Wonderful Relation of one Mary Moore, whose Husband died some time ago, and left her with two Children, who was reduced to great Want; How she wandered about the Country asking Relief, and went two Days without any food. How the Devil appeared to her, and the many great Offers he made to her to deny Christ, and enter into his Service; and how she confounded Satan by powerful Arguments. How she came to a Well of Water, when she fell down on her Knees to pray to God, that he would give that Vertue to the Water that it might refresh and satisfy her Children's Hunger; with an Account how an Angel appeared to her and relieved her; also declared many things that shall happen in the Month of March next; shewing likewise what strange and surprizing Accidents shall happen by means of the present War; and concerning a dreadful Earthquake, etc.

EDINBURGH : PRINTED IN THE YEAR 1741.

THE

𝔚itch of the 𝔚oodlands;

OR, THE

COBLER'S NEW TRANSLATION.

Here Robin the Cobler for his former Evils,
Is punish'd bad as Faustus with his Devils.

PRINTED AND SOLD IN ALDERMARY CHURCH YARD,
BOW LANE, LONDON.

HERE the old Witches dance, and then agree,
How to fit Robin for his Lechery;
First he is made a Fox and hunted on,
'Till he becomes an Horse, an Owl, a Swan.

At length their Spells of Witchcraft they withdrew,
But Robin still more hardships must go through;
For e'er he is transform'd into a Man,
They make him kiss their bums and glad he can.

This is the argument of the story, which is too broad in its
humour to be reprinted, but the following two illustrations show
the popular idea of his Satanic Majesty and his dealings with
witches.

THE HISTORY OF

DR. JOHN FAUSTUS.

THERE is very little similarity between this history and Goethe's beautiful drama. This is essentially vulgar, and perfectly fitted for the popular taste it catered for ; but we, who are familiar with Goethe's masterpiece, can hardly read it without a shudder. It has been given at length, because it is a type of its class.

The History of Faust (who, as far as one can learn, existed early in the sixteenth century) has been repeatedly written, especially in Germany, where it first appeared in 1587, published at Frankfurt-on-the-Main, and it was soon translated into English by P. K. Gent. Marlowe produced his " Tragicall History of D. Faustus " in 1589, and in an entry in the Register of the Stationers' Company it appears that in the year 1588 "A Ballad of the Life and Death of Doctor Faustus, the great Congerer," was licensed to be printed,* so that it soon became well rooted in England. It has been a favourite theme with dramatists and musicians, and has even been the subject of a harlequinade, " The Necromancer ; or Harlequin Dr. Faustus " (London, 1723). It was a popular Chap book, and many versions were published of it in various parts of the country. J. O. Halliwell Phillips, Esq., has an English edition of Faustus printed 1592, unknown to Herbert or Lowndes.

---

* Probably the original of that ballad, " The Judgment of God shewed upon one J. Faustus Dr. in Divinity," of which the British Museum possesses two versions—Rox. II. 235 and $\frac{643 \text{ m. 10,}}{55.}$ the date of both being attributed 1670.

THE HISTORY

OF

Dr. John Faustus,

SHEWING

How he sold himself to the Devil to have power to do what he pleased for twenty-four years:

ALSO

STRANGE THINGS DONE BY HIM AND HIS SERVANT
MEPHISTOPHOLES.

With an Account how the Devil came for him, and tore him in Pieces.

PRINTED AND SOLD IN ALDERMARY CHURCH YARD,
BOW LANE, LONDON.

THE HISTORY OF
DR. JOHN FAUSTUS.

CHAP. I.

THE DOCTOR'S BIRTH AND EDUCATION.

DR. JOHN FAUSTUS was born in Germany: his father was
a poor labouring man, not able to give him any manner of
education; but he had a brother in the country, a rich man,
who having no child of his own, took a great fancy to his
nephew, and resolved to make him a scholar. Accordingly
he put him to a grammar school, where he took learning
extraordinary well; and afterwards to the University to study
Divinity. But Faustus, not liking that employment, betook
himself to the study of Necromancy and Conjuration, in
which arts he made such a proficiency, that in a short time
none could equal him. However he studied Divinity so
far, that he took his Doctor's Degree in that faculty; after
which he threw the scripture from him, and followed his
own inclinations.

CHAP. 2.

DR. FAUSTUS RAISES THE DEVIL, AND AFTERWARDS MAKES HIM APPEAR AT HIS OWN HOUSE.

FAUSTUS whose restless mind studied day and night, dressed his imagination with the wings of an eagle, and endeavoured to fly all over the world, and see and know the secrets of heaven and earth. In short he obtained power to command the Devil to appear before him whenever he pleased.

One day as Dr. Faustus was walking in a wood near Wirtemberg in Germany, having a friend with him who was desirous to see his art, and requested him to let him see if he could then and there bring Mephistopholes before them. The Doctor immediately called, and the Devil at the first summons made such a hedious noise in the wood as if

heaven and earth were coming together. And after this made a roaring as if the wood had been full of wild beasts. Then the Doctor made a Circle for the Devil, which he danced round with a noise like that of ten thousand waggons running upon paved stones. After this it thundered and lightened as if the world had been at an end.

Faustus and his friend, amazed at the noise, and frighted at the devil's long stay, would have departed; but the Devil cheared them with such musick, as they never heard before. This so encouraged Faustus, that he began to command

Mephistopholes, in the name of the prince of Darkness, to appear in his own likeness; on which in an instant hung over his head a mighty dragon.—Faustus called him again, as he was used, after which there was a cry in the wood as if Hell had been opened, and all the tormented souls had been there—Faustus in the mean time asked the devil many questions, and commanded him to shew a great many tricks.

Chap. 3.

Mephistopholes comes to the Doctor's House; and of what passed between them.

Faustus commanded the spirit to meet him at his own house by ten o'clock the next day. At the hour appointed he came into his chamber, demanding what he would have? Faustus told him it was his will and pleasure to conjure him to be obedient to him in all points of these articles, viz.

First, that the Spirit should serve him in all things he asked, from that time till death.

Secondly, whosoever he would have, the spirit should bring him.

Thirdly. Whatsoever he desired for to know he should tell him.

The Spirit told him he had no such power of himself, until he had acquainted his prince that ruled over him. For, said he, we have rulers over us, who send us out

and call us home when they will; and we can act no farther
than the power we receive from Lucifer, who you know for his
pride was thrust out of heaven. But I can tell you no more,
unless you bind yourself to us—I will have my request replied
Faustus, and yet not be damned with you—Then said the spirit,
you must not, nor shall not have your desire, and yet thou art
mine and all the world cannot save thee from my power. Then
get you hence, said Faustus, and I conjure thee that thou come
to me at night again.

Then the spirit vanished, and Doctor Faustus began to consider by what means he could obtain his desires without binding himself to the Devil.

While Faustus was in these cogitations, night drew on, and
then the spirit appeared, acquainting him that now he had
orders from his prince to be obedient to him, and to do for him
what he desired, and bid him shew what he would have.—
Faustus replied, His desire was to become a Spirit, and that
Mephistopholes should always be at his command; that whenever he pleased he should appear invisible to all men.—The
Spirit answered his request should be granted if he would sign
the articles pronounced to him viz, That Faustus should give

This is a rough copy of the frontispiece to Gent's translation, ed. 1648.

himself over body and soul to Lucifer, deny his Belief, and become an enemy to all good men; and that the writings should be made with his own blood.—Faustus agreeing to all this, the Spirit promised he should have his heart's desire, and the power to turn into any shape, and have a thousand spirits at command.

Chap. 4.

Faustus lets himself blood, and makes himself over to the Devil.

The Spirit appearing in the morning to Faustus, told him, That now he was come to see the writing executed and give him power. Whereupon Faustus took out a knife, pricked a vein in his left arm, and drew blood, with which he wrote as follows:

"I, John Faustus, Doctor in Divinity, do openly acknowlege That in all my studying of the course of nature and the elements, I could never attain to my desire; I finding men unable to assist me, have made my addresses to the Prince of Darkness, and his messenger Mephistopholes, giving them both soul and body, on condition that they fully execute my desires; the which they have promised me. I do also further grant by these presents, that if I be duly served, when and in what place I command, and have every thing that I ask for during the space of twenty four years, then I agree that at the expiration of the said term, you shall do with Me and Mine, Body and Soul, as

you please. Hereby protesting, that I deny God and Christ and all the host of heaven. And as for the further consideration of this my writing, I have subscribed it with my own hand, sealed it with my own seal, and writ it with my own blood.

JOHN FAUSTUS."

No sooner had Faustus sent his name to the writing, but his spirit Mephistopholes appeared all wrapt in fire, and out of his mouth issued fire ; and in an instant came a pack of hounds in full cry. Afterwards came a bull dancing before him, then a lion and a bear fighting. All these and many spectacles more did the Spirit present to the Doctor's view, concluding with all manner of musick, and some hundreds of spirits dancing before him.—This being ended, Faustus looking about saw seven sacks of silver, which he went to dispose of, but could not handle himself, it was so hot.

This diversion so pleased Faustus, that he gave Mephistopholes the writing he had made, and kept a copy of it in his own hands. The Spirit and Faustus being agreed, they dwelt together, and the devil was never absent from his councils.

Chap. 5.

How Faustus served the Electoral Duke of Bavaria.

Faustus having sold his soul to the Devil, it was soon reported among the neighbours, and no one would keep him company, but his spirit, who was frequently with him, playing of strange tricks to please him.

Not far from Faustus's house lived the Duke of Bavaria, the Bishop of Saltzburg, and the Duke of Saxony, whose houses and cellars Mephistopholes used to visit, and bring from thence the best provision their houses afforded.

One day the Duke of Bavaria had invited most of the gentry of that country to dinner, in an instant came Mephistopholes and took all with him, leaving them full of admiration.

If at any time Faustus had a mind for wild or tame fowl, the Spirit would call whole flocks in at the window. He also taught Faustus to do the like so that no locks nor bolts could hinder them.

The devil also taught Faustus to fly in the air, and act many things that are incredible, and too large for this book to contain.

Chap. 6.

Faustus Dream of Hell, and what he saw there.

After Faustus had had a long conference with the Spirit concerning the fall of Lucifer, the state and condition of the fallen angels, he in a dream saw Hell and the Devils.

Having seen this sight he marvelled much at it, and having Mephistopholes on his side, he asked him what sort of people they was who lay in the first dark pit? Mephistopholes told him they were those who pretended to be physicians, and had poisoned many thousands in trying practices ; and now said the spirit, they have the very same administered unto them which they prescribed to others, though not with the same

effect ; for here, said he, they are denied the happiness to die.
—Over their heads were long shelves full of vials and gallipots
of poison.

Having passed by them, he came to a long entry exceeding
dark, where was a great crowd : I asked what they were? and
the Spirit told me They were pick pockets, who, because they
loved to be in a crowd in the other world, were also crowded
here together. Among these were some padders on the highway, and others of that function.

Walking farther I saw many thousand vintners and some
millions of taylors ; insomuch there was scarce room enough
for them in the place destined for their reception.

A little farther the Spirit opened a cellar door, from which
issued a smoke almost enough to choak me, with a dismal
noise ; I asked what they were? and the Spirit told me, They
were Witches, such as had been pretended Saints in the other
world, but now having lost their veil, they squabble, fight and
tear one another.

A few steps farther I espied a great number almost hid
with smoke ; and I asked who they were? The Spirit told me
they were Millers and bakers ; but, good lack! what a noise
was there among them! the miller cried to the baker and
the baker to the miller for help, but all in vain, for there was
none that could help them.

Passing on farther I saw thousands of Shop keepers, some
of whom I know, who were tormented for defrauding and
cheating their Customers.

Having taken this prospect of Hell, my Spirit Mephistopholes took me up in his arms, and carried me home to my
own house, where I awaked, amazed at what I had seen in my
dream.

Being come to myself I asked Mephistopholes in what
place Hell was? he answered, Know thou that before the Fall,
Hell was ordained : As for the substance or extent of Hell, we
Devils do not know it ; but it is the wrath of God that makes
it so furious.

CHAP. 7.

DR. FAUSTUS'S TRICK ON TWENTY STUDENTS.

THIRTEEN students meeting seven more near Faustus's house, fell to words, and at length to blows; the thirteen was took hard for the seven. The Doctor looking out at a window saw the fray, and seeing how much the Seven were overmatched by the thirteen, he conjured them all blind, so that they could not see each other; and in this manner they continued to fight, and so smote each other, as made the public laugh heartily. At length he parted them, leading them all to their own homes, where they immediately recovered their sight, to the great astonishment of all.

CHAP. 8.

FAUSTUS HELPS A YOUNG MAN TO A FAIR LADY.

THERE was a galant young gentleman that was in love with a fair Lady, who was of a proper personage, living at Wirtemberg near the Doctors house. This gentleman had long sought the lady in marriage, but could not obtain his desire; and having placed his affections so much upon her, he was ready to pine away, and had certainly died with grief, had he not made his affairs known to the Doctor, to whom he opened the whole matter. No sooner had the gentleman told his case

to the Doctor, but he bid him not fear, for his desire should
be fulfilled, and he should have her he so much admired, and
that the gentlewoman should love none but him, which was
done accordingly ; for Faustus so changed the mind of the
damsel, by his practices, that she could think of nothing else
but him, whom she before hated ; and Faustus's device was
thus : He gave him an inchanted ring, which he ordered him
to slip on her finger, which he did : and no sooner was it on
but her affections began to change, and her heart burned with
love towards him. She instead of frowns could do nothing
else but smile on him, and could not be at rest till she had
asked him if he thought he could love her, and make her a
good husband : he gladly answered yes, and he should think
he was the happiest man alive ; so they were married the next
day, and proved a very happy couple.

CHAP. 9.

FAUSTUS MAKES SEVEN WOMEN DANCE NAKED IN
THE MARKET.

FAUSTUS walking in the Market place saw seven jolly women
setting all on a row, selling butter and eggs, of each of them he

bought something and departed; but no sooner was he gone, but all their butter and eggs were gone out of their baskets, they knew not how. At last they were told that Faustus had conjured all their goods away; whereupon they ran in haste to the Doctor's house, and demanded satisfaction for their wares. —He resolved to make sport for the townspeople; made them pull off all their cloaths, and dance naked to their baskets; where every one saw their goods safe, and found herself in a humour to put her cloaths on again.

Chap. 10.

How Faustus served a Countryman driving Swine.

Faustus, as he was going one day to Wirtemberg, overtook a country fellow driving a herd of Swine, which was very head-strong, some running one way and some another way, so that the driver could not tell how to get them along. Faustus taking notice of it made every one of them dance upon their hind legs, with a fiddle in one of their fore feet and a bow in the other, and so dance and fiddle all the way to Wirtemberg, the countryman dancing all the way before them, which made the people wonder—After Faustus had satisfied himself with this sport, he conjured the fiddles away; and the countryman offering his pigs for sale, soon sold them and got the money; but before he was gone out of the house, Faustus conjured the pigs out of the market, and sent them to the countryman's house. The man who had bought them, seeing the swine gone, stopped the man that sold them, and forced him to give back the money; on which he returned home very sorrowful, not knowing what to do; but to his great surprize found all the pigs in their sties.

Chap. 11.

Faustus begins to contemplate upon his latter End.

Faustus having spun out his twenty four years within a month or two, began to consider what he could do to cheat the devil, to whom he had made over both body and soul, but could find no ways to frustrate his miserable end; which now was drawing near. Whereupon in a miserable tone he cried out, O lamentable wretch that I am! I have given myself to the devil for a few years pleasure to gratify my Carnal and devilish appetites, and now I must pay full dear; Now I must have torment without end. Woe is me, for there is none to help me; I dare not, I cannot look for mercy from God, for I have abandoned him; I have denied him to be my God, and given up myself to the Devil to be his for ever; and now the time is almost expired, and I must be tormented for ever and ever.

Chap. 12.

Faustus warned by the Spirit to prepare for his end.

Faustus's full time being come, the Spirit appeared to him, and shewed him the writings, and told him that the next day

the Devil would fetch him away.   This made the Doctor's heart
to ache ; but to divert himself he sent for some Doctors, Masters
and Batchelors of Arts, and other students to dine with him for
whom he provided a great store of varieties, with musick and
the like ; but all would not keep up his spirits, for his hour
drew near—Whereupon his countenance changing, the doctors
asked the reason of his confusion ?   To which Faustus answered, O ! my friends, you have known me these many years,
and that I practised all manner of wickedness.   I have been a
great conjuror, which art I obtained of the devil ; selling myself
to him soul and body, for the term of twenty four years ; which
time expiring to night, is the cause of my sorrow ; I have called
you, my friends, to see my miserable end ; and I pray let my
fate be a warning to you all, not to attempt to search farther
into the secrets of nature than is permitted to be known to
man, lest your searches lead you to the Devil, to whom I must
this night go, whether I will or no.

About twelve o'clock at night the house shook so terribly
that they all feared it would have tumbled on their heads, and
suddenly the doors and windows were broke to pieces, and a
great hissing was heard as though the house had been full of
snakes ; Faustus in the mean time calling out for help but all in
vain.   There was a vast roaring in the hall, as if all the Devils
in Hell had been there ; and then they vanished, leaving the
hall besprinkled with blood, which was most terrible to behold.

FINIS.

THE

HISTORY

Of the Learned

FRIAR BACON.

PRINTED AND SOLD IN ALDERMARY CHURCH YARD,
LONDON.

ROGER BACON was born at Ilchester, Somersetshire, in 1214, and was educated at Oxford and Paris, where he was made D.D. He seems to have settled at Oxford about 1240, and entered the order of St. Francis. He devoted himself body and soul to the study of natural philosophy, mathematics, and chemistry, and obtained such celebrity by his discoveries, that they were assigned to evil spirits, and he himself was branded as a magician. He was confined to his cell and forbidden to lecture. A copy of his " Opus Majus " being sent to Clement IV. on his elevation to the Papal chair, he promised his protection, which continued until his death; when Bacon was more severely persecuted, his works were prohibited, and he was imprisoned about ten years. When released, he returned to his beloved Oxford, where he died, June 11, 1292. Why the popular idea of him in after times should be always associated with the ludicrous, I cannot say, but it is so, even in Greene's play, " The Honourable Historie of frier Bacon, and frier Bongay," of which the earliest edition extant is 1594; but it must have been earlier, for in Henslowe's Diary, under 1591–92, is an entry, " Rd at fryer bacone, the 19 of febrary satterdaye xvij^s ii^d." Indeed, every history makes fun about him, and almost all his deeds are comic. In this book, for instance, the king, being about four miles from Oxford, naturally desired to see the great philosopher, and sent a nobleman to bring him. Bacon could not go quietly, but he caused a great mist to spring up, and the nobleman lost his way; whilst Bacon was straightway transported into the king's presence, when at the royal request he waved his wand, and caused beautiful music to sound. Another wave, and a banquet appeared, of which the king and queen partook, and then it vanished, leaving the place sweetly perfumed. " Then waving the fourth time, came in Russians Persians and Polanders clad with the finest furs and richest silks in the universe, which he bid them feel; and then the strangers all dancing after their fashion vanished. . . . During this, the gentleman of the bed chamber came in puffing and blowing, all bemired and dirty, his face and hands scratched with bushes and briars. The King asked him why he stayed so long and how he came in that condition? Oh! the plague, said he, take Friar Bacon and all his Devils, they have led me a dance to the endangering my neck; but the dog is here, I'll be revenged on him. Then he laid his hand upon his sword; but Bacon waving his wand, fixed it in the scabbard, that he could not draw it, saying, I fear not thy anger, thou hadst best be quiet, lest a worse thing befal thee."

He had a hypocritical servant, who on Good Friday would not take a bit of bread and a cup of wine when offered by his master, but went privately to eat a pudding, which, by Bacon's enchantments, stuck fast in his mouth, in which condition he was found by the friar, who fastened him by the pudding to the college gate, and there left him to be exposed to the jeers of the passers-by.

After he had perfected his famous brazen head, which was to speak at some time or other unknown, within two months after being finished, and required careful watching, this man Miles had his turn of guard. When the head uttered the words "Time is," instead of at once informing his master, he chaffed the head, and it said "Time was." He still went on bantering, when the head called out, "Time is past," and then, with a horrible noise, it fell down and broke in pieces. Bacon and Bungay rushed in, and on questioning Miles he told them the truth, and was punished by his enraged master with the loss of speech for the space of two months.

A

Timely Warning

To Rash and Disobedient

CHILDREN.

Being a strange and wonderful RELATION of a young
Gentleman in the Parish of *Stepheny* in the Suburbs of *London*,
that sold himself to the Devil for 12 Years to have the Power
of being revenged on his Father and Mother, and how his
Time being expired, he lay in a sad and deplorable Condition
to the Amazement of all Spectators.

EDINBURGH : PRINTED ANNO 1721.

BATEMAN'S TRAGEDY,

OR THE

𝔓𝔢𝔯𝔧𝔲𝔯𝔢𝔡 𝔅𝔯𝔦𝔡𝔢 𝔧𝔲𝔰𝔱𝔩𝔶 𝔯𝔢𝔴𝔞𝔯𝔡𝔢𝔡;

BEING THE

HISTORY

OF THE

UNFORTUNATE LOVE

OF

German's Wife and Young Bateman.

NEWCASTLE: PRINTED IN THIS PRESENT YEAR.

THE story of this very popular Chap book can be very well epitomized by the headings of the chapters, which give an excellent idea of the tale.

CHAPTER I.

How young Bateman, riding through Clifton Town, accidentally espied fair Isabella, a rich Farmer's Daughter, standing at her Father's door, and fell in love with her, enquiring who she was, and his resolution to let her know his passion.

CHAPTER II.

How the fair Isabella fell sick for Love of Bateman, though a Stranger, and his Abode unknown to her, when she was given over, he came in the Habit of a Physician, discovered himself to her, and she recovered her health by that means, to the unspeakable joy of her Parents.

CHAPTER III.

How being invited to her Father's House, he walked abroad with her and discovered his passion to her at large. Of the Encouragement he found to proceed in his Suit, and the prospect there was of a happy marriage between them.

CHAPTER IV.

How he came and asked her Father's consent, but was refused. How one German attempted to kill him, but was wounded by him : and how he made his escape.

CHAPTER V.

How being banished from her Father's house, his lovely mistress, upon sending a letter, came to him in disguise, in a neighbouring wood, and there they sealed their love by solemn vows, and breaking a piece of gold between them.

Chapter VI.

How upon her coming back, her going was discovered, and she confined to her chamber, where German courted her with tears presents and the proffer of a great estate; she at the instance of her parents, renounced her vows, sent back her gold, and married him, whereupon Bateman hanged himself.

Chapter VII.

How, upon Bateman's hanging himself before her door, she grew malancholy, fancying she saw him with a ghostly face, putting her in mind of her broken vows; and how after having been delivered of a child, a spirit carried her away.

THE
Miracle of Miracles.

Being a full and true Account of *Sarah Smith*, Daughter of *John Symons* a Farmer, who lately was an Inhabitant of Darken Parish in Essex, that was brought to Bed of a Strange Monster, the Body of it like a Fish with Scales thereon: it had no Legs but a pair of great Claws, Tallons Like a Liands, it had Six Heads on its Neck, one was like the Face of a Man with Eyes Nose and Mouth to it, the 2d like the Face of a Cammel, and its Ears Cropt, Two other Faces like Dragons with spiked Tongues hanging out of their Mouths, another had an Eagles Head with a Beak instead of a Mouth at the end of it, and the last seeming to be a Calves head. Which eat and fed for some time, which Monster has surprised many Thousand people that came there to see it. Daily, Spectators flock to view it, but it was by Command of the Magistrates knock'd on the Head, and several Surgeons were there to dissect it. Also you have a Funeral Sermon on the Woman who brought it forth, a very wicked Liver, and disobedient to her Parents, and one that was mightily given to Wishing, Cursing and Swearing. With a Prayer before and after the said Sermon. It being very fit and necessary to be had in all Families for a Warning to Disobedient Children. This strange and unheard of Monster was brought into the World in May last, and if any doubt the truth thereof, it will be certify'd by the Minister and Church-Wardens of the said Parish of Darkins in Essex as aforesaid.

ENTRED IN THE HALL BOOK ACCORDING TO ORDER.

A wonderful and Strange

RELATION

OF A

SAILOR

IN

St. Bartholomew's Hospital, London;

WHO

Slept for Five Days and Nights together and then awaking
gave an Account of the Blessedness of those in Heaven, and
the woful Estate of the Damned in Hell. And also of the
STATE of two of his Companions who dy'd whilst he was in
his sleep. All which is attested by the Minister and many who
were present and Ear Wittnesses to the Relation.

TO WHICH IS PREFIXED

The Greatest Light to Sinners

Occasioned and Explain'd by the late

SLEEPING MAN'S DREAM.

LICENSED AND ENTERED ACCORDING TO ORDER.

The Children's Example.

SHEWING

How one Mrs. Johnson's Child of Barnet was tempted by the
Devil to forsake God and follow the Ways of other Wicked
Children, who us'd to Swear, tell Lies, and disobey their
Parents; How this pretty innocent Child resisting Satan, was
Comforted by an Angel from Heaven, who warned her of her
approaching Death; Together with her dying Speeches desiring
young Children not to forsake God, lest Satan should gain a
Power over them.

ENTER'D ACCORDING TO ORDER.

THIS style of Chap-book, although always a favourite among a certain section of society, is such rubbish that one extract will suffice :—

> " As this Child went to School one Day,
> Through the Church Yard she took her Way,
> When, lo ! the Devil came and said,
> Where are you going, pretty Maid?
> To School I am going Sir (said she)
> Pish, child, don't mind the same, (saith he)
> But hast to your Companions dear,
> And learn to lie, and curse and swear.
> They bravely spend their time in Play,
> God they don't value ; no, not they ;
> It is a Fable, Child he cry'd.
> At which his Cloven Foot she spy'd.
> I'm sure there is a God, said she,
> Who from your Power will keep me free ;
> And if you should this thing deny,
> Your Cloven Foot gives you the Lie.
> Satan avoid hence out of Hand
> In name of JESUS I command !
> At which the Devil instantly
> In flames of Fire away did fly," etc., etc.

There is another somewhat similar one, presumably of same date "to the tune of 'The Children's Example,'" entitled "The Pious Virgin; or Religious Maid. Being a Relation of the Wonderful and Divine Speeches of Sarah Shrimpton, Daughter to Mrs. Shrimpton, living in Rochester, who falling into a Trance declared the Wonderful Things she had seen ; desiring Young Children to serve the Lord in the Time of their Youth, in order to obtain Salvation ;" but it is not worth an extract.

Indeed, speculative young ladies of this class do not seem to have been uncommon, for a Miss Katherine Atkinson of Torven, in the parish of Ulverstone in the county palatine of Lancaster, also indulged in the luxury of a trance, which is described as follows :—

𝔄 𝔑𝔢𝔴 𝔓𝔯𝔬𝔭𝔥𝔢𝔰𝔶; 𝔬𝔯, 𝔄𝔫

ACCOUNT

Of a young Girl, not above Eight Years of Age; Who being in a Trance, or lay as dead for the Space of Forty Eight Hours. With an Account of the Strange and Wonderful Sight that she see in the other World. With an Alarm from Heaven to the Inhabitants of the Earth; Giving an Account how crying Sins of the Day and Time do provoke the Almighty. With strange and wonderful Things, as a Warning to this last and worst Age, agreeable to the Holy Scriptures and Divine Revelation. The like never published; That the Saying of the Almighty may be fulfilled, That out of the Mouth of Babes and Sucklings God will perfect Praise.

LICENSED AND ENTERED ACCORDING TO ORDER.

GOD'S JUST JUDGMENT ON

BLASPHEMERS,

Being a Terrible Warning Piece to repining Murmurers, set forth in a dreadful Example of the Almighty's Wrath, on one Mr. Thomas Freeburn a Farmer, near Andover in Wiltshire, who utter'd those horrid and blasphemous Expressions, That God never did him any good in his Life, and he believed did not know what he did himself; with other words too monstrous and devilish to be repeated: Upon which he was immediately struck Speechless, Motionless and almost without sign of Life, and fell down as in a dead Sleep; and no strength of Men or Horses, has been able hitherto to remove him from the ground.

Also an Account of his wicked Life and Actions for 24 Years before this just Judgment fell upon him, with his coming to his Speech again, in four Months and twenty Day's time, and the terrible Sights he saw in the other World, which he has discover'd to some thousands of Spectators.

LICENSED AND ENTERED ACCORDING TO ORDER.

A Dreadful Warning

To all Wicked and Forsworn
SINNERS.

Shewing the sad and dreadful Example of Nicholas Newsom and David Higham, who were drinking in a Public House in Dudley near Birmingham on Thursday; the 5th day of March 1761. Giving an Account, how they laid a Wager, whether could swear the most blasphemous Oaths, and how they were struck Deaf and Dumb, with their Tongues hanging out of their Mouths.

To which is added a Sermon, preached on this Occasion, by the Rev. Dr. Smith from the following Text. Matt. 5. 34. 35. Swear not at all neither by Heaven for it is Gods Throne; nor by the earth for it is his Footstool.

Here is a full and true

RELATION

OF ONE

Mr. RICH LANGLY, a Glazier,

Living over against the Sign of the Golden Wheat Sheaf in Ratcliff Highway, London, that lay in a Trance for two Days and one Night. He also saw the Joys of Heaven and the Terrors of Hell.

You have also an Account when he came out of his Trance, how he declared to the Minister, that he had but 5 Days to live in this World, before he should depart. As soon as the Minister was gone out of the Room, it is said the Devil appearing to him, and asking of him if he would Sell his Soul and Body to Him, proffering him in the shape of a Gentleman, a bag of Gold, but he crying out against it, and saying, Lord Jesus receive my soul.

Having an account how the Devil Vanished away in a Flame of Fire, you have also in this Book, a Good and Godly Sermon, that was Preached on him at his Funeral, by that Reverend and Learned Divine, Dr. Pede, Minister, of the Parish Church of Clakenwell London.

LICENSED ACCORDING TO ORDER.

London: Printed for T. Bland near Fleet Street.

A Full, True and Particular

ACCOUNT

of the Ghost or Apparition of the Late Duke of Buckingham's Father, which several Times appeared in Armor to one of the Duke's Servants; and for about half a Year before foretold the Dukes death.

PRINTED BY F. C. IN THE OLD BAILEY.

THIS account of the apparition of Sir George Villiers purports to be an " Extract a Monsieur d'Ablancour, le Vie le Grand Duc de Buckingham," but in reality is taken word for word from Clarendon's " History of the Rebellion," book i. pars. 89 to 93; according to which, the apparition appeared three times to an officer of the king's wardrobe, in Windsor Castle, and commanded him to tell the Duke of Buckingham "that if he did not somewhat to ingratiate himself to the People, or at least, to abate the Extream Mallice they had against him, he would be suffer'd to live but a Short Time." He is reported to have seen the duke, and left him much troubled. Soon afterwards the duke was murdered by Felton.

There were many strange stories similar to this afloat. Lilly the conjuror gave a version in his " Observations on the Life and Death of King Charles," which Dr. Robert Plot contradicted, and gave an altogether fresh one, in all probability as veracious.

That the duke received warnings of danger to himself is undoubted. Sir Henry Wotton, in his "Short View of the Life and Death of George Villiers Duke of Buckingham" (1642), admits it, but he denies any supernatural warning. He says, "I have spent some enquiry whether he had any ominous presagement before his end; wherein though both ancient and modern Stories have been infected with much vanity; yet oftentimes things fall out of that kind which may bear a sober constitution, whereof I will glean two or three in the Duke's Case.

" Being to take his leave of my Lords Grace of *Canturbury* the only Bishop of *London*, whom he knew well planted in the King's unchangeable affection, by his own great abilities, after cortesies of courage had passed between them; My Lord, sayes the Duke, I know your Lordship hath very worthily good accesses unto the King our Soveraign, let me pray you to put His Majesty in minde to be good, as I no way distrust, to my poor wife and children; at which words, or at his countenance in the delivery, or at both, My Lord Bishop being somewhat troubled, took the freedom to aske him where [? whether] he had never any secret abodements in his minde, No (replyed the Duke) but I think some adventure may kill me as well as another man," etc.

THE

PORTSMOUTH GHOST

OR A

Full and true Account of a Strange, wonderful, and dreadful Appearing of the Ghost of Madam Johnson, a beautiful young Lady of Portsmouth

SHEWING

1. Her falling in Love with Mr. John Hunt, a Captain in one of the Regiments sent to Spain.

2. Of his promising her Marriage, and leaving her big With Child.

3. Of her selling herself to the Devil to be revenged on the Captain.

4. Of her ripping open her own Belly, and the Devil's flying away with her Body, and leaving the Child in the room.

5. Of the Captain's Fleet being drove back by a Storm to St. Helen's.

6. Of her appearing to several Sailors, acquainting them who she was.

7. Of her Carrying him away in the night in a flame of fire.

PRINTED AND SOLD BY CLUER DICEY AND CO. IN ALDERMARY CHURCH YARD, BOW LANE.

THIS book is useful, as it shows the early date of the firm of Dicey in Aldermary Churchyard. It must have been published very early in the century, for her ghost appeared to him whilst on his voyage to Vigo; the date of the famous capture of the galleons and the large quantity of snuff, which augmented, if it did not almost inaugurate, the taste for snuff-taking in England, being 1702. The catastrophe of the poem is graphically told.

> "The next time that she came again
> For to have perish'd on the main,
> They all expected for to rue
> So violent the storm it grew.
>
> They all at fervent prayers were,
> At length this sailor, I declare,
> Did speak to her, and thus did say,
> What ails thy troubled spirit pray?
>
> The truth she quickly then did tell.
> Saying Him I'll have, then all is well
> Then with a visage fierce and Grim,
> She strait approached unto him,
>
> He went to turn and hide his face,
> She cry'd False man it is too late,
> She clasp'd him in her arms straitway,
> But no man knew his dying day.
>
> In a flash of fire many see
> She dragged him into the sea
> The storm is soon abated where
> They all returned thanks by prayer
>
> Unto the Lord that sav'd their lives
> And delivered them from that surprise
> Let this a warning be to all
> That reads the same both great and small."

THE
GUILFORD GHOST.

Being an Account of the Strange and Amazing Apparition or Ghost of Mr. Christopher Slaughterford; with the manner of his Wonderful Appearance to Joseph Lee his Man, and one Roger Voller, at Guildford in Surrey, on Sunday and Monday Night last, in a sad and astonishing manner, in several dreadful and frightful Shapes, with a Rope about his Neck, a flaming Torch in one hand and a Club in the Other, crying Vengeance, Vengeance. With other amazing particulars.

London : Printed for J. Wyat in Southwark, 1709.

THERE is a contemporary Chap-book with this, printed by A. Hinde in Fleet Street, 1709 : "The Birth, Parentage, and Education, Life and Conversation of Mr. Christopher Slaughterford, who was Executed at Guildford in Surrey, on Saturday the 9th July, 1709, for the Barbarous Murther of Jane Young, his Sweetheart," etc.

There was a peculiarity about this case—for the man protested his innocence to the last, although the evidence was very strongly circumstantial against him—and public opinion being exercised thereon, the necessary " catchpenny " was forthcoming. His ghost seems to have appeared to several people, and the book winds up : " P.S. Just now we have an Account from the Marshálsea Prison in Southwark, that he was seen there by several of the Prisoners on Tuesday Night last, and that he has been heard to make his Fetters jingle in·the Whyte Lyon, being the place where he was put after his condemnation ; insomuch, that those who have heard the said unaccountable Noise are afraid to go near the said Place after Day light."

THE

𝕬𝖑𝖔𝖓𝖉𝖊𝖗 𝖔𝖋 𝕬𝖑𝖔𝖓𝖉𝖊𝖗𝖘

BEING

A Strange and Wonderful Relation of a Mermaid, that was seen
and spoke with, on the Black Rock nigh Liverpool, by John
Robinson Mariner, who was tossed on the Ocean for Six days
and Nights; Together with the Conversation he had with her,
and how he was preserved; with the Manner of his Death five
days after his return Home.

LICENSED AND ENTERED ACCORDING TO ORDER.

ON the 29th of April last one Mr. James Dixon Captain and Commander of the Ship Dolphin in her passage from Amsterdam in Holland, was beat back by a tempestuous Wind and all the Men perished except a young Man named John Robinson, who was taken very ill on board the Ship, and was left to Almighty Providence, and to the Mercy of the Seas and Winds, and was also in great Fear and dreadful fright on the Main Ocean, for the said John Robinson dreamt that he was on the top of an high Mountain, whose top he thought reach'd up to the Heavens, and that there was a fine Castle, about the Circumference of a Mile, and furnished with all sorts of Diamonds, and precious Stones, and likewise on the top of the Mountain was a well, which Water was as sweet as Honey and as white as Milk, that whomsoever drank of that Water should never be dry again; with all sorts of Musick very delightful to hear, so one would think, as one suppos'd seven Years in that Place, not so long as a Day.

After having view'd the Castle round he observed to his great Admiration, a beautiful young Lady, who was guarded by Seven Serpents, very frightful to behold.

Suppose the young Lady was very beautiful, yet he wish'd rather to be a Thousand Miles off than in the Sight of those Serpents; and looking round about, he espy'd (to his great Comfort) a green Gate, and a street pav'd with blue Marble, which open'd at his coming to it, and so he got away from the Serpents; But coming to the top of the Hill, he did not know how to get down, it being very high and steep, but he found a Ladder to his Comfort; it being very slender, was afraid to venture, but at last was oblig'd to go down it, for one of the Serpents having taken Notice of him pursued him so very close that he was in great Danger, and thought he fell and broke his leg, and that the Serpent fell upon him, which awaked him in great Fright, and almost made him mad.

By this you may think what a great trouble he was in, awaked alone on the Main Ocean, when missing all the rest of the Ships Crew, and also the great Danger he was in.

But to his great Amazement, he espy'd a beautiful young

Lady combing her head, and toss'd on the Billows, cloathed all in green (but by chance he got the first word with her) then she with a Smile came on board and asked how he did. The young Man being Something Smart and a Scholar, reply'd Madam I am the better to see you in good Health, in great hopes trusting you will be a comfort and assistance to mè in this my low Condition ; and so caught hold of her Comb and Green Girdle that was about her Waist. To which she replied, Sir, you ought not to rob a young Woman of her Riches, and then expect a favour at her Hands ; but if you will give me my Comb and Girdle again, what lies in my power, I will do for you.

At which Time he had no Power to keep them from her, but immediately delivered them up again ; she then smiling, thank'd him, and told him, If he would meet her again next Friday she wou'd set him on shore. He had no power to deny her, so readily gave his Consent ; at which time she gave him a Compass and desired him to Steer South West ; he thank'd her and told her he wanted some News. She said she would tell him the next opportunity when he fulfilled his promises ; but that he would find his Father and Mother much grieved about him, and so jumping into the Sea she departed out of his sight.

At her departure the Tempest ceased and blew a fair Gale to South West, so he got safe on shore ; but when he came to his Father's House he found every Thing as she had told him. For she told him also concerning his being left on Ship board, and how all the Seamen perished, which he found all true what she had told him, according to the promise made him.

He was still very much troubled in his Mind, concerning his promise, but yet while he was thus Musing, she appeared to him with a smiling Countenance and (by his Misfortune) she got the first word of him, so that he could not speak one Word, but was quite Dumb, yet he took Notice of the Words she spoke ; and she began to Sing. After which she departed out of the young Mans sight, taking from him the Compass.

She took a Ring from off her Finger, and put it on the

young Man's, and said, she expected to see him once again with more Freedom. But he never saw her more, upon which he came to himself again, went home, and was taken ill, and died in five Days after, to the wonderful Admiration of all People who saw the young Man.

FINIS.

DREAMS AND MOLES

WITH THEIR

Interpretation and Signification

Made far more Manifest and Plain than any Published, to the very meanest Capacities, by the most ancient as well as the most modern Rules of Philosophy.

To which is prefixed, A Collection of choice and valuable Receipts concerning Love and Marriage.

FIRST COMPILED IN GREEK, AND NOW FAITHFULLY RENDERED INTO ENGLISH BY A FELLOW OF THE ROYAL SOCIETY, AND A TRUE LOVER OF LEARNING.

PRINTED AND SOLD IN ALDERMARY CHURCH YARD, BOW LANE.

THE
Old Egyptian Fortune-Teller's Last Legacy

CONTAINING

1. The Wheel of Fortune by pricking with a Pin.
2. The Wheel of Fortune by the Dice.
3. The Signification of Moles.
4. The Art of Palmistry.
5. The Interpretation of Dreams.
6. The Art of Physiognomy; with the Signification of Lines in the Face.
7. Omens of good and bad luck.

PRINTED AND SOLD IN ALDERMARY CHURCH YARD,
BOW LANE, LONDON.

THE engravings in this Chap-book are very numerous, but neither they nor the subject-matter are worth reproducing in their entirety. Two extracts will suffice to give an idea of the book.

"THE SIGNIFICATION OF MOLES.

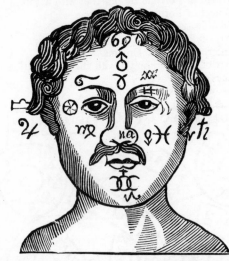

A Mole on the right Shoulder, denotes happiness to man or woman.

A Mole on the left shoulder, denotes a man to be quarrelsome but a woman to have many husbands.

A Mole on the left cheek, denotes fruitfulness in man or woman.

A Mole on the left ribs denotes a Man very cruel, and a woman to be vain and proud.

A Mole near the right Shoulder, denotes a Man to be a slave to love, and shews that a woman will be beloved of great Men.

A Mole under the right loin, signifies an industrious man, and good to a woman.

A Mole on the buttock denotes honour to a man, and Riches to a woman.

A Mole on the right side the belly, denotes a Man to flow in riches, and a woman to be happy in Marriage.

One under the right breast, denotes good Fortune.

One on the back denotes Riches and honour.

One on the right hip signifies good fortune in wedlock to man or woman.

One near the navel signifies many Children.

It is a most certain truth. That if the second toe, near the great toe, be as long as the great toe, the person will be very rich and happy.

THE SIGNIFICATION OF DREAMS.

To dream of musick signifies speedy marriage.

To dream of falling out denotes constancy.

To dream a ring falls from off your finger, signifies the loss of a friend.

To dream of meeting a coffin, signifies the death of a friend.

To dream of birds singing, signifies joy.

To dream of having teeth drawn, loss of friends.

To fight with and destroy serpents, denotes victory over enemies.

To dream of kisses denotes love from a friend.

To dream of a ring put on your finger, denotes a speedy marriage.

To fly high, signifies praise.

To dream of gathering fruit from trees well loaden, is gain and profit.

To dream of fire, and not being able to quench it, signifies quarrels.

To dream of being at a wedding, signifies the death of friends.

To dream of vermin, and to be troubled in killing them signifies much riches.

To see the Sun or Moon greater than ordinary, signifies increase of honour.

To be at a feast and eat greedily, signifies sickness.

To speak with an Angel that reveals secrets to you denotes preferment.

To dream of losing blood by the nose is of ill consequence.

To find difficulty in passing a river, signifies hard labour.

To dream of falling from a high place without hurt is good.

If you lay a bunch of rosemary under your head, on Easter eve, you will dream of the party you shall enjoy."

A NEW

FORTUNE BOOK.

BEING A NEW ART OF COURTSHIP

Open'd for young Men and Maids, Widows, Widowers and
Batchelors, Instructions for young Men and Maids, how they
may know their good or bad Fortune, shewing the signification
of Moles, the Interpretation of Dreams, the famous Secret and
New invented Art of making the true and false Love Powder;
to make the Enchanted Ring that will cause Love. Also how
to cure a Drunken Husband or a Scolding Wife, secondly, how
to cure the Ague, Thirdly how to cure the Tooth Ache.

SOLD AT CIRENCESTER.

THE

HISTORY

OF

𝕸𝖔𝖙𝖍𝖊𝖗 𝕭𝖚𝖓𝖈𝖍 𝖔𝖋 𝖙𝖍𝖊 𝖂𝖊𝖘𝖙

CONTAINING

Many Rarities out of her Golden Closet of Curiosities.

PRINTED AND SOLD AT THE LONDON AND MIDDLESEX PRINTING OFFICE. NO 81 SHOE LANE, HOLBORN.

THE HISTORY OF

MOTHER BUNCH

Is not particularly interesting, except for its scraps of folk-lore, and both parts consist principally of receipts for girls to get husbands. A few examples may be acceptable.

"Take a St. Thomas's onion, pare it, and lay it on a clean handkerchief under your pillow; put on a clean smock, and as you lie down, lay your arms abroad, and say these words

> Good St. Thomas, do me right
> And bring my love to me this night,
> That I may view him in the face,
> And in my arms may him embrace.

Then lying on thy back, with thy arms abroad, go to sleep as soon as you can, and in your first sleep you shall dream of him who is to be your husband, and he will come and offer to kiss you; do not hinder him, but catch him in thy arms, and strive to hold him, for that is he.

"Yet I have another pretty way for a maid to know her sweetheart which is as follows: Take a summer apple, of the best fruit, stick pins close into the apple, to the head, and as you stick them, take notice which of them is the middlemost, and give it what name you fancy; put it into thy left hand glove, and lay it under thy pillow on Saturday night, after thou gettest into bed, then clap thy hands together, and say these words.

> If thou be he that must have me
> To be thy wedded bride,
> Make no delay, but come away
> This night to my bedside.

And in thy sleep thou shalt see him come in his shirt, and if he offer thee any abuse, he will be great with another woman ; but if he puts his hand over thee be not afraid, for it is a sign he'll prove a good husband ; and this is a good way for a young man to know his sweetheart, giving the middlemost pin that name he fancies best, putting an apple in his right hand glove, and laying it under his pillow when he is in bed, saying,

> If thou be she that must have me
>   In wedlock for to join,
> Make no delay, but come away
>   Unto this bed of mine.

And that night he may see her, as if she came in her shift and petticoat she will prove a civil woman—but if she comes with her shift only, she will prove a ranter, and so better lost than found."

"On Midsummer Eve three or four of you must dip your shifts in fair water, then turn them wrong side outwards, and hang them on chairs before the fire, and lay some salt on another chair, and speak not a word. In a short time the likeness of him you are to marry will come and turn your smocks, and drink to you; but if there be any of you will never marry, they will hear a bell, but not the rest."

" *Another way quickly tried.*

" Take hemp seed, and go into what place you will by your-self, carry the seed in your apron, and with your right hand throw it over your shoulder, saying,

> Hemp seed I sow, hemp seed I sow,
> And he that must be my true love,
> Come after me and mow.

And at the ninth time expect to see the figure of him you are to wed, or else to hear a bell as before."

" *Another way.*

" The first change of the New Moon in the New Year, the

first time you see it, hold your hands across, saying this three times.

> New Moon, New Moon, I pray thee,
> Tell me this night who my true love will be.

Then go to bed without speaking a word, and you will certainly dream of the person you shall marry."

A GENTLEMAN GOING TO CONSULT WITH
MOTHER BUNCH.

MOTHER BUNCH'S FUNERAL.

Thus all her Art at length could not her save,
From death's dire stroke, and mould'ring in the Grave.

THE

HISTORY

OF

MOTHER SHIPTON.

PRINTED AND SOLD IN ALDERMARY CHURCH YARD, LONDON.

THE HISTORY OF

MOTHER SHIPTON.

ALL tradition agrees with the Chap-book version, that Mother Shipton was born at Knaresborough, in Yorkshire. According to this Chap-book, her father was the devil, and she was born in 1488, in a violent storm of thunder and lightning. "The strange physiognomy of the infant frighted the gossips; its body was long, and very big boned, great goggling, sharp and fiery eyes, and unproportionable nose, full of crooks, turnings and red pimples, which gave such light that needed not a candle to dress her by; as it was likewise observed that as soon as she was born, she fell a grinning and laughing after a jeering manner; and immediately the tempest ceased." This interesting child was christened by the Abbot of Beverley by the name of Ursula, and she took the surname of Sontibles, after her mother, who, when her child was two years old, repented of her evil ways, and retired to the convent of St. Bridget, near Nottingham. At the age of twenty-four, Ursula married Toby Shipton, a carpenter, and it is related they lived comfortably together, but never had any children. The wonders she worked are all jocular, and some rather broad in their humour, but it is by her prophecies that she is more generally known. Many are attributed to her, which she probably never uttered, and those in the Chap-book are mainly local. She prophesied that Cardinal Wolsey should never see York; and "at divers other times when persons of quality came to visit her she delivered these prophecies.

"FIRST PROPHECY.

"Before Oose bridge and Trinity Church meet, they shall build by day and it shall fall by night; until they get the uppermost stone of Trinity Church to be the lowest stone of Oose Bridge.

"*Explanation.*

"This came to pass, for Trinity steeple in York was blown down by a tempest and Oose Bridge broke down by a rapid flood, and what they repaired by day fell down by night, until they laid the highest stone of the steeple as a foundation of the Bridge.

"SECOND PROPHECY.

"A time shall come when a ship will come sailing up the Thames till it is opposite London, and the master of the ship asks the Captain of the ship why he weeps, since he has made so good a voyage ; and he shall say, Ah ! what a grand city was this ? none in all the world comparable to it, and now there is scarce a house left.

"*Explanation.*

"These words were verified after the dreadful Fire of London in 1666, not one house being left on the Thames side from the Tower to the Temple," etc., etc.

There are more, but these are a fair sample, and two illustrations are also given, showing the then popular idea of a *Walpurgisnacht.*

Mother Shipton is said to have died in 1561, but her life and prophecies were not published till 1641, in a small quarto tract, "The Prophesie of Mother Shipton in the raigne of Henry the eighth. Foretelling the death of Cardinal Wolsey, the lord Percy, and others, as also what should happen in insuing times. London : Printed for Richard Lownds at his shop adjoyning to Ludgate. 1641."

NIXON'S
CHESHIRE PROPHECY

AT LARGE

Published from Lady Cowpers correct
Copy in the reign of Queen Ann.

WITH

HISTORICAL AND POLITICAL REMARKS;

AND

*Several Instances wherein it has been
Fullfilled*

ALSO HIS LIFE

Nixon unfolds the dark decrees of fate
Foretells our Second George shall make him great;
That Gallia's Politicks are all a Trance,
For Brunswick's Arms shall conquer wily France.

PRINTED AND SOLD IN ALDERMARY CHURCH YARD, BOW LANE,
LONDON.

ROBERT NIXON.

Judging from Mother Shipton, and this portrait of Nixon, our native prophets are not remarkable for their good looks. The latter, especially, seems to have owed very little to nature, for he is described as being "a short squab fellow, had a great head and goggle eyes, that he used to drivel as he spoke, which was very seldom, and was extremely surly.

"Against Children he particularly had a spite, especially if they made any sport of him, and would run after them and beat them. At first he was a plough boy to Farmer Crowton of Swanton, and so stubborn, they could make him do nothing without beating. They could seldom get any thing out of him but Yes and No, unless he was pinched with hunger ; for he had a very good stomach, and could eat up a shoulder of mutton at one meal, with a good hunch of bread and cheese after it."

The spirit of prophecy seems to have come suddenly upon him, and his recorded vaticinations are purely local.

His end was sad. " The noise of Nixon's predictions coming to the ears of the King [presumably James I.] he would needs see this fool ; he cried, and made much ado that he might not go to court, and the reason he gave was that he should be starved. The King being informed of Nixon's refusing to come, said He would take particular care that he should not be starved ; and ordered him to be brought up. Nixon cried out he was sent for again—and soon after the messenger arrived, who brought him up from Cheshire. How or whether he prophesied to his Majesty no body can tell but he is not the first fool that has made a good court prophet.—That Nixon might be well provided for, it was ordered he should be kept in the kitchen ; but he grew so troublesome in licking and picking the meat, that the cooks locked him up in a hole, and the King going on a sudden from Hampton Court to London, they forgot Nixon in the hurry, and he was starved to death." The first printed book relating to him is " The Cheshire Prophesy ; with Historical and Political Remarks. (By John Oldmixon) London printed and sold by A. Baldwin, in Warwick Lane, price 3*d*." (1714).

REYNARD THE FOX.

OF the antiquity of this story there is no doubt; the only difficulty is to say how old it is. A poem in Flemish, called " der Reinaert," was known in the eleventh century; and in two *serventes*, or verses of the Troubadours, attributed to our Richard I., the names of Isegrim the Wolf and Reinhart are found. It was, however, reserved to England to have first printed it, as Caxton did in 1481. This rare book is in the British Museum, and winds up " Prayeng alle them that shal see this lytyl treatis to correcte and amende Where they shal fynde faute / For I haue not added ne mynusshed but haue folowed as nyghe as I can my Copye whiche was in dutche / and by me Willm Caxton translated in to this rude and symple englyssh in thabbey of Westmestre + fynysshed the vj daye of Juyn the yere of our lord mcccclxxxj and the xxj yere of the regne of Kynge Edward the iiijth /." Roscoe * says the earliest printed German copy would appear to be 1498, written in the dialect of Lower Saxony ; though there was a Dutch romance in prose bearing the same title, " Historie van Reynaert de Vos," published at Delft in 1485. Goethe ennobled the subject by his poem in 1794.

This Chap-book version is somewhat condensed, but it gives a very good account of the romance, and, as it is not very well known, it is given *in extenso*.

* " German Novelists," vol. i.

THE HISTORY

REYNARD THE FOX

PRINTED AND SOLD IN ALDERMARY CHURCH YARD
BOW LANE. LONDON
1780.

Chap. i.

A GREAT FEAST PROCLAIMED BY THE LION, AT WHICH THE WOLF, HIS WIFE AND THE HOUND COMPLAIN AGAINST REYNARD THE FOX.

IT was when the woods was cloathed with green attire, and the meadows adorned with fragrant flowers ; when birds chaunted forth their harmonious songs, the Lion made a great feast at his palace at Sanden ; and issued a proclamation for all the beasts and birds to come thereto without delay, on pain of his contempt.

Now being assembled before the King, there were some beasts found there that made great complaints against the Fox (who was absent) particularly Isegrim the Wolf who thus began :

Dread Sovereign,

I beseech thee to take pity on me and my wife, for the injuries we have sustained by that false creature Reynard the Fox ; who came into my house by violence and befouled my children in such a rank manner that they became instantly blind ; for which I expect from him amends, and from your Majesty Justice.

When the Wolf had ended, up starts Curtis the Hound, and complaining against Reynard, said, That in the cold season of the Winter, when he was kept from all manner of prey, and half-starved, having but one poor pudding left, the said Reynard had taken it from him.

Tibert the Cat, upon this got up, and falling before the King, said, My Lord, I must confess that Reynard the Fox is much complained against, yet each of these will find enough for his clearing; for concerning the offence against the Hound it was committed long since; the puding was mine, though I complained not, for I got it out of the Mill by night when the miller lay asleep.

Here the Panther interrupted the Cat, saying, It was just and good to complain against Reynard, for all the world knows he is a thief, murderer, and ravisher; and false to every creature: I will tell you what I saw him do yesterday to Kayward the Hare, who is now standing in the King's presence. He promised to teach him his Credo, and make him a good chaplain; but had I not come by he had killed him, for he had got poor Kayward between his legs, and was squeezing his throat: therefore, O my Lord if you suffer him to go unpunished that hath broken the peace, your Children hereafter will bear the shadow of this evil—Certainly Panther, said Isegrim, what you say is true.

Chap. 2.

Grimbard the Brock's Speech in Behalf of Reynard.

Grimbard the Brock who was Reynard's Sister's Son, being moved with anger, said, Isegrim, you are malicious and as the proverb is, Malice never speaks well of any one: I wish you would agree that he who hath done the most injury of either my Cousin Reynard or you, should die the death; was he here at Court, and in favour as you are, he would make you ask forgiveness, for have you not bitten and torn him with your venemous teeth? have you forgot how you cheated him of his plaice, of which you left him nothing but the bones; also of the flitch of bacon; the taste of which was so good, that you eat it up from him alone, though he got it at the danger of his own life; I must confess that my kinsman lay with his wife, but it was seven years before Isgrim married her; so what credit gets he by slandering his wife, when she is troubled at it.

Now comes Kayward the Hare with his complaint, which is but a trifle; for if he would not learn his lesson, can you blame his schoolmaster Reynard for giving due correction; and lastly, for Curtise had he not stole the pudding himself? and who can blame Reynard for taking away stolen goods from a thief; my uncle is a gentleman, a true man, and cannot endure false-hood; he does nothing but by the Council of a priest; and since the King hath made peace, he hath hurt no body; he eats but once a day, wears a hair shirt, and hath eat no meat for this year past; he hath forsaken his Castle, a poor hermitage retains him; he hath distributed all his wealth, and lives upon alms, and doth infinite penance for his Sins.

Chap. 3.

The Cock's Complaint against Reynard; and the King's Answer.

THUS while Grimbard stood preaching was brought upon a bier by Canticleer the Cock, a dead Hen, whose head Reynard had bitten off: On each side stood two sorrowful Hens, sisters to the deceased, each bearing a burning torch, and crying out, Alack-and-a-well-a-day for the loss of our sister Copple: and being come before the King, they kneeled down, and said

Most mighty King,

Vouchsafe to redress the great injuries that Reynard the Fox hath done me and my children, now weeping before you.

In April last, in fair weather, and I in the midst of my pride, having seven fair daughters, was envied by Reynard, who made many attempts to get at us by scaling the wall, but was repulsed, and had his skin tore by the dogs : but at last he came like a hermit with a letter to read, signed with your Majesty's seal, in which I found you had made peace throughout your whole realm, and that no beast nor fowl should hurt one another ; and as for him he was become a Monk, did penance for his sins, shewed me his books and beads, the hair shirt next his skin, and vowed to eat no more flesh ; and saying his Credo, laid himself down under a bench.—I was glad to hear this, and took no heed, but clucked my children together ; but false Reynard crept between us and the gate, seized on, bore away, and destroyed fifteen of them ; and yesterday Copple my daughter, now on the bier, was rescued from him by a kennel of Hounds : so for all this, I beg of your Majesty, Justice.

The King then turning to Grimbard, said, Your Uncle hath prayed and fasted well, hath he not ? I vow he shall suffer for this—Mr. Canticleer I have heard your complaint and will grant your request ; give your daughter solemn burial, and I will consult with my Lords to give you right against the murderer.—This the King immediately did, and it was agreed to send Bruin the Bear to summon Reynard to appear before the King to answer to the heavy crimes laid to his charge.

CHAP. 4.

BRUIN THE BEAR UNFORTUNATE IN HIS MESSAGE TO REYNARD THE FOX.

THE next morning went Bruin to Malepardus, a high mountain where Reynard had a castle, and knocked at the gate, he cried aloud, Sir Reynard, are you at home ? I am Bruin your kinsman, come to summons you to Court, to answer to several complaints laid against you ; and if you appear not to your summons, the King vows you shall answer it with your life.—

Reynard hearing this, ran into one of his holes, where he plotted how he might bring the Bear to disgrace, whom he knew loved him not. At last he came out of his holes saying, Dear uncle you are welcome, I was busy when you spoke, in saying my evening devotion. I am sorry you have taken this long journey, for I intended to have been at court to-morrow; indeed I wish we were there now, since I have left off eating meat, my body is swelled and distempered with eating so many honey combs through wantonness, that I fear its consequence. —How! quoth Bruin do you make so light of honey combs, which is meat for the Emperor? Nephew help me to some and I will be your friend for ever—Quoth the Fox, well I will bring you to a place where you shall have as much of it as you can eat: at this the Bear laughed till he could hardly stand. Well, thought Reynard, you will soon laugh on the other side of the mouth. So he brought him to a Carpenter's Yard where in stood a great oak tree with two great wedges in it and the clift open. Dear Uncle, said the Fox, be careful, for within this tree is much honey; pray eat moderate, for a surfeit is dangerous.—Never fear you that, said Bruin; so he entered the tree with eagerness, and thrust his head into the cleft quite over his ears; which the Fox perceiving, pulled out the wedges, and the Bear was locked fast in, and roared out hedieously; while the Fox at a distance said, Is the honey good, Uncle? do you like it? pray do not surfeit yourself with it: then left him and went to his Castle. The Bears noise brought out the Carpenter and his neighbours with great sticks and staves; and the Bear seeing so many enemies, at last wrenched his head out of the tree, leaving behind him his skin and ears; upon this the people fell on him and beat him most woefully; however at last he got from them, bitterly cursing the Fox, who had brought him to this misery. In great pain and grief he at length arrived at the King's Court, where he cried out, Behold, dread Sovereign, for doing your Royal will and pleasure I am come to this disgrace. Then said the King, How durst he do this? I swear by my crown I will take such revenge as shall make him tremble.

Upon this was summoned another council, when it was agreed to send Tibert the Cat.

CHAP. 5.

TIBERT THE CAT'S AMBASSY TO REYNARD, WITH THE BAD SUCCESS OF IT.

TIBERT was loath to go on this message, but at length, fearing the King's displeasure, undertook it; and arriving at Male-pardus, he found the Fox standing at his Castle gate, to whom he thus addressed himself. Health to my Cousin Reynard: the King by me summonses you to the Court, on sure pain of death for the refusal—Welcome Cousin, I obey the command, and wish my sovereign all happiness; only let me desire you to stay all night, and early in the morning I will go with you— I am content to stay, says Tibert, you speak like a gentleman— Truly says the Fox, I have but one honeycomb left, what think you of it for supper? I had rather have a mouse, replied Tibert—A Mouse dear Cousin!, here is a parson hard by that hath a barn full of mice. Dear Reynard, lead me thither, and I will be your friend for ever—Now the Fox had the night before got into the parson's barn and stole a fat hen, which so exasperated the priest, that he sat a snare to catch him, of which the Fox being apprized, had escaped: To this hole brings the Cat, saying Go in here, and you will soon get your bellyfull. I will wait for you till you come out.

But may I go in safety said the Cat, for Priests are very subtle. Cousin, said the Fox, I never knew you a Coward before. Puss being ashamed at this reproof, sprung in, and was quickly caught by the Neck; which as soon as the Cat felt, he leaped back again, so that the snare closed faster and had like to have strangled him, so that he exclaimed bitterly against Reynard, who scornfully said, Tibert, dost thou love mice? but the Cat mewed sadly. The priest rising out of his bed called up his servant, saying, We have caught the Fox that stole our Hens; and coming to Tibert, smote him with a great Staff, and struck out one of his eyes. The Cat thinking his death near, leaped between the Priests legs and fastened his Claws into them; which when his wife saw, swore she would rather lose the whole offering of seven years, than see him so abused—This threw the priest into a swoon, so they all left the Cat, and the Fox returned to his Castle, thinking Tibert past recovery; but he, seeing his foes busy about the priest gnawed the Cord asunder, and made her escape out of the hole, going roaring to court with the loss of one eye, and a bruised body; so that when the King beheld him he was angry and took Council once more how to be revenged on the Fox.

Chap. 6.

The Brock's Embassy to Reynard, the Fox's Confession and their Arrival at Court.

Then said the King, Go you Sir Grimbard, but take heed, Reynard is very subtle. Brock thanked his Majesty, and taking his leave, went to Malepardus, and found Reynard and his wife sporting with their young ones—Having saluted them, he said, Take heed uncle, that absence from the Court doth not do you more harm than you think for; the complaints against you are many and great; this is the third summons, and if you delay coming, you and yours will find no mercy, for in three days your Castle will be demolished, all your kindred made slaves, and you a publick example; unless you can make your innocence appear; and the which I doubt not you have discretion to do.—Very true nephew, replied Reynard, I will go with you, not only to clear myself, but to the shame of my enemies; many of which I have at court: so taking leave of his family he and Grimbard set out for Sandem the King's Palace—On their way Reynard made the following confession unto his nephew Grimbard; Blame me not dear cousin, if my life be full of Care; for I strive to blot out my sins by repentance, that my soul may be at quiet: I have grievously offended against Canticleer the Cock and his Children; my uncle Bruin the Bear and Tibert the Cat; nay I've abused and slandered the King and Queen; I have betrayed Isegrim the Wolf by calling him Uncle, when he is no kin to me; I made him bind his foot to the bell rope to teach him to ring, but the peal had like to have cost him his life; I taught him to catch fish, by which he was sorely banged; I led him to the parson's house to steal bacon; I stole a fine fat hen set before the priest for his dinner, in doing which he espied and pursued me, when I was obliged to let the hen go and creep into a hole; but the priest espying Isegrim, cried this is he, strike! strike! So my enemies fell upon the Wolf and almost killed him—But for all this I ask forgiveness.

Here on their way they met a Pullen, at which the Fox glanced his eye (for the ill that was bred in the bone stuck) which Brock taking notice of, said, Fie, dissembling Cousin why wander your eyes after the Pullin?—You wrong me, nephew, said the Fox, my eyes wandered not; I was just saying a Pater Noster for the Souls of the Pullens I have formerly slain; in which devotion you hindered me.

By this time they were come to the palace, and Reynard quaked for fear, on account of the many and great crimes he had to answer for.

CHAP. 7.

REYNARD'S EXCUSE BEFORE THE KING HIS TRIAL AND CONDEMNATION.

AT the news of Reynard's arrival, all sorts of the King's Subjects from the highest to the lowest, prepared themselves to accuse him—Though Reynard's heart trembled, yet he kept his countenance, and went as proudly and unconcerned through the streets, as though he were the King's Son, and entirely innocent of any offence—When he came before the King, he said, Heaven preserve your Majesty, there never came before you a more loyal subject than myself, and so will die; I know there are several in your court that seek my life; but I am persuaded your Majesty hates slanderers.—Peace, traiterous Reynard, replied the King, thinkest thou to deceive me also; Know that the peace which I commanded, you have broken; therefore, thou Devil among the good, with what face can you pretend to love me? when all these before me can testify against thee?—Said the Fox, my Liege, if Bruin's crown be bloody with stealing honey; and Tibert loses her eye by getting into the Priest's barn to steal mice; when they should have been diligent in your majesty's embassy, can I help that? O my dread Sovereign, I am as innocent as the Child unborn; however, use me as you please. Upon this, Bruin the Bear, Bellin the Ram, Kaward the Hare, Isegrim the Wolf, Bruel the Goose, Boulden the Ass, Borell the Bull, and Canticleer the

Cock, with their Children, all with one voice cried out against the Fox; all which caused the King to order his trial to be immediately brought on.

A parliament was summoned, and after a long trial, in the course of which the Fox answered every thing with much craft, he was condemned; whereupon Grimbard, and the rest of his kindred left the Court, as not enduring to see him executed. The King seeing so many depart, said, Though Reynard had some faults, yet he had many friends. This musing of the King made the Cat, the Bear, and the Wolf jealous lest the King should retract Reynard's sentence, and was angry at the delay of his execution; to forward which Tibert produced the Cord in which he was hanged in the priests house, and they put it round Reynard's neck, who said, I do not fear death; I saw my father die, and he soon vanished; death is familiar to me: but I beseech your Majesties (who were both seated to see the execution) to grant me but one request before I die; that is that I may unload my Conscience, and beg the assistance of your prayers, that I may be made happy hereafter.

Chap. 8.

Reynard's Confession and Pardon.

Now every one began to pity Reynard, and prevailed with the King to grant his request; which being done he thus began;

Help me ye powers above, for I can see none but whom I have offended ; in my youth I used to be much with the lambs, delighting in their bleating, till at last biting one of them, I tasted the Sweetness of their blood, and could not forbear ever since. This drew me into the woods among the goats, where I slew and eat some young Kids ; this made me more hardy, so I fell to killing Hens, Geese, and other Pullin ; for all was fish that came to net. Afterwards I fell into bad company, as Isegrim, who pretended to be my kinsman ; we grew at last so intimate, that he stole the great things and I the small ; he murdered the Nobles, and I the meaner subjects ; I speak thus plainly, he had plate and jewels more than ten carts could carry.—Ah ! said the King, where is all this treasure ? It was stolen, my Liege, said the Fox, but had it not been stolen as it was, it might have cost your Majesty's life—Discover the matter immediately, said the Queen.—I am willing to discharge my Conscience before I die : it is true the King was to have been killed by his own subjects, I must confess by some of my nearest kindred ; it was thus, My father digging in the ground found the King's treasure, whereupon he was so proud, that he scorned the rest of the beasts of the wilderness ; at last he caused Tibert the Cat to go to Bruin the Bear in the forest of Arden, to do him homage, and promised to set the crown upon Bruin's head ; then he sent for his wife, Isegrim the Wolf, and Tibert the Cat, amongst whom it was agreed to murder your Majesty, and make Bruin king ; but it happened that my nephew Grimbard being got drunk, discovered it to Sluggard his wife, who in great secrecy told it my wife and she discovered it to me. It grieved me to think a ravenous Bear should depose you ; but being desirous to find out this treasure which my father had hid, I at last by constant watching did, and I and my wife removed it. The plot being thus carried on with secrecy, when my father went to the cave and found his treasure all taken away, he for madness hanged himself—All this is true, I am now ready to die, my conscience being eased.

The King and Queen hearing this, hoping to get from Reynard this treasure, released him from the gibbet, desiring him to discover where it lay.—Rather you than my enemies, said the Fox—Fear not Reynard, said the Queen, the King shall spare thy life—Madam, replied the King, will you believe, the Fox? know you not his quality is to lie and steal? In these circumstances, my Lord, you may believe him.—Well, Madam, for this time I will be ruled by you, and pardon him, all his offences, with this promise, That if ever he offends again, he and all his posterity shall be destroyed.

Chap. 9.

Reynard restored to favour and preferred.

Then said the King, Reynard, you shall do us homage; and for your discoveries I will make you one of the Lords of my Council; discharge your trust, and govern by truth and equity; henceforth I will be ruled by your wisdom, and under me you shall be chief governor.

Reynard's friends thanked the King, and returned with the Fox, who was glad he had sped so well, having caused Bruin and Tibert to be destroyed, who sought his life.

Arriving at Malepardus there was great feasting and rejoicing at the Fox's good fortune; after which Reynard thanked them for the love and honour done him, protesting to be their friend and servant for ever; and so shaking hands, they departed.

FINIS.

VALENTINE AND ORSON.

THIS romance is undoubtedly of French origin, and an edition of it was printed at Lyons by Jac. Maillet in 1489, whilst one, probably as early, was printed by Wynkyn de Worde, of which only a fragment of four leaves is in existence. This is in the Duke of Devonshire's library, and was found in the binding of an oak-covered volume in his library at Bolton Abbey. William Coplande also printed two editions—one "The Hystorye of the two Valyaunte Brethren Valentyne and Orson, sōnes vn to the Emperour of Grece. Imprented at London ouer agaynst S. Margaretes Church in Lothbery be William Coplande," quarto, black letter; and the other, "The Hystorye of the two Valyaunte Brethren Valentyne and Orson Sonnes vnto the Emperour of Greece (translated out of French by Henry Watson) Lond. by Wylliam Coplande at the sygne of the Rose Garland," quarto—whilst in the British Museum there are illustrations of the romance in a manuscript, " 10 E. IV. Royal," pp. 120, etc., and several beautifully printed early French versions, notably those of Lyons, 1539, and Paris, 1540. The idea of children being nursed by wild beasts is very common and stories of such are told in quite modern times.

THE

HISTORY OF

𝕍alentine and Orson.

Reader; you'll find this little Book contains
Enough to answer thy Expence and Pains;
And if with Caution you will read it thro'
'Twill both Instruct thee and Delight thee too.

PRINTED AND SOLD IN ALDERMARY CHURCH YARD
BOW LANE, LONDON.

Chap. i.

The Banishment of the Lady Bellisant who is delivered of Valentine and Orson at one birth in a wood.

IT is recorded, That PEPIN King of France had a fair sister named Bellisant, who was married to Alexander, the Emperor of Greece, and by him carried to his capital at Constantinople; from whence, after having lived with great virtue, she was banished, through the means of a false accuser, whom she had severely checked for his impudence; and though at that time she was big with child, yet she was compelled to leave her husband's empire, to the great regret of the people, attended only with a Squire named Blandiman.

After great fatigue and travel she arrived in the forest of Orleans, where finding her pains come thick upon her, she dismissed her attendant for a midwife, but before his return was delivered of two lovely children, one of which was conveyed away by a she bear, but she, willing to save it pursued on her

hands and knees, leaving the other behind. But before her return, King Pepin being a hunting in the forest, came to the tree where she left the other babe, and causing it to be taken up, sent it to nurse, and when it grew up called its name Valentine —Blandiman at length came back, and instead of finding his mistress found her brother Pepin, at the tree, to whom he declared all that had happened, and how his sister had been banished through the false suggestions of the arch priest; which when King Pepin heard he was greatly enraged against the Lady Bellisant, saying, that the Emperor ought to have put her to death; so leaving Blandiman, he returned with his Nobles to Paris.

The Lady Bellisant having followed the Bear to no purpose, returned to the place where she had left the other babe, but great was her sorrow when Blandiman said, He had seen her brother Pepin, but could tell nothing of the child, and having comforted her for the loss of it, they went to the sea side, took shipping, and arrived at the castle of the Giant Feragus, in Portugal.

All this while the Bear nourished the infant among her young ones, until at length it grew up a wild hairy man, doing great mischief to all that passed through the forest; in which we will leave him, and return to the arch Priest, who did great mischief, till he was impeached by a merchant, of having wrongfully accused the Empress, upon which they fought, and the merchant conquering, made the Priest confess all his treasons, when the Emperor acquainting the King of France of it, he was hanged.

CHAP. 2.

VALENTINE CONQUERS HIS BROTHER ORSON IN THE FOREST OF ORLEANS.

Now was Valentine grown a lusty young man, and by the King as greatly beloved as if he had been his own child; commanding him to be taught the use of Arms, in which he soon became so expert, that few in the Court dare to encounter him; which made Hufray and Henry, the King's bastard sons exceedingly envy him—At this juncture great complaints were made against the Wild Man, from whom no Knight had escaped with his life, that had encountered him; which made the King promise a thousand marks to any that should bring him dead or alive, which offer none dare accept; but Hufray and Henry desired King Pepin to send Valentine, with a view of getting rid of so powerful a rival in the King's favour, but his Majesty seeing their malice was very angry, telling them he had rather lose the best Baron in the land.

However Valentine desired leave of his Majesty to go to the forest, resolving either to conquer the wild man or die in the attempt. Accordingly having furnished himself with a good horse and arms, he set forward on his journey, and after two days travelling he arrived in the forest. In the evening he tied his horse to a large spreading oak; and got up into a tree himself for his security, where he rested that night.

Next Morning he beheld the Wild man traversing the forest in search of his prey, and at length he came to the tree where Valentine's horse stood from whom he pulled many hairs, upon

which the horse kicked him. The Wild man feeling the pain was going to tear him to pieces, which Valentine seeing, made signs as if he would fight him, and accordingly he stepped down and gave him a blow; but the Wild Man caught him by the arm and threw him to the ground. Then taking up Valentines shield, he beheld it with amaze, with respect to the divers colours thereon emblazoned.

Valentine being much bruised, got up, and came towards his brother in great anger; but Orson ran to a tree and then they engaged; but both being terribly wounded, gave out by consent; after which Valentine signified to Orson, That if he would yield to him, he would order matters so, as he should become a rational creature.

Orson thinking that he meant him no harm, stretched forth his hand to him. Upon which he bound him, and then led him to Paris, where he presented him to King Pepin, who had the Wild Man baptized by the name of Orson, from his being taken in a wood. Orson's actions during their stay there, very much amused the whole court, that at length the Duke of Acquitain sent letters importing, That whoever should overthrow the Green Knight, a Pagan Champion, should have his daughter Fazon in marriage. Upon which proposition Valentine set out for that province, attended by his brother Orson, by which means he came to the knowledge of his parents, as we shall find hereafter.

CHAP. 3.

THE FIGHT BETWEEN ORSON AND THE GREEN KNIGHT.

AFTER a long journey, Valentine and Orson arrived at Duke Savary's palace in Acquitain; and making known the reason that they came there, was presented to Fazon, to whom Valentine thus addressed himself.

"Sweet creature, King Pepin has sent me hither with the bravest Knight in all his realm to fight the Green Knight, who, though he is dumb and naked, is endued with such valour, that no Knight under the sun is able to cope with him."

During this speech she viewed Orson narrowly and he her; but Supper coming in, interrupted them, and they sat down to eat.

Whilst they were in the midst of all their feasting, the Green Knight entered, saying Duke Acquitain, hast thou any more Knights to cope with me for thy daughter—Yes, replied the Duke, I have seventeen, and then shewed them to him— The Green Knight then said to them Eat your fill, for tomorrow will be your last—Orson hearing what he said, was much incensed against him and suddenly rising from the table, threw the Green Knight with such force against the wall, as laid him dead for some time; which very much pleased the whole company.

Next day many Knights went to fight the Green Knight, but he overcame and slew them all; till at last, Orson being armed in Valentine's armour, came to the Green Knight's pavilion, and defying him they began the most desperate combat as was ever heard of, and the Green Knight made so great a stroke at him, as to cut off the top of the helmet, and half his shield, wounded him very much. But this served only to enrage the valiant Orson, who coming up to him on foot took hold of him, and pulling him from his horse, got astride him, and was just going to kill him, but was prevented by the sudden arrival of Valentine, who interceded with Orson to spare his life on condition of his turning Christian, and acquainted King Pepin how he was conquered.

The Green Knight having promised to perform all that was desired, they led him prisoner to the city of Acquitain; and the Duke received them with great joy, and offered the Lady Fazon to Orson; but he would not marry her till his brother had won the Green Knight's sister Lady Clerimond, nor till they had talked with the Enchanted Head of Brass to know his Parents, and get the proper use of his tongue; which when the lady knew she was very sorrowful, because she loved Orson, and was resolved to marry none but him, who had so nobly conquered the Green Knight.

VALENTINE AND ORSON GO IN SEARCH OF LADY CLERIMOND, WHO HAD THE BRAZEN HEAD IN HER POSSESSION.

VALENTINE and Orson having taken their leave of the Duke of Acquitain, and his daughter Fazon, proceeded upon their journey, in search of the Lady Clerimond, and at last came to a tower of burnished brass; which upon enquiry, they discovered to be kept by Clerimond, sister to Feragus and the defeated Green Knight, and having demanded entrance, was refused it by the centinal who guarded the gate ; which provoked Valentine to that degree, that he ran against him with such fury, that the centinell fell down dead immediately.

The Lady Clerimond beheld all this dispute, and seeing them brave knights received them courteously—Valentine having presented tokens from the Green Knight, told her, he came there for the love of her, and to discourse with the All knowing Head, concerning their parents. After dinner, the Lady took them by the hand, and led them to the chamber of

Rantus, where the head was placed between four pillars of pure jasper ; when as they entered, it made the following speeching to Valentine.

" Thou famous Knight of Royal extract, art called Valentine the Valiant, who of right ought to marry the Lady Clerimond. Thou art Son to the Emperor of Greece and the Empress Bellisant, who is now in the Castle of Feragus in Portugal, where she has resided for twenty years, King Pepin is thine uncle, and the Wild man thy brother; the Empress Bellisant brought ye two forth in the forest of Orleans; he was taken away by a ravenous Bear, and thou wast taken up by thine Uncle Pepin, who brought thee up to man's estate— Moreover, I likewise tell thee that thy brother shall never speak till thou cuttest the thread that grows under his tongue."

The Brazen head having ended his speech, Valentine embraced Orson, and cut the thread which grew under his tongue; and he directly related many surprising things. After which Valentine married Lady Clerimond, but not before she had turned Christian.

In this Castle lived a dwarf, named Pacolet, who was an Enchanter, and by his art had contrived a horse of wood, and in the forehead a fixed pin, by turning of which he could convey himself to the farthest part of the world.

This enchanter flies to Portugal and informs Ferragus of his sister's nuptials, and of her turning Christian; which so enraged him that he swore by Mahomet he would make her rue it; and thereupon got ready his fleet, and sailed towards the Castle of Clerimond, where when he arrived, he concealed his malice from his sister, and also the two Knights, telling them that he came to fetch them into Portugal, the better to solemnize their Marriage, and he would turn Christian at their arrival at his castle; all which they believed, and soon after embarked with him—When he had got them on board, he ordered them to be put in irons, which so grieved his sister Clerimond, that she would have thrown herself into the sea, had she not been stopped.

CHAP. 5.

PACOLET COMFORTS THE LADIES AND DELIVERS VALENTINE AND ORSON OUT OF PRISON.

WHEN they were come to Portugal, he put Valentine and Orson in a dungeon, fed them with bread and water, but allowed his sister Clerimond to meet the Empress Bellisant, who had been confined twenty years in the Castle of Feragus. She, seeing her so full of grief, comforts her, enquiring the reason, which she told her. The Empress was mightily grieved, but Pacolet comforted them, telling them he would release them all that evening, the which he accordingly did in the following manner:

In the dead of the night he goes to the dungeon, where lay Valentine and Orson, bound in chains, and touching the doors

with his magical wand, they flew open; and coming to the Knights, he released them and conducted them to the apartment where Bellisant and Clerimond was, who were exceedingly transported; but Pacolet hindered them from discoursing long, by telling them they must depart before the guards of Ferrajus awaked, which would put a stop to his proceedings. So Pacolet led them to the gates of the Castle, and having prepared a ship, he conveyed them to Lady Fazon, at the city of Acquitain. Next morning when Ferragus heard of their escape, he was enraged to the last degree.

The Knights and Ladies being out of danger, soon arrived at Acquitain, to the great joy of Lady Fazon, who was soon after married to Orson with great solemnity; upon which tilts and tournaments were performed for many days; but Valentine carried the prize, overthrowing at least an hundred brave Knights.

Chap. 6.

Ferragus raises a mighty army, and lays Siege to the City of Acquitain.

Ferragus, to be revenged on them assembled an Army, and laid close siege to it with a vast army of Saracens, which when Duke Savary perceived, he resolved to give them battle the very next morning, and accordingly he sallied forth with all his forces, but venturing too far, he was taken by the Saracens and carried to Ferragus's tent.

Now Orson was resolved to set him free, or lose his life; so putting on the arms of a dead Saracen, he called Pacolet and went through the enemy without being molested, until they

arrived at the tent where the Duke was confined; which done they gave him a horse, and rode to the Christian army: on their return a general shout was made by all the army, Long live the Duke of Acquitain; which so dismayed the Saracens, that they fled away in confusion, and the Christians pursued them till the night obliged them to give over.

Soon after this victory Valentine, Orson, the Ladies Bellisant, Clerimond and Fazon, set out for Constantinople, to see the Emperor their father, after they had taken leave of Duke Savary and his Nobles, and was received with great joy.

At length the Emperor set out from Constantinople after taking leave of his family, to visit a strong Castle he had in Spain.—While he was absent, Brandiser brother to Feragus invaded the Empire with a very great army, and at length besieged Constantinople, where lay Valentine and Orson, the Green Knight and all the Ladies.

Valentine seeing the condition they all were in, resolved to give Brandiser battle, and thereupon divided his army into ten battalions, commanded by ten Knights, and sallying out of the City, began to fight with the Saracens, who were drawn up in readiness to receive them.

In the mean time the Emperor was at sea, returning homeward, and in his way he met a fleet going to the assistance of Brandiser, which bore upon him with full sails : whereupon exhorting his companions to behave like men, they made eady to receive them ; and after a most bloody and obstinate battle, the Emperor got the victory, having slain many of the Pagans, and dispersed all their ships.

After this victory the Emperor commanded his men to put on the Arms of the Vanquished, as he did himself, thinking thereby the better to fall upon the beseigers, his enemies ; but the Stratagem proved most fatal to him, as we shall hereafter find.

All this while the Christians and Valentine bravely encountered Brandiser and his men before the Walls of Constantinople, sometimes getting, and sometimes losing ground ; but at length Valentine came to the standard of Brandiser, where an Indian King run against him with great force, but Valentine avoided him, struck him with such fury as cleft him down the Middle. On the other hand Orson and the Green Knight were not idle, but with their brandished swords cut themselves a passage quite through the Pagan army, destroying all that opposed them.

Soon after news came that a mighty fleet of Saracens were entering the harbour ; whereupon Valentine judged it necessary to go thither, and oppose their landing, but it proved fatal ; for

in his fleet was the Emperor his father, who being clad in
Saracen armour, Valentine by mistake ran him quite through
the body with his spear; which when he knew, he was going
to kill himself, had not his brother and the Green Knight
prevented him; but getting an horse with an intent to lose
his life, he rushed into the midst of the enemy, overthrew all
that opposed him, till he came to the Giant Brandiser, who
when he saw Valentine, encountered him so fiercely, that both
fell to the ground; but Valentine recovering, gave him a stab
which sent him to hell, to see his false prophet Mahomet—

The Pagans seeing their King dead, threw down their arms
and run, and the Christians pursued them with a mighty
slaughter—At last the pursuit being over, they returned to
Constantinople and Orson acquainted the Empress of the
death of his father, but concealed by whom it was done.

Upon which it was concluded, That Valentine and Orson should govern the Empire by turns, with their wives the ladies Fazon and Clerimond, whose brother the Green Knight was crowned King of the Green Mountain; the people of which were much delighted to have so brave a warrior for their King.

Chap. 7.

VALENTINE DIES AND ORSON TURNS HERMIT.

Now Valentine being greatly vexed in mind for the death of his father, whom he had killed out of a mistake, resolved to make a pilgrimage to the Holy Sepulchre; and therefore taking leave of his wife Clerimond, and giving the government of the Empire unto his brother, he departed to the great sorrow of all, particularly his brother, Bellisant, and the fair Clerimond.

Valentine after seven years absence returned, dressed like a poor palmer begging victuals at the gate of his own palace; and at length, being sick, and about to die, he called for Clerimond, and made himself known unto her, at which she was ready to give up the ghost.

At last having recommended the care of her to his brother, and the Empress his dear mother, and blessing them he turned on one side, and breathed out his noble soul from his illustrious body to the great grief of all the valiant Knights of Christendom to whom he had been a noble example, and a generous reliever of. But Clerimond never could espouse any one, but betook her to a single life, always lamenting the loss of her beloved husband.

After his death, Orson governed the Empire with great wisdom and justice for Seven Years, till at length seeing the fragile state of human affairs, he gave the charge of his Empire, Wife and Children, to the Green Knight, and then turning hermit, he became a resident in the forests and woods, where after living to a great age, this magnanimous and invincible hero surrendered up his body unto never sparing death, and his soul to the immortal deities of whose attributes it had a true resemblance.

> Thus Reader you may see that none withstand
> Tho' great in valour, or in vast command
> The mighty force of Death's all conquering hand.

FINIS.

FORTUNATUS.

THE first notice of this romance I can find, is " Fortunatus, Augsp. zu trucken verordnet durch J. Heybler 1509," quarto, and it seems to have been popular, for there was a Fren-h edition, "Histoire des aventures de Fortunatus, *trad. de l'Espagn.* Rouen 1656," 12mo. The earliest English edition with an absolute date, seems to be that of Thomas Churchyarde (1676), but it is not perfect, and consists only of ninety-five leaves. In the British Museum is "The History of Fortunatus (Translated from the Dutch)," black letter, quarto ; but it is catalogued as doubtful whether it was printed in London, and whether the supposed date of 1650 is correct. It is also imperfect. The edition of 1682 is, however, perfect, and is very curious. It is entitled, "The right, pleasant and variable trachical history of Fortunatus, whereby a young man may learn how to behave himself in all worldly affairs and casual chances. First penned in the Dutch tongue ; there hence abstracted and now published in English by T. C." The Chap-book very fairly follows the romance, but of course is much condensed.

THE

HISTORY OF FORTUNATUS

CONTAINING

Various Surprising Adventures.

AMONG WHICH HE ACQUIRED A PURSE THAT COULD NOT BE EMPTIED.

And a Hat that carried him wherever he wished to be.

PRINTED AND SOLD IN ALDERMARY CHURCH YARD. BOW LANE. LONDON.

Chap. I.

Of the Birth of Fortunatus.

In the famous Isle of Cyprus there is a stately city called Famagosta, in which lived a wealthy citizen named Theodorus. He, being left young by his parents, addicted himself to all manner of pleasures, often frequenting the Courts of princes,

where he soon wasted great part of his wealth in riotous living, to the grief of his friends, who thinking to make him leave his idle courses, got him married to a rich citizen's daughter named Gratiana with whom he lived virtuously for some time.

In one year after his Marriage, Gratiana was brought to bed of a son, who was named Fortunatus—Theodorus in a short time began to follow his old bad courses, insomuch that he began to sell and mortgage all his estate, so that he fell into extreme poverty; Gratiana being forced to dress her meat and wash her clothes herself, not being able now to keep one single servant, or hire the meanest assistance.

Theodorus and his wife sitting one day at a poor dinner, he could hardly refrain weeping, which his son, (who was now about eighteen years old, and experienced in hunting, hawking, and playing the lute,) perceiving, he said Father, what aileth you? for I observe, when you look upon me, you seem sad; Sir, I fear I have some way offended you—Theodorus answered,

My dear Son, thou art not the cause of my grief, but my self
has been the sole cause of the pinching poverty we all feel.
When I call to mind the wealth and honour I so lately enjoyed,
and when I consider how unable I am now to succour my
child, it is that which vexeth me.—To this his son replied—
Beloved father, do not take immoderate care for me, for I am
young and strong. I have not been so brought up but I can
shift for myself; I will go abroad and try my fortune; I fear
not but I shall find employment and preferment.

Soon after without the least ceremony, Fortunatus set out
with a hawk in his hand, and travelled towards the sea side
where he espied a galley of Venice lying at anchor. He
inquired what ship she was and where bound, hoping he might
here find employment. He was told the Earl of Flanders was
on board, and had lost two of his men. Fortunatus wishing

that he could be entertained as one of his servants, and so
get away from his native place, where his poverty was so well
known, steps up to the Earl, and making a low bow, says,
I understand, noble Lord, you have lost two of your men, so,
if you please, I desire to be received into your service. What
wages do you ask? says the Earl. No wages, replied Fortunatus,
but to be rewarded according to my deserts. This answer
pleased the Earl, so they agreed and sailed to Venice.

CHAP. 2.

OF FORTUNATUS'S SAILING WITH THE EARL OF FLANDERS, WITHOUT THE KNOWLEDGE OF HIS PARENTS.

THE Earl was now returned back and joyfully received by his subjects, and welcomed by his neighbours; for he was a very affable and just Prince.

Soon after his return, he married the Duke of Cleve's daughter, who was a very beautiful lady; Fortunatus went to the wedding, to which came several Lords and Gentlemen, and were present at a tilt and tournament held there before the Ladies; and though there was so many gentlemen, yet none behaved so well as Fortunatus—After all the Nobles had finished their triumphs and delightful games, the Duke and the bride and bridegroom agreed to let their servants try their manhood at several pastimes for two Jewels, each to be esteemed worth an hundred crowns, and he that obtained the said prize should have it, which made all the servants glad, every one striving to do his best. The Duke of Burgundy's servants won one, and Fortunatus the other, which displeased the other servants. Upon which they desired the Duke's Servants to challenge Fortunatus to fight him before the ladies, which should have them both; which challenge he accepted. Coming to the tilt yard, they encountered each other very briskly, and at last Fortunatus hoisted the Duke's servant quite

off his horse at spears length. Whereupon he obtained the victory, and got the Jewels, which encreased the envy of the other servants, but much rejoiced the Earl.

Among the Earl's servants was a crafty old fellow who consulted with the rest of the servants, and agreed for ten crowns to make Fortunatus quit his master's service of his own accord. To accomplish the affair, he pretended great friendship to Fortunatus, treating him and praising him much for his great courage. At last he told him he had a secret to reveal to him, which was, That the Lord having conceived a Jealousy of his two Chamberlains, of whom Fortunatus was one, he had a design secretly to kill them. This much amazed Fortunatus, who desired his fellow servant to inform him how to convey himself away; for said he I had rather wander as a vagabond than stay here and be slain. Says Robert, I am sorry I told thee any thing since I shall now lose thy company. Being resolved to go off, he desired Robert to conceal his departure.

When Fortunatus had rode ten Miles, he bought another horse, and returned the Earl's, that he might not pursue him; but when the Earl found he was gone, without his leave, not knowing the cause, he was offended, and demanded of the

servants if they knew the occasion? which they all denied; and he went to the ladies and gentlemen, and enquired of them if they knew any thing of his departure? and they answered No. Then said the Earl, Though the cause of his departure is concealed from me, yet I am perswaded he is not gone without some cause, which I will find out if it be possible.

When Robert found his Lord was so vexed for the loss of Fortunatus, he went and hanged himself, for fear of being discovered.

Chap. 3.

Of the Travels of Fortunatus after he left his Master.

Fortunatus having sent home his master's horse, travelled with all speed to Calais, where he took shipping and arrived safe in England—Coming to London, he met with some young Cyprus Merchants, his countrymen, who riotously spent his money in gaming and wenching; so that in about half a years time their cash was quite spent. Fortunatus having least his was soonest exhausted. Being moneyless, he went to some of his Landladies to borrow three Crowns, telling them he wanted to go to Flanders, to fetch four hundred crowns that were in his uncle's hands; but he was denied, and none they would lend him. He then desired to be trusted a quart of wine, but they refused, and bid the servants fetch him a pint of small beer.

He then took shipping, and soon arrived at Piccardy in France. Travelling through a wood, and being benighted, he made up to an old house, where he hoped to find some relief, but there was no creature in it ; Then hearing a noise among the Bears, he got up into a tree where one of them had climbed. Fortunatus being surprised, drew his sword, and stuck the bear, that he fell from the tree.

The rest of the beasts being gone, Fortunatus came down from the tree, and laying his mouth to the wound, he sucked out some of the blood, with which he was refreshed ; and then slept until the Morning.

CHAP. 4.

LADY FORTUNE BESTOWS UPON FORTUNATUS A FAMOUS PURSE; SO THAT AFTERWARDS HE NEVER WANTED MONEY.

As soon as Fortunatus awoke, he saw standing before him a fair Lady with her eyes muffled—I beseech thee said he, sweet virgin, for the love of God to assist me, that I may get out of this wood, for I have travelled a great way without food. She asked what country he was of? he replied Of Cyprus, and I am constrained by poverty to seek my fortune—Fear not, Fortunatus, said she, I am the Goddess of Fortune, and by permission of heaven have the power of Six gifts, one of which I will bestow on thee, so chuse for yourself: they are, Wisdom, Strength, Riches, Health, Beauty, and Long Life—Said Fortunatus, I desire to have Riches, as long as I live. With that she gave him a purse, saying, As often as you put your hand into this purse, you shall find ten pounds of the coin of any nation thou shalt happen to be in.

Fortunatus returned many thanks to the Goddess. Then she bid him follow her out of the wood, and so vanished. He then put his hands in his purse, and drew out the first fruits of the Goddess's bounty, with which he went to an inn and refreshed himself. After which he paid his host, and instantly departed, as doubting the reality of his money, notwithstanding the evidence of his hands and eyes.

Chap. 5.

Fortunatus buys some Horses out of an Earls Hands; for which he is taken up and examined about his Purse.

Two miles from this wood was a little town and castle, where dwelt an Earl, who owned the wood.—Fortunatus here took up his lodgings at the best inn, and asked the host if he could help him to some good horses—The host told him there was a dealer, who had several fine ones, of which the Earl had chosen three, but was refused though he offered three hundred crowns for them. Fortunatus went to his Chamber and took out of his purse six hundred crowns, and bid the host to send for the dealer with his horses—The host at first supposed he had been in Jest, seeing him so meanly apparelled; but on being convinced by the sight of the money, the dealer and horses were sent for, and Fortunatus with a few words bargained for two of those the Earl had cheapened, and gave three hundred crowns for them. He bought also costly saddles and furniture, and desired his host to get him two servants.

The Earl hearing that the two horses had been bought out of his hands, grew angry, and sent to the innkeeper to be informed who he was—The Earl being told he was a stranger, commanded him to be apprehended, imagining he had com-

mitted some robbery, and being examined who he was, answered, He was born in Cyprus, and was the son of a decayed gentleman. The Earl asked him how he got so much money? He told him he came by it honestly—Then the Earl swore in a violent passion, that if he would not discover, he would put him to the rack.—Fortunatus proposed to die rather than reveal it.—Upon this he was put upon the rack, and being again asked how he got so many crowns, he said he found them in a wood adjoining.—Thou villain, said the Earl the money found is mine, and thy body and goods are forfeited. O, my gracious Lord, said he, I knew not it was in your jurisdiction—But said the Earl, this shall not excuse you, for to day I will take thy goods, and tomorrow thy life.

Then did Fortunatus wish he had chose Wisdom before Riches.

Then Fortunatus earnestly begged his life of the Earl, who at the entreaty of some of his nobles spared his life and re-stored him the crowns and the purse, and charged him never to come into his jurisdiction—Fortunatus rejoiced that he had so well escaped, and had not lost his Purse.

After that he had travelled towards his own country, having got horses and servants to attend him, he arrived at Famagosta, where it was told him that his father and mother were dead. He then purchased his fathers house, and pulled it down, and built a stately palace. He also built a fine Church, and had three tombs made, one for his father and mother, the other for the wife which he intended to marry, and the last for his heirs and himself.

Chap. 6.

Of Fortunatus's Marriage with Lord Nemains youngest Daughter.

Not far from Famagosta lived a Lord who had three daughters; one of which the King of Cyprus intended to bestow on Fortunatus: but gave him leave to take his choice. When Fortunatus had asked them some questions, he chose the youngest, to the great grief of the other two sisters; but the Countess and Earl approved the match. Fortunatus presented the Countess her mother, and her two sisters, with several rich jewels.

Then did the King proffer to keep the wedding at his court, but Fortunatus desired to keep it at his own palace, desiring the King and Queen's Company—Then said the King, I'll come with my Queen and all my relations—After four days the King and all his Company went to Fortunatus's house where they were entertained in a grand manner. His house was adorned with costly furniture, glorious to behold. This feasting lasted forty days. Then the king returned to his Court, vastly well satisfied with the entertainment.—After this, Fortunatus made another feast for the citizens, their wives and daughters.

CHAP. 7.

OF FORTUNATUS HAVING TWO SONS BY HIS WIFE.

FORTUNATUS and his Wife Cassandra lived long in a happy state, and found no want of any thing but Children; and he knew the virtues of his purse would fail at his death, if he had no lawfully begotten heirs; therefore he made it constantly the petition in his prayers to God, that he would be pleased to send him an heir; and at length, in due time his lady brought forth a son, and he named him Ampedo. Shortly after she had another son, for whom he provided the best of tutors to take care they had an education suitable to their fortunes.

Fortunatus having been married twelve years, took it into his head to travel once more, which his wife much opposed, desiring him, by all the love he bore to her and to her dear children, not to leave them, but he was resolved, and soon after took leave of his wife and Children, promising to return again in a short space. A few days after, he took shipping for Alexandria, where having stayed some time, and got acquainted with the Soldan, he gained such favour of him, as to receive letters to carry him safe through his dominions.

Chap. 8.

Fortunatus artfully gets possession of a Wishing Hat.

Fortunatus after supper, opened his Purse, and gave to all the Soldan's servants very liberally. The Soldan being highly pleased, told Fortunatus he would shew him such curiosities as he had never seen. Then he took him to a strong marble tower, in the first room were several very rich vessels and jewels; in the second he shewed several vessels of gold coin; with a fine wardrobe of garments, and golden candlesticks, which shined all over the room, and mightily pleased Fortunatus. —Then the Soldan shewed him his bed chamber, which was finely adorned, and likewise a small felt Hat, simple to behold, saying I set more value on this Hat, than all my jewels, as such another is not to be had; for it lets a person be wherever he doth wish. Fortunatus imagined his Hat would agree very well with his Purse, and thereupon put it on his head saying. He should be very glad of a Hat that had such virtues. So the Soldan immediately gave it him; With that he suddenly wished himself in his ship, it being then under Sail, that he might return to his own country. The Soldan looking out at

his window, and seeing the Ship under sail, was very angry, and
commanded his men to fetch him back; declaring, if they took

him, he should immediately be put to death. But Fortunatus
was too quick for them, and arriving safe at Famagosta, very
richly laden, was joyfully received by his wife, his two sons
and the Citizens.—He now began to tender the advancement
of his children; he maintained a princely court, providing
masters to instruct his children in all manner of chivalry,
whereof the youngest was most inclined to behave manfully,
which caused Fortunatus to bestow many Jewels for his
exploits. When he had many years employed all earthly
pleasures, Cassandra died, which so grieved Fortunatus, that
he prepared himself for death also.

Chap. 9.

Fortunatus declares the Virtues of his Hat and Purse to his Son.

Fortunatus perceiving his death to approach, said to his two
sons, God has taken away your mother, which so tenderly
nourished you; and I perceiving death at hand, will shew you
how ye may continue in honour unto your dying day.—Then
he declared to them the virtues of his Purse, and that it would
last no longer than their lives. He also told them the virtues
of his Wishing Hat, and commanding them not to part with

those Jewels, but to keep them in common, and live friendly together, and not to make any person privy to their virtues; for,

said he I have concealed them forty years, and never revealed them to any but you.—Having said this, he ceased to speak, and immediately gave up the ghost.—His sons buried him in the magnificent church before mentioned.

FINIS.

GUY, EARL OF WARWICK.

THE earliest known printed edition of this romance is French, "Cy commence Guy de Waruich, chevalier d'Angleterre, qui en son temps fit plusieurs prouesses et conquestes en Angleterre, en Allemaigne, Ytalie et Dannemarche, et aussi sur les infidelles ennemys de la chrestieneté. Par Fr. Regnault, 7 Mars 1525," small folio, Gothic letter; and Ebert mentions an earlier undated edition. Hazlitt says the Bodleian library possesses a fragment of one leaf, containing thirty lines on a page, and printed with the types of Wynkyn de Worde's "Memorare Novissima." In *Notes and Queries*, 2nd Series, vol. x. p. 46, E. F. B. writes: "On recently examining a copy of the Sarum Ordinale edited by Master Clerke, Chantor of King's Coll. Cambridge, and printed by Pynson in 1501, I found three fly leaves of a book of earlier date, respecting which I should be glad to be informed; and therefore I subjoin a passage by which it may or may not be identified with the romance of Sir Guy. The type is of the Gothic character.

> " Wyth that the lumbardis fledde away
>   Guy Guy and heraude and terrey pfay
>   Chased after theym gode wone,
>   They slowe and toke many one,
>   The Lumbardis made sory crye.
>   For they were on the worse partye,
>   Of this toke duke otton gode hede,
>   And fledde to an hylle gode spede;
>   That none sued of theym echone,
>   But syr heraude of arderne alone,

> Heraude hym sued as an egyr lyon
> And euer he cryed on duke otton,
> Heraude had of hym no doubte,
> Nor he sawe no man ferre aboute,
> But only theymselfe two."

The earliest copy in the British Museum is 1560?, "The Booke of the most victoryous Prince Guy of Warwicke," and it was "Imprynted at London in Lothbury, ouer agaynst saynt Margarits Church, by Wylliam Copland," quarto, imperfect. This is in verse, beginning—

> "Sithen the tyme that God was borne
> And Chrisendom was set and sworne
> Many aduentures haue befall
> The which that men knew not all."

There is a fine fourteenth-century illumination in the royal manuscripts in the British Museum (20 A. ii. fo. 4*b*) of Guy as a hermit.

The mute witnesses of Guy's wonderful deeds, preserved in Warwick Castle, have been proved apocryphal in these investigating and matter-of-fact days. His breastplate, or helmet, is the "croupe" of a suit of horse armour; another breastplate is a "poitrel." His famous porridge-pot or punch-bowl is a garrison crock of the sixteenth century, and his fork a military fork, *temp.* Henry VIII.

THE

HISTORY

OF

𝕲𝖚𝖞. 𝕰𝖆𝖗𝖑 𝖔𝖋 𝖂𝖆𝖗𝖜𝖎𝖈𝖐

PRINTED AND SOLD IN ALDERMARY CHURCH
YARD, LONDON.

Chap. i.

Guy's Praise. He falls in love with the Fair Phillis.

In the blessed time when Athelstone wore the crown of the English nation, Sir Guy, Warwick's Mirror, and all the world's wonder, was the chief hero of the age; whose prowess so surpassed all his predecessors, that the trump of fame so loudly sounded Warwick's praise, that Jews, Turks, and Infidels became acquainted with his name.

But as Mars the God of Battle was inspired with the beauty of Venus, so our Guy, by no means conquered, was conquered by love; for Phillis the fair, whose beauty and virtue was inestimable, shining with such heavenly lustre that Guy's poor heart was ravished in adoration of this heavenly Phillis, whose beauty was so excellent, that Helen the pride of all Greece, might seem as a Black, a Moor to her.

Guy resolving not to stand doating at a distance, went to Warwick Castle, where Phillis dwelt, being daughter and heiress to the Earl of Warwick; the Earl, her father hearing of Guy's coming, entertained him with great joy; after some time the Earl invited Guy to go a hunting with him; but finding himself unable to partake of the diversion, feigned himself sick. The Earl troubled for his friend Guy, sent his own Physician to him. The Doctor told Guy his disease was dangerous, and without letting blood there was no remedy. Guy replied, I know my body is distempered; but you want skill to cure the inward inflammation of my heart; Galen's herbal cannot quote the flower I like for my remedy. I know my own disease, Doctor, and I am obliged to you.

The Doctor departed, and left Guy to cast his eyes on the heavenly face of his Phillis, as she was walking in a garden full of roses and other flowers.

CHAP. 2.

GUY COURTS THE FAIR PHILLIS, SHE AT FIRST DENIES, BUT AFTER GRANTS HIS SUIT ON CONDITIONS WHICH HE ACCEPTS.

GUY immediately advanced to fair Phillis, who was reposing herself in an arbour, and saluted her with bended knees, All hail, fair Phillis, flower of beauty, and jewel of virtue, I know great princes seek to win thy love, whose exquisite perfections might grace the mightiest monarch in the world; yet may they come short of Guy's real affection, in whom love is pictured with naked truth and honesty, disdain me not for being a steward's son, one of thy father's servants.

Phillis interrupted him saying, Cease, bold youth, leave off this passionate address :—You are but young and meanly born, and unfit for my degree; I would not that my father should know this.

Guy, thus discomfited, lived like one distracted, wringing his hands, resolving to travel through the world to gain the love of Phillis, or death to end his misery. Long may dame Fortune frown, but when her course is run she sends a smile to cure the hearts that have been wounded by her frowns; so Cupid sent a powerful dart, representing to her a worthy Knight of Chivalry, saying, This Knight shall be so famous in the world, that his actions shall crown everlasting posterity. When Phillis found herself wounded, she cried, O pity me gentle Cupid, sollicit for me to my Mother, and I will offer myself up at thy shrine.

Guy, little dreaming of this so sudden a thaw, and wanting the balm of love to apply to his sores, resolves to make a second encounter. So coming again to his Phillis, said, fair Lady, I have been arraigned long ago, and now am come to receive my just sentence from the Tribunal of Love; It is life or death, fair Phillis, I look for, let me not languish in despair, give Judgment, O ye fair, give Judgment, that I may know my doom; a word from thy sacred lips can cure a bleeding heart, or a frown can doom me to the pit of misery. Gentle Guy, said she, I am not at my own disposal, you know my father's name is great in the nation, and I dare not match without his consent.

Sweet Lady, said Guy, I make no doubt, but quickly to obtain his love and favour; let me have thy love first, fair

Phillis, and there is no fear of thy father's wrath preventing us. It is an old saying, Get the good will of the daughter, and that of the parent will soon follow.

Sir Guy, quoth Phillis, make thy bold achievements and noble actions shine abroad, glorious as the sun, that all opposers may tremble at thy high applauded name and then thy suit cannot be denied.

Fair Phillis, said Guy, I ask no more.—Never did the hound mind more his game, than I do this my new enterprize. Phillis, take thy farewell, and accept of this kiss as the signal of my heart.

Chap. 3.

Guy wins the Emperor's Daughter from several Princes, He is set upon by Sixteen Assassins, whom he overcomes.

Thus noble Guy at last disengaged from Love's cruelty, he now arms himself like a Knight of Chivalry, and crossing the raging ocean, he quickly arrived at the Court of Thrace, where he heard that the Emperor of Almain's fair daughter Blanch, was to be made a prize for him that won her in the field, upon which account the worthies of the world assembled to try their fortunes—The golden trumpets sounded with great joy and triumph, and the stately pampered steeds prance over the ground, and each He there thought himself a Cæsar, that none could equal;—Kings and Princes being there to behold who should be the conqueror, everyone thinking that fair Blanch should be his.

After desperate charging with horse and man, much blood was shed, and Princes no more valued than common persons; but our noble Guy appearing laid about him like a lion, among the princes; here lay one headless, another without a leg or an arm, and there a horse. Guy, still like Hercules, charged desperately and killed a German Prince and his horse under him. Duke Otto vowing revenge upon our English Champion, gave Guy a fresh assault, but his courage soon cooled. Then

Duke Poyner would engage our favourite knight; but with as little success as the rest, so that no man could encounter Guy any more; by which valor he won the Lady in the field as a prize, being thus approved Conqueror.

The Emperor being himself a spectator, he sent a messenger for our English Knight. — Guy immediately came into the Emperor's presence, and made his obeysance, when the Emperor as a token of his affection, gave him his hand to kiss and withal resigned him his daughter, the falcon and the hound—

Guy thanked his Majesty for his gracious favour, but for fair Phillis's sake left fair Blanch to her father's tuition, and departed from that graceful court only with the other tokens of victory.

Now Guy beginning to meditate upon his long absence from his fair Phillis, and doubting of her prosperity, or that she might too much forget him, because the proverb says, Out of

L

Sight out of Mind! prepared for England, and at last arrived at the long wished for haven of his love; and with this sort of salutation greeted his beloved mistress; Fair foe, said he, I am now come to challenge your promise, the which was, upon my making my name famous by martial deeds, I should be the master of my beloved mistress,—Behold, fair Phillis, part of the prize I have won in the field before kings and princes.

Worthy Knight, quoth Phillis, I have heard of thy winning the Lady Blanch from Royal Dukes and Princes, and I am glad to find that Guy is so victorious. But, indeed Guy thou must seek more adventures.

Guy, discomfited at this answer, taking leave of his fair Phillis, clad himself again in Belona's livery, and travelled towards Sedgwin, Duke of Nouvain, against whom the Emperor of Almain had then laid siege. But as Guy was going his intended journey, Duke Otto, whom Guy had disgraced in battle, hired sixteen base traytors to slay him. Guy being set upon by these rogues, drew his sword, and fought till he had slain them all; and leaving their carcasses to the fowls of the air, he pursued his Journey to Louvain, which he found close besieged, and little resistance could the Duke make against the Emperor's power—Guy caused the Levinians to sally forth, and made a most bloody slaughter among the Almains; but the Emperor gathering more forces renewed the siege, thinking to starve them out; but Guy in another sally defeated the Almains, slaying in these two battles about thirteen thousand men.

After this Guy made a perfect league between the Emperor and the Duke, gaining more praise thereby than by his former victories.

CHAP. 4.

GUY HAVING PERFORMED GREAT WONDERS ABROAD, RETURNS TO ENGLAND, AND IS MARRIED TO PHILIS.

AFTER a tedious journey Guy sat down by a spring to refresh himself, and he soon heard a hedious noice, and presently espied a Lion and a Dragon fighting, biting, and tearing each other; but Guy perceiving the Lion ready to faint, encountered the Dragon, and soon brought the ugly Cerberes roaring and yelling to the ground.—The Lion in gratitude to Guy, run by his horse's side like a true-born spaniel, till lack of food made him retire to his wonted abode.

Soon after Guy met with the Earl of Terry, whose father was confined in his castle by Duke Otto; but he and the Lord posted thither, and freed the castle immediately; and Guy in an open field slew Duke Otto hand to hand; but his dying words of repentance moved Guy to pity and remorse.

But as Guy returned through a desart he met a furious boar that had slain many Christians. Guy manfully drew his sword and the boar gaping, intending with his dreadful tusks to devour

our noble champion; but Guy run it down his throat, and slew the greatest boar that ever Man beheld.

At Guy's arrival in England, he immediately repaired to King Athelstone at York, where the King told Guy of a mighty Dragon in Northumberland, that destroyed men, women, and children.—Guy desired a guide, and went immediately to the dragon's cave, when out came the monster, with eyes like a flaming fire: Guy charged him courageously, but the monster bit the lance in two like a reed; then Guy drew his sword, and cut such gashes in the dragon's sides that the blood and life poured out of his venemous carecase. Then Guy cut off the head of the monster, and presented it to the King, who in the memory of Guy's service caused the picture of the Dragon, being thirty feet in length to be worked in a cloth of arras, and hung up in Warwick Castle for an everlasting monument.

Phillis hearing of Guy's return and success, came as far as Lincoln to meet him, where they were married with much joy and great triumph; King Athelstone, his Queen, the chief Nobles and Barons of the land being present.

No sooner were their nuptials celebrated but Phillis's father died, leaving all his estate to Sir Guy; and the King made him Earl of Warwick.

Chap. 5.

GUY LEAVES HIS WIFE AND GOES A PILGRIMAGE TO THE HOLY LAND.

IN the very height of Guy's glory, being exalted to his father's dignities, Conscience biddeth him repent of all his former sins, and his youthful time; so Guy resolved to travel to the Holy Land like a Pilgrim. Phillis perceiving this sudden alteration enquires of her Lord what was the cause of this Passion? Ah! Phillis, said he, I have spent much time in honouring thee, and to win thy favour, but never spared one minute for my soul's health in honouring the Lord.

Phillis, though very much grieved, understanding his determination, opposed not his will. So with exchanging their rings, and melting kisses, he departed like a stranger from his own habitation, taking neither money nor scrip with him, and but a small quantity of herbs and roots, such only as the wild fields could afford, were his chief diet; vowing never to fight more but in a just cause.

Guy, after travelling many tedious miles, met an aged person oppressed with grief, for the loss of fifteen sons, whom Armarant a mighty Giant had taken from him, and held in strong captivity. Guy borrowed the old mans sword, and went directly up to the

Castle gate, where the Giant dwelt, who, coming to the door, asked grimly, How he durst so boldly knock at the gates? vowing he would beat his brains out. But Guy laughing at him, said, Sirrah, thou art quarrelsome; but I have a sword has often hewn such lubbards as you asunder:—At the same time laying his blade about the Giant's shoulders, that he bled abundantly, who being much enraged, flung his club at Guy with such force, that it beat him down; and before Guy could recover his fall Armarant had got up his club again. But in the end Guy killed this broad back dog, and released divers captives that had been in thrawldom a long time, some almost famished, and others ready to expire under various tortures. They returned Guy thanks for their happy deliverance; after which he gave up the castle and keys to the old man and his fifteen sons.

Guy pursued his intended journey and coming to a grave, he took up a worm-eaten skull, which he thus addressed:— Perhaps thou wert a Prince, or a mighty Monarch, a King,

a Duke, or a Lord?—But the King and the Beggar must all return to the earth; and therefore man had need to remember his dying hour. Perhaps thou mightest have been a Queen, or a Dutchess, or a Lady varnished with much beauty; but now thou art worm's meat, lying in the grave, the Sepolchre of all creatures.

While Guy was in this repenting solilude, fair Phillis, like a mourning widow, cloathed herself in sable attire, and vowed chastity in the absence of her beloved husband. Her whole delight was in divine meditations and heavenly consolations, praying for the welfare of her beloved Lord, fearing some savage monster had devoured him.—Thus Phillis spent the remainder of her life in sorrow for her dear Lord ; and to shew her humility she sold her Jewels and costly robes, with which she used to grace King Athelstones Court, and gave the money freely to the poor ; she relieved the lame and the blind, the widow and the fatherless, and all those that came to ask alms ; building a large hospital for aged and sick people that they may be comforted in their sickness and weak condition. And according to this rule she laid up treasure in heaven, which will be paid again with life everlasting.

Meantime Guy travelled through many lands and nations ; at last in his Journey he met the Earl of Terry, who had been exiled from his territories by a merciless traytor. Guy bid him not be dismayed, and promised to venture his life for his restoration. The Earl thanked Guy most courteously, and they travelled together against Terry's enemy. Guy challenged him into the field, and then slew him hand to hand, and restored to the Earl his lands.

The Earl begged to know the name of his Champion, but Guy insisted to remain in secret, neither would he take any gratuity for his services.

Thus was the noble Guy successful in all his actions, and finding his head crowned with silver hairs, after many years travel, he resolved to lay his aged body in his native country, and therefore returning from the Holy Land, he came to England, where he found the nation in great distress, the Danes having invaded the land, burning Cities and towns, plundering the country, and killing men, women and children ; insomuch that King Athelstone was forced to take refuge in his invincible city of Winchester.

CHAP. 6.

GUY FIGHTS WITH THE GIANT COLBORN, AND HAVING OVER-
COME HIM, DISCOVERS HIMSELF TO THE KING, THEN TO
HIS WIFE, AND DIES IN HER ARMS.

THE Danes having intelligence of King Athelstone's retreat
to Winchester, drew all their forces hither, and seeing there was
no way to win the City, they sent a summons to King Athelstone desiring that an Englishman might combat with a Dane,
and that side to lose the whole whose champion was defeated.

On this the mighty Colborn singled himself from the
Danes, and entered upon Morn Hill, near Winchester, breath-
ing venemous words, calling the English cowardly dogs, that
he would make their carcasses food for ravens.

What mighty boasting said he, hath there been in the
foreign nations, of these English Cowards, as if they had done
deeds of wonder, who now like foxes hide their heads.

Guy hearing proud Colborn could no longer forbear, but
went immediately to the King, and on his knee begged a
Combat; the King liking the courage of the pilgrim bid him
go and prosper. Guy walking out of the North Gate to Morn
Hill, where Colborn, the Danish Champion was—When Colborn espied Guy he disdained him, saying, Art thou the best
Champion England can afford? Quoth Guy, it is unbecoming
a professed champion to rail, my sword shall be my Orator.
No longer they stood to parley, but with great Courage fought
most Manfully, but Guy was so nimble, that in vain Colborn
struck for every blow, fell upon the ground. Guy still laid
about him like a dragon, which gave great encouragement to
the English; but Colborn in the end growing faint, Guy
brought the giant to the ground; upon which the English all
shouted with so much Joy, that peals of ecchoes rung in the air
—After this battle the Danes retired back again to their own
Country.

King Athelstone sent for this Champion to honour him, but
Guy refused honours, saying, My Liege, I am a mortal man,

and have set the vain world at defiance. But at the King's earnest request, on promise of concealment, Guy discovered himself to him, which rejoiced his heart, and he embraced his worthy champion; but Guy took leave of his sovereign, and went into the fields where he made a cave living very pensive and solitary; and finding his hour draw nigh, he sent a messenger to Phillis, at the sight of which she hasted to her Lord,

where with weeping joy they embraced each other—Guy departed this life in her tender arms, and was honourably interred. His widow grieving at his death died 15 days after him.

THEIR EPITAPH.

Under this marble lies a pair,
Scarce such another in the world there are.
Like him so valiant or like her so fair,
His actions thro' the world have spread his fame,
And to the highest honours rais'd his name.
For conjugal affection and chaste love,
She's only equal'd by the blest above,
Below they all perfections did possess,
And now enjoy consummate happiness.

FINIS.

THE FAMOUS

HISTORY

OF

GUY EARL OF WARWICK

NEWCASTLE : PRINTED IN THIS PRESENT YEAR.

THE letter-press in this Chap-book is nearly identical with the previous one, but there are two engravings which the other lacks.

GUY AND THE NORTHUMBRIAN DRAGON.

GUY HAVING SLAIN ARMARANT.

THE HISTORY

OF THE

LIFE AND DEATH

OF THAT NOBLE KNIGHT

SIR BEVIS

OF

SOUTHAMPTON

NEWCASTLE: PRINTED IN THIS PRESENT YEAR.

ACCORDING to Ebert, the French editions of this romance are very early ; he quotes two, " Le livre de Beufoes de Hantonne et de la Belle Josienne sa mye. Par. Verard." no date, folio, G.L., and " Beufues Danthonne nouvellement imprimé a Paris. Par le Noir 1502," small folio, Gothic letter; whilst the British Museum possesses an earlier Italian book on the subject, " Buovo de Antona di Guidone Palladius Rezunto & reuisto. Caligula di Bazalieri. Bologna 1497," octavo, Gothic letter. The Bodleian Library possesses a very early English copy of " Sir Beuys of Hamton," " Emprynted by Rycharde Pynson in Flete-strete at the Sygne of the George," quarto, black letter ; and Hazlitt says there also is a fragment of two leaves by Wynkyn de Worde, printed with the same types as the " Memorare Novissima."

The frontispiece is an engraving belonging to an edition of 1690. Sir Bevis was born in the reign of Edgar, and his parents were Sir Guy of Southampton, and a daughter of the King of Scotland, who was desperately in love with Sir Murdure, brother of the Emperor of Almaine. She managed to keep up appearances for some years after the birth of Bevis, until her passion for Sir Murdure became uncontrollable, and she sent a message to him to come over to England and slay her husband. He obeyed, and with his men lay in wait for Sir Guy, who was hunting for a wild boar for his wife. They assaulted him, and, after a desperate resistance on his part, killed him, and Sir Murdure was received joyfully by the false wife, and duly installed in her husband's stead. Naturally, Bevis was wroth, and having expressed his opinion freely, was duly hated by his mother, who sent to Sir Sabere, her husband's brother, to privately murder him. Sir Sabere, however, dressed him in old clothes and put him to keep sheep, whilst he showed Bevis's blood-stained garments, as a token of having killed him. However, the impulsive Bevis could not brook the situation, but went to the castle, crook in hand, and with it knocked Sir Murdure under the table, and would have murdered his mother, had not better thoughts prevailed. His mother was furious, and ordered Sir Sabere and another knight to cast him into the sea, which they promised to do; but meeting with merchants of Armony, they sold Bevis to them.

The merchants presented him to the king (Ermine), who was prepossessed with his looks, and on questioning him, remembered having heard of the prowess of his father Sir Guy. " I have but one fair Daughter, said the King, and if thou wilt forsake thy God, and serve *Apoline* our God, thou shalt have my Daughter to Wife, and enjoy my Kingdom after me. Not so, my Lord, said Bevis, for all the Beauties in the World, I would not deny my Creator; Then, said the King, wilt thou be my Chamberlain, and when I find thy Desert, I'll dub thee a Knight, and thou shalt bear my Standard in the Field against my Foes. What you please to command me, my Lord, said he, save the denying of my God, I will do.

" Bevis was so beloved of the king that none durst speak against him; nay *Josian* the King's daughter was in love with him." But it happened, one Christmas Day, Bevis met sixty Saracens, who, taunting him with his religion, he encountered, and slew them all. At which the king swore he should die. But Josian on her knees begged his life, which was granted; she dressed his wounds, nursed him, and he was in as great favour as ever.

He next, after many difficulties, slew a mighty wild boar of cannibal propensities, and won great honour thereby.

Josian must have been fair indeed, for, all through the story, Bevis is perpetually getting into trouble through her fatal beauty. It now happened to have attracted King Brandmond, who sent to King Ermine demanding her hand, or he would depose him. The nobles were for yielding; but Josian suggested that if Bevis were made general, and invested with command, things would speedily be righted. This was done; he was dubbed knight, and Josian armed him, and gave him a sword, Morglay, and a wonderful steed, Arundel. He defeated Brandmond, and took him prisoner. " So Bevis returned with great Victory and was royally entertained by the King, and then *Josian* broke her mind to *Bevis;* quoth she, by *Mahomed*, I do desire to be thy Love: Not so, Lady, said *Bevis*, I'll wed no

Heatheness; which words she took very scornfully." But her love prevailed, and she went to Bevis, offering to do anything, even turn Christian, could she but win his love. Sir Bevis could only act as he did—take her in his arms, and kiss her. Her speech and behaviour being reported to the king, he was mad, and wrote letters to Brandmond, to put Sir Bevis to death, and gave them to him, to be the unconscious bearer of his own death-warrant.

Meanwhile, Sir Sabere had sent his son, Terry, travelling in search of Sir Bevis, and the two met near Damas; but Bevis did not make himself known. He rode into Damas, insulted the inhabitants by asking them, "What devil do you serve here?" and pulled down their idol Mahomed, throwing it into the gutter. This naturally exasperated the Saracens, and they set upon him; but before they could secure him, two hundred of them were slain. He was brought before the king, who read the letters of which he was the bearer. Bevis, finding he had only himself to trust to, went Berserk again and killed sixty more Saracens, was overpowered and thrown into a dungeon with two dragons, which, however, he slew with the truncheon of a spear he opportunely found, "and then he was at rest awhile."

Josian's fatal beauty was to bring trouble. "Father, said *Josian* where is *Bevis?* He reply'd he is gone to his own country. At this Time came King *Jour*, Intending for to wed *Josian* which he obtained. And *Ermine* gave *Jour*, *Arundel* and *Morglay*, which belonged to Bevis; this *Josian* could in no way avoid."

Bevis's captors thought they would go and see him, and as he had been in prison seven years, fed only on bread and water, they thought he would be weak; but he killed them all, and seizing on a horse, escaped. He met with a giant whom he slew, and then proceeded on his search for Josian. He met a poor palmer who told him that in that castle opposite lived King Jour and his wife, the fair Josian. They exchanged clothes, and Bevis entered the castle. He saw and conversed with Josian, who did not know him; but when Arundel heard

him speak, he " broke seven Chains asunder, and neighed ; "
and then Josian recognized him. The sequel may be imagined.
King Jour was sent off on an imaginary errand, and Josian
and Bevis eloped, taking with them the chamberlain Boniface.
They were pursued, and hid in a cave, where, Bevis being
absent hunting for their sustenance, two lions entered, killed
and eat Boniface, and then meekly laid their heads in Josian's
lap.   On Bevis's return, she called out to him the state of
things, when he told her to let the lions loose, and he killed
them.

They then continued their journey, until they were stopped
by Ascapart, " an ugly Giant, who was thirty Foot high, and a
Foot between his Eyebrows ; he was bristled like a Swine, and
his Blubber Lips hung on one side."   Naturally he had to be
fought and overcome, and on his life being spared, he promised
to be a faithful servant.   They reached the shore, where they
wanted to take ship, but, being unable to procure a boat, they
first had to fight and slay many Saracens, and then Ascapart
waded to the ship, carrying Sir Bevis and Josian, and tucking
Arundel under his arm.   They reached the land of Colen,
where the bishop was a relation of Bevis.   Josian was baptized,
but Ascapart refused the rite.

" *Bevis* being in bed heard a Knight cry, I rot, I rot, at
which Noise *Bevis* wondered ; and the next Morning he ask'd
what was the Cause of that Noise ; He was a Knight, they
said, that coming through the street, the Dragon met him
and cast her Venom upon him, whereof he rotted and died."
Bevis could not stand this, but sought and encountered
the dragon, which he slew, after the hardest of his many
fights.

Then he set about recovering his lost inheritance, and
sailed for England, landing near Southampton.   But no sooner
was his back turned than the Earl of Milo, having got rid of
Ascapart by stratagem, married Josian ; but she strangled him in
bed, whereupon she was sentenced to be burned.   Ascapart,
however, had broken prison, joined Bevis, and they together
arrived just in the nick of time to save Josian.

Sir Bevis and Sir Sabere then seriously took Sir Murdure in hand, defeated him, and boiled him in a cauldron of pitch and brimstone; which treatment had such an effect on the mother of Sir Bevis, that she threw herself from the top of her castle and broke her neck. Sir Bevis then, somewhat tardily, married Josian, and went to do homage to Edgar; but the king's son, having been refused Arundel at any price, went to take him by force, and had his brains kicked out by the horse. Sir Bevis was banished, and having left his estates in the hands of his uncle Sabere, started on his journey, when Josian, whilst passing through a forest, was taken ill and delivered of twins. She had requested her husband, Terry, and Ascapart to leave her alone for a time; so the former two went one way, and the latter another. But when Sir Bevis and Terry returned, they found the two boys, but not the mother, who had been carried off by Ascapart. Bevis left his children with a forester, with strict injunctions to return them to one Bevis of Hampton in seven years' time; but Sabere and twelve knights tracked and slew the villain Ascapart, and restored Josian to her husband. They redeemed the children; and then, finding there was war between the kings Ermine and Jour, Bevis naturally helped his father-in-law, and captured Jour, whose ransom was "twenty Tun of Gold and three hundred White Steeds."

King Ermine turned Christian, and before his death crowned his grandson Guy King of Armony, and knighted his grandson Miles. Not unnaturally King Jour hated Sir Bevis, and beseiging him in Armony, was of course overcome and slain, and Bevis took possession of his kingdom, and converted all the inhabitants to Christianity.

But his troubled life was drawing to a close. King Edgar had disinherited Sabere's wife, so he, Bevis, and Josian, with their two sons Guy and Miles, marched to London with a great army, fought the king, slew two thousand of his men, and then went back to Southampton. The king wisely parleyed with them, and ultimately agreed to marry his eldest daughter to Miles, whom he created Earl of Cornwall; after which they all separated and went home. Bevis and Josian retired to the late King Jour's capital of Mambrant, where both he and Josian fell sick, and died the same day. "They were solemnly interred in one Grave, by Guy their Son, who raised a stately Tomb over them, to the everlasting Memory of so gallant a Knight, and his most royal and constant Lady.

> So I conclude his famous Acts here penn'd,
> For Time and Death brings all Things to an End."

THE
LIFE AND DEATH

OF

𝕾𝔱. 𝕲𝔢𝔬𝔯𝔤𝔢

THE NOBLE

CHAMPION OF ENGLAND.

PRINTED AND SOLD IN ALDERMARY CHURCH YARD
BOW LANE LONDON

ALTHOUGH there are, as may be expected from the great popularity of this patron saint of England, very numerous illustrations of him in manuscripts, even as far back as the eleventh century, yet there seems, with the exception of the "Legenda Aurea" of Caxton and Wynkyn de Worde, to be very little early printed matter about him, although Dibdin (Ames) notices "The Lyfe of that glorious Martyr Saint George," quarto, printed by Pynson.

Alban Butler gives a very etherealized life of this saint, and says, "George is usually painted on horseback and tilting at a dragon under his feet; but this representation is no more than an emblematical figure, purporting, that by his faith and Christian fortitude he conquered the Devil, called the Dragon in the Apocalypse."

Caxton's "Legenda Aurea" ("Westmestre, 1483") gives the following account of the Cappadocian saint, and his encounter with the Dragon :—"Saynt George was a knyght and borne in capadose /　On a tyme he came to the prouynce of Lybye to to a cyte which is sayd Sylene /　And by this cyte was a stagne or a ponde lyke a see / wherein was a dragon whyche envenymed alle the contre /　And on a tyme the peple were assemblid for to slee hym /　And whan they sawe hym they fledde /　And whan he came nyghe the citte / he venymed the peple wyth his breeth /　And therfore the peple of the citte gaue to hym euery day two sheep for to fede hym / by cause he shold doo no harme to the peple /　And whan the sheep fayled there was taken a man and a sheep /

"Thenne was an ordenaunce made in the towne / that there shold be taken the chyldren and yonge peple of them of the towne by lotte /　And eueryche as it fyl were he gentil or poure shold be delyuered whan the lotte fyl on hym or hyr / So it happed that many of them of the towne were thenne delyuerd /　In soo moche that the lotte fyl vpon the kynges doughter /　Wherrof the kyng was sory and sayd vnto the people /

"For the loue of the goddes take golde and syluer and alle that I haue / and lett me haue my doughter / they sayd how syr ye haue made and ordeyned the lawe / and our chyldren been now deed / And now ye wold doo the contrarye / your doughter shal be gyuen / or ellys we shal breune you & your hows. Whan the kyng saw he myght nomore doo he began to wepe and sayd to his doughter / Now shal I neuer see thyn espousayls / Thenne retorned he to the peple and demauded viij dayes respyte And they graunted hit to hym / and whan the viij dayes were passed they came to hym and sayd / thou seest that the cyte perissheth / Thenne dyd the kyng doo * araye his doughter / lyke as she shold be wedded / and embraced hyr kyssed hir and gaue hir his benedyccion / And after ledde hyr to the place where the dragon was / whan she was there / saynt george passed by / And whan he sawe the lady / he demaunded the lady what she made there, And she sayd / goo ye your waye fayre yonge man / that ye perysshe not also /

"Thenne sayd he telle to me what haue ye / and why ye were / and doubte ye of no thynge / whan she sawe that he wold knowe she sayde to hym how she was delyuered to the dragon / Thenne sayd saynt george / Fayre doughter doubte ye no thynge herof / For I shall helpe the in the name of Jhesu Cryste / She said for goddes sake good knyght goo your waye / and abyde not wyth me / for ye may not delyuer me /

"Thus as they spake to gyder the dragon apperyd & came rennyng to them and saynt George was vpon his hors & drewe out his swerde & garnysshed hym wyth the signe of the Crosse / and rode hardely ageynst the dragon which came toward hym and smote hym with hys spere and hurte hym sore & threwe hym to the grounde / And after sayde to the mayde / delyuer to me your gyrdel and bynde hit about the necke of the dragon / and be not aferde / whan she had doon soo the dragon folowed hyr as it had been a make beest and debonayr / Thenne she ledde hym in to the cyte / & the peple fledde by mountayns and valeyes / and sayd / alas / alas / we shal be alle deed / Thenne saynt George sayd to them /

* Dyd doo, *i.e.* caused to be.

ne doubte ye no thynge / without more byleue ye in god Jhesu
Cryste / and doo you to be baptysed / and I shal slee the
dragon /

"Thenne the kyng was baptysed and al his peple / and
saynt george slewe the dragon and smote of his heed / And
commaunded thathe shold be throwen in the feldes / and they
took iiij cartes wyth oxen that drewe hym out of the cyte /
Thenne were there wel fyftene thousand men baptised without
wymmen and chyldren / And the kyng dyd doo make a
chirche there of our lady and of saynt George / In the whiche
yet sourdeth a founteyn of lyuynge water whiche heleth seek
peple that drynke therof / After this the kyng offred to Saint
george as moche money as there myght be nombred / but he
refused alle and commaunded that it shold be gyuen to poure
peple for goddes sake / and enioyned the kynge iiij thynges /
that is / that he shold haue charge of the Chyrches / and that
he shold honoure the preestes / and here theyr seruyce
dylygently / and that he shold haue pite on the poure peple /
And after kyssed the kyng and departed /"

The Chap-book version is far more marvellous, and is, as
the reader will note, strangely similar, in some places, to the
romance of Sir Bevis.

Coventry, not Cappadocia, is made his birth-place; his
father was "a renowned peer named Lord Albert," and his
mother was the King's daughter, who before St. George's birth
dreamed her child would be a dragon. So Lord Albert went to

consult the enchantress Kalyb, which he did by blowing a
trumpet at the entrance of her cave, when a voice replied that
his son should be as fierce as a dragon in deeds of chivalry.
The mother died in childbirth, and St. George was stolen in his
infancy by Kalyb, which so grieved Lord Albert that he died.

Kalyb grew very fond of the boy, and in a moment of con-
fidence she showed him the brazen castle where the other six
champions of Christendom were confined, and made him a
present of some invincible armour. She also lent him her

magic wand, a kindness which he requited by enclosing her in
a rock. He then released the six champions, who went their
several ways, and he went to Egypt. There he found the
whole kingdom desolate because of a dragon which every day
devoured a virgin, and had destroyed all but the king's
daughter, who was that day to be given to him unless some one

should slay the dragon, in which case she would be given in marriage to her deliverer. St. George, of course, undertook the adventure, and reached the place soon after the king and queen had taken leave of their daughter.

St. George held a short parley with the damsel, whose name was Sabra, when the dragon approached and the combat took

place. We know its issue—St. George cut off the dragons head, released Sabra, and entered the city, but was withstood by some of the inhabitants, stirred up by Aminder, King of Morocco, in love with Sabra, whom he had to fight and overcome.

The king, however, received him graciously; but Aminder spread reports of St. George trying to convert the princess to Christianity, and the king wrote a letter to the Sultan of Persia, making St. George the bearer, asking him to slay him. On its delivery St. George was thrown into a dungeon, and when he had been there two days, they let down two hungry lions to devour him, but he killed them with an old sword he found.

He was seven years in prison, during which time Sabra had been forced by her father to marry Aminder, when one day he found an iron crowbar and effected his release, stole a horse, was stopped by and fought with a giant, whom he killed. He journeyed on till he came to where Sabra lived, changed clothes with a peasant, applied to her for alms, showed her a ring which she had given him, and was immediately recognized.

Accompanied by a servant, they fled; met with two lions, who eat the servant but did Sabra no harm. and were duly killed by St. George.

He returned to Coventry, where he was but a little while, when St. David and the other champions asked him for his assistance against the pagans who had invaded Hungary. He went with them, leaving Sabra at home, and duly overthrew the pagans. Then came messengers to him saying that Sabra, who it appears the Earl of Coventry had attempted to seduce, had stabbed and killed him, and was condemned to die unless a champion could be found to fight for her. St. George came at the right moment, fought, conquered, and freed Sabra. They now lived quietly, and three sons, Guy, Alexander, and David, were born to them, who were sent to Rome, England, and Bohemia, to be educated at the Courts of the several sovereigns. After eighteen years' absence they all returned, and after they had rested a few days a hunt was proposed, in which Sabra joined. Her horse, however, fell and threw her "into a thorny briar, which tore her tender flesh so terribly, that she found she had not long to live, whereupon calling to St. George and her sons, she very affectionately embraced them, not being able to speak, and soon died."

St. George undertook a pilgrimage to Jerusalem, and on his return home he fought with a dragon on Dunsmore Heath and slew it. "But this proved the most fatal of all his adventures, for the vast quantities of poison thrown upon him by that monsterous beast, so infected his vital spitals, that two days afterwards he died in his own house."

PATIENT GRISSEL.

"I WOL you tell a Tale which that I
 Lerned at Padowe of a worthy clerk
 As preved by his wordes and his werk :
 He is now ded and nailed in his cheste,
 I pray to God to yeve his soule reste.
 Fraunceis Petrark, the Laureate poete,
 Hight this clerk whos retherike swete
 Enlumined all Itaille of poetrie"—

so says Chaucer in the prologue to the "Clerkes Tale," but
Petrarch was not the author of this ever favourite story. It
seems to have been the undoubted offspring of Boccaccio's fancy,
even Mr. Baring Gould failing to trace an Indian source for it,
as he has done in so many tales of the "Decameron." * In fact,
Petrarch, although intimately acquainted with Boccaccio, never
saw the tale until 1374, just before his death at Arquà. He at
once fell in love with it, and translated it into Latin, with alter-
ations. This translation was never printed, but there is a copy
in the library at Paris, and another at Magdalen College, Oxford.
It was dramatized in France in 1393, under the title of "Le
Mystere de Griseildis Marquis de Salucas ; " again in England,
"The Pleasant Comedie of Patient Grissill. As it hath been
sundrie times lately plaid by the right honorable the Erle of
Nottingham (Lord high Admirall) his seruants. London : Imprinted for Henry Rocket, and are to be solde at the long Shop
vnder S. Mildreds Church in the Poultry. 1603." † There was
also a comedy by Ralph Radcliffe, called "Patient Griseld,"
but this was never printed ; and in modern times it has been
dramatized by Mr. Edwin Arnold.

* "Bouchet,. in his *Annales d'Aquitaine*, I. iii., maintains that Griselda
flourished about the year 1025, and that her real history exists in manuscript
under the title of ' Parement des Dames.' "—*Notes and Queries*, 3rd Series,
vol. iii. p. 389.

† Of this play only two copies are known.

THE

HISTORY

OF THE NOBLE

MARQUIS OF SALUS

AND

Patient GRISSEL

Printed and Sold in Aldermary Church
Yard, Bow Lane London.

Chap. 1.

The Marquis of Salus is sollicited by his Nobles to Marry; he consents, and falls in Love with a poor Countryman's Daughter.

Between the mountains of Italy and France, towards the South, lies the territory of Salus, a country flourishing with excellent towns, and some castles, and peopled with the best sort of gentry and pheasants.—Among them lived not long since a nobleman of great reputation and honour, who was Lord of the country, and by name Gualter, Marquis of Salus; to whom, as the government appertained by his right of inheritance, so their obedience attended by desert of his worthiness. He was young in years and never had thought of marriage until pressed to it by the desires and petitions of his people, who often importuned him thereto—At last he consented to it, and fame soon spread the report abroad, and each Princess was filled with hopes of being the Marquis's happy partner.

All this time the Marquis continued his hunting, and usually resorted to a little village not far from Selus where lived a poor

countryman named Janicola, overworn in years, and overcome with distress, having nothing to make his life comfortable but an only daughter, who was exceedingly beautiful, modest, and virtuous. But as fire will not lay hid where there is matter of combustibles, so virtue cannot be obscured if there is tongues and ears; for the report of her reached the Marquis, who being satisfied of the truth, and finding her a fit woman to be his wife, resolved to forward the business.—In the mean time the Court was furnished, a Crown and rich apparel prepared for the Queen; but who she was the Nobles all wondered, and the damsels marvelled; while the people in general flocked to see who was to be the happy woman.

At last the nuptial day arrived, and each one looked for a bride, but who she was the next Chapter must discover.

Chap. 2.

The Marquis demands, and Marries the Old Man's Daughter.

When all things were prepared, the Noble Marquis took with him a great Company of Earls Lords Knights Squires, Gentlemen, Ladies, and Attendants, and went from the palace into the country, towards Janicola's house, where the fair maid Grissel, ignorant of what had happened, or of what was to come, had made herself and house clean, determining with the rest of the neighbouring virgins to see this solemnity; at which instant arrived the Marquis with his Company, meeting Grissel with two pitchers of Water which she was carrying home. He asked

where her father was? She answered, in the house—Go then, replied he, and tell him I would speak with him. The poor man came forth to him somewhat abashed, until the Marquis taking him by the hand, said That he had a secret to impart to him ; and taking him from the rest of the Company spoke to him in the following manner :

" Janicola,

I know thou always lovedst me, and I am satisfied thou dost not hate me now ; you have been pleased when I have been pleased, and you will not now be sorrowful if I am satisfied ; nay I am sure if it lies in your power, you will further my delight ; for I am come with the intention of begging your daughter to be my wife ; and I to be your son in law, will you take me for your friend, as I have chose you for a father."

The poor old man was so astonished, that he could not speak for Joy, but when the extasy was over, he thus faintly replied ;

" Most gracious Sovereign,

You are my Lord, and therefore I must agree to your will ; but you are generous, and therefore take her in God's name, and make me a glad father ; and let that God which raiseth up the humble and meek, make her a befitting wife and a fruitful mother."

Why then, quoth the Marquis, let us enter your house, for I must ask her a question before you. So he went in, the company tarrying without in vast astonishment—The fair maid was busied in making it as handsome as she could, and proud to have such a guest under her roof, amazed why he came so accompanied, little conjecturing so great a blessing ; but at last the Marquis took hold of her hand and used these speeches. To tell you this blush becomes you, were but a folly ; or that your modesty has graced your comliness, is unbecoming my greatness ; but in one word, your father and I have agreed to make you my wife, therefore, delays shall not entangle you with suspicion, nor two days longer protract the kindness, only I must be satisfied in this, if your heart affords willing entertainment to the motion, and your virtue and constancy to the following resolution ; that is, not to repine at my pleasure in anything, nor presume on contradiction when I command ; for as good soldiers must obey without disputing the business, so must virtuous wives dutifully consent without reproof; therefore be advised how you answer, and I charge thee take heed that thy tongue utters no more than thy heart conceits. All this time was Grissel wondering at these words; but thinking nothing impossible with God, made the Marquis the following answer:

"My gracious Lord,

I am not ignorant of your greatness, and know my own weakness. There is nothing worthy in me to be your servant, therefore can have no desert to be your wife. Notwithstanding, because God is the author of Miracles, I yield to your pleasure, and praise him for the fortune. Only this I will be bold to say. That your will shall be my delight; and death shall be more welcome to me, than a word of displeasure against you."

After this the Ladies adorned Grissel with robes befitting her state; the Marquis and all the company returned back to Salus, where in the Cathedral, in the sight of the people according to the fullness of religious ceremonies they were by the priest essentially joined together.

CHAP. 3.

LADY GRISSELS PATIENCE TRIED BY THE MARQUIS.

To the other blessinge in process of time, there was added the birth of a daughter, that rejoiced the mother and gladded the father; the country triumphed, and the people clapped their hands with joy—Notwithstanding this, fortune had a trick to check her pride; and prosperity must be seasoned with some crosses or else it would corrupt us too much. Whereupon the Marquis determined to prove his wife, and to make trial of her virtues indeed; and so taking a convenient season, after the child was weaned, he one day repaired secretly to her chamber, and seeming angry, imparted to her some of his mind.

The lady hearing him, sorrowfully apprehended the Marquis's resolution to her grief (though every word was like an arrow in her side) yet admitted of the temptation, and disputing with herself to what end the virtues of patience, modesty, forbearance, fortitude and magnanimity was ordained, if they had not proper subjects to work upon.

When the Marquis saw her constancy, he was pleased with her modest behaviour, and said but little at that time, but between joy and fear departed; resolving to make a farther trial of her.

Chap. 4.

The Marquis's Daughter is taken from her Mother and sent to Bologne to be there brought up.

Not long after this Conference between the Marquis and his Lady, he called a faithful servant, to whom he imparted the secret, and what he meant to do with his child; and then sent him to his wife with an unsavoury message—When she had heard him out, remembering the conference the Marquis had with her, and apprehending there was no room for dispute, feared it was ordained to die; so taking it up in her arms with a mothers blessing she kissed it, being not once amazed or troubled, since her lord would have it so, only she said, I must, friend, intreat one thing at your hand, that out of humanity and Christian love, you leave not the body to be devoured by beasts and birds, for she is worthy of a grave.

The man, having got the Child, durst not tarry, but returned to his master, repeating every circumstance of her answer that might aggrandise her constancy.

The Marquis considering the great virtue of his wife, and looking on the beauty of his daughter, began to entertain some compassion, and to retract his wilfulness; but at last resolution won the field of pity, and having, as he thought so well begun, would not soon give over. But with the same secrecy he had taken her from his wife, he sent her away to his sister the Dutchess of Bologne, with presents of worth, and letters of recommendation, containing in them the nature of the business, and the manner of her bringing up, which she accordingly put into practice.

Chap. 5.

The Marquis makes a farther Trial of his Wife's Patience.

As this patient and wonderful lady was one day sporting with her infant son, like a tempest did this messenger of death interpose; yet as if he was conscious of disquieting her greatness, he came forward with preamble, craving pardon of the lady, that the message might seem blameless. He was not so sudden in his demand, as she was in her despatch; for she immediately gave him this child also, with the same enforcements as she had done the former.—

In the like manner he returned to the Marquis, who had

still more cause for astonishment, and less reason to abuse so obedient a wife; but for a time sent this child likewise to his sister, who understanding her brother's mind brought up the children in such a manner, that tho' no man ever knew whose children they were, yet they supposed them to belong to some great potentate.

The ordering the business in this manner, made the Marquis once again settle himself in Salus, where he kept an open house to all comers, and was proud of nothing but the love of his wife; for although he had more than once tried her patience, yet she never complained, but seemed to love him the more.

By this time his unkindness to her got spread among the people, who all admired and wondered at her for her constancy and patience.

CHAP. 6.

GRISSEL DISROBED, AND SENT HOME TO HER FATHER BY HER HUSBAND; HER SON AND DAUGHTER BROUGHT HOME, UNDER PRETENCE OF THE MARQUIS'S MARRYING HER; GRISSEL IS SENT FOR TO MAKE PREPARATIONS, AND HER CONDESCENSION THEREON.

AFTER this the Marquis was resolved to put her to another trial, so sent for her cloaths, and commanded her to go home again to her father's naked, except her shift; when, being in the midst of her nobility she disrobed herself, and returned back to her father's Cottage. They could not but deplore the alteration of fortune; yet she could not but smile that her virtue was predominant over her passion. They all exclaimed against the cruelty of her Lord; but she used no invective. They wondered at her so great virtue and patience; she answered, They were befitting a modest woman.

By this time they approached the house and old Janicola having been acquainted with it; and seeing his daughter only in her smock, amidst such honourable company, he ran into the house and brought the robes she formerly wore, and putting them on said Now, thou art in thy element, and kissing her bid

her welcome. The Company was in amaze at his moderation, and wondered how nature could be so restrained from passion, and that any woman could have so much grace and virtue. In which amaze not without some reprehension of fortune and their Lord's cruelty, they left her to the poverty of the Cell, and returned to the glory of the palace, where they recounted to the Marquis how she continued in her moderation and patience; and the father comforting her in her condition.

Not long after came the Dutchess of Bologne, with her glorious company, she sending word beforehand she should be at Salus such a day. Whereupon the Marquis sent a troop to welcome her, and prepared a court for her entertainment. The effects of which were not agreeable; some condemned the Marquis whilst others deplored his wife's misfortunes. Some were transported with the gallant youth and comely virgin that came along with the Dutchess, the latter of whom it was reported the Marquis was going to marry; nor did the Duke nor Princess know themselves to be the Children of the Marquis, but appeared as strangers designed to be at this new Marriage.

The next morning after their arrival he sent a messenger for Grissel bidding her come and speak with him just in the dress she then was; upon which she immediately waited upon her Lord. At her appearance he was somewhat abashed, but recovering his spirits he thus addressed her:

Grissel, the Lady with whom I must marry will be here

to-morrow by this time, and the feast is prepared according—
Now, because there is none so well acquainted with the secrets
of my palace and disposition of myself but you, I would have
you, for all this base attire, address your wisdom to the ordering of the business, appointing such officers as are befitting,
and disposing of the rooms according to the degrees and
estates of the persons. Let the Lady have the privilege of the
marriage chamber, and the young Lord the pleasure of the
gallery. Let the wines be plentiful, and the ceremonies be
maintained—In a word, let nothing be wanting which may set
forth my honour and delight the people.

My Lord, said she, I ever told you, That I took pleasure in
nothing but your Contentment, and in whatsoever might conform
to your delight. Herein consisted my joy and happiness,
therefore make no question of my diligence and duty in this or
anything you shall please to impose upon me. And so, like
a poor servant she presently addressed herself to the business
of the house performing all things with such dispatch and
quickness that each one wondered at her goodness and fair
demeanor ; and many murmured to see her put to such a trial.
But the day of entertainment being come, and when the fair
lady approached, she looked exceeding beautiful, insomuch
that some began not to blame the Marquis for his change. At
length Grissel, taking the lady by the hand, thus addressed

her : Lady, if it were not his pleasure, that may command, to
bid you welcome, yet methinks there is a kind of over ruling

grace from nature in you, which must extort a respect unto you.—And as for you young Lord, I can say no more, but if I might have my desires, they should be employed to wish you well—To the rest I afford all that is fit for entertainment, hoping they will excuse whatever they see amiss. And so conducted them to their several apartments, where they agreeably reposed themselves till it was dinner time. When all things were thus prepared, the Marquis sent for his Grissel, and standing up, took her by the hand, and thus expressed himself to her :

You see the Lady is here I mean to marry, and the Company assembled to witness it ; are you therefore contented I shall thus dispose of myself? and do you submit quietly to the alteration?

My Lord, replied she, before them all, in what as a woman I might be found faulty, I will not now dispute ; but because I am your wife, and have devoted myself to obedience, I am resolved to delight myself in your pleasure ; so, if this match be designed for your good, I am satisfied and more than much contented. And as for your lady, I wish her the delights of marriage, the honour of her husband, many years happiness, and the fruits of true and chaste wedlock—Only, great Lord, take care of one thing, That you try not your new bride, as you did your old wife; for she is young, and perhaps wants the patience which poor I have endured.

Till this he held out bravely, but now could not forbear bursting into tears, and all the company wondered at it ; but the next Chapter will happily conclude the whole Story.

Chap. 7.

The Marquis's Speech to his Wife and the Discovery of the Children.

After the Marquis had recovered himself, he thus addressed his patient wife Grissel :—Thou Wonder of Women, and Champion of true Virtue ! I am ashamed of my imperfections, and tired with abusing thee ; I have tried thee beyond all modesty.—Believe me therefore, I will have no wife but thyself, and therefore seeing I have used you so unkindly heretofore, I protest never to disquiet thee any more ; and wherein my cruelty extended against thee in bereaving thee of thy Children, my love shall now make amends in restoring thee thy son and daughter ; for this my new bride is she, and this young Lord, her brother. Thank this good Lady my sister for the bringing them up ; and this man, you know him well enough, for his secrecy. I have related the truth, and will confirm it with my honour and this kiss ; only sit down till the dinner is come, and then bid the company welcome even in this poor array.

The Marquis thus tenderly treating her, and discovering who the young Lord and Lady was, gave the Nobility a fresh opportunity to shew their obedience ; the which they immediately did to all three ; and the dinner being over, none was so ready to attire Grissel, as her daughter, who was more glad than disappointed by this so sudden a change—Janicola was sent for to Court, and ever afterwards he was the Marquis's counsellor. The servant was also well rewarded for his fidelity ; and the Dutchess returned to her palace, leaving her brother and sister to reign in peace.—In length of time the Marquis died, and Grissel lived thirty three years after him, and then died in a good old age ; being a pattern for all women after, who might have their virtue or patience tried in the like, or other manner, not to distrust an all wise Providence, who, when he seemeth most to frown, oftentimes is about blessing his creatures with the Sunshine of prosperity.—On the other hand her example should teach us Content, though in meek and abject circumstances ; considering it is not the pleasure of the Divine Will to bless all people alike with affluence.

FINIS.

The Pleasant and Delightful

HISTORY

OF

JACK AND THE GIANTS

PART THE FIRST

NOTTINGHAM
PRINTED FOR THE RUNNING STATIONERS.

THE SECOND PART OF

JACK and the GIANTS

GIVING

A full Account of his Victorious Conquests over the North Country Giants; destroying the inchanted Castle kept by Galligantus; dispers'd the fiery Griffins; put the Conjuror to Flight; and released not only many Knights and Ladies, but likewise a Duke's Daughter, to whom he was honourably married.

NEWCASTLE: PRINTED AND SOLD BY J. WHITE. 1711

THE

HISTORY

OF

JACK and the GIANTS

PRINTED AND SOLD IN ALDERMARY CHURCH
YARD, BOW LANE, LONDON

THE origin of this romance is undoubtedly Northern.

The Edda of Snorro contains a similar story to that of the Welsh Giant. Thor and the giant Skrimner were travelling together, and when they slept, Skrimner substituted a rock, as Jack did a billet, for his person. Thor smote it with his mighty hammer, and the giant asked whether a leaf had fallen from a tree. Again he smote, and this time the giant suggested an acorn had fallen. Yet still one mightier blow than all, but the provoking Skrimner thought it was only some moss fallen on his face.

Also in the second relation of Ssidi Kur, a Calmuck romance, the wonderful shoes of swiftness are to be found.*

This romance used to be a never-failing source of delight to children, but a long version of it is now seldom found. The Chap-books give two parts, and all agree in their story. The date is laid in King Arthur's time, and Jack was the son of a wealthy farmer near Land's End in Cornwall, and he was of great strength and extremely subtle. The country at that time seems to have been under the terrorism of a race of giants, and Jack's mission was their destruction. For the greater part, as we shall see, they were a very simple and foolish race, very ferocious, but with no brains, and they fell an easy prey to the astute

* The Chan steals a pair from the Tchadkurrs, or evil spirits, by means of a cap which made him invisible, which he won from some quarrelling children whom he met in a forest.

Jack. He tried his 'prentice hand on a fine specimen, the Giant Cormoran, eighteen feet high and three yards in circumference, who dwelt on the Mount of Cornwall. Jack's preparations were simple. He took a horn, a pickaxe, and a shovel, and with the two latter dug a pit twenty-two feet deep, and covered it over; then he blew his horn. The Giant came out and fell into the pit, when Jack killed him with his axe (Plates Nos. 1 and 2). This earned him his sobriquet of the Giant-Killer. The Giant Blunderbore, hearing of this feat, vowed vengeance, and meeting Jack in a lonely part of Wales, he carried him on his shoulders to his castle, locked him in an upper room, and started off to invite a brother giant to supper. But, alas for the blindness of these huge dunderheads! two strong cords had been left most imprudently in Jack's room, in which he made running nooses, and, as the giants were unlocking the gates, he threw the ropes over their heads and strangled them, cut off their heads, and delivered their captives.

In Flintshire he met with an abnormal specimen, a giant with two heads; and, as perhaps they were "better than one," this giant was crafty, pretended friendship, and took Jack home with him to sleep. Luckily for Jack, the giant had a bad habit of soliloquy, and he overheard him say—

> "Tho' here you lodge with me this night,
> You shall not see the morning's light.
> My club shall dash your brains out quite."

"Forewarned is forearmed;" so Jack substituted a billet of wood for himself, which the giant duly belaboured, and, being utterly astounded at seeing Jack alive and well in the morning, asked him how he slept—whether he had been disturbed? "No," said the self-possessed Jack; "a rat gave me three or four flaps with his tail."

Crafty Jack, however, made the foolish giant destroy himself, as follows :—"Soon after the Giant went to breakfast on a great bowl of hasty pudding, giving Jack but little quantity; who being loath to let him know he could not eat with him, got a leather bag, putting it artfully under his coat, into which he put his pudding, telling the Giant he would shew him a trick ; so taking a large knife he ripped open the bag which the Giant thought to be his belly, and out came the hasty pudding ; which the Welsh Giant seeing, cried out, Cot's plut, hur can do that hurself; and taking up the knife he ripped open his belly from top to bottom, and out dropped his tripes and trullibubs, so that he immediately fell down dead."

King Arthur's son was travelling about, and meeting with Jack, they joined company. The prince seems to have been too lavish with his money, and soon was in want. Jack then proposed they should sup and sleep at the house of a *three-*headed giant, who rather prided himself upon his fighting qualities. Stratagem succeeded ; Jack made the giant believe that the prince was coming with a thousand men to destroy him, and the human Cerberus (who, although he was a match for five hundred, did not dare to overweight himself with double that number) begged Jack to bolt and bar him in a vault till the prince had gone. Jack and the prince ate and drank of the best, slept well, and in the morning took the giant's cash. When the prince was well on his way, Jack let the big stupid lubber out, and he out of gratitude gave his preserver a coat which would render him invisible, a cap which would furnish him with knowledge, a miraculously sharp sword, and shoes of incredible swiftness.* Jack took them and followed the prince, whose life he afterwards saved, and, besides, made himself useful in casting an evil spirit out of a lad.

In the Second Part Jack turns professional giant-slaughterer,

---

* To show the northern origin of this tale, it is only necessary to point out that the coat is identical with the magic garment known in ancient German as the "Nebel Kappe," or cloud cloak, fabled to belong to King Alberich and the other dwarfs of the Teutonic Cycle of Romance, who, clad therein, could walk invisible. To them also belongs the "Tarn hut," or Hat of Darkness. Velent, the smith of the Edda of Sæmund, forged a "Sword of Sharpness," which in the Wilkina Saga is called Balmung. It was so sharp that when Velent cleft his rival Æmilius, it merely seemed to the latter like cold water running down him. "Shake thyself," said Velent. He did so, and fell in two halves, one on each side of the chair. The Shoes of Swiftness were worn by Loke when he escaped from Valhalla.

and of course these overgrown simpletons had no chance against Jack's magic paraphernalia. They had to give up their prisoners (Plate 4) ; they were cut in pieces without seeing their assailant (Plate 3) ; their very weight sometimes proved their destruction —notably one Thundel, who will always live in memory as the talented author of

> " Fe, fa, fum
> I smell the blood of an Englishman,
> Be he alive, or be he dead,
> I'll grind his bones to make me bread."

This Thundel was beguiled on to a drawbridge, which broke with his weight (see frontispiece, Newcastle edition), and, floundering in the moat, fell an easy prey. But Jack's supreme effort was masterly, and well rewarded him. A hermit told him of a giant, one Galligantus, who lived in an enchanted castle, in which, by the aid of a conjuror and two fiery dragons, he had imprisoned a duke's daughter, transforming her into a deer. Could Jack resist this charming adventure? Impossible. Clad in his invisible coat, he got into the castle, found that the way to break the enchantment was to blow a certain trumpet, did so—an act which had the effect of temporarily depriving the giant and sorcerer of their presence of mind, a fact which Jack took advantage of by decapitating Galligantus ; at which sight the conjuror mounted in the air, and disappeared in a whirlwind. The two dragons, considering these proceedings equivalent to a notice of ejectment, promptly took their departure ; whilst a quantity of beasts and birds resumed their former shapes of knights and ladies, and the castle vanished.

Needless to say, King Arthur prevailed on the duke to reward Jack with his daughter's hand, and he himself gave him " plentiful estate ; " so there is very little reason to doubt the announcement which closes this veracious history, that " he and his Lady lived the residue of their days in joy and content.

A pleasant and delightful
HISTORY
OF
𝕿𝖍𝖔𝖒𝖆𝖘 𝕳𝖎𝖈𝖐𝖆𝖙𝖍𝖗𝖎𝖋𝖙

NEWCASTLE, PRINTED BY AND FOR M. ANGUS AND SON, IN THE SIDE—

Where is always kept on Sale, a choice and extensive Assortment of Histories, Songs, Children's Story Books, School Books &c &c.

THIS worthy does not seem to have been an absolute myth, if we can trust Sir Henry Spelman, who in his " Icenia sive Nor-folciæ Descriptio Topographica," p. 138, speaking of Tilney in Marshland Hundred, says, " Hic se expandit insignis area, quæ à planitie nuncupatur *Tylney-smeeth*, pinguis adeo & luxurians ut Padua pascua videatur superasse. . . . Tuentur eum indigenæ velut Aras and Focos, fabellamque recitant longa petitam vetustate de *Hikifrico* (nescio quo,) *Haii* illius instar in Scotorum Chronicis, qui Civium suorum dedignatus fugam, Aratrum quod agebat, solvit ; arrepto que Temone furibundus insiliit in hostes, victoriamque ademit exultantibus. Sic cum de agri istius finibus acriter olim dimicatum esset inter fundi Dominum et Villarum Incolas, nec valerent hi adversus eum consistere ; cedentibus occurrit *Hikifricus*, axem que excutiens a Curru quem agebat, eo vice Gladii usus ; Rotâ, Clypei ; invasores repulit ad ipsos quibus nunc funguntur terminos. Ostendunt in cæmeterio Tilniensi, Sepulcrum sui pugilis, Axem cum Rota insculptum exhibens."

Sir William Dugdale also says, "They to this day shew a large gravestone near the east end of the Chancel in Tilney Churchyard, whereon the form of a Cross is so cut or carved, as that the upper part thereof (wherewith the carver had adorned it) being circular they will therefore have it to be the gravestone of Hickifrick as a memorial of his Courage."

In Chambers's " History of Norfolk," vol. i. p. 492, it says, "The stone coffin which stands out of the ground in Tilney Churchyard, on the north side of the Church, will not receive a person above six feet in length ; and this is shewn as belonging formerly to the giant Hickafric. The cross said to be a repre-sentation of the cart wheel, is a cross pattée on the head of a staff, which staff is styled an axletree."

THE

HISTORY

OF

THOMAS HICKATHRIFT

PART THE FIRST

PRINTED IN ALDERMARY CHURCH YARD. LONDON

Chap. 1.

Tom's Birth and Parentage.

In the reign of William the Conqueror I have read in antient records, there lived in the Isle of Ely in Cambridgeshire, a man named Thomas Hickathrift, a poor labourer, yet he was an honest stout man, and able to do as much work in a day as two ordinary men. Having only one Son he called him after his own name Thomas. The old man put his son to School, but he would learn nothing.

God called the old man aside, his Mother being tender of her son, maintained him by her own labour as well as she could; but all his delight was in the chimney corner, and he eat as much at once as would serve five ordinary men. At ten years old he was six feet high and three in thickness, his hand was like a shoulder of mutton, and every other part proportionable; but his great strength was yet unknown.

Chap. 2.

How Tom Hickathrift's great Strength came to be Known.

Tom's Mother being a poor widow, went to a rich farmer's house, to beg a bundle of straw, to shift herself and her son Thomas. The farmer being an honest charitable man, bid her take what she wanted. She, going home to her son Thomas said, Pray go to such a place and fetch me a bundle of straw; I have asked leave.—He swore he would not go—Nay, prythee go, said his poor old Mother.—Again he swore he would not go, unless she would borrow him a cart rope, she being willing to pleasure him, went and borrowed one.

Then taking the Cart rope, away he went, and coming to the farmer's house, the master was in the barn, and two men threshing.

Tom said, I am come for a burden of Straw. Tom, said the farmer, take as much as thou can'st carry. So he laid down his Cart rope, and began to make up his burden.

Your rope, Tom, said they is too short, and jeered him. But he fitted the farmer well for his joke; for when he had made up his burthen, it was supposed it might be two thousand weight— But says they, what a fool art thou? for thou can'st not carry the tythe of it.—But however he took up his burthen, and made no more of it than we do an hundred pound weight, to the great admiration of master and men.

Now Tom's strength beginning to be known in the town, they would not let him lie basking in the chimney corner, everyone hirting him to work, seeing he had so much strength, all telling him, it was a shame for him to lie idle as he did from day to day; so that Tom finding them bate at him as they did, went first to one work and then to another.

At last a man came to him and desired him to go to the wood to help him to bring a tree home; so Tom went with him and four other men.

And when they came to the wood, they set the cart by the tree, and began to draw it by pullies; but Tom seeing them not able to stir it, said aloud, stand aside fools—And set it on one end, and then put it in to the cart—There, said he, see what a man can do? Marry, said they, that's true.

Having done, and come through the wood they met the woodman, and Tom asked him for a stick to make his mother a fire with.

Aye, said the woodman, take one.

So Tom took up a tree bigger than that on the cart, and put it on his shoulder, and walked home with it faster than the six horses in the cart drew the other.

This was the second instance of Tom's shewing his strength; by which time he began to know that he had more natural strength than twenty common men; and from this time Tom began to grow very tractable; he would jump, run, and take delight in young company, and go to fairs and meetings, to see sports and diversions.

One day going to the wake, where the young men were met, some went to wrestling, and some to cudgels, some to throwing the hammer and the like.

Tom stood awhile to see the sport, and at last he joined the company throwing the hammer; at length he took the hammer

in his hand, and felt the weight of it, bidding them stand out
of the way, for he would try how far he could throw it—Aye,
said the old smith, you will throw it a great way I warrant you—

Tom took the hammer, and giving it a swing, threw it into
a river five or six furlongs distant, and bid them fetch it out.

After this Tom joined the wrestlers; and though he had no
more skill than an ass, yet by main strength he flung all he
grappled with; if once he laid hold, they were gone; some he
threw over his head, and others he laid down gently. He did
not attempt to lock or strike at their heels, but threw them
down two or three yards from him, and sometimes on their
heads, ready to break their necks. So that at last none durst
enter the ring to wrestle with him; for they took him to be
some devil among them.

Chap. 3.

Tom becomes a Brewer's Servant; and of his killing a Giant, and gaining the Title of Mr. Hickathrift.

Tom's fame being spread, no one durst give him an angry
word; for being fool hardy, he cared not what he did; so that
those who knew him would not displease him. At last a
brewer of Lynn, who wanted a lusty man to carry beer to the
Marsh, and to Wisbeach, hearing of Tom, came to hire him;
but Tom would not hire himself, until his friends persuaded

him, and the master promised him a new suit of cloaths from top to toe, and besides that he should eat and drink of the best. At last Tom consented to be his man, and the master shewed him which way he was to go; for there was a monsterous Giant, who kept part of the Marsh, and none durst go that way; for if the Giant found them, he would either kill them, or make them his slaves.

But to come to Tom and his master; Tom did more in one day than all the rest of his men did in three; so that his master seeing him so tractable, and careful in his business, made him his head man, and trusted him to carry beer by himself, for he needed none to help him; Thus Tom went each day to Wisbeach, which was a long Journey of twenty miles.

Tom going this journey so often, and finding the other road, the Giant kept, nearer by the half, and Tom having encreased his strength by being so well kept, and improved his courage by drinking so much strong ale; one day as he was going to Wisbeach, without saying any thing to his master, or any of his fellow servants, he resolved to make the nearest road, or lose his life; to win the horse, or lose the saddle; to kill or be killed if he met the Giant.

Thus resolved, he goes the nearest way with his cart, flinging open the gates in order to go through; but the Giant soon espied him, and seeing him a daring fellow, vowed to stop his journey, and make a prize of his beer; but Tom cared nothing for him; and the Giant met him like a roaring lion, as though he would have swallowed him.

Sirrah, said he, who gave you authority to come this way? Do you not know that I make all stand in fear of my sight; and you, like an impudent rogue, must come and fling open my gates at pleasure. Are you so careless of your life that you care not what you do? I'll make you an example to all rogues under the sun. Dost thou not see how many heads hang on yonder tree, that have offended my laws? thine shall hang above them all.

Who cares for you, said Tom, you shall not find me like one of them. No, said the Giant, why you are but a fool, if you come to fight me, and bring no weapon to defend yourself. Cries Tom I have got a weapon here shall make you know I am your Master. Aye, say you so, Sirrah, said the Giant, and then ran to his Cave to fetch his Club, intending to dash out his brains at one blow. While the Giant was gone for his club,

Tom turned his cart upside down, taking the axle tree and wheel for his sword and buckler, and excellent weapons they was on such an emergence.

The Giant coming out again began to stare at Tom to see him take the wheel in one hand and the axle tree in the other.

Oh! Oh! said the Giant, you are like to do great things with these instruments. I have a twig here that will beat thee and thy axle tree, and thy wheel to the ground. Now that

which the giant called a twig was as thick as a millpost; with
this the giant made a blow at Tom with such force as made

his wheel crack. Tom nothing daunted, gave him as brave a
blow on the side of his head, which made him reel again.—
What, said Tom, are you got drunk with my small beer already?
The Giant recovering, made many hard blows at Tom; but
still, as they came, he kept them off with his wheel, so that he
received but very little hurt.

In the mean time Tom plied him so well with blows, that
the sweat and blood ran together down the Giant's face; who
being fat and foggy, was almost spent with fighting so long,
begged Tom to let him drink, and then he would fight him
again. No said Tom, my mother did not teach me such wit;
who is fool then? whereupon finding the Giant grow weak,
Tom redoubled his blows till he brought him to the ground.
The Giant finding himself overcome, roared hediously, and
begged Tom to spare his life, and he would perform anything
he should desire, even yield himself unto him, and be his
servant.

But Tom having no more mercy on him than a bear upon
a dog, laid on him till he found him breathless, and then Cut
off his head, after which he went into the cave and there
found great store of gold and silver, which made his heart leap
for Joy.

When he had rumaged the cave and refreshed himself a
little, he restored the wheel and axletree to their former places,

and loaded his beer on his cart, and went to Wisbeach, where he delivered his beer and returned home the same night as usual.

Upon his return to his master, he told him what he had done, which though he was rejoiced to hear, he could not altogether believe, till he had seen it was true. Next morning Tom's master went with him to the place, to be convinced of the truth; as did most of the inhabitants of Lynn. When they came to the place they were rejoiced to find the giant dead: and when Tom shewed them the head, and what gold and silver there was in the Cave, all of them leaped for joy; for the giant had been a great enemy to that part of the Country.

News was soon spread that Thomas Hickathrift had killed the giant, and happy was he that could come to see the giant's cave; and bonfires were made all round the country for Tom's success.

Tom by the general consent of the country took possession of the giant's cave, and the riches. He pulled down the Cave and built himself a handsome house on the spot. Part of the Giant's lands he gave to the poor for their Common, and the rest he divided and enclosed for an estate, to maintain him and his mother. Now Tom's fame spread more and more thro' the country, and he was no longer called plain Tom but Mr. Hickathrift; and they feared his anger now, almost as much as they did that of the Giant before.

Tom now finding himself very rich, resolved his neighbours should be the better for it; he enclosed himself a park and kept deer; and just by his house he built a church, which he dedicated to St. James, because on that Saint's day he killed the Giant.

Chap. 4.

How Tom kept a Pack of Hounds, and of his being attacked by four Highwaymen.

Tom not being used to have such a stock of riches could hardly tell how to dispose of it; but he used means to do it;

for he kept a pack of hounds and men to hunt them; and who but Tom! he took such delight in sports and exercises, that he would go far and near to a merry meeting.

One day as Tom was riding, he saw a company at Football, and dismounted to see them play for a wager; but he spoiled all their sport, for meeting the football he gave it such a kick that they never found it more; whereupon they began to quarrel with Tom, but some of them got little good by it; for he got a Spar, which belonged to an old house that had been blown down, with which he drove all opposition before him, and made way wherever he came.

After this, going home late in the evening, he was met by four highwaymen well mounted, who had robbed all the passengers that travelled this road. When they saw Tom, and found he was alone, they were cock sure of his money, and bid him stand and deliver—What must I deliver, cries Tom?—Your money, sirrah, says they.—Aye, said Tom, but you shall give me better words for it first, and be better armed too.—Come, come, said they, we came not here to prate, but for your money, and Money we will have before we go. Is it so said Tom, then get it and take it.

Whereupon one of them made at him with a trusty sword, which Tom immediately wrenched out of his hand, and attacked the whole four with it, and made them set spurs to their horses; but seeing one had a portmantua behind him, and supposing it contained money, he more closely pursued them, and cut their journey short, killing two of them, and sadly wounding the other two; who begging hard for their lives, he let them go; but took away all their money, which was above two hundred pounds, to bear his expenses home.

When Tom came home, he told them how he had served the poor football players; and also related his engagement with the four thieves; which produced much laughter amongst the whole company.

Chap. 5.

Tom meets with a Tinker and of the Battle they fought.

Some time afterwards as Tom was walking about his estate, to see how his workmen went on, he met upon the skirts of the forest a very sturdy Tinker, having a good staff on his shoulder, and a great dog to carry his budget of tools. So Tom asked the Tinker from whence he came and whither he was going? as that was no highway. And the Tinker being a very sturdy fellow, bid him go look, what was that to him? but fools must always be meddling—Hold said Tom, before you and I part I will make you know who I am.—Ay—said the Tinker, it is three Years since I had a combat with any man; I have challenged many a one, but none dare face me, so I think they are all cowards in this part of the country; but I hear there is a man hereabouts named Thomas Hickathrift, who killed a Giant; him I'd willingly see to have a bout with.—Aye, said Tom, I am the man, what have you to say to me? Truly said the Tinker, I am glad we are so happily met that we may have one touch—Surely, said Tom, you are but in jest—Marry said the Tinker, I am in earnest—A match, said Tom—It is done, said the Tinker.—But, said Tom, will you give me leave to let me get a twig—Aye, said the Tinker, I hate him that fights with a man unarmed.

So Tom stepped to a gate, and took a rail for a staff. To it they fell, the Tinker at Tom, and Tom at the Tinker like two Giants. The Tinker had a leather coat on, so that every blow Tom gave him made him roar again; yet the Tinker did not give way an inch, till Tom gave him such a bang on the side of the head as felled him to the ground.—Now, Tinker, where art thou? said Tom.—But the Tinker being a nimble fellow leaped up again, and gave Tom a bang, which made him reel, and following his blow took Tom on the other side, which made him throw down his weapon, and yield the Tinker the best of it.

After this Tom took the Tinker home to his house, where we shall leave them to improve their acquaintance, and get themselves cured of the bruises they gave each other.

FINIS.

TOM THUMB.

THIS prose version is made from the ballad, the original of which was printed for John Wright in 1630; the second and third parts were written about 1700. Like most of its class, it seems to have had a northern origin. The German "Daumerling," or little Thumb, was, like Tom, swallowed by a cow; and there is a Danish book which treats of "Svend Tomling, a man no bigger than a thumb, who would be married to a woman three ells and three quarters long." But tradition has it that Tom died at Lincoln, which was one of the five Danish towns of England, and there was a little blue flagstone in the cathedral, said to be his tombstone, which got lost, or at least never replaced, during some repairs early in this century. The first mention of him is in Scot's "Discoverie of Witchcraft," 1584, where he is classed with "the puckle, hobgobblin, *Tom Tumbler* boneles, and such other bugs," or bugbears.

The Famous History of

TOM THUMB

Wherein is declared,

𝕳is 𝕸arvellous 𝕬cts of 𝕸anhood

FULL OF WONDER AND MERRIMENT

PART THE FIRST.

PRINTED AND SOLD IN ALDERMARY CHURCH YARD, LONDON.

" In Arthur's court Tom Thumb did live
    A man of mickle might,
Who was the best of the table round,
    And eke a worthy Knight.

" In stature but an inch in height,
    Or quarter of a span,
How think you that this valiant knight
    Was proved a valiant man.

" His father was a ploughman plain,
    His mother milked the Cow,
And yet the way to get a son
    This couple knew not how.—

" Until the time the good old man
    To learned Merlin goes,
And there to him in deep distress,
    In secret manner shews,

" How in his heart he'd wish to have
    A child in time to come,
To be his heir, though it might be
    No bigger than his Thumb.

" Of this old Merlin then foretold,
    How he his wish should have ;
And so a son of stature small
    This charmer to him gave."

It is needless to say that this marvellous being was under special fairy protection.

" Tom Thumb, the which the Fairy Queen
    Did give him to his name,
Who with her train of goblins grim
    Unto the Christening came."

Of his childhood nothing very particular is told until

> " Whereas about Christmas time,
>   His mother a hog had kill'd,
> And Tom would see the pudding made,
>   For fear it should be spoil'd.

> " He sat the candle for to light
>   Upon the pudding bowl,
> Of which there is unto this day,
>   A pretty Story told.

> " For Tom fell in and could not be
>   For some time after found,
> For in the blood and batter he
>   Was lost and almost drown'd."

In cooking, the pudding behaved so curiously—

> " As if the devil had been boil'd
>   Such was the mother's fear,"

that she at once gave it to a passing tinker, who put it in his
"budget;" but hearing Tom cry out, threw both bag and
pudding away; and Tom, by some unexplained means having

got out, returned home, where his mother, when she went milking, tied him to a thistle to keep him safe. Whilst she was busy milking, the cow eat the thistle, and Tom with it; but his

mother missed him, and calling for him was answered by Tom from the cow's interior. Naturally unaccustomed to such internal commotion, the cow took the earliest opportunity of getting rid of Tom by natural means, and

> " Now all besmeared as he was
>   His mother took him up
> And home to bear him hence, poor Lad,
>   She in her apron put."

But Tom from his size was a prey to accidents from which ordinary mortals were exempt, for we find—

"Now by a raven of great strength,
    Away poor Tom was borne,
And carried in the Carrion's beak,
    Just like a grain of corn.

"Unto a Giant's castle top
    Whereon he let him fall
And soon the Giant swallowed up
    His body, cloaths and all."

* This illustration is from another edition.

But Tom, like most small men, was rather self-assertive.

> "But in his belly did Tom Thumb
>   So great a rumbling make
> That neither night nor day he could
>   The smallest quiet take.

> "Until the Giant him had spew'd
>   Full three miles in the sea;
> There a large fish took him up,
>   And bore him hence away."

The fish was sent to King Arthur; Tom was discovered, and taken into high favour at Court.

> "Among the deeds of courtship done,
>   His Highness did command
> That he should dance a galliard brave
>   Upon the Queen's left hand.

" All which he did, and for the same
  Our king his signet gave,
Which Tom about his middle wore
  Long time a girdle brave."

The king used to take him out hunting, and Tom was made proficient in martial exercises—so much so that at one tourney we read:

" And good Sir Lancelot du Lake
  Sir Tristram and Sir Guy,
Yet none compar'd to brave Tom Thumb
  In acts of Cavalry."

Nay, his prowess was such that he beat all comers, "Sir Khion and the rest;" even the invincible Lancelot had his horse clean run through.

Indeed, it was through his exertions in this manner that he fell sick and finally died, and was buried with great pomp. His death is forcibly and graphically told.

> " He being both slender and tall,
>   The cunning Doctors took
> A fine perspective glass thro' which
>   They took a careful look,

> " Into his sickly body down,
>   And therein saw that death
> Stood ready in his wasted guts
>   To take away his breath."

But to a being so wonderful, ordinary death was a mere nothing.

> " The Fairy Queen she lov'd him so
>   As you shall understand,
> That once again she let him go
>   Down to the Fairy Land.

> " The very time that he return'd
>   Unto the Court again,
> It was, as we are well inform'd,
>   In good King Arthur's reign.

> " When in the presence of the King,
>   He many wonders wrought,
> Recited in the Second Part,
>   Which now is to be bought

> " In Bow Church Yard, where is sold
>   Diverting Histories many ;
> And pleasant tales as e'er was told
>   For purchase of One Penny."

The Second Part commences with Tom's return to earth from Fairy Land, but his *début* was neither agreeable nor romantic. The Fairy Queen had determined

"To send him to the lower World,
  In triumph once again ;
So with a puff or blast him hurl'd
  Down with a mighty pain :
With mighty force it happened,
  Did fall, as some report,
Into a pan of firmity,
  In good King Arthur's * Court.

The Cook that bore it then along
  Was struck with a surprise,
For with the fall the firmity
  Flew up into his eyes."

The cook let the dish fall, and Tom was extricated ; but the
Court, disappointed of dinner, looked very evilly on him.

"Some said he was a fairy elf
  And did deserve to die."

To escape this fate, Tom, unperceived, jumped down a miller's
throat, but evidently behaved ungratefully in his asylum of
safety :

"Tom often pinched him by the tripes,
  And made the Miller roar,
Alas ! Alas ! ten thousand stripes
  Could not have vexed him more."

* The chronology is somewhat involved. The king could not have
been King Arthur, for Tom was not remembered by him, and at the end
of the book it says—

"And to his memory they built
  A monument of gold
Upon King Edgars dagger hilt
  Most glorious to behold."

At length the Miller got rid of him, and Tom was turned into a river, and swallowed by a salmon. The same thing occurred to him as before. The fish was caught, sent to the king, and Tom found by his old enemy the cook, who had not forgiven the loss of the firmity.

> " He stared strait, and said, Alas !
>   How comes this fellow here ?
> Strange things I find have come to pass,
>   He shall not now get clear.
> Because he vow'd to go thro' stitch,
>   And him to Justice bring,
> He stuck a fork into his breech
>   And bore him to the King."

The king, however, was busy, and ordered Tom to be brought before him another time ; so the cook kept him in custody in a mouse-trap.

The king, on hearing Tom's story, pardoned him " for good King Arthur's sake," took him into favour, and allowed him to go hunting with him, mounted on a mouse.

This, however, was the cause of his second death.

"For coming near a Farmer's house,
　　Close by a Forest side,
A Cat jump'd out and caught the mouse
　　Whereon Tom Thumb did ride.
She took him up between her Jaws,
　　And scower'd up a tree,
And as she scratch'd him with her claws,
　　He cry'd out, Woe is me !
He laid his hand upon his sword,
　　And ran her thro' and thro' ;
And he for fear of falling roar'd,
　　Puss likewise cry'd out Mew.
It was a sad and bloody fight
　　Between the Cat and he ;
Puss valu'd not this worthy Knight,
　　But scratch'd him bitterly."

He was taken home ; but his wounds were too bad, and he died, and was taken again to Fairy Land, and did not reappear on earth till Thunston's (?) reign.

————————

The Third Part opens with the Fairy Queen again despatching Tom to earth, and also, as before, his advent is unpropitious.

"Where he descended thro the Air,
　　This poor unhappy man,
By sad mishap as you shall hear
　　Fell in a close stool pan."

He was rescued, but narrowly escaped death, and was brought before King Thunston.

> " In shameful sort Tom Thumb appear'd
>   Before his Majesty,
>   But grown so weak could not be heard,
>   Which caused his malady."

He recovered and was taken into high favour by the king, who

> " For lodgings—Now the King resolv'd
>   A palace should be fram'd
>   The walls of this most stately place
>   Were lovely to behold.
>   For workmanship none can take place
>   It look'd like beaten gold
>   The height thereof was but a span,
>   And doors but one inch wide.
>   The inward parts were all Japan,
>   Which was in him great pride."

And not only was he lodged so magnificently, but the king did all in his power to make him happy.

> " All recreation thought could have
>   Or life could e'er afford,
>   All earthly Joys that he would crave,
>   At his desire or word.

*　　　*　　　*　　　*　　　*　　　*

"Of smallest mice that could be found,
    For to draw his coach appears
Such stately steeds his wish to crown
    Long tails with cropped ears."

But the morals of this ungrateful little wretch had evidently grown lax during his stay in Fairy Land, and he forgot all his obligations to his benefactor.

"For his desires were lustful grown
    Against her Majesty,
Finding of her one day alone,
    Which proved his tragedy."

The queen was naturally furious.

"That nothing would her wrath appease
    To free her from all strife,
Or set her mind at perfect ease,
    Until she had his life."

Tom hid himself, and tried to escape on the back of a butterfly;

but the insect flew into the palace, and Tom was captured. He was duly tried, and found guilty.

> " So the King his sentence declar'd,
>   How hanged he should be,
> And that a gibbet should be rear'd,
>   And none should set him free.
> After his sentence thus was past,
>   Unto a prison he was led.
> For in a Mousetrap he was fast,
>   He had no other bed.

*   *   *   *   *   *

> " At last by chance the cat him spy'd,
>   And for a mouse did take,
> She him attacked on each side,
>   And did his prison break.
> The Cat perceiving her mistake,
>   Away she fled with speed,
> Which made poor Tom to flight betake,
>   Being thus from prison freed.
> Resolving there no more to dwell
>   But break the Kings decree,
> Into a spider's web he fell,
>   And could not hence get free.
> The spider watching for his prey
>   Took Tom to be a fly,
> And seized him without delay,
>   Regarding not his cry.

The blood out of his body drains,
　He yielded up his breath ;
Thus he was freed from all his pains,
　By his unlook'd for death."

Thus sadly ended the favourite of immortals and of kings ;
but, from the fact that we hear no more of his going to Fairy
Land, it is probable that his immoral conduct could not be
condoned by the " good people."

The Shoemaker's Glory

OR THE

PRINCELY HISTORY

OF THE

GENTLE CRAFT

SHEWING

What renowned Princes, Heroes, and Worthies have been of the Shoemakers Trade, both in this and in other Kingdoms Likewise why it is called the *Gentle Craft;* and that they say a Shoemaker's son is a Prince born &c.

Crispin. Crispianus.

NEWCASTLE : PRINTED AT THE PRINTING OFFICE IN PILGRIM STREET.

THE
SHOEMAKER'S GLORY.

Or, The Princely History of the

GENTLE CRAFT

SHEWING

What renowned Princes, Heroes, and Worthies have been of the Shoemaker's Trade, both in this and other Kingdoms. Likewise, Why it is called the Gentle Craft; and that they say, A Shoemakers Son is a Prince born.

PRINTED AND SOLD IN ALDERMARY CHURCH YARD. BOW LANE LONDON.

THIS book is in reality two : one, the history of Sir Hugh, and the other, of Crispin and Crispianus. Sir Hugh seems to have been the son of Arviragus, King of Powisland in Britain, and Genevra, daughter of a king in North Wales. He went abroad for his education, and there distinguished himself by slaying monsters and giants, and by fighting against the Saracens—so much so, that he was knighted by the Roman Emperor, and

promised one of his daughters as a wife ; but this he would not have, although the princess loved him dearly.

He returned home, and whilst visiting Donvallo, King of Flintshire, fell in love with his daughter Winnifred. Finding her one day reading in her bower in the garden, he declared his love, but was courteously, though firmly, declined by the prin-

cess. Grieved at this disappointment, Sir Hugh went again

abroad, was shipwrecked, and finally returned to Harwich in a destitute condition. Here he fell in with some shoemakers, and tarried with them a whole year, learning their trade.

In Chap-books one does not look for extreme historical accuracy, so we are not surprised that Diocletian came over to England, and sent Winnifred to prison for refusing to worship idols. Sir Hugh heard of this, and in order to join her, spoke loudly in favour of the Christian religion, and soon had his wish gratified. In prison, journeymen shoemakers brought him relief, and were so kind to him, that he styled them all gentlemen of the "gentle craft;" but the tale winds up informing us that "Sir Hugh and Winnifred remained a long time in prison, and were at last, for their steadfastness to the Christian religion, put to death by order of this cruel tyrant."

Crispin and Crispianus seem to have lived in Britain in the reign of Maximinius, and were the sons of King Logrid. Maximinius sent for them in order to slay them, but their mother, Queen Esteda, disguised them, and caused them to flee. They wandered to Faversham, where, tired out, they knocked at the door of a shoemaker, who took them in, and finally apprenticed them to himself. Crispianus, however, could not "stick to his last," so he went to assist the King of France against the Persians; whilst Crispin, whose master was the Court shoemaker, being a handsome young man, used to be sent there with shoes, and the Princess Ursula fell violently in love with him, declared her passion for him, and they were privately married under an oak tree in the park.

Crispianus, meanwhile, had been performing prodigies of valour, and at length returned to Maximinius with letters of commendation from the French king; whilst the Princess Ursula, whose confinement drew nigh, did not know how to screen herself. Love, however, is proverbially sharp-witted; so a false rumour of an enemy having landed being spread by means "*of firing a gun*," she escaped in the confusion, and took refuge in the shoemaker's house, where a son was born, whence the saying, "A shoemaker's son is a prince born." Maximinius received Crispianus with effusion, sent for his mother, acknow-

ledged his birth, and would have given him his daughter in marriage could she have been found. At this juncture the young couple turned up, were forgiven, " and they lived very happy all their lives afterwards."

The original of this book seems to have been written by Thomas Deloney; an edition of it was printed in 1598, and it was entered on the Stationers' Books on October 19, 1597, as " a booke called the gentle Crafte, intreatinge of Shoomakers."

The Famous History of the Valiant

LONDON PRENTICE

NEWCASTLE: PRINTED IN THIS PRESENT YEAR.

A YOUTH named Aurelius was the son of wealthy parents in the county of Chester, and, being of singular beauty, caused a flutter in all the feminine hearts in his neighbourhood ; one young lady, named Dorinda, even going so far as to write him a most unmaidenlike love letter, which, being dropped by accident, was found by one of the young lady's lovers, who, taking counsel with three others, set upon Aurelius as he was going through a wood. It is needless to say that he speedily overcame them ; but his parents, fearing revenge, and wishing to remove him from the wiles of Dorinda, sent him to London, and bound him apprentice to a Turkey merchant on London Bridge. Here the young gentleman, after some time, must needs fall in love with his master's daughter; but, unlike the usual course of events in such cases, his passion was not reciprocated, so in dudgeon he applied for, and obtained, the merchant's leave for him to go to Turkey as his factor.

He set out with a gallant equipage, and was well received by the English merchants in Turkey. Merchants at that time do not seem to have been of the same prosaic class as they are now ; for, on the occasion of a tournament held in honour of a marriage, Aurelius must go fully armed, in order to take part in the joust. His blood boiled to see the knights of other nations overthrown by the Turkish champions; so he joined in the fray, soon disposed of the Turkish chivalry, and killed Grodam, the son-in-law of the Great Turk, who, in his rage, ordered " the English boy" to be sent to prison, and afterwards to be cast alive to two lions, who were kept fasting many days.

" The day of his death, as appointed being come, and the King, his nobles, and all his ladies seated to behold the execution, the brave Aurelius was immediately brought forth in his shirt of Cambric, and the drawers of white Satin, embroidered with gold and a crimson cap on his head, but had scarce ime to bow respectfully to the ladies, who greatly praised his manly beauty, and began highly to pity his misfortunes ere the lions were let loose, who at the sight of their prey, casting their eyes upon him, began to roar horridly, insomuch that the spectators trembled and beheld Aurelius whom death could not daunt, laying aside all fear, as they came fiercely to him, with open mouths, he thrust his hands into their throats and ere they had power to get from his strong Arms, he forced out their hearts, and laid them dead at his feet, demanding of the King what other dangerous enterprises they had to put on him, as he would gladly do it for the Queen and his country's sake ; when immediately the Emperor descended from his throne, tenderly embracing him, swearing he was some Angel withal pardoning him, and gave him the beautiful Teoraza his daughter in marriage, with great riches, who for his sake became a Christian ; and after spending some time in that place, they both returned to England with great joy, where they lived many years very loving and happy."

THE
LOVER'S QUARREL

OR

CUPID'S TRIUMPH

Being the Pleasant and Delightful

HISTORY

OF

FAIR ROSAMOND

WHO WAS BORN IN

SCOTLAND.

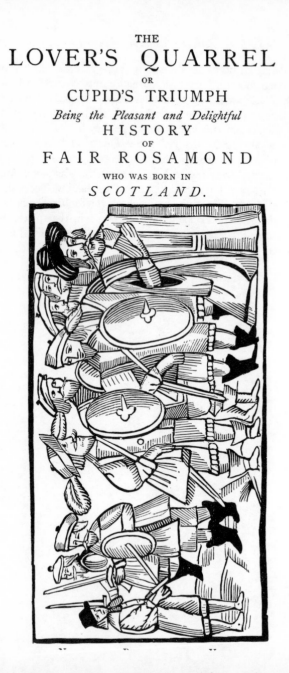

THIS metrical romance is more commonly known by the name of " Tommy Potts," and somewhat extravagantly recounts

the love between him and fair Rosamond, daughter of the Earl of Arundel, who, being wooed by Lord Phœnix, confessed her passion to him, to his natural and great disgust; but their marriage being settled by their friends, as a last resource she sent her little foot page to Tommy Potts, telling him of her dilemma, and begging him to meet her on Guildford Green. Tommy, whose position was only that of a servant at Strawberry Hall, sent back word by her messenger that he would be there, and went and asked his master for leave, which his master not only readily granted, but offered to enrich him so that their fortunes might be equalized ; also, he wished to furnish him with an armed force—both of which offers Tommy declined. He met Rosamond and Lord Phœnix at Guildford Green, was taunted by the latter with his menial position, and challenged him to a course of spears, at a future day, on that very spot. His master behaved very kindly to him, and reiterated his offers, which were again refused, Potts only accepting the loan of an old white horse and a suit of armour. The combatants duly met, and Tom Potts was run through the thick of the thigh. He bound up his wound with his handkerchief, and continued the combat, this time running Lord Phœnix through the right arm. He doctored Lord Phœnix, and offered to resume the fight, which his lordship refused, and they agreed to refer their claims to the lady herself. She, of course, chose Tommy ; but to prove her still more, Lord Phœnix pretended to fight with Tommy behind a wall, and reported to her that he had slain him. The lady declared she would spend all her fortune rather than Lord Phœnix should not be hanged, and then swooned. From this time everything prospered with the lovers. Lord Arundel joyfully gave his consent to their marriage, and made Tommy his heir.

There is a Second Part, but it lacks the interest of the first.

I cannot trace any connection between the Chap-book and the frontispiece ; but it is evidently the proper thing, as it occurs in the same place in the black-letter edition of 1675, which is the earliest I can find. It is entitled, "The Lovers Quarrel, or *Cupid's Triumph* being The Pleasant History of fair Rosamond of Scotland. Being Daughter to the Lord *Arundel* whose Love was obtained by the Valour of *Tommy Pots :* who conquered the Lord *Phenix*, and wounded him, and after obtained her to be his wife. Being very delightful to read. London. Printed by A. P. for F. Coles, T. Vere and J. Wright."

THE

HISTORY

OF THE

KING and the COBLER

PART THE FIRST

PRINTED AND SOLD AT THE LONDON AND MIDDLESEX PRINTING
OFFICE 81. SHOE LANE HOLBORN.

"It was the custom of King Henry 8 to walk late in the night into the City disguised, to observe how the constables and watch performed their duty; not only in guarding the City gates but also diligently watching the inner part of the city, that they might prevent those dangers and casualities that happens to great and populous Cities, in the night time—This he did oftentimes, without the least discovery who he was, returning home to Whitehall early in the morning.—Now on his return home through the Strand he took notice of a certain Cobler, who was always up at work whistling and singing every morning, so he resolved to see him, in order which he immediately knocks the heel off his shoe by hitting it against the Stones."

The King gives the shoe to be mended, and tells the cobbler to bring it to him at the opposite inn when done. The cobbler obeys. The king gives him liquor, and they hobnob in the most familiar manner; the king telling him his name was Harry Tudor, that he belonged to the Court, and should be very glad to see the cobbler whenever he liked to call. In fact, they became so friendly, that the cobbler would insist on the king's going over to his cellar, and trying some wonderful brown ale and a Cheshire cheese; and there they kept it up

until Joan, the cobbler's wife (who slept in the same apartment), awoke, and then the King retired.

The cobbler sadly missed his boon companion, and at length, with his wife's permission, he started to pay him a visit, Joan having made him as spruce as possible.

On his arrival at Whitehall, he asked for Harry Tudor, and by the King's express command, was immediately ushered into his presence.

This so bewildered the cobbler that he turned and fled ; but being captured, and once more brought to the king, the

* This illustration is from another edition.

latter, on hearing his tale, bids him go to the cellar and he will send Harry Tudor to him.

The king disguises himself and joins the cobbler, and they have a jovial tune together, until their noise attracts some of the nobility, who enter, and then the cobbler discovers who his boon companion really is.

Bluff King Hal, however, must needs reward his humble friend, so he gave him a pension of forty marks yearly, with the freedom of his cellar, and made him " one of the courtiers "—a position which he must have graced, judging by his deportment as depicted in the illustrations.

The earliest book on this subject I can find, is the " Cobler turned Courtier, being a Pleasant Humour between K. Henry 8th and a Cobler," 1680, quarto.

* This illustration is from another edition.

The First Part of the

FRYAR AND BOY.

OR THE

Young PIPER'S pleasant Pastime

CONTAINING

The witty Adventures betwixt the Fryar and Boy in relation to his Step Mother, whom he fairly fitted for her unmerciful cruelty.

NEWCASTLE: PRINTED IN THIS YEAR.

THE

FRIAR AND BOY

OR THE

Young PIPER'S

PLEASANT PASTIME

CONTAINING

His witty Pranks in Relation to his Step Mother,
whom he fitted for her unkind Treatment.

PART THE FIRST

PRINTED AND SOLD IN ALDERMARY CHURCH YARD LONDON

The father of the "boy" Jack had married a second time,
and Jack's stepmother behaved most harshly to him, and half
starved him.

> "Nay, tho' his meat and drink was poor
>   He had not half enough.
> Yet, if he seem'd to crave for more
>   His ears she strait did cuff."

His father, however, behaved kindly, and to get the lad
away, proposed he should look after the cows all day, taking
his provision with him.   One day, an old man came to him
and begged for food, on which Jack offered him his dinner,
which the old man thankfully took and eat.

Indeed, he was so grateful that he told Jack he would give
him three things, whatever he liked to choose.   Jack replied—

" The first thing I'd have thee bestow
    On me without dispute,
Pray let it be a cunning bow,
    With which I birds may shoot.
Well thou shalt have a bow, my son,
    I have it here in store,
No archer ever yet had one
    Which shot so true before.
Take notice well of what I say.
    Such virtues are in this
That wink or look another way
    The mark you shall not miss."

Jack also asked for a pipe, and the old man said—

" A pipe I have for thee my son,
    The like was never known,
So full of mirth and mickle joy,
    That whensoe'er 'tis blown,
All living creatures that shall hear
    The sweet and pleasant sound
They shan't be able to forbear
    But dance and skip around."

The third thing Jack chose was, that whenever his step-mother looked crossly at him, she should, against her will, behave in a rude and unseemly manner, which was also granted.

The old man left him; and at evening Jack took the cattle home, and as he went, he tried his pipe with wonderful effect.

> " His Cows began to caper then,
>   The Bulls and Oxen too,
> And so did five and twenty men
>   Who came this sight to view,
> Along the road he piping went,
>   The Bulls came dancing after,
> Which was a fit of merriment,
>   That caus'd a deal of laughter.
> For why, a friar in his gown
>   Bestrides the red cow's back,
> And so rides dancing thro' the town,
>   After this young wag Jack."

He found his father at home, and telling him how he had disposed of his dinner, the good man handed him a capon; at which his mother-in-law frowned, and, to her great disgust, her punishment was prompt, and she had to retire, Jack bantering her. She vowed vengeance, and

> " A Friar whom she thought a saint,
>   Came there to lodge that night;
> To whom she made a sad complaint,
>   How Jack had sham'd her quite.

> Said she, For sweet St. Francis sake,
>   To-morrow in the field,
> Pray thrash him till his bones you break
>   No shew of comfort yield."

The friar went the next morning to give Jack his thrash-

ing, but Jack begged him not to be angry, and he would show
him something; so he took his bow and shot a pheasant, which
fell in a thorn bush. The friar ran to secure the bird, and
when well in the bush, Jack played his pipe, with woeful effects
as regards the friar, who in his involuntary dancing got literally
torn to pieces, till he begged Jack—

* This illustration is from another edition.

"For Good St. Francis sake,
Let me not dancing die."

He naturally told his pitiful tale when he reached Jack's father's house, and the father asked him if it were true, and if so, to play the pipe and make them dance. The friar had already experienced the sensation, and

"The Friar he did quake for fear
And wrung his hands withal.
He cry'd, and still his eyes did wipe,
That work kills me almost;
Yet if you needs must hear the pipe,
Pray bind me to a post."

This was done; the pipe struck up, and every one began their involuntary dance, to the delight of the father, and the great disgust of the stepmother and the friar, who

"was almost dead,
While others danced their fill
Against the post he bang'd his head,
For he could not stand still.
His ragged flesh the rope did tear,
And likewise from his crown,
With many bangs and bruises there
The blood did trickle down."

The lad led them all into the street, where every one joined in the mad scene, until his father asked him to stop. Then the friar summoned him before the proctor, and the gravity of the court was disturbed by Jack's playing his pipe at the proctor's request. All had to dance, nor would Jack desist until he had a solemn promise that he should go free. Here the First Part ends, as also does the first printed version of the romance, which is entitled, "Here begynneth a mery Geste of the Frere and the Boye, emprynted at London in Flete strete at the sygne of the sonne by Wynkyn de Worde." There is no date, and there is a copy in the public library, Cambridge. It has been reprinted both by Ritson and Hazlitt. Ritson says, "From the mention made in v. 429 of the city of 'Orlyance,' and the character of the 'Offycial,' it may be conjectured that this poem is of French extraction; and, indeed, it is not at all improbable that the original is extant in some collection of old Fabliaux."

It is a most popular Chap-book, and went through many editions. A Second Part was afterwards added, but it is coarser in its humour. The Newcastle frontispiece is extremely quaint.

The Pleasant History of

JACK HORNER

CONTAINING

His witty tricks and pleasant pranks, which he play'd from his youth to his riper years : Right pleasant and delightful for winter and summer recreations.

NEWCASTLE: PRINTED IN THIS PRESENT YEAR.

THIS is somewhat similar to "The Friar and the Boy," but is even coarser.

> "Jack Horner was a pretty lad,
>   Near London he did dwell,
> His father's heart he made full glad
>   His mother lov'd him well;
> She often set him on her lap,
>   To turn him dry beneath
> And fed him with sweet sugar'd pap,
>   Because he had no teeth.
> While little Jack was sweet and young,
>   If he by chance should cry,
> His mother pretty sonnets sung,
>   With a Lulla ba by;
> With such a dainty, curious tone,
>   As Jack sat on her knee,
> So that e'er he could go alone,
>   He sung as well as she.
> A pretty boy, of curious wit,
>   All people spoke his praise
> And in the corner he would sit
>   In Christmas holy-days:
> When friends they did together meet,
>   To pass away the time;
> Why, little Jack, he sure would eat
>   His Christmas pye in rhime.
> And said, Jack Horner, in the corner,
>   Eats good Christmas pye,
> And with his thumbs pulls out the plumbs,
>   And said Good boy am I.
> These pretty verses which he made
>   Upon his Christmas cheer,
> Did gain him love, as it is said,
>   Of all both far and near."

Jack Horner was a dwarf, and never exceeded thirteen inches in height. His first exploit was to frighten a tailor who stole some of his cloth, by putting on the head of a goat lately killed, and pretending to be the devil. He had a fight with a cook-maid who chastised him for making a sop in the dripping-pan, in which he got the best of it. An old hermit being desirous of a jug of beer, Jack brought it to him, and in return the hermit presented him with a coat in which he should be invisible, and a pair of enchanted pipes, both of which he tried on some fiddlers, making them dance sorely against their will. He had many adventures, but his last was with a giant who had seized and imprisoned a knight's daughter. Jack armed himself, and mounting on a badger, rode down the giant's throat, and with his pipes and sword created such a disturbance in his inside, that the giant died, and Jack delivered the lady, whom he afterwards married.

MAD PRANKS

OF

TOM TRAM

Son in Law to Mother Winter

TO WHICH IS ADDED.

*His Merry Jests, odd Conceits and Pleasant Tales, being
very delightful to read.*

NEWCASTLE : PRINTED IN THIS PRESENT YEAR.

THE

MAD PRANKS

OF

Tom Tram

Son in Law to Mother Winter

TO WHICH IS ADDED.

His Merry Jests, odd Conceits and pleasant
Tales, very delightful to Read.

THE FIRST PART.

PRINTED AND SOLD IN ALDERMARY CHURCH YARD,
BOW LANE LONDON.

"THERE was an old woman, named Mother Winter, who had a son in Law, whose name was Thomas, who though he was at man's estate, yet would do nothing but what he pleased, which grieved his mother to the heart. One day being at market, she heard a proclamation that those who would not work should be whipped; On this she ran home and told Tom of the proclamation that was issued out; replied Tom, I will not break the decree. Upon which the old woman left her son, and went to market.

"She was no sooner gone, but Tom looked into a stone pot she used to keep her small beer in, and seeing the beer did not work, he with his cartwhip lays on the pot as hard as he could. The people seeing him, told his mother, who said, The knave will be hanged, and in that note went home—Tom seeing her coming, laid on as hard as he could drive, and broke the pots, which made the old woman say, O what hast thou done, thou villain? O dear mother said he, you told me it was proclaimed, that those who did not work must be whipped; and I have so often seen our pots work so hard that they foamed at the mouth; but these two lazy knaves will never work. So I have whipped them to death to shew their fellows to work, or never look me in the face again."

Mother Winter once sent him to buy a pennyworth of soap, and bade him be sure and bring her the change back safely; so he got two men with a hand barrow to carry the soap, and

hired four men with "brown bills" to guard it, and gave them the elevenpence for their pains. But Tom was quite as much knave as fool, and, as the anecdotes relating to him are not very amusing, only those illustrating the Newcastle title-page will be made use of.

Whilst staying at an inn, he saw some turkeys in the yard. He killed two of them by running pins into their heads, and then persuaded his hostess to throw them away, as there was a sickness among the birds. Of course he took them away with him, but, finding them heavy to carry, had recourse to strata-gem to help himself. He saw a man leading his horse down the hill, and "Tom fell down, crying as if he had broke a leg and made great lamentation of his being five or six miles from any town, and was likely to perish. The man asked where he lived? Tom replied, With such a Knight. He, knowing the

gentleman, set him on his horse. Tom then bid him give him his master's turkies, and then galloped away as fast as he could, crying out I shall be killed, I shall be killed—The man seeing he was gone without the turkies, knew not what to do, for he thought if he left the turkies behind the Knight might take it amiss. So carrying them on foot, lugging, fretting, and sweat-ing to the next town, where he hired a horse to overtake Tom, but could not till he arrived at the Knight's house, where Tom stood ready, calling to him, Oh! now I see thou art an honest fellow; I had thought you had set me on a headstrong horse on purpose to deceive me of my two turkies. But he replied

Pox on your turkies and you too; I hope you will pay me for the horse I got."

The story of the house on fire in the top left hand of the title-page is thus told : " It happened one evening there came a number of Gypsies to town, whom Tom meeting, asked what they did there ? they said, To tell people their fortunes, that they might avoid approaching danger. Where do you lie to night said Tom ? We cannot tell, said they. If you can be content to lie in the straw, says Tom, I will show you where you may lie dry and warm. They thanked him, and said they would tell him his fortune for nothing. He thanked them, and conveyed them to a little thatched house filled with straw, and which had a ditch round it, close to the wall of the house, and there left them to take their rest, drawing up the bridge after him. In the dead of the night he got a long pole with a large whisp of straw, and set the house on fire. One of the Gypsies seeing the house in flames, calling to the rest, and thinking to cross the bridge, fell into the ditch, crying out for help ; while by Tom's means great part of the town stood to see the Jest. As the Gypsies came out of the ditch, the people let them go to the fire to warm themselves ; when Tom told them, That seeing they could not foretel their own fortunes he would, which was on the morrow morning they should be whipt for cheats, and in the afternoon charged for setting the house on fire.

" The Gypsies hearing this having made haste to dry themselves, got out of the town before day break, and never came there afterwards."

The right-hand upper portion of the engraving represents Tom cutting some shavings of wood from the gallows, to put in the ale of some persons who had played a practical joke upon him.

There are three parts, but the other two are uninteresting both as to matter and illustrations.

THE

Birth, Life, and Death

OF

JOHN FRANKS

With the Pranks he played
Though a meer Fool

PRINTED AND SOLD IN ALDERMARY CHURCH YARD. LONDON.

FROM the preface, and its general internal evidence, this Chap-book seems to be recollections of a real person, who was locally famous, and whose actions were traditionally handed down. Only a few of the sayings and deeds of this half-witted jester are worth repeating.

THE PREFACE.

"John Franks, the reputed son of John Ward, was born at Much Eaton in Essex, within three miles of Dunmow. He had no friends to take care of him, but his being such a fool was the cause of his well being; for every one was in love with the sport he made.

"When he was grown to be of man's stature, there was a worthy Knight, who took him to keep, where he did many strange pranks.

"He was a comely person, and had a good complexion, his hair was of a dark flaxen. He was of a middle stature, and good countenance. If his tongue had not betrayed his folly, he might have been taken for a wise man."

"The Knight where Jack lived kept a poor taylor in his house, who lay with the fool.

"One morning they wondered that the taylor nor Jack did not come down; one of the servants going up, found the door fast, and calling to them, Jack only answered them; so calling more assistance and breaking open the door, they found the

taylor dead in his bed with his neck broke, and the fool set astride on a high beam, whence he could not come down without help. They asked Jack how it was? he said the Devil came upstairs, clink, clink, clink, and came to my bed side, and I cried, Good devil do not take me take the taylor; so the devil broke the taylor's neck, and set me upon the beam. Jack was strictly examined at Chelmsford Assizes, and several times after; but he always kept in one story, and never seemed concerned."

"Jack was often upon the ramble; one day he went up to a yeoman's house, who loved to make sport with him. The servants being all busy and abroad, none but the fool and he was together. Mr. Sorrel, says Jack, shall we play at Blind Man's Buff? Ay, says he, with all my heart, Jack—You shall be blinded says Jack—That I will, Jack, says he. So pinning a napkin about his eyes and head; Now turn about, says Jack; but you see Mr. Sorrel, you see; No, Jack, said he I do not see. Jack shuffled about the kitchen, in order to catch him, still crying, you see, but when he found he did not see he ran to the chimney and whipt down some puddings, and put them

into his pockets; this he did every time he came to that end of the room, till he had filled his pockets and breeches. The doors being open, away runs Jack, leaving the good man blindfolded, who wondering he did not hear the fool, cried out, Jack, Jack; but finding no answer, he pulled off the napkin, and seeing the fool gone, and that he had taken so many puddings with him, was so enraged that he sent his blood hounds after him; which when Jack perceived, he takes a pudding and flings it at them; the dogs smelling the pudding, Jack gained ground the time: and still as the dogs pursued, he threw a pudding at them; and this he did till he come to an house. This was spread abroad to the shame and vexation of the farmer.

"Some time after Mr. Sorrel and some other tenants went to see the fool's master. Jack espying them, went and told his Lady that Mr. Sorrel was come. The lady being afraid the fool might offend him by speaking of the puddings, told Jack he should be whipped if he mentioned them. But when they were at dinner, Jack went and shaked Mr. Sorel by the hand, saying, How is it Mr. Sorel? then, seeming to whisper, but speaking so loud that all the Company heard him, said, Not a word of the puddings, Mr. Sorel.—At this they all burst into a laughter, but the honest man was so ashamed, that he never came there again. Ever since it is a bye-word to say, Not a word of the puddings."

"A Justice of the Peace being at his Lord's table one day, who delighted to jest with every one, and Jack being in the room to make them some sport, and having then a new calf-skin suit on, red and white spotted, and a young puppy in his arms, much of the same colour; he said to the justice, as he jogged him, Is not this puppy like me? The justice said It is very much like thee; now there are two puppies Jack, ha! ha!

ha !—Jack after going downstairs to dinner, returned again and striking the Justice on the back with his fist the Justice seemed angry. How is it Justice, said Jack, are you angry, let us shake hands and be friends. The Justice gave him his hand, and the fool cried out laughing, Now here are two fools, Justice, two fools, two fools. At this they all laughed heartily, to see this great wit affronted by a fool ; especially a gentleman whom the Justice had but a few minutes before abused by his jesting ; for he was of that temper that he would jest but never take one.

> It is not safe to play with edged tools
> Nor is it good to Jest too much with fools."

Simple Simon's Misfortunes

AND HIS

𝔚𝔦𝔣𝔢 𝔐𝔞𝔯𝔤𝔢𝔯𝔶'𝔰 𝔆𝔯𝔲𝔢𝔩𝔱𝔶

WHICH BEGAN

The very next Morning after their Marriage

Printed and Sold in Aldermary Church Yard
London

SIMPLE SIMON married a shrew named Margery, who brought him a "considerable fortune; forty shillings in money, and a good milch cow, four fat weathers, with half a dozen ewes and lambs, likewise geese, hens, and turkies; also a sow and pigs, with other moveables." She began scolding him the day after marriage, and the poor fellow found out he had a hard bargain. "Ud swaggers, I think I have a woeful one now." He went out, and meeting with one Jobson, an old friend, proceeded to an alehouse with him; but his wife, coming there with her gossips, "snatched up Jobsons oaken staff from off the table, and gave

poor Simon such a clank upon the noddle, as made the blood spin," and afterwards treated Jobson to a sound thrashing, and then she and her gossips got "as drunk as fishwomen."

Simon sneaked away, but when he got home he found his wife before him, and "not forgetting the fault he had com-

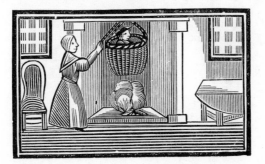

mitted, she invented a new kind of punishment; for having a
wide chimney, wherein they used to dry bacon, she, taking him
at a disadvantage, tied him hand and foot, bound him in a
basket, and by the help of a rope drew him up to the beam
of the chimney, and left him there to take his lodging the
second night after his wedding; with a small smoaky fire under
him; so that in the morning he was reezed like a red herring.
But at length he caused his wife to shew him so much pity
as to let him down."

He was undoubtedly a great fool, for, his wife having sent
him to the mill with a sack of corn, he was induced by a
stranger to lay it on the back of his spare horse, and of course
the man made off with it.

Simon had to take a basket of eggs to market, but finding
that "two butter women had fallen out, and to that degree,

that they had taken one another by the quoif, their hair and their fillets flying about their ears," he essayed to part them, but got pushed down, and his eggs were all broken. The constable, coming up, thought they were drunk, and clapped them in the stocks, where, being between the combatants, he had to endure their scolding. On his release he went home, only to endure his customary beating. So he lay all night in the hog-stye, and on the morrow, " in the presence of some of his dearest friends he begged pardon on his knees, of his sweet wife Margery."

One day his wife went to a " gossiping," leaving Simon at home to fill and boil the kettle. He made the fire and hung the kettle over it, then started to fill his pail at the well. He put down his pail in order to stop a runaway ox, which led him a chase of three or four miles. On his return he found his pail

stolen, and, when he reached home, the bottom was burnt out of the kettle. When his wife came back, it is needless to say that " she let fly an earthen pot at his head, which made the blood run about his ears. This done she took him by the collar and cuft him about the kitchen at a most horrid rate."

No doubt he was very vexing, as he could not be trusted with the most ordinary concerns of life. He had to get some soap, but, whilst passing over a bridge, he was frightened by some crows, and dropped the money into the water. Knowing what the consequences would be, he stripped and went into the water to search after it, but a larcenous old ragman came by and stole his clothes. He had to go home naked, where

his wife administered his usual correction—" taking the dog whip, she jerked poor Simon about, making him dance the Canaries for two hours."

Many more mishaps and punishments happened to the poor wretch, until at last even he could stand it no longer ; so he attempted to poison himself, but, by mistake, drank his wife's bottle of sack (*vide* frontispiece), and consequently got drunk. He was duly cudgelled ; but, either this determination of his, frightened his wife, or she saw the folly of going on in the way they were doing, for the tale winds up with, " For now he leads a happy life."

THE

HISTORY

OF

TOM LONG the Carrier

PRINTED AND SOLD IN ALDERMARY CHURCH YARD
BOW LANE

ALTHOUGH the address "To the Reader" says—

> "Of all the Toms that ever yet was nam'd,
> Was ever Tom like TOM LONG fam'd,
> Tom Tram, who mad pranks shews,
> Unto Tom Long, will prove a Goose.
> Tom Thumb is dumb until the pudding creep,
> In which he was entomb'd, then out doth peep.
> The fool may go to school, but ne'er be taught,
> Such rare conceits with which Tom Long is fraught.
> Tom Ass but for his ugly ears, might pass,
> Since no such jewels as our Tom he wears.
> Tom Tell Truth is but froth, the truth to tell,
> From all the Toms, TOM LONG doth bear the bell,"

yet the Chap-book is very dreary fun, not even being enlivened by any good illustrations—those supplied belonging to other books—but it is valuable for its frontispiece, which represents a Chapman of Elizabethan or Jacobean time, a veritable Autolycus. The other edition in the British Museum, "Printed and Sold at Sympson's Warehouse in Stone Cutter Street, Fleet Market," has a bad copy of this engraving.

THE

WORLD

TURNED

UPSIDE DOWN

OR THE

FOLLY OF MAN

EXEMPLIFIED

IN TWELVE COMICAL RELATIONS

UPON

UNCOMMON SUBJECTS

Illustrated with Twelve curious Cuts
Truly adapted to each Story

PRINTED AND SOLD IN LONDON

"Philosophers of old will tell us,
  As Tycho, and such merry fellows,
  That round this habitable ball
  The beamy sun did yearly fall;
  No wonder then the world is found
  By change of place Turn'd Upside Down;
  If revolutions strange appear
  Within the compass of the sphere;
  If men and things succession know,
  And no dependance reigns below;
  Since tis allow'd the world we dwell in,
  Is always round the sun a sailing;
  Experience to our knowledge brings;
  That times may change as well as things,
  And art than nature wiser grown,
  Turns every object upside down,
  Whim's epidemic takes her rise,
  And constancy's become a vice.
  He that to do is fortunate,
  The darling minions of his fate!
  To morrow feels his fate's displeasure,
  Spoil'd his hoarded idol treasure!
  And like this man, his emblem shows,
  A sudden revolution knows.

His fortune grows profoundly scurvy
Turns the poor earthworms topsy turvy,
Becomes the tennis ball of fools,
Things quite form'd out of nature's rules.
Such as you see Atlas bear
Upon their backs this mighty sphere.
The young, the old, the middle aged,
Are all in this great task engaged;
And strive with wondrous eagerness
Which all the greatest part possess.
Since folly then has got the ascendant,
He's most a fool that han't a hand in't;
And as the mad brain'd world runs round
Still keeps towards the rising ground."

This is quite enough for a specimen of the style of this poem, and, luckily, the illustrations explain themselves.

THE OX TURNED FARMER.

THE OLD SOLDIER TURNED NURSE.

THE REWARD OF ROGUERY, OR THE ROASTED COOK.

THE DUEL OF THE PALFRIES.

THE MAD SQUIRE AND HIS FATAL HUNTING.

THE OX TURNED BUTCHER.

GALLANTRY—A LA MODE—OR THE LOVERS CATCHED
BY THE BIRD.

THE HONEST ASS AND MILLER.

THE HORSE TURNED GROOM.

THE WATER WONDER, OR FISHES LORDS OF THE
CREATION.

SUN, MOON, STARS AND EARTH TRANSPOSED.

A Strange and Wonderful

RELATION

OF THE

OLD WOMAN

WHO WAS DROWNED AT

RATCLIFFE HIGHWAY

A Fortnight ago.

TO WHICH IS ADDED

THE OLD WOMAN'S DREAM,

A little after her Death.

PART THE FIRST.

PRINTED AND SOLD IN LONDON.

THIS book is somewhat of a curiosity; it is the only one of its kind in the whole series of Chap-books, and has been several times reprinted in the country. It is illustrated, in every edition, with engravings which have no connection with the text, which, however, would be an impossible task, as the following page or so of the commencement will show. The frontispiece has nothing whatever to do with the book, but it is curious and valuable, as giving a representation of the ducking-stool. There are two parts, but they both consist of such rodomontade as the following :—

" It was the last Monday Morning about four o'clock in the afternoon before sun rising, going over Highgate Hill I asked him if the Old Woman was dead that was drowned at Ratcliffe Highway a few nights ago. He told me he could not tell, but if I went a little farther I should meet with two young men on horseback, riding under a mare, in a blue red jerkin and a pair of white freestone breeches, and they would give intelligence. So when I came up with the women they thought I was a Hector that was come to rob them and therefore ran to me, but I most furiously pursued before them, so that one of them for meer madness, seeing him dead, drew out his sword and directly killed him. The horse for vexation seeing himself dead ran away as fast as he could, leaving them to go on foot upon another horse's back forty miles—Friend, said I, I mean you no good, but pray inform me if the Old woman be dead yet that was drowned at Ratcliff Highway a fortnight ago? and they told me they could not tell; but if I went a little farther I should meet with two women driving an empty cartful of apples, and a Mill Stone in the midst, and they would give me particular intelligence—But when I came up with them they would not satisfy me neither; but told me if I went down to the waterside, there lived one Sir John Vang, and he would give me true intelligence. So going by the waterside, I hooped and hallowed, but I could make nobody see. At last I heard Six Country Lads and Lasses, who were all fast asleep playing at nine pins under a hay cock, piled up of pease straw in the midst of the Thames, and eating of a roasted bran pudding freezing hot," etc., etc.

THE WISE MEN OF GOTHAM.

WRIGHT, in his "Early Mysteries," 1838, published some poems, by an anonymous writer, which he assigned to the thirteenth century, called "Descriptus Norfolciensum," by which it would appear that these tales had their origin in Norfolk; and the "Folcs of Gotham" are mentioned as early as the fifteenth century in the Townley "Mysteries." But be that as it may, "The Merie Tales" are undoubtedly the work of Andrew Borde, or Boorde, who lived in the fifteenth and sixteenth centuries. He was born at Holmesdale in Sussex, was educated at Oxford, and afterwards became a Carthusian monk. At the persecution, *temp*. Henry VIII., he escaped abroad, and travelled over many parts of Europe and some portion of Africa. He settled at Montpellier, became a physician, and practised as such on his return to England. For some reason, he was imprisoned in the Fleet, where he died, April, 1549. There are two black-letter editions without dates, and there is one in the Bodleian library, with a woodcut of the hedging in the cuckoo, "The Merry Tales of the Mad Men of Gotham. Gathered together by A.B. of Physick Doctor," 1630; but Ant. à Wood, in his "Ath. Oxon." (Bliss. edition), says it was printed in the reign of Henry VIII.

Gotham is a village about six miles from Nottingham, and the name of the "Cuckoo bush" is still given to a place near the village.

THE

𝕸𝖊𝖗𝖗𝖞 𝕿𝖆𝖑𝖊𝖘

OF THE

WISE MEN OF GOTHAM.

PRINTED AND SOLD IN ALDERMARY CHURCH YARD BOW LANE
LONDON.

TALE 1.

THERE was two Men of Gotham, and one of them was for going to Nottingham market to buy sheep ; and the other came from the Market, and both met on Nottingham Bridge.—Well met, said one to the other, Whither are you going, said he that came from Nottingham ; Marry, said he that was going thither, I am going to the market to buy sheep—To buy sheep! said the other, which way will you bring them home? Marry, said the other, I will bring them over this bridge—By Robin Hood, said he that came from Nottingham, but thou shalt not—By Maid Margery, said the other, but I will—You shall not, said the one. I will, said the other.

Then they beat their staves one against the other, and then against the ground, as if a hundred sheep had been between them. Hold then there said the one. Beware of my sheep leaping over the bridge, said the other—I care not said the one —They shall all come this way, said the other—But they shall not, said the one—Then said the other, if thou make much ado, I will put my finger in thy mouth. The Devil thou wilt said the one. And as they were in contention, another Wise Man that belonged to Gotham, came from the market with a sack of meal on his horse.; and seeing his neighbours at strife about sheep, and none betwixt them, said he, Ah ! fools, will you never learn wit ! help me to lay this sack upon my shoulder ; and they did so, and he went to the side of the bridge, and shook out the meal into the river, saying, How much meal is there in the sack, neighbours? Marry, said they, none.— By my faith, replies this Wise Man, even so much wit is there in your two heads to strive for that which you have not.

Now which was the Wisest of these three, I leave you to judge.

TALE 2.

THERE was a man of Gotham that rode to the market with two bushels of wheat, and because his horse should not be damaged by carrying too great a burden, he was determined to carry the corn himself on his own neck and still kept riding upon the horse until the end of his journey.—Now I will leave you to judge which is the wisest, his horse or himself.

Tale 3.

On a time the Men of Gotham fain would have pinned in the Cuckow, that she might sing all the year; all in the midst of the town they had a hedge made round in Compass, and got a cuckow, and put her into it, and said, Sing here, and you shall lack neither meat nor drink all the year—The Cuckow when she perceived herself encompassed within the hedge, flew away. A vengeance on her, said these Wise Men, we made not the hedge high enough.

Tale 4.

There was a Man of Gotham who went to Nottingham market to sell Cheese, and going down the hill to Nottingham bridge one of the cheeses fell out of his wallet, and ran down the hill. Whoreson, said the fellow, what can you run to the market alone?—I'll now send one after another; then laying down his wallet, taking out the cheeses, he tumbled them down the hill, one after another; some ran into one bush, and some into another; however he charged them to meet him in the market place—The man went to the market to meet with the cheeses, and staid till the market was almost over, then went and enquired of his neighbours, if they saw the cheeses come to market? Why, who should bring them? said one—Marry themselves, said the fellow, they knew the way very well—A vengeance on them, they run so fast I was afraid they would run beyond the market; I suppose by this time they are got as far as York:—so he immediately rode to York, but was very much disappointed; and to this day no man has ever heard of his cheeses.

TALE 5.

A Man of Gotham, bought at Nottingham market a trivet or bar iron, and going home with it, his shoulder grew weary of the carriage ; he set it down, and seeing it had three feet, said Whoreson, thou hast three feet, and I but two, thou shalt bear me home, if thou wilt—so set himself down on it saying

> Bare me along as I have bore thee,
> For if thou dost not thou shalt stand still for me.

The Man of Gotham seeing that his trevit would not move, Stand still, said he, in the Mayor's name, and follow me if thou wilt ; and I can shew thee the way.—When he went home, his wife asked him where the trivet was ? he told her it had three legs, and he but two, and he had taught him the ready way to his house ; and therefore he might come home himself if he would. Where did you leave the trevit ? said the woman. At Gotham bridge, said he. So she immediately went and fetched the trevit, otherwise she must have lost it, on account of her husband's want of wit.

TALE 6.

A certain Smith of Gotham had a large wasp's nest in the straw at the end of his forge, and there coming one of his neighbours to have his horse shod, and the wasps being exceeding busy, the man was stung by one of them ; and being grievously affronted, he said, Are you worthy to keep a forge or no, to have men stung with these wasps ?—O neighbour, said the smith, be content, and I shall put them from their nest presently. Immediately he took a Coulter, and heated it red hot and thrust it into the straw, at the end of the forge, and set it on fire and burnt it up.—Then said the smith, I told thee I'd fire them out of their nest.

Tale 7.

ONE Good Friday the Men of Gotham consulted together what to do with their white herrings, red herrings, sprats, and salt fish, and agreed that all such fish should be cast into the pond or pool in the middle of the town, that the number of them might encrease against the next year. Therefore every one that had any fish left did cast them immediately into the pond—Then said one, I have as yet gotten left so many red herrings, Well, said another, and I have left so many whitings—Another immediately cried out, I have as yet gotten so many sprats left;—And, said the last, I have as yet gotten so many salt fishes, let them go together in the great pond without distinction, and we may be sure to fare like Lords the next year—At the beginning of the next Lent they immediately went about drawing the pond, imagining they should have the fish; but were much surprised to find nothing but a great eel. Ah! said they, a mischief on this eel, for he hath eaten up our fish. What must we do with him, said one to the other. Kill him, said one. Chop him in pieces, said another. Nay, not so, said the other, let us drown him.—Be it accordingly so, replied them all.—So they immediately went to another pond, and cast the eel into the water. Lie there, said these wise men, and shift for thyself, since you may not expect any help of us—So they left the eel to be drowned.

Tale 8.

ON a time the men of Gotham had forgotten to pay their rent to their landlords, so one of them said to the other, To morrow must be pay day, by whom can we send our money that is due to our landlord? upon which one of them said, I have this day taken a hare, and he may carry it, for he is very quick footed. Be it so, replied the rest, he shall have a letter and a purse to put our money in, and we can direct her the right way. When the letter was written, and the money put in a purse, they immediately tied them about the hare's neck saying, You must go to Loughboro' and then to Leicester, and at Newark is our landlord; then commend us unto him, and there is his due. The hare, as soon as she got out of their hands ran quite a contrary way—Some said, Thou must go to Loughborough—Others said, let the hare alone for she can tell a nearer way than the best of us—let her go.

TALE 9.

A MAN of Gotham that went mowing in the meads, found a large grasshopper; he immediately threw down his scyth, and ran home to his neighbours, and said that the devil was there in the field, and was hopping amongst the grass. Then was every man ready with their clubs and staves, with halberts and other weapons to kill the grasshopper. When they came almost to the place where the grasshopper was, said one to the other, Let every man cross himself from the Devil, for we will not meddle with him—So they returned again and said—We were blest this day that we went no farther—O ye cowards! said he that left his scyth in the mead, help me to fetch my scyth. No, answered they, it is good to sleep in a whole skin; it is much better for thee to lose thy scyth than to marr us all.

TALE 10.

ON a certain time there were twelve men of Gotham, that went to fish, and some stood on dry land. And in going home, one said to the other, We have ventured wonderfully in wading, I pray God that none of us come home to be drowned—Nay, Marry, said one to the other, let us see that, for there did twelve of us come out—Then they told themselves, and every one told eleven. Said the one to the other, There is one of us drowned.` They went back to the brook where they had been fishing and sought up and down for him that was drowned, making great lamentation.

A Courtier coming by, asked what it was they sought for,

and why they were sorrowful? Oh! said they, this day we
went to fish in the brook; twelve of us came out together, and
one is drowned—Said the Courtier, tell how many there be of
you. One of them said eleven, and he did not tell himself.
Well, said the Courtier, what will you give me and I will find
the twelfth man. Sir, said they, all the money we have got.
Give me the money, said the Courtier, and began with the first,
and gave him a stroke over the shoulders with his whip, which
made him groan, saying Here is one; and so he served them
all, and they all groaned at the matter. When he came to the
last, he paid him well, saying Here is the twelfth man.—God's
blessings on thy heart, said they, for thus finding our dear
brother.

TALE 11.

A MAN of Gotham riding along the highway, saw a cheese, so
drew his sword and pricked it with the point in order to take it
up. Another man came by, and alighted, and picked it up,
and rode away with it. The man of Gotham rides back to
Nottingham to buy a long sword to pick up the cheese, and
returning to the place where the cheese did lie, he pulled out
his sword, and pricking the ground, he said, if I had this
sword at the first, I should have gotten the cheese myself, but
now another has got it from me.

TALE 12.

A MAN of Gotham who did not love his wife, she having fair
hair, her husband said divers times, He would cut it off, but
durst not do it when she was awake; so resolved to do it when
she was asleep: therefore one night he took up a pair of sheers
and put them under his pillow, which his wife perceiving, said
to one of her maids, Go to bed to my husband, for he thinks
to cut off my hair to-night; let him cut off thy hair, and I will
give thee as good a kirtle as ever thou didst see. The maid
did so, and feigned herself asleep; which the man perceiving,
cut off the maids hair and wrapped it about the sheers, and

laid them under his pillow and went to sleep; then the maid arose and the wife took the hair and sheers and went into the hall, and there burnt the hair. The man had a fine horse that he loved much; and the good wife went into the stable, cut off the tail of the horse, wrapping the sheers up in it, and then laid them under the pillow again. Her husband seeing her combing her head in the morning, he marvelled very much thereat—The girl seeing her master in a deep study, said, What the Devil ails the horse in the stable, he bleeds so prodigiously? The man ran into the stable, and found the horse's tail was cut off; then going to his bed, he found the sheers wrapped up in his horse's tail. He then went to his wife, saying, I cry thee mercy, for I intended to have cut off my horses tail. Yea, said she, self do, self have—Many men think to do a bad turn but it turneth oftimes to himself.

Tale 13 is rather too broad in its humour to be reproduced.

TALE 14.

A MAN of Gotham took a young buzzard, and invited four or five gentlemen's servants to the eating of it; but the old wife killed an old goose and she and two of her gossips eat up the buzzard, and the old goose was laid to the fire for the gentlemen's servants. So when they came and the goose was set before them, What is this? said one of them. A fine buzzard, said the man. A buzzard! said they, why it is an old goose, and thou art a knave to mock us; and in anger departed home.

The fellow was very sorry that he had affronted them, and took a bag, and put in the buzzard's feathers; but his wife desired him before he went to fetch her a block of wood, and in the intrim, she pulled out the buzzard's feathers, and put in the gooses. Then the man taking the bag went to the gentlemen's servants, and said, Pray be not angry with me; you shall see I had a buzzard, for here be the feathers. Then he opened the bag and shook out the goose's feathers. They said, Why thou knave, could you not be content to mock us at home but art come here to mock us? The one took a cudgel and gave him a dozen stripes, saying, Heretofore mock us no more.

Tale 15 is too silly, and not worth reproducing.

TALE 16.

A YOUNG man of Gotham went a wooing to a fair maid; his mother warned him before hand, saying, whenever you look at her, cast a sheep's eye at her and say, How dost thou do, my sweet pigsnie! * The fellow went to the butchers shop and bought seven or eight sheeps eyes; and then when this lusty wooer was at dinner, he would look upon his fair wench, and cast in her face a sheep's eye, saying how do you do, my sweet pigsnie?—How do you do, swine's face? said the wench; what do you mean by casting a sheep's eye at me?—O sweet pigsnie, have at thee another.—But I defy thee, swine's flesh, said the wench.—What, my sweet old pigsnie be content, for if you live till next year, you will be a foul sow.—Walk knave, walk, said she, for if you live till next year, you will be a fool.

TALE 17.

THERE was a man of Gotham who would be married, and when the day of marriage was come, they went to church. The priest said, Do you say after me. The priest said say not after me such words but say what I shall tell you— Thou dost play the fool to mock with the Holy Bible concerning

---

* A term of endearment, generally used towards a young girl :

> "And here you may see I have
> Even such another,
> Squeaking, gibbering, of everie degree.
> The player fooles dear darling *pigsnie*
> He calls himselfe his brother,
> Come of the verie same familie."
>
> TARLTON'S *Horse Loade of Fooles.*

Chaucer, in "The Milleres Tale," says—

> "Hire shoon were laced on her legges hie ;
> She was a primerole (primrose), a piggesnie."

Matrimony. Then the fellow said, Thou dost play the fool to mock with the Holy Bible concerning Matrimony. The priest could not tell what to say, but answered, what shall I do with this fool? And the man said, What shall I do with this fool.— So the priest departed, and would not marry him—But he was instructed by others how to do and was afterwards married— And thus the breed of Gothamites has been perpetuated even unto this day.

TALE 18.

THERE was a Scotchman who dwelt at Gotham, and he took a house, a little distance from London, and turned it into an inn, and for a sign he would have a Boars head; accordingly he went to a Carver, and said, Make me a Bare heed. Yes, said the Carver. Then says he, Make me a bare heed and thous have twenty pence for thy hire. I will do it, said the Carver.— So on St. Andrew's day, before Christmas the which is called Youl in Scotland, the Scot came to London for his Boar's head to set up at his door. I say, to speak, said the Scotchman, hast thou made me a bare's heed. Yes, said the Carver. Aye then thous a good fellow. He went and brought a man's head that was bare, and said here is your bare head! Aye, said the Scot, the mickle devil! is this a bare heed? Yes, said the carver. I say, said the Scotchman, I will have a bare heed, like a heed that follows the sow that has gryces. Sir, said the Carver, I don't know a sow and gryces. What! whoreson, know you not a sow that will greet and groan, and her gryces will run after and cry Aweek, aweek. O, said the Carver it is a pig—Yes said the Scotchman, let me have her heed made in timber, and set on her scalp, and let her sing, whip, whire. The Carver said he could not.—You whoreson, said he, gang as she'd sing Whip, whire.—This shews that all men delight in their fancy.

TALE 19.

IN old times, during these tales, the wives of Gotham got into an alehouse, and said, They were all profitable to their husbands ; which way, good gossips ? said the alewife.—The first said, I tell you all, good gossips, I can brew or bake, so I am every day alike ; and if I go to the alehouse, I pray to God to speed my husband, and I am sure my prayers will do him more good than my labour. Then said the second, I am profitable to my husband in saving candle in the winter ; for I cause my husband and all my people to go to bed by daylight, and rise by the same.—The third said, I am profitable in sparing bread, for I drink a gallon of ale, care not how much meat and drink at home, so I go to the tavern at Nottingham and drink wine and such other things, as God sends me.—The fourth said, A man will for ever have more company in another's house than his own, and most commonly in an alehouse. The fifth said, My husband has flax and wool to spare, if I go to other folks houses to do their work.—The sixth said, I spare both my husbands wood and coals, and talk all the day at other folks fire. The seventh said, beef, mutton and pork are dear, wherefore I take pigs, hens, chickens, conies which be of a lower price.—The eighth said I spair my husband's lie and soap, for whereas I should wash once a week, I wash but once a quarter ; then said the alewife, and I keep all my husband's ale that I brew from sowering, for, as I used to drink it most up, now I never leave a drop.

Tale 20.

One Ash Wednesday the Minister of Gotham would have a Collection of his parishioners, and said unto them, My friends the time is come that you must use prayer, fasting and alms ; but come ye to shrift, I will tell you more of my mind ; but as for prayer, I don't think that two men in the parish can say half the Pater Noster. As for fasting, ye fast still, for ye have not a meal's victuals in a year. As for alms deed, what should they do to give that have nothing to take ? But as one came to shrift and confessed himself to have been drunk divers times in the year, but especially in Lent : the priest said In Lent you should most refrain from drunkenness and refrain from drink—

No, not so, said the fellow, for it is an old proverb that fish would swim. Yes, said the priest—it must swim in the water; I say you mercy, quoth the fellow, I thought it should have swum in fine ale, for I have been so.—Soon after the man of Gotham came to shrift, and even the priest knew not what penance to give; he said, If I enjoin prayer, you cannot say your Pater Noster. And it is but a folly to make you fast, because you never eat a meals meat. Labour hard and get a dinner on Sunday, and I will come and partake of it—Another man he enjoined to fare well on Monday, and another on Tuesday, and one after another, that one or the other would fare well once in a week, that he might have part of their meat. And as for alms deeds the priest said, ye be beggars all except one or two so therefore bestow your alms among yourselves.

FINIS.

JOE MILLER'S

JESTS

BEING

A COLLECTION

OF

The most Brilliant JESTS and most pleasant
short Stories in the English Language—

*The greater Part of which are taken from the Mouth of that
facetious Gentleman whose Name they bear.*

PRINTED AND SOLD IN LONDON

JOE MILLER

WAS a comedian, born 1684, died August 15, 1738; but, although he might have originated the jests, he did not collect them, which was done by John Mottley, a dramatist, in 1739. Miller was buried in St. Clement's burial-ground, in Portugal Street, Clare Market—now destroyed—and his tombstone was to be seen in 1852. Part of his epitaph was—

" HERE LYE THE REMAINS OF

HONEST JO. MILLER

WHO WAS

A TENDER HUSBAND

A SINCERE FRIEND

A FACETIOUS COMPANION

AND AN EXCELLENT COMEDIAN," etc.

Hogarth is said to have engraved a ticket for his benefit on April 25, 1717, when he played Sir Joseph Wittol in Congreve's " Old Batchelor."

All jokes marked with an asterisk are in the first edition, but the book has been somewhat expurgated.

" Joe Miller going with a friend one day along Fleet Street, and seeing old Cross the Player, who was very deaf, and un-willing that any one should know it, on the other side of the way, told his friend he should see some Sport; so beckoning Cross with his finger, and stretching open his mouth as wide as ever he could, as if he hallooed to him, though he said nothing; the old fellow came puffing from the other side of the way. What a pox do you make such a noise for, do you think one can't hear ?

* " Joe Miller another day sitting in the window at the Sun tavern in Clare Street, while a fish woman was passing by,

crying, Buy my soul—buy my maids ! Ah ! you wicked creature, said Joe, are you not content to sell your own soul, but
you must sell your maid's also.

"A person of quality coming into a church where several of
his ancestors lay buried, after he had praised them very much
for worthy men, Well, said he, I am resolved, if I live, to be
buried as near them as possible.

"One man told another who used not to be clothed very
often, that his new coat was too long for him ; That's true
answered the other, but it will be longer before I get another.

* "A poor man who had a termagant wife, after a very long
dispute, in which she was resolved to have the last word, told
her, if she spoke another crooked word more he would beat
her brains out : Why then, Ram's Horns, you dog, said she
if I die for it.

"A certain Country Squire asked a Merry Andrew why he
played the fool ? For the same reason, said he, as you do, for
want ; you do it for want of wit, I for want of money.

* "A Welshman bragging of his family, said, that his father's
effigy was set up in Westminster Abbey ; being asked where-
abouts, he said, In the same monument with Squire Thynne,
for he was his coachman.

"A very harmless Irishman was eating an apple pie with some
quinces in it. Arrah now, dear honey, said he, if so few of
these quinces give such a flavour, how would an apple pye taste
made all of quinces.

* "An Irish lawyer of the Temple having occasion to go to
dinner, left this direction in the keyhole ; Gone to the Elephant
and Castle, where you will find me, and if you cannot read this,
carry it to the stationer's and he will read it for you.

* "Two Oxford Scholars meeting on the road with a Yorkshire ostler, they fell to bantering him ; and told him, That
they would prove him to be an horse or an ass, Well, said the
ostler, I can prove your saddle to be a mule. A mule, said one
of them, how can that be ? Because said the Ostler, it is something between a horse and an ass.

* "The Chaplain's boy of a man of war, being sent out of

his own ship on an errand to another, the boys were conferring notes about their manner of living. How often do you go to prayers now? Why, answered the other, in case of a storm or the apprehension of any danger from an enemy. Aye, said the first, there is some sense in that; but my master makes us go to prayers when there is no more occasion for it, than for my leaping overboard.

* "King Henry VIII. designing to send a nobleman on an embassy to Francis I. at a very dangerous juncture, he begged to be excused, saying, Such a threatening message to so hot a prince as Francis I. might go near to cost him his head. Fear not said old Harry: if the French King should offer to take away your life, I will revenge it by taking off the heads of the Frenchmen now in my power.—But of all these heads, replied the Nobleman, not one would fit my shoulders.

* "A prince laughing at one of his nobles whom he had employed in several embassies, told him he looked like an owl. I know not, said the Courtier, what I look like; but this I know, that I have had the honour several times to represent your Majesty's person.

* "A Mayor of Yarmouth, in antient times, being by his office a justice of the peace, and one who was willing to dispense the laws in the wisest manner, though he could hardly read, got himself a statute book, where finding a law against firing a beacon, or causing one to be fired, read it, Frying bacon or causing it to be fried; and according went out the next night upon the scent, and being directed by his nose to the Carriers house he found the man and his wife both frying bacon, the husband holding the pan, while the wife turned it. Being thus caught in the fact and having nothing to say for themselves his worship committed them both to prison without bail or mainprize.

* "A gentleman who had been a shooting brought home a small bird with him, and having an Irish servant, he asked him if he had shot that little bird? Yes, he told him. Arrah, by my shoul, honey, replied the Irishman, it was not worth the powder and shot, for this little thing would have died in the fall.

* "The same Irishman being at a tavern, where the Cook was dressing some Carp, he observed some of the fish moved, after they were gutted and put in the pan, which much surprised honest Teague.—Well, now by my faith, said he, of all the Christian creatures that ever I saw, this same carp will live the longest after it is dead.

* "A young fellow riding down a steep hill, doubting if the foot of it was boggish, called out to a clown that was ditching, and asked if it was hard at the bottom? Aye, answered the countryman, it is hard enough at the bottom, I will warrant you. But in half a dozen steps the horse sunk up to the saddle girts, which made the young gallant whip, spur, curse, and swear; Why you whoreson of a rascal, said he to the ditcher, didst thou not tell me that it was hard at the bottom? Aye, said the ditcher, but you are not halfway to the bottom yet.

* "An Englishman and a Welshman disputing in whose Country was the best living; said the Welshman, there is such noble housekeeping in Wales, that I have known above a dozen cooks to be employed at one wedding dinner. Aye, replied the Englishman, that was because every man toasted his own cheese.

* "One losing a bag of money of about Fifty pounds, between the Temple Gate and Temple Bar, fixed up a paper, offering a reward to those who took it and should return it. Upon which, the person that had it came and wrote underneath it to the following effect: Sir, I thank you for the offered reward, but indeed you really bid me to my loss.

* "A very humourous countryman having bought a barn in partnership with a neighbour of his, neglected to make the least use of it, while the other had plentifully stored his part with corn and hay. In a little time the latter came to him, and conscientiously expostulated with him about laying out his money to so little purpose. Why, neighbour, said he, pray never trouble your head, you may do what you will with your part of the barn, but I will set mine on fire.

* "The famous Tom Thynne, who was remarkable for his good housekeeping and hospitality, standing one day at his gate in the Country, a beggar came up to him and craved a mug of his small beer. Why, how now, said he, what times are these, when beggars must be choosers! I say, bring this fellow a mug of strong beer.

* "A profligate young Nobleman being in company with some sober people, desired leave to toast the Devil. The gentleman who sat next to him, said he had no objection to any of his Lordship's particular friends.

* "A certain Lady of quality, sending her Irish footman to fetch home a pair of new stays, strictly charged him to take a coach if it rained, for fear of wetting them. But a great shower falling, the fellow returned with the stays dripping wet; and being severely reprimanded for not doing as he was ordered, he said he had obeyed his orders. How then, answered the lady, could the stays be wet if you took them into the coach with you? No replied honest Teague, I know my place better, I did not get into the Coach, but rode behind, as I always used to do.

"Two honest gentlemen, who dealt in brooms, meeting one day in the street, one asked the other, how the devil he could afford to undersell him as he did, when he stole the stuff, and made the brooms himself? Why, you silly dog, replied the other, I steal them ready made.

"A cowardly servant having been out a hunting with his master, they killed a wild boar. The fellow thinking the boar stirred, betook himself to a tree; upon which his master called to him, and asked him, what he was afraid of, as the boar's guts were out? No matter for that, said he, his teeth are in.

"One Irishman meeting another, asked, what was become of their old acquaintance Patrick Murphy? Arrah! now, dear honey, answered the other, he was condemned to die, but he saved his life by dying in prison.

"One asked his friend, why he, being such a proper man himself, had married so small a wife? Why, friend, said he, I thought you had known that of evils we should chuse the least.

"Two gentlemen, one named Chambers and the other Garret, riding to Tyburn, said the first, This would be a pretty tenement, if it had a garret. You fool, says Garret, don't you know there must be Chambers first.

"Two Irishmen having travelled on foot from Chester to Barnet, were much tired and fatigued with their journey, and the more so when they were told that they had still ten miles to London. By my shoul and St. Patrick, cries one of them, it is but five miles apiece, let's e'en walk on.

* "A country clergyman meeting a neighbour who never came to church although an old fellow about sixty, he gave him some reproof on that account and asked him if he never read at home? No, replied the clown, I cannot read. I dare say, said the parson, You don't know who made you? Not I, in troth, said the countryman. A little boy coming by at the time—Who made you, child? said the parson. God, sir, said the boy. Why, look you there quoth the clergyman, are you not ashamed to hear a child five or six years old tell me who made him, when you, who are so old a man, cannot? Ah! said the countryman it is no wonder that he should remember ; he was made but the other day, and it is a long while, measter, since I was made."

A

WHETSTONE

FOR

DULL WITS

OR A

𝕻𝖔𝖊𝖘𝖞

OF NEW AND INGENIOUS

RIDDLES

Of Merry Books this is the Chief,
'Tis as a purging Pill ;
To carry off all heavy Grief
And make you laugh your Fill

Printed & Sold in London

Question. Into this world I came hanging,
    And when from the same I was ganging,
  I was cruelly batter'd and Squeez'd,
    And men with my blood, they were pleas'd.

Answer. *It is a Pipping pounded into Cyder.*

Q. A Wide Mouth, no ears nor eyes,
    No scorching flames I feel—
  Swallow more than may suffice
    Full forty at a meal.

A. *It is an Oven.*

Q. Tho' of great age   My mouth it is round
    I'm kept in a Cage   And when Joys do abound
    Having a long tail and one   O' then I sing wonderful clear.
     ear,

A. *It is a Bell in a Steeple; the Rope betokens a Tail, & the Wheel an ear.*

Q. The greatest travellers that e'er were known
    By Sea and land were mighty archers twain;
No armor proof, or fenced walls of stone,
    Could turn their arrows; bulwarks were in vain.
Thro' princes courts, and kingdoms far and near,
    As well in foreign parts as Christendom,
These travellers their weary steps then steer,
    But to the deserts seldom come.

A. *'Tis Death and Cupid, whose arrows pierce thro' the walls of Brass or strong Armour in all Courts and Kingdoms in the habitable World.*

Q. Two Calves and an Ape   They travell'd together
   They made their escape   In all sorts of weather
   From one that was worse   But often were put in a fright.
      than a spright;

A. *'Tis a Man flying from his scolding wife ; the two Calves
and an Ape, signify the calves of the legs and the Nape of his
neck, which by travelling was expos'd to the weather.*

Q. A thing with a thundering breech
   It weighing a thousand welly,
     I have heard it roar
     Louder than Guys wild boar,
   They say it hath death in its belly.

A. *It is a Cannon.*

Q. It flies without wings, And leaves as you'll find
   Between silken strings It's guts still behind.

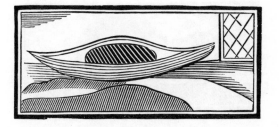

A. *It is a Weaver's Shuttle.*

Q. Close in a cage a bird I'll keep,
   That sings both day and night,
   When other birds are fast asleep
   It's notes yield sweet delight.

A. *It is a Clock.*

Q. To the green wood   Yet yields us no good
    Full oft it hath gang'd,   Till decently hang'd.

A. *It is a hog fattened with Acorns, which makes good bacon when hanged a drying.*

Q. Rich, yellow, and bright,   Now tell unto me,
    Long, slender and white,   What this Riddle may be,
    Both one in another there   Then will I your wisdom
      are ;   declare.

A. *A Diamond ring on a Lady's finger.*

Q. A Visage fair   Which is with us
    And voice is rare,   Most ominous
    Affording pleasant charms ;   Presaging future harms.

A. *A Mermaid, which betokens destruction to Mariners.*

Q. To ease men of their care   Yet tho' I do,
    I do both rend and tear   There are but few
    Their mother's bowels still ;   That seem to take it ill.

A. *'Tis a Plough which breaks up the bowels of the Earth for the sowing of Corn.*

Q. By sparks in lawn fine
   I am lustily drawn,
   But not in a chariot or
   Coach ;

I fly, in a word,
More swift than a bird,
That does the green forest
   approach.

A. *An Arrow drawn in a Bow by a Gentleman Archer.*

Q. By the help of a guide
   I often divide
   What once in a green forest
   stood ;

Behold me, tho' I
Have got but one eye,
When that is stopt I do the
   most good.

A. *A Hatchet, with which they cleave Wood ; till the Eye is
stopped with the Haft, it cannot perform business.*

Q. My back is broad, my belly   Where mortal man has never
    is thin,   been
  And I am sent to pleasure   Tho' strange it is a naked
    youth ;   truth.

A. *A Paper Kite which mounts the lofty air.*

THE TRUE

TRIAL

OF

UNDERSTANDING:

OR

𝔚it 𝔑ewly 𝔕ebib'd

BEING A BOOK OF

RIDDLES

Adorned with Variety of

PICTURES.

New Riddles make both Wit and Mirth
The Price of a Penny, yet not half the Worth.
By S. M.

PRINTED AND SOLD IN
LONDON.

Q. Tho' it be cold I wear no cloaths,
   The frost and snow I never fear,
   I value neither shoes nor hose,
   And yet I wander far and near;
   Both meat and drink are always free,
   I drink no cyder, mum, nor beer,
   What Providence doth send to me
   I neither buy, nor sell, nor lack.

A. *A Herring swimming in the Sea.*

Q. Once hairy scenter did transgress,
  Whose dame, both powerful and fierce,
  Tho' hairy scenter took delight
  To do the thing both fair and right,
  Upon a Sabbath day.

A. *An old Woman whipping her Cat for Catching Mice on a Sunday.*

Q. Promotion lately was bestow'd
Upon a person mean and small;
Then many persons to him flow'd,
Yet he return'd no thanks at all;
But yet their hands were ready still
To help him with their kind good will.

A. *It is a Man pelted in the Pillory.*

Q. There was a sight near Charing Cross,
   A creature almost like a horse;
   But when I came the beast to see,
   The head was where the Tail should be.

A. *A Mare tied with her tail to the Manger.*

Q. As I walked thro' the street,
It was near twelve o'clock at night;
Two all in black I chanc'd to meet,
Their eyes like flaming fire bright.
They passed by, and nothing said,
Therefore I was not much afraid.

A. *Two long lighted Links carried along the street.*

Q. Three men near the flowing Thames, ·
   Much pains and labour they did take
   They did both scratch and claw their wems,
   Until their very hearts did ache.
   It is as true as e'er was told,
   Therefore this riddle now unfold.

A. *Three Fidlers in Thames Street, who played up a bridegroom in the Morning, who gave them nothing to drink.*

Q. There is a steeple standing fair,
   'Tis built upon a rock of care,
   Therein a noise both fierce and shrill,
   Tho' here was neither clock nor bell.

A. *An old woman scolding in a high crown'd Hat.*

Q. My weapon is exceeding keen,
  Of which I think I well may boast,
  And I'll encounter Colonel Green
  Together with his mighty host.
  With me they could not then compare,
  I conquer them both great and small,
  Tho' thousands stood before me there
  I stood and got no harm at all.

A. *A Man mowing of Grass with a Scyth, which took all before it.*

Q. I saw five birds all in a cage,
 Each bird had but one single wing,
 They were an hundred years of age,
 And yet did fly and sweetly sing.
 The wonder did my mind possess,
 When I beheld their age and strength ;
 Besides, as near as I can guess,—
 Their tails were thirty feet in length.

A. *A Peel of Bells in a Steeple.*

The whole Trial and Indictment of
SIR JOHN BARLEYCORN, KNT.

*A Person of noble Birth and Extraction and well known by Rich and Poor
throughout the Kingdom of Great Britain ; Being accused of several
Misdemeanours, by him committed against his Majesty's Liege People ;
by killing some, wounding others, and bringing Thousands to Beggary,
and ruins many a poor family.*

Here you have the substance of the Evidence given in against him on
his Trial ; with the Names of the Judges, Jury and Witnesses. Also the
comical Defence Sir John makes for himself, and the Character given him
by some of his Neighbours, namely Hewson the Cobler, an honest Friend
of Sir John's, who is entomb'd as a Memorandum, at the Two Brewers
in East Smithfield.

Taken in Short Hand by Thomas Tosspot, Foreman of the Jury.

LICENSED AND ENTERED ACCORDING TO ORDER.

THE

Arraigning and Indicting

OF

SIR JOHN BARLEYCORN, KNT.

Newly Composed

BY A WELL WISHER TO SIR JOHN,
AND ALL THAT LOVE HIM.

PRINTED AND SOLD IN ALDERMARY CHURCH YARD
LONDON.

THIS Chap-book not only contains the following ballad, but
sets forth the offences of which Sir John is guilty, and witnesses
are called to prove them.   They consist principally of his
making people quarrelsome, etc.   For the defence it is asserted
that "there is not such another in the land that can do what
he can and hath done for he can make a cripple to go, he can
make a coward to fight with a valiant soldier ; nay he can make
a good soldier to feel neither hunger or cold."   It is needless
to say he is triumphantly acquitted.

"A NEW SONG.

"*To the Tune of Old Sir John Barleycorn, Or Jack of
all Trades.*

> "ALL you that be good fellows,
>   Come listen unto me,
>   If that you love the alehouse
>   And merry company.

> "Attend unto my story,
>   It makes my heart full sorry,
>   Which I fear is too true
>   And many doth it rue.

" 'Tis of a gallant noble Knight,
 Which many know full well,
An honest man, I witness can,
 If I the truth may tell.

" His name is Sir John Barleycorn,
 Who makes both beer and bread,
What would do all that now are born,
 If Barleycorn was dead ?

" For as I abroad did walk,
 I heard a piteous cry,
And many a man did talk
 That Barleycorn must die,

" His enemies increase so fast,
 At board, and eke at bed,
I fear their malice will not cease,
 Till they cut off his head.

" For Smut the honest blacksmith,
 With many tradesmen more ;
And Snip the nimble Taylor,
 Doth vow that he shall die.

" And Will the Weaver doth complain,
 With many thousands more ;
I hope their labour is in vain,
 Therefore they may give o'er.

" Yet now awhile give ear,
 You that are standers by,
And you presently shall hear
 Sir John condemned to die.

" All you that love poor Barleycorn,
 A good word for him give,
And he that speaks against him,
 I wish he may not live."

The foregoing is nothing like so witty, or funny, as the Black-Letter ballad. A copy is in the British Museum (Rox. i. 343), which, although it has been reprinted, is not generally known, and is too good to lose.*

" A pleasant new Ballad to Sing both Even and Morne,
    Of the bloody Murther of Sir John Barleycorne.

" To the tune of *Shall I lye beyond thee.*

" As I went through the
        North Countrey,
    I heard a merry greet-
        ing,
A pleasant toy, and full of
        joy,
    two noble men were
        meeting.

" And as they walked for to
        sport,
    vpon a Sommers day,
Then with another noble
        man
    they went to make a fray.

" Whose name was sir John
        Barleycorne
    he dwelt down in a dale ;
Who had a kinsman dwelt
        him nigh
    they cal'd him Thomas
        Goodale.

" Another named Richard
        Beere,
    was ready at that time ;

Another worthy Knight was
        there,
    call'd sir William White
        Wine.

" Some of them fought in a
        blacke Jacke,
    some of them in a Can ;
But the chiefest in a blacke
        pot,
    like a worthy noble man.

" Sir John Barleycorne fought
        in a Boule
    who wonne the victorie ;
And made them all to fume
        and sweare
    that Barleycorne should
        die.

" Some said kill him, some
        said drowne,
    others wisht to hang him
        hie :
For as many as follow
        Barleycorne
    shall surely beggers die.

* This ballad, which is circa 1640, was stolen wholesale by Robert Burns, as an examination of " John Barleycorn " will prove.

"Then with a plough they
     plowed him vp
     and thus they did deuise,
To burie him quicke within
     the earth
     and swore he should not
     rise.

"With horrowes strong they
     combed him
     and burst clods on his
     head:
A joyfull banquet then was
     made,
     when Barleycorne was
     dead.

"He rested still within the
     earth
     till raine from skies did
     fall
Then he grew vp in
     branches greene,
     which sore amazed them
     all.

"And so grew vp till Mid-
     sommer,
     which made them all
     afeard;
For he was sprouted vp ón
     hie
     and got a goodly beard.

"Then he grew till S. James
     tide
     his countenance was wan,

For he was growne vnto his
     strength,
     and thus became a man.

"With hookes and sickles
     keene,
     into the field they hide,
They cut his legs off by the
     knees,
     and made him wounds
     full wide.

"Thus bloodily they cut him
     downe
     from place where he did
     stand,
And like a thiefe for
     treachery,
     they bound him in a
     band.

"So then they tooke him vp
     againe
     according to his kind;
And packt him vp in
     seuerall stackes
     to wither with the wind.

"And with a pitchfork that
     was sharpe,
     they rent him to the
     heart,
And like a thiefe for treason
     vile
     they bound him in a cart.

" And   tending him with
          weapons strong,
       vnto the towne they
          hie,
    And straight they mowed
          him in a mow
       and there they let him
          lie.

" Then he lay groaning by the
          wals,
       till all his wounds were
          sore ;
    At length they took him vp
          againe
       and cast him on the
          floore.

" They hyred two with holly
          clubs,
       to beat on him at once,
    They thwacked so on Barly-
          corne
       that flesh fell from the
          bones.

" And then they tooke him
          vp againe
       to fulfill womens mind
    They dusted and they sifted
          him,
       till he was almost blind.

" And then they knit him in
          a sacke
       which grieued him full
          sore ;

They steep'd him in a Fat,
          God wot,
       for three dayes space and
          more,

" Then they tooke him vp
          againe,
       and laid him for to drie,
    They cast him on a chamber
          floore,
       and swore that he should
          die.

" They   rubbed and they
          stirred him
       and still they did him
          turne,
    The Malt man swore that
          he should die
       his body he would burne.

" They spightfully tooke him
          vp againe
       And threw him on a
          kill :
    So dried him then with fire
          hot,
       and thus they wraught
          their will.

" Then they brought him to
          the mill,
       and there they burst his
          bones,
    The Miller swore to murther
          him
       betwixt a pair of Stones.

" Then they tooke him vp
againe,
and seru'd him worse than
that
For with hot scalding liquor
score
they washt him in a
Fat.

" But not content with this,
God wot,
that did him mickle
harme,
With threatning words they
promised
to beat him into barme

" And lying in this danger
deep
for feare that he should
quarrell,
They took him straight out
of the fat
and tunn'd him in a
barrell.

" And then they set a tap to
him,
euen thus his death
begun ;
They drew out euery drain
of blood,
whilst any drop would
run,

" Some brought iacks vpon
their backs
some brought bill and
bow,
And euery man his weapon
had,
Barlycorne to overthrow.

" When sir John Goodale
heard of this
he came with mickle
might
And there he took their
tongues away,
their legs or else their
sight.

" And thus sir John in each
respect
so paid them all their
hire,
That some lay sleeping by
the way
some tumbling in the
mire—

" Some lay groning by the
wals,
some in the streets down
right,
The best of them did
scarcely know
what they had done ore
night.

"All you good wiues that brew good ale
　　God turne from you all teen,
　But if you put too much water in
　　the devill put out your eyne.

" FINIS.

" LONDON, PRINTED FOR JOHN WRIGHT, AND ARE TO BE SOLD AT HIS
　SHOP IN GUILTSPURRE STREET, AT THE SYNE OF THE BIBLE."

LONG MEG OF WESTMINSTER.

THERE can be very little doubt but that this virago was a living being, for the first edition known of her " Life and Pranks "— which was published in 1582, and which differs materially from the Chap-book version—bears internal evidence of her reality ; and she must have lived in the reign of Henry VIII., for, in chapter ii. she finds, on her arrival in London, her mistress drinking with Doctor Skelton (poet laureate, who died 1529), Will Summers the King's Jester, and a Spanish knight called Sir James of Castille. As the 1582 edition does not mention her death, she might then have been alive. The Chap-book version says, " After marriage she kept a house at Islington." This may have been true, but she also seems to have had one on the Southwark side of the river, for a scarce tract, called " Holland's leaguer," etc. (London, 1632), says, " It was out of the *Citie* yet in the view of the *Citie* only divided by a delicate *River ;* there was many handsome buildings, and many hearty neighbours, yet at the first foundation, it was renowned for nothing so much as for the memory of that famous Amazon, *Longa Margarita*, who had there for many years kept a famous *infamous* house of open Hospitality," and on the tract is a woodcut of the house. That she was well known, appears in an old book, " Pierces Supererogation, on a new prayse of the Olde Asse," by Gabriell Harvey, 1593, p. 145 : " Phy, Long Megg of Westminster would have been ashamed to disgrace her Sonday bonet with her Satterday witt. She knew some rules of Decorum ; and although she were a lustie bounsing rampe, somewhat like Gallemella or maide Marian, yet was she not such a roinish rannell, or such a dissolute gillian-flurtes, as this wainscot-faced Tomboy.'

It is probable from this, as speaking of her in the past tense, that she was then dead, and this is the more likely, as there is an entry in the curious diary of Philip Henslowe, proprietor of the Rose Theatre near Bankside, Southwark, relating to her. He kept a register of all the plays performed by the servants of Lord Strange and the Lord Admiral, and by other companies, between February 19, 1591–2, and November 5, 1597. Against each entry was put the sum he received as a proprietor from either a part or the whole of the galleries; so we read, " R the 14 of febreary 1594, at long mege of westmester (18 *) *l.*iii. *s.*ix. *d.*o." It was performed at the theatre at Newington Butts, which Howes, in his continuation of Stowe's " Chronicles " (1631), mentions as having been there " in former time." By whom it was acted seems uncertain, as the heading reads, " *In the name of God, Amen, beginning at* newington *my* lord admirell men, *and* my lord chamberlen men, as followeth, 1594."

It is a singular coincidence that on this very February 14, 1594, the Registers of the Stationers' Company should have an entry : " xiiij Febr. John Danter. Entred for his Copie &c. a ballad entituled The mad merye pranckes of Long Megg of Westm(inster) . . . vj*ᵈ*."

That the play was popular, is evidenced by the fact that in N. Field's play, " Amends for Ladies " (1618), Meg is not only mentioned, but the play is spoken of by Fee simple : " Faith, I have a good mind to see Long Meg and the Ship at the Fortune."

---

* This shows how popular the play was, as it notes it had the long run of eighteen representations.

THE WHOLE

𝕷𝖎𝖋𝖊 𝖆𝖓𝖉 𝕯𝖊𝖆𝖙𝖍

OF

LONG MEG

OF

WESTMINSTER

PRINTED AND SOLD IN ALDERMARY CHURCH YARD.
LONDON

CHAP. I.

WHERE MEG WAS BORN, HER COMING UP TO LONDON, AND HER USAGE TO THE HONEST CARRIER.

IN the reign of Henry VIII. was born in Lancashire, a maid called LONG MEG. At eighteen years old she came to London to get her a service; Father Willis the Carrier being the Waggoner, and her neighbour, brought her up with some other lasses. After a tedious journey, being in sight of the desired city, she demanded why they looked sad? We have no money said one, to pay our fare. So Meg replies, If that be all, I shall answer your demands, and this put them in some comfort. But as soon as they came to St. John's Street, Willis demanded their money. Say what you will have, quoth she. Ten shillings a piece, said he. But we have not so much about us, said she.—Nay, then I will have it out of your bones.—Marry, content, replied Meg; and taking a staff in her hand, so belaboured him and his man, that he desired her for God's sake to hold her hand.—Not I, said she, unless you bestow an angel on us for good luck, and swear e'er we depart to get us good addresses.

The Carrier having felt the strength of her arm, thought it best to give her the money, and promised not to go till he had got them good places.

CHAP. 2.

OF HER BEING PLACED IN WESTMINSTER, AND WHAT SHE DID AT HER PLACE.

THE Carrier having set up his horses, went with the lasses to the Eagle in Westminster, and told the landlady he had brought her three fine Lancashire lasses, and seeing she often asked him to get her a maid, she might now take her choice. Marry, said she I want one at present, and here are three gentlemen

who shall give their opinions—As soon as Meg came in, they
blessed themselves, crying

Domine, Domine, viee Originem.*

So her mistress demanded what was her name ; Margaret, for-
sooth, said she briskly—And what work can you do? She
answered she had not been bred unto her needle, but to hard
labour, as washing, brewing, and baking, and could make a
house clean—Thou art, quoth the hostess, a lusty wench, and
I like thee well, for I have often persons that will not pay—
Mistress, said she, if any such come let me know, and I'll make
them pay, I'll engage.—Nay, this is true, said the Carrier, for
my carcase felt it ; and then he told them how she served him
—On this Sir John de Castile, in a bravado, would needs make
an experiment of her vast strength ; and asked her, If she durst
exchange a box o' the ear with him. Yes, quoth she, if my
mistress will give me leave. This granted, she stood to receive
Sir John's blow, who gave her a box with all his might, but it
stirred her not at all ; but Meg gave him such a memorandum
on his ear that Sir John fell down at her feet.—By my faith,
said another, she strikes a blow like an ox, for she hath knocked
down an Ass.—So Meg was taken into Service.

* In the 1582 edition the passage runs, "As soon as they saw long
Meg they began to smile, and Dr. Skelton in his mad merry vain blessing
himself began thus,

Domine, Domine, Vid : Origin."

CHAP. 3.

THE METHOD MEG TOOK TO MAKE ONE OF THE VICARS PAY
HIS SCORE.

MEG so bestirred herself, she pleased her mistress, and for her tallness was called Long Meg of Westminster.

One of the lubbers of the Abbey had a mind to try her strength, so coming with Six of his associates one frosty morning calls for a pot of Ale, which being drank, he asked what he owed? To which Meg answers, Five Shillings and Threepence.

O thou foul scullion, I owe thee but three shillings and one penny, and no more will I pay thee. And turning to his landlady, complained how Meg had charged him too much. The foul ill take me, quoth Meg, if I misreckon him one penny, and therefore, Vicar, before thou goest out of these doors, I shall make thee pay every penny; and then she immediately lent him such a box on the ears, as made him reel again. The Vicar then steps up to her, and together both of them went by the ears.—The Vicars head was broke, and Megs Cloaths torn off her back. So the Vicar laid hold of her hair, but he being shaved she could not have that advantage; so laying hold of his ears, and keeping his pate to the post, asked him how much he owed her? As much as you please said he.—So you knave, quoth she, I must knock out of your bald pate my reckoning. And

with that she began to beat a plain song between the post and his pate. But when he felt such pain, he roared out he would pay the whole—But she would not let him go, until he laid it down, which he did, being jeered by his friends.

CHAP. 4.

OF HER FIGHTING AND CONQUERING SIR JAMES OF CASTILE
A SPANISH KNIGHT.

ALL this time Sir James continued his suit to Meg's mistress but to no purpose. So coming in one day and seeing her melancholy, asked what ailed her? for if any one has wronged you I will requite you—Marry, quoth she, a base knave in a white sattin doublet has abused me, and if you revenge my quarrel, I shall think you love me—Where is he? quoth Sir James.—Marry—said she, he said he would be in St. George's Fields—Well, quoth he, do you and the Doctor go along with me, and you shall see how I'll pumel the knave.

Unto this they agreed, and sent Meg into St. George's Fields beforehand. Yonder, said she, walks the fellow by the windmill. Follow me, hostess, said Sir James, I will go to him. But Meg passed as if she would have gone by. Nay, stay, said Sir James, you and I part not so; I am this gentle-woman's champion, and fairly for her sake will have you by the ears—With that Meg drew her sword, and to it they went.

At the first blow she hit him on the head, and often endangered him—At last she struck his weapon out of his hands, and stepping up to him, swore all the world should not save him—O, save me, Sir, said he, I am a Knight and it is but a woman's matter; do not spill my blood. Wer't thou twenty Knights, said Meg, and was the King here himself, I would not spare thy life, unless you grant me one thing—Let it be what it will, you shall be obeyed—Marry, said she, that this night you wait on my plate at this woman's house, and confess me to be your master.

This being yielded to, and a supper provided, Thomas Usher and others was invited to make up the feast; and unto whom Sir James told what had happened.—Pho! said Usher, jeeringly, it is no such great dishonour for to be foiled by an English gentleman, since Cæsar the Great was himself driven back by their extraordinary courage. At this juncture, Meg came in, having got on her man's attire. Then said Sir James, This is that valiant gentleman whose courage I shall ever esteem. Hereupon she pulling off her hat, her hair fell about her ears, and she said I am no other than Long Meg of Westminster; and so you are heartily welcome.

At this they all fell a laughing, nevertheless at supper time, according to agreement, Sir James was a proper page; and she, having leave of her mistress, sat in state like her Majesty —Thus Sir James was disgraced for his love, and Meg was counted a proper woman.

CHAP. 5.

HER USAGE TO THE BAILIFF OF WESTMINSTER, WHO CAME INTO HER MISTRESS'S AND ARRESTED HER FRIEND.

A BAILIFF having for the purpose took forty shillings, arrested a gentleman in Meg's mistress's house, and desired the company to keep peace. She, coming in, asked what was the matter? O, said he, I'm arrested. Arrested! and in our house! Why this unkind act to arrest one in our house; but, however take an Angel, and let him go. No, said the Bailiff, I cannot, for the creditor is at the door. Bid him come in said she, and I'll make up the matter. So the creditor came in: but being found obstinate she rapped him on the head with a quart pot, and bid him go out of doors like a knave; he can but go to prison, quoth she, where he shall not stay long, if all the friends I have can fetch him out.

The creditor went away with a good knock, and the Bailiff was going with his prisoner. Nay, said she, I'll bring a fresh pot to drink with him. She came into the parlour with a rope, and knitting her brows, Sir Knave, said she, I'll learn thee to arrest a man in our house, I'll make thee a spectacle for all catchpoles; and tossing the rope round his middle, said to the gentleman, Sir, away, shift for yourself, I'll pay the bailiff his fees before he and I part. Then she dragged the bailiff unto the back side of the house, making him go up to his chin in a pond, and then paid him his fees with a cudgel; after which he went away with the amends in his hands; for she was so well beloved that no person would meddle with her.

CHAP. 6.

OF HER MEETING WITH A NOBLEMAN, AND HER USAGE TO HIM AND TO THE WATCH.

Now it happened she once put on a suit of man's apparel. The same night it fell out, that a young nobleman being disposed for mirth, would go abroad to see the fashions, and coming down the Strand, espies her, and seeing such a tall fellow, asked him whither he was going? Marry, said she, to St. Nicholas's to buy a calve's head. How much money hast thou? In faith, said she, little enough, will you lend me any?—Aye, said he, and putting his thumb into her mouth, said—There's a tester. She gave him a good box on the ear, and said, There's a groat, now I owe you twopence. Whereupon the Nobleman drew, and his man too; and she was as active as they, so together they go; but she drove them before

her into a little Chandler's shop, insomuch that the Constable came in to part the fray, and, having asked what they were, the nobleman told his name, at which they all pulled off their caps—And what is your name? said the Constable.   Mine, said she is Cuthbert Curry Knave—Upon this the constable commanded some to lay hold on her, and carry her to the Compter.   She out with her sword and set upon the watch, and behaved very resolutely; but the constable calling for clubs, Meg was forced to cry out, Masters, hold your hands, I am your friend, hurt not Long Meg of Westminster—So they all staid their hands, and the nobleman took them all to the tavern; and thus ended the fray.

CHAP. 7.

MEG GOES A SHROVING, FIGHTS THE THIEVES OF ST. JAMES'S
    CORNER AND MAKES THEM RESTORE FATHER WILLIS THE
    CARRIER HIS HUNDRED MARKS.

NOT only the cities of London and Westminster, but Lancashire also, rung of Meg's fame: so they desired old Willis the Carrier to call upon her, which he did, taking with him the other lasses. Meg was joyful to see them, and it being Shrove Tuesday, Meg went with them to Knightsbridge, and there spent most of the day, with repeating tales of their friends in Lancashire, and so tarried the Carrier, who again and again enquired how all did there; and made the time seem shorter than it was.   The Night growing on, the carrier and the two other lasses were importunate to be gone, but Meg was loath to set out, and so stayed behind to discharge the reckoning, and promised to overtake them.

It was their misfortune at St. James's Corner to meet with two thieves who were waiting there for them and took an hundred marks from Willis the Carrier, and from the two wenches their gowns and purses.—Meg came up immediately after, and then the thieves, seeing her also in a female habit, thought to take her purse also; but she behaved herself so well that they began to give ground.   Then said Meg, Our gowns and purses against your hundred marks; win all and wear all.   Content, quoth they.—Now, lasses, pray for me, said Meg—With that she buckled with these two knaves, beat one and so hurt the other, that they entreated her to spare their lives—I will, said she, upon conditions.—Upon any condition, said they—Then, said she, it shall be thus: 1. That you never hurt a woman, nor any company she is in.

2. That you never hurt lame or impotent men.

3. That you never hurt any Children or innocents.

4. That you rob no carrier of his money.

5. That you rob no manner of poor or distressed.

Are you content with these conditions? We are, said they. I have no book about me, said she, but will you swear on my smock tail? which they accordingly did, and then she returned the wenches their gowns and purses, and old Father Willis the Carrier an hundred marks.

The men desiring to know who it was had so lustily beswinged them, said, To alleviate our sorrow pray tell us your name? She smiling, replied, If any one asks you who banged your bones, say Long Meg of Westminster once met with you.

Chap. 8.

Meg's fellow servant pressed; her Usage of the Constable; and of her taking Press Money to go to Bologne.

In those days were wars between England and France, and a hot press about London. The Constables of Westminster pressed Meg's fellow servant and she told them if they took him her mistress was undone.

All this could not persuade the Constable, but Harry must go, on which she lent the Constable a knock—Notice being given to the Captain, he asked who struck him—Marry, quoth Meg, I did, and if I did not love soldiers, I'd serve you so too. So taking a Cavalier from a mans hand, she performed the exercise with such dexterity, that they wondered; whereupon she said, Press no man, but give me press money, and I will go myself. At this they all laughed, and the Captain gave her an Angel. Whereupon she went with him to Bologne.

CHAP. 9.

OF HER BEATING THE FRENCHMEN OFF THE WALLS OF BOLOGNE, FOR WHICH GALLANT BEHAVIOUR SHE IS REWARDED BY THE KING WITH EIGHT PENCE PER DAY FOR LIFE.

KING HENRY passing the seas took Bologne; hereupon the Dauphin with a great number of men surprised and retook it. Meg being a Laundress in the town, raised the best of the women, and with a halberd in her hand, came to the walls, on which some of the French had entered, and threw scalding water and stones at them, that she often obliged them to quit the town before the soldiers were up in arms—And at the sally she came out the foremost with her halberd in her hand to pursue the Chace.

The report of this deed being come to the ears of the King, he allowed her for life, eight pence a day.

CHAP. 10.

OF HER FIGHTING AND BEATING A FRENCHMAN BEFORE BOLOGNE.

DURING this, she observed one who in a bravado tossed his pike; she seeing his pride, desired a drum, to signify that a young soldier would have a push at pike with him. It was agreed on, and the place appointed, life against life.

On the day the Frenchman came, and Meg met him, and without any salute fell to blows; and, after a long combat, she overcame him, and cut off his head, Then pulling off her hat her hair fell about her ears.

By this the Frenchman knew it was a woman, and the English giving a shout, she by a Drummer sent the Dauphin his soldier's head, and said, An English Woman sent it.

The Dauphin much commended her, sending her an hundred crowns for her Valour.

CHAP. 11.

OF HER COMING TO ENGLAND, AND BEING MARRIED.

THE Wars in France being over, Meg came to Westminster, and married a soldier, who, hearing of her exploits, took her into a room and making her strip to her petticoat, took one staff, and gave her another, saying, As he had heard of her manhood, he was determined to try her—But Meg held down her head, whereupon he gave her three or four blows, and she in submission fell down upon her knees desiring him to pardon her—For, said she, whatever I do to others, it behoves me to be obedient to you ; and it shall never be said, If I cudgel a knave that injures me, Long Meg is her husband's master ; and therefore use me as you please—So they grew friends, and never quarrelled after.

CHAP. 12.

LONG MEG'S USAGE TO AN ANGRY MILLER.

MEG going one day with her neighbours to make merry, a miller near Epping looking out, the boy they had with them about fourteen years old, said, Put out, miller, put out.— What must I put out? said he.—A thief's head and ears, said the other.

At this the Miller came down and well licked him, which Meg endeavoured to prevent, whereupon he beat her ; but she wrung the stick from him, and then cudgelled him severely ; and having done, sent the boy to the Mill for an empty sack, and put the Miller in, all but his head ; and then fastening him to a rope she hawled him up half way, and there left him hanging. The poor Miller cried out for help, and if his wife had not come he had surely been killed, and the mill, for want of corn, set on fire.

Chap. 13.

Of her keeping House at Islington, and her Laws.

After Marriage she kept a house at Islington. The Constable coming one night, he would needs search Meg's house, whereupon she come down in her shift with a cudgel, and said, Mr. Constable take care you go not beyond your Commission, for if you do, I'll so cudgel you, as you never was since Islington has been.—The Constable seeing her frown, told her he would take her word, and so departed.

Meg, because in her house there should be a good decorum, hung up a table containing these principles ; First—If a Gentleman or Yeoman had a charge about him, and told her of it, she would repay him if he lost it, but if he did not reveal it, and said he was robbed, he should have ten bastinadoes, and afterwards be turned out of doors.

Secondly, whoever called for meat and had no money to pay, should have a box on the ear, and a cross on the back that he might be marked and trusted no more.

Thirdly. If any good fellow came in, and said he wanted money, he should have his belly full of meat and two pots of drink.

Fourthly. If any rafler came in, and made a quarrel, and would not pay his reckoning, to turn into the fields and take a bout or two with Meg, the maids of the house should dry beat him, and so thrust him out of doors.

These and many such principles, she established in her house, which kept it still and quiet.

FINIS.

MERRY FROLICKS

OR THE

Comical Cheats

OF

SWALPO

A NOTORIOUS PICK POCKET

And the Merry Pranks of

ROGER the CLOWN

PRINTED AND SOLD IN ALDERMARY CHURCH YARD
BOW LANE LONDON

NOWADAYS, Swalpo would have made a fortune as a presti-digitateur, for his was the high art of pocket-picking, and people used to employ him to show his talents for their amuse-ment, even after he had become virtuous, and steward to a nobleman.   The frontispiece represents him meeting with a countryman at Bartholomew Fair, and cautioning him against pickpockets.   The countryman tells him he has a broad piece, which he puts in his mouth.   Swalpo instructs a confederate boy, who tumbles and falls down in front of the countryman, scattering a lot of change, which he held in his hand.   The people round about help to pick up the money, and the boy declares he has got it all except a broad piece of gold.   Swalpo then comes up, and says he saw the countryman put it in his mouth ; it is discovered, and the countryman gets as badly used as a " welsher " at a race meeting.

The next engraving shows how " Swalpo steals a fine Coat from a Nobleman's back."

" The whole Company being greatly pleased with the ingenuity of the last trick, Swalpo said, Alas, gentlemen, this trick is not worth talking of, such as this, we send our boys about.   There is now a Nobleman going by the door, I will wager a guinea I steal his coat from off his back before all his followers.   The gentlemen staked each their guinea, and Roger and Swalpo covered them as before.   Then out went Swalpo, and dogged the Nobleman to a tavern ; as soon as he was conducted upstairs, Swalpo went to the barkeeper, and desired to borrow an apron for the Nobleman his master would only be served by himself ; he ran so nimbly, and did everything so handily, that the Company were mightily pleased with him, taking him for a servant to the house ; he never came into the room but he passed some merry jest, and when they spoke to him, his answers pleased them all mightily.

" When he found them in a good humour, he resolved not to trifle, wherefore as he waited behind the Lord's chair he took out his knife, and made a slit in the back seam of his coat, and ran downstars for more liquor, when he returned, as soon as he came near his Lordship he started back, asking what taylor

made that coat, which would not hold one day? Some of the Company rising and seeing the slash, said the taylor had affronted my Lord—Said he I paid him his price, and he shall hear of it—My Lord, said Swalpo, it is only the end of a thread has slipt, such things often happen; there is a fine drawer of my acquaintance lives in the next street, if your Lordship pleases, I will convey it under my master's cloak, and return immediately. The Nobleman borrows a great coat of one of the Company, and gave it unto Swalpo, who immediately came down to the vintner, and told him what had happened, and to prevent its being seen in the streets, desires him to lend him his Cloak. The Vintner shewed him where it was, which Swalpo put on, as also a hat which hung on the next pin; thus he walks off with them, and coming to the tavern at which the gentlemen waited, he went into a room, changed his cloaths, then returns and salutes them. Says one, Instead of a coat you come in a cloak; so then opening the cloak they were surprised to see the rich embroidered Coat. Then Roger laughed heartily; but when he told them how he had performed it, they all burst into a great laughter."

Space will only admit of one more story of his dexterity in picking pockets after notice given:—

"The Nobleman hearing of his dexterity in taking watches desired him to do it. Swalpo bid the Nobleman be on his guard; so he walked up and down the room as did also Swalpo. While the Lord was disputing warmly with some of the Company, Swalpo who watched his opportunity, gently tickles the Lord with a feather under the right ear; which makes him on a sudden quit the watch to scratch himself, and clapping his hand to his fob again, he found it gone.   He looks behind him, and sees Swalpo with the watch in his hand, bowing, which occasioned much laughter."

THE

𝕷𝖎𝖋𝖊 𝖆𝖓𝖉 𝕯𝖊𝖆𝖙𝖍

OF

SHEFFERY MORGAN

THE

Son of Shon ap Morgan

NEWCASTLE; PRINTED IN THIS YEAR

THERE are several editions of this book, and parts of it are amusing.

Sheffery was the son of a small farmer, and received some slight education. His father sent him to the university, where he wasted his time, and learnt nothing; but his father, considering his studies were sufficient and complete, got the promise of a living from the bishop, provided Sheffery could preach a sermon he could approve of. The day came and he knew nothing that he should say—in fact, he had not brains enough to compose a sermon—but " Sheffery no sooner enters the church, but he steps into the pulpit, and so begun as followeth. ' Good people, all hur knows, there's something expected from hur by way of Discourse, and seeing we are all met together, take the following matter as an undeniable truth; There are some things that I know and you know not, and there are some things that neither you nor I know; For thus, as I went over a stile, I tore my breeches; that I know, and you know not; but what you'll give me towards the mending of them, that you know and I know not; but what the knave the taylor will have for mending them, that neither you nor I know."

This sermon did not gain Sheffery his proposed living, so he started for London to seek his fortune. On the road, he joined two Welsh drovers, who asked him to help them and they would share with him the shilling they were to receive. "At last they came to Smithfield where the owner gave them a whole shilling, then was their care to part this one piece equally amongst three; Sheffery being ingenious said, ' We'll go shange it for three groats :' to which they consented : So going from street to street, at last they came to Lombard Street, where Sheffery spies a tray full of groats, and cry'd Here, hur will do it, if ever. The gentleman of the shop being at dinner, the hatch was shut, and nobody in the shop but an old jacka- napes chained, upon the cáunter; Sheffery leaning over the hatch said ' Good sir, will you give hur three groats for a shilling?' and held the shilling forth, which the jackanapes took, and put it down into the place where he used to see his master put money, and minded Sheffery no more ; but hur was very urgent with the jackanapes for hur change ; and said ' Good Sir, what does hur intent to do ? Will hur give her three groats for a shilling or no ; But the jackanapes not minding, stirred hur Welsh blood up, fearing that the old shentleman was minded to sheat them, which caus'd a great croud about the door, so that the gentleman of the house heard them, and coming into the shop to see what was the matter, began to be rough with them, doubting they intended to rob his shop ; but they cried out, that they were poor Welshmen that thought no hurt but desired to have three groats for a shilling. The gentleman finding them to be three poor ignorant fellows, asked them for their shilling ; they immediately told him they had given it to hur poor aged father. The gentleman in great wrath cry'd out, You villains, do you think I'm the son of a jackanapes. And threatening to set them by the heels ; but discovering their simplicity asked them what the jackanapes did with it. Quoth they, he put it into that hole. So he supposed it might be, and gave them three groats, bidding them be gone, so away went Sheffery's countrymen to their places provided for them, but Sheffery had hur fortune to seek."

Which he did with varying success ; married the widow of a physician, set up as doctor, got a wonderful reputation, and finally died, leaving his practice to his son Shon ap Morgan.

There is a Second Part to this history.

THE

WELCH TRAVELLER;

OR THE

Unfortunate Welchman

By HUMPHREY CORNISH

NEWCASTLE. PRINTED IN THE PRESENT YEAR

THIS is another of the satires against the Welsh, which were
so frequent in the seventeenth and early eighteenth centuries.
It was written in the latter part of the seventeenth century, as
the first edition shows.

"The Welch Traveller, or the Unfortunate Welchman ;

> "If any Gentleman do want a Man,
> As I doubt not but some do now and than,
> I have a Welchman though but meanly clad—
> Will make him merry be he nere so sad :
> If that you read, read it quite ore I pray,
> And you'l not think your penny cast away.

> "By Humphry Crouch.

"London printed for William Whitwood at the Sign of the
Bell in Duck Lane near Smithfield 1671."

The engraving to that edition is exactly similar to the
Chap-book frontispiece.

As the frontispiece to the Aldermary edition (from which
the subjoined illustrations are taken) is almost similar to "The
Life and Death of Sheffery Morgan," one from a Newcastle
Chap-book of about the same age has been substituted. This
is a metrical story of the adventures of a Welshman who was
going along star-gazing.

> "For as hur gaz'd upon the Sky,
> For want of better wit,
> Poor Taffy fell immediately
> Into a great deep pit.

> " Had not a shepherd been hur friend,
>   And help'd hur quickly out,
> Hur surely then had had an end,
>   Hur makes no other doubt."

Hungry and weary, he arrived at an alehouse, where the hostess gave him rotten eggs, which he cast in her face, and fled.   Seeing an apple tree, he climbed it in order to assuage his hunger.

> " Up into the tree hur gets,
>   The owner came anon,
> Made hur almost besides hur wits,
>   A cruel fight began.

> " He pelted hur with large huge stones
>   And hur did apples cast ;
> The stones did so benumb her pones
>   That down hur come at last."

He fled, and lying down under a hedge, saw a couple of lovers, one of whom dropped a gold ring, which he picked up and appropriated.   But

> " Going thro' a town, God wot,
>   Against some ill bred curs,
> Hur shewed it to a chattering trot
>   Who said the ring was hers."

An altercation ensued, and it ended in their going before

a justice, where the Welshman, calling the justice a "great Boobie," was sent to the stocks. Whilst there, the lovers passed him, and he told them that the woman had the ring. She was apprehended and put with him in the stocks.

"Now Taffy had his hearts desire
  He had her company,
But when he did begin to jeer,
  She in his face did fly."

He was released, and finding a house open and the proprietor absent, he entered and began feeding on the bacon smoking up the chimney, sitting astride of it; but fell down, bacon and all, when the owner and his wife were sitting by the fire. The man beat him severely, and he ran away. Joining some gipsies on the road, they agreed to rob the house of its bacon, by letting Taffy down the chimney with a rope. This was done.

> " They let him down, to work he falls,
>   The bacon strait doth bind,
>   The gipsies up the bacon haul
>   And leave the fool behind."

He went to the larder and helped himself to the bread and butter, and by his sooty and begrimed appearance he frightened the maid, who thought he was the devil ; and she alarmed her

master, who came with a sword, but was appalled by the sight of the pseudo-fiend. He walked away, frightening the children, till the women of the town determined to drive the devil out ; and sorely they beat poor Taffy, who took refuge in the church, where he was captured by the sexton, who was not afraid of him, carried before a justice, and condemned to stand for " one long hour or more " in the pillory, where the history leaves him.

JOAKS UPON JOAKS.

OR

No Joak like a true Joak.

BEING THE

Diverting Humours of Mr. John Ogle a Life Guard Man

THE

MERRY PRANKS OF LORD MOHUN AND THE EARLS OF WARWICK AND PEMBROKE

WITH

Rochesters Dream, his Maiden Disappointment and his Mountebanks Speech

TOGETHER WITH

The diverting Fancies and Frolicks of Charles 2 and his three Concubines

PRINTED AND SOLD IN LONDON.

SPACE will only admit of a few of these "Joaks," even if their quality would permit them to be reproduced for general perusal. "Another time Ogle wanted a pair of boots which were brought to him. They fitting him he walks up and down the shop to settle them to his feet, but espying an opportunity, he ran out of the shop, and the shoemaker followed him, crying, Stop thief, stop thief—No, gentlemen, it is for a wager, I am to run in boots, and he shoes and stockings. Then, said the mob, Well done boots, shoes and stockings can never overtake thee—So Ogle got clear off with the boots."

"One time the Earl of Warwick being out late one night and in company of an officer who had an artificial leg, they went into the Dark house near Billingsgate, but by the way the wary Warwick scraped a deal of dust out of a rotten post, and as he was putting it up before several people, one asked him what that powder was good for? Warwick said, it is good for all manner of bruises, sores, and scalds. And to shew the excellency of it, he desired them to bring him a kettle of scalding hot water. Then rubbing the powder on his friends artificial leg, he put it into the water. Now, the people seeing he was not hurt, soon bought up all the powder, so that his lordship very shortly raised between three and four pounds. Soon after this a very ingenious drayman who had purchased some of the powder, being in company with some of his calling, and having laid a wager that he could put his leg into a kettle of scalding water without hurting himself. The wager being laid, he, like

a cunning dog, got into a private room, to rub the powder of rotten post upon his leg. Which done, he returns to the kitchen, and plunged his leg into the kettle of scalding hot water which made him roar out like a town bull, and what was worst, he had like to have lost his leg."

Lord Pembroke was once playing the fool with a woman of low degree, when she persuaded him to strap her child upon his back, which when done, she ran away, and left him the child to take care of.

The frontispiece is supposed to represent the following scene :—" The Earl of Rochester being out of favour at the Court took private lodgings on Tower Hill, where being in disguise, he set up a mountebank's stage upon the hill, and spoke to the Mob in the following manner.

" Gentlemen and Ladies.

" Here is my famous Unguentum Aureum, or Golden Ointment, so very famous for curing all kinds of distempers in men, women and children. Look here, good people, this is my noble Tinctura Hyperboriacorum prepared only by myself. This will make the blind to see, the deaf to hear and the dumb to speak ; nay there is nothing can restore life so soon as this ; for with three drops of this tincture I restored a gentleman to life who had lost his head seven years ; but he being a state criminal, the Emperor made me fly to Germany for my great exploit ; Therefore I am come here to seek my fortune, with my incomparable and famous tincture, which cures all manner of sickness, hectick fever, jaundice, looseness, megrims, and all other distempers incident to mankind," etc.

THE

HISTORY

OF

ADAM BELL. CLIM OF THE CLOUGH.

AND

WILLIAM OF CLOUDESLIE.

Who were three Archers good enough
The best in the North Country.

NEWCASTLE: PRINTED IN THIS PRESENT YEAR.

THIS Chap-book follows the old poem very closely, and, in its main facts, is almost identical with an edition of 1550.*

The story is briefly as follows :—Of the three outlaws, only one, William of Cloudeslie, was married, and he longed to see his wife and children at Carlisle. He went, was welcomed by his wife, but was betrayed to the sheriff by an old woman whom he had kept out of charity over seven years. His house was surrounded, and, as no entrance could be forced, it was set on fire. William let down his wife and children out of a back window, and at last he was compelled to sally forth in order to escape being burnt. He was overcome and captured, and sentenced to be hanged next day. A little boy heard of this, and ran and told Adam Bell and Clim, who went to Carlisle, and, in spite of fearful odds against them, rescued William when on his road to execution. They performed prodigies of valour, killed the justice, and sheriff, and hundreds of the citizens, and finally got clear off. William's wife joined them, and, fearful of the consequences of their deeds, they set off at once to London to sue for pardon from the king. At first he would not hear of it, but at the queen's intercession he relented and pardoned them, just before a letter arrived from Carlisle narrating their evil doings. The pardon could not be recalled, but the king, having heard of their wonderful shooting, determined that they should beat all his archers or die. William did so, by cleaving a hazel wand at four hundred paces, and then shooting an apple off his son's head at a hundred and twenty paces. The king was so struck with these marvellous feats that—

> " Now God forbid, then said the King,
>   That thou should shoot at me.
> I give thee Eighteen pence a Day,
>   And my Bow shalt thou bear,
> Yea, over all the North Country,
>   I make thee Chief Keeper.
> Ill give thee Thirteen pence a Day,

---

* " Adam bel Clym of the cloughe and wyllyym of cloudesle. (colophon) Imprinted at London in Lothburye by Wyllyam Copland." Black letter.

Said the Queen, by my fay
Come fetch the payment when thou wilt
No man shall say thee Nay.
William, I make thee Gentleman,
Of Clothing and of Fee,
Thy Brethren of my Bedchamber
For they are lovely to see.
Your Son, for he's of tender age,
Of my Cellarists shall be ;
And when he comes to Man's Estate
Better preferr'd shall be ;
And William bring your wife, said she,
I long full sore to see ;
She shall be chief Gentlewoman
To govern my Nursery."

It will be seen from the foregoing short description, that the frontispiece has nothing to do with the book. It is very evidently belonging to some history of Robin Hood, as he is represented in the centre at the top, having on one side either the Bishop of Carlisle or the Abbot of St. Mary's, and on the other the beggar, tinker, or shepherd who thrashed him, while at the bottom are Little John, Friar Tuck, and Maid Marian.

A.

TRUE TALE

OF

ROBIN HOOD.

Printed and sold in Aldermary Church Yard
London

WHILST the poems and ballads on Robin Hood are more plentiful than on any other Englishman, the Chap-books are comparatively scarce, probably on account of the impossibility of condensing his numerous adventures and exploits into the conventional twenty-four pages. There are several editions printed in London, all having similar engravings, of which, however, but three or four belong properly to the work, which are reproduced below, the first being Robin Hood and the Abbot of St. Mary.

> " He bound the Abbot to a tree,
>   And would not let him pass
> Before that to his men and he,
>   His Lordship had said Mass."

The next is Robin's attack on the Bishop of Ely.

> " He riding down towards the North,
>   With his aforesaid train
> Robin and his men did issue forth,
>   Them all to entertain.
> And with the gallant grey goose wing,
>   They shew'd to them such play,
> That made their horses kick and fling,
>   And down their riders lay.

Full glad and fain the Bishop was,
    For all his thousand men,
To seek what means he could to pass
    From out of Robin's ken.
Two hundred of his men were kill'd,
    And fourscore horses good,
Thirty who did as captives yield,
    Were brought to the Green Wood—
Which afterwards were ransomed
    For twenty marks a man,
The rest set spurs to horse and fled
    To the town of Warrington."

And there is the representation of the treacherous monk
bleeding him to death.

" This sad perplexity did cause
    A fever as some say,
Which him into confusion draws,
    Tho' by a stranger way.
This deadly danger to prevent,
    He hy'd him with all speed
Unto a Nunnery with intent
    For health's sake there to bleed.
A faithless friar did pretend
    In love, to let him blood,
But he by falsehood wrought the end
    Of famous Robin Hood."

THE
HISTORY
OF THE
BLIND BEGGER
OF BEDNAL GREEN.

Young *Monford* Riding to the Wars where he unhapily lost his Eye-fight

Licenfed and Enter'd according to Order

THE illustrations to this very scarce Chap-book are evidently of earlier date than 1715, to which it is assigned, and, with the exception of the one of the blind beggar and his dog, have probably very little to do with the letter-press. The frontispiece is more likely to represent " Prince Rupert and his dogge Pudle" than "Young Monford Riding to the Wars." The ballad is well known, and extremely popular in England ; it was written in the reign of Elizabeth, to commemorate the tradition of Henry de Montfort, a son of Simon de Montfort, the famous Earl of Leicester, founder of the House of Commons, who was slain at the battle of Evesham, August 4, 1265. His son, Henry, who was left for dead on the field, was found, according to the ballad, by a baron's daughter, who had come to search for her father, but finding young Montfort half dead and deprived of sight by his wounds, she "was moved with pitye and brought him awaye."

> " In secret she nurst him, and swaged his paine,
> While hee through the realme was beleev'd to be slaine ;
> At length his faire bride she consented to bee,
> And made him glad father of prettye Bessee.
> And now lest oure foes oure lives sholde betraye,
> Wee clothed ourselves in beggar's arraye ;
> Her jewelles shee sold, and hither came wee ;
> All our comfort and care was our prettye Bessee."

The Chap-book differs somewhat in detail from the ballad. It places the time in the wars with France, and the scene itself in France, whither Monford went, accompanied by his wife in man's attire. He was wounded and blind, and was discovered on the field by his wife and servant, and on his recovery to health they all returned to England ; but his relations, for some unknown reason, treated him very coldly, and this their high spirits could not brook, so it ended in their settling down at Bethnal Green, where she spun and he turned beggar.

Here a professional beggar named Snap introduced himself to him, and "invited him to their Feasts, or Rendezvouse in

White chappel, whither he having promised to come, and they between them tipp'd off four black Pots of Hum, they at that time parted." His wife took him to the "rendezvouse," where he not only thoroughly enjoyed himself, but the beggars presented him with a dog trained to the business.

Soon after this pretty Betty was born, and at fifteen years of age was a marvel of beauty, and a paragon of accomplishments. Betty then left her parents, and obtained a situation at an inn at Rumford, where she found plenty of lovers, all of whom, except the knight, withdrew their pretensions to her hand when they heard she was only the daughter of a blind beggar. The knight, however, was constant, and they had just set out together to see old Monford, when the knight's uncle came

up, and, having followed them, created a scene at the beggar's
residence, when, to end it, Monford proposed to give angel for
angel with the knight's uncle, as a fortune for the young
people.   The uncle's servant was sent for coin, and the two old
gentlemen set themselves to their task of dropping angels
against each other; but the beggar kept producing cats' skins
filled with gold, and beat the knight's uncle.   This money was
made up to £3000 by Monford, who also gave Bessie " a hundred more to buy her a gown."   Monford declared his pedigree ;
everybody was pleased and happy, and the young couple were
duly married.

The young Knight
that Married pretty *Betty*

THE HISTORY OF THE

BLIND BEGGAR

Of Bethnal Green;

SHEWING

HIS BIRTH AND PARENTAGE.

His going to the Wars, losing his sight, and turning
Beggar at Bethnal Green. Of his getting Riches, and
the Education of his Daughter; who is courted by a
young Knight.—Of the Beggar's dropping Gold with
the Knight's Uncle.—Of the Knight's Marriage with the
Beggar's Daughter; and the Discovery of his famous
Pedigree

PRINTED AND SOLD IN ALDERMARY CHURCH YARD
BOW LANE LONDON

"The Beggar Trav'lling with his Dog,
  Brings home good store of Wealth to prog

With which he does outvie the Knight,
And weds his Child to her delight."

THE BLIND BEGGAR RECEIVING ALMS.

MONTFORT RETURNING FROM THE BEGGARS' FEAST

PRETTY BESSIE RECEIVING HER FATHER'S BLESSING
WHEN GOING TO SEEK HER OWN LIVELIHOOD.

BESSIE AND THE KNIGHT GOING TO SEE HER FATHER.

The HISTORY of

The Two Children in the WOOD.

The most Lamentable and Deplorable

HISTORY

OF THE

TWO CHILDREN IN THE WOOD:

CONTAINING

The happy Loves and Lives of their Parents, the Treachery and barbarous Villany of their Unkle, the duel between the Murdering Ruffians, and the unhappy and deplorable death of the two innocent Children.

As also an Account of the Justice of God that overtook the Unnatural Unkle; and of the deserved Death of the two murdering Ruffians.

TO WHICH IS ANNEX'D

THE OLD SONG UPON THE SAME

LONDON : PRINTED BY AND FOR W.O., AND SOLD BY THE BOOK-SELLERS.

THE date given to this rare and most interesting Chap-book is 1700, but though the frontispiece apparently points to an earlier date, it seems to have been executed specially for this work, as the nearest approach to it, a ballad in the Bagford Collection (British Museum, $\frac{643, \text{ m. } 10}{44}$), varies from it in some slight particulars, and this is undoubtedly the finest engraving of the subject extant. Almost all the ballads of the seventeenth, and the Chap-books of the eighteenth, century give a similar treatment: the duel between the ruffians, the birds covering the children with leaves, the deserved chastisement of the good robber, and the fearful punishment that fell upon the wicked uncle thus described in this book. "But tho' he had contriv'd all this so privately, yet Divine vengeance follow'd him; affrighting Dreams terrifying him in his Sleep, and the image of the murther'd children still staring him i' th' Face; and he that egg'd him on to all this wickedness, now in most horrid Shapes appear'd to him, and threat'ning every Moment to destroy him. Besides, most of his Cattle dy'd of the Murrain, his Corn was blasted, and his Barns were fir'd by Lightning; Mildews and Catter-pillars destroy'd all his Fruits; two of his Sons, for whom he coveted his Brother's Lands, were cast away at Sea. His company was hated by all honest Men, and he was forc'd to herd with Rogues and Villains out of meer necessity, amongst whom when he had profusely lavish'd his Estate, he run in Debt, and was cast into Prison, where through Despair and Want he dy'd unpitied."

"The Old Song upon the Same" is identical with the earliest (1640) in the British Museum (Rox. I. 284), and may be considered as the standard ballad. Indeed, another ballad (Rox. III. 588) in the same collection (1720) has been corrected in ink from this model.

" THE NORFOLK GENTLEMAN'S LAST WILL AND TESTAMENT, ETC.

" Now ponder well, you Parents dear, these words which I shall
    write,
A Doleful Story you shall hear, in time brought forth to light ;
A Gentleman of good account, in Norfolk dwelt of late,
Whose Wealth and Riches did surmount, most men of his
    Estate.
Sore sick he was, and like to dye, No help that he could have ;
His Wife by him as sick did lye, and both possess'd one Grave,
No love between these two was lost, each was to other kind,
In love they liv'd, in love they dy'd, and left two Babes behind.
The one a fine and prity Boy, not passing three Years old,
The other a Girl more young than he, and made in Beauty's
    Mould ;
The Father left his little Son, as plainly doth appear,
When he to perfect Age should come, three hundred Pounds a
    year.
And to his little Daughter Jane, five hundred Pound in Gold,
To be paid down on Marriage day, which might not be
    controul'd ;
But if the Children chance to dye, e're they to Age should
    come,
Their Uncle should possess their Wealth, for so the Will did
    run.
' Now, brother, (said the dying Man) look to my children dear,
' Be good unto my Boy and Girl, no Friends else I have here :
' To God and you I do commend my children night and day,
' A little while be sure we have within this world to stay.
' You must be Father and Mother both, and Uncle all in one ;
' God knows what will become of them, when I am dead and
    gone.
' With that bespoke their Mother dear, O Brother kind quoth
    she, ·
' You are the Man must bring my Babes to Wealth or Misery.

' If you do keep them carefully, then God will you reward.

' If otherwise you seem to deal, God will your Deeds regard.

With lips as cold as any stone, he kist the Children small,

' God bless you both, my Children dear ; with that the tears did fall.

These Speeches then their Brother spoke, to this sick Couple there,

' The keeping of your Children dear, sweet Sister, do not fear ;

' God never prosper me nor mine, nor aught else that I have,

' If I do wrong your Children dear, when you are laid in Grave.

Their Parents being dead and gone, the Children home he takes,

And brings them home unto his House, and much of them he makes.

He had not kept those prity Babes, a Twelvemonth and a Day,

But for their Wealth he did devise to make them both away.

He bargain'd with two Ruffians rude, that were of furious Mood,

That they should take the Children young, and slay them in a Wood.

And told his Wife and all he had, he did the Children send

To be brought up in fair London, with one that was his friend.

Away then went these prity Babes rejoycing at that Tide,

Rejoycing with a merry mind, they should on Cock horse ride :

They prate and prattle pleasantly, as they rode on the way,

To those that should their Butchers be, and work their Lives decay.

So that the prity speech they had, made Murtherers hearts relent,

And they that took the Deed to do, full sore they did repent.

Yet one of them more hard of heart, did vow to do his charge,

Because the wretch that hired him, had paid him very large.

The other would not agree thereto, so here they fell at Strife,

With one another they did fight àbout the Children's Life :

And he that was of mildest mood, did slay the other there,

Within an unfrequented Wood, where Babes did quake for fear.

He took the Children by the hand, when tears stood in their eye,

And bade them come and go with him, and look they did not
cry :

And two long Miles he led them thus, while they for Bread
complain,

Stay here, quoth he, I'll bring ye Bread, when I do come again.

These prity Babes with hand in hand, went wandering up and
down,

But never more they saw the Man, approaching from the Town :

Their prity lips with Black berries, were all besmear'd and dy'd,

And when they saw the darksome night, they sat them down
and cry'd.

Thus wandered these two prity Babes, till death did end their
grief ;

In one another's arms they dy'd as Babes wanting Relief ;

No Burial these prity Babes of any Man receives,

Till Robin red breast painfully, did cover them with Leaves.

And now the heavy Wrath of God upon their Uncle fell,

Yea, fearful Fiends did haunt his house, his Conscience felt an
Hell :

His barns were fir'd, his goods consum'd, his lands were barren
made,

His Cattle dy'd within the Field, and nothing with him staid.

And in the Voyage of Portugal, two of his sons did dye ;

And to conclude, himself was brought unto much Misery ;

He pawn'd and mortgag'd all his land, e're seven years came
about ;

And now at length this wicked Act, did by this means come
out :

The Fellow that did take in hand these Children for to kill,

Was for a Robbery judg'd to dye, as was God's blessed Will ;

Who did confess the very Truth of what here is exprest ;

Their Uncle dy'd while he for debt, did long in Prison rest.

All you that be Executors made, and Overseers eke,

Of Children that be Fatherless, and Infants mild and meek ;

Take you Example by this thing, and yeild to each his Right,

Least God with such like Misery, your wicked Minds requite.

" FINIS."

In "The History of the Children in the Wood ; or Murder Revenged," published in Aldermary Churchyard, and all other Chap-books, the name of the father is changed from Arthur Truelove to Pisaurus, the wicked uncle is called Androgus, and the children are named Cassander and Jane.

The three illustrations therefrom tell their own story.

THE
HISTORY
OF
SIR RICHARD WHITTINGTON
THRICE
Lord Mayor of London.

PRINTED AND SOLD IN ALDERMARY CHURCH YARD.
BOW LANE.

THE common version of Whittington's story is well known, and not worth repeating at length. The headings of the chapters tell the tale succinctly, and are all that is wanted to explain the illustrations.

"Chap. 1. Of Whittington's obscure Birth and hard Fortune; and of his being drove to London.

"Chap. 2. Of Mrs. Alice putting him under the Cook, with her cruel Usage to him; and Mrs. Alice's interposition in his favour.

"Chap. 3. Of his being troubled with Vermin in his Garret; of his buying a Cat to destroy them; and of his sending her for a venture abroad.

"It was a custom with the worthy merchant Mr. Hugh Fitz Warren, that God might give him a greater blessing to his endeavours, to call his servants together when he sent out a ship, and cause every one to venture something in it to try their fortune; for which they was to pay nothing for freight or custom."

The two illustrations, one taken from a Chap-book published at Newcastle (1770?), show Fitzwarren receiving his servants' ventures.

"Chap. 4. Of Whittington's Elopement on Allhallow's Day; and his Return on hearing Bow Bells ring; and of the Disposal of the Cat by the Factor abroad."

This illustration shows the dreadful condition of the Court of Barbary as regards rats, and by the style the cat is killing her foes, the casket of jewels, valued at £300,000, was not too dear for her purchase.

"Chap. 5. Of the Riches received for the Cat; the Unbelief of Whittington on their Arrival; and of his Liberality to some of his Fellow Servants.

"Chap. 6. Of Mr. Whittington's Comely Person and Deportment; of Mrs. Alice's falling in Love with him and marrying him, and of his being Sheriff of London.

Chap. 7. Of his being thrice Lord Mayor, his entertainment of Henry V., and his Death, Burial, etc."

As a matter of fact, the common story of Sir Richard Whittington is full of error. So far from being a poor obscure boy, he was the third son of Sir William Whittington, lord of the manor of Pauntley, in Gloucestershire, who died in 1360. He was sent to London to be a merchant, then a not unusual course to pursue with cadets of good families, and eventually

became enormously rich.   He was thrice Lord Mayor of
London, in 1397, 1406, and 1419, besides having been named
by Richard II. to succeed a Mayor who died in his year of
office.   He was a mercer, and enjoyed royal patronage, his
invoices of the wedding trousseau of the Princesses Blanche and
Philippa, daughters of Henry IV., being still in existence.   He
died, leaving no issue, in 1423.   He rebuilt Newgate, founded
the library in Guildhall, and the Grey Friars, repaired St.
Bartholomew's Hospital, and materially contributed towards
the rebuilding of the nave of Westminster Abbey.   These are
the bare facts of his life.   His cat still remains a mystery.   It
has been said that he made money by carrying coals in vessels
called cats or "cattes."   Mr. Riley, who edited the famous
"Liber Albus" (which compilation we owe to Whittington),
suggests that his fortune was made by "achats," which was the
French name for trading; and Mr. Lysons, in his charming

book, " The Model Merchant of the Middle Ages," defends the ordinary story on these grounds :

1st. From the ancient and generally received tradition ;

2nd. From the scarcity and value of domestic cats at that period ;

3rd. From its not being a solitary instance of a fortune made by such means ;

4th. From the ancient portraits and statues of Whittington in connection with a cat, some of which may be reasonably traced up to the times and orders of his own executors.

The reader may decide which of the three theories he prefers.

THE

HISTORY

OF

WAT TYLER

AND

JACK STRAW.

PRINTED AND SOLD IN ALDERMARY CHURCH YARD.

THIS Chap-book gives a very fair account of the domestic troubles of Richard II.'s reign, especially of the poll-tax rising of 1381 ; but it stigmatizes as " scum," " rake shames," and "rake hells " those poor men who then rose against oppression.

The frontispiece represents Sir William Walworth, and gives due prominence to the famous dagger, with which he is said to have killed Wat Tyler, and which is still shown at Fishmonger's Hall.

There was a play, " The Life and Death of Iake Straw, a notable Rebell in England ; who was kild in Smithfield by the Lord Maior of London—Printed at Lond. by Iohn Danter and are to be sold by William . Barley 1593 ; " and a tract, which was taken from the " Chronicle of the Schoolmaster of St. Albans," called " The just Reward of Rebels, or the Life and Death of Jack Straw and Wat Tyler 1642." There was also another little book, of which two editions appeared in 1654, called " The Idol of the Clownes or Insurrection of Wat the Tyler."

THE
HISTORY
OF
JACK OF NEWBURY

CALLED

THE CLOTHIER
OF ENGLAND.

PRINTED AND SOLD IN LONDON.

OF Jack of Newbury, as he is familiarly called, very little is
known certainly. He lived in the reigns of Henry VII. and
VIII., and was said to be the largest clothier or clothmaker in
England. He sumptuously entertained Henry VIII. and
Queen Catherine on their visit to the town, and built the vestry
to the church, besides having liberally contributed towards its
improvement. He also left £40 for the same object. In his
will he describes himself as "John Smalwoode the Elder aīs
John Wynchcombe." He was twice married, and left his wife
Joan behind him. There is a brass to him and his first wife :
"Off yo charitie pray for the soule of John Smalwode als
Wynchcom & Alys hys Wyfe. John dyed the 15 day of
February A° Dm. M°CCCCC°XIX."

The Chap-book version is, that he was apprenticed to a rich
clothier at Newbury, and married his master's widow, and a
great portion of the book is taken up with their courtship.
"Shortly after the king had occasion to raise an army against
the Scots, who were risen against the English, Jack of Newbury
raised at his own expense one hundred and fifty men, and
cloathed them with white coats, red caps and yellow feathers,
and led them himself." This was to the famous battle of
Flodden.

Jack's wife died, and he married one of his maids, whose

father came to see her, and was astonished at Jack's magnificent establishment, making a speech which would delight the Philological Society. "Sir, quoth the old man, I wize you be abominable rich, and cham content you should have my daughter, and God's blessing and mine light on you both. I waith cham of good exclamashon amongst all my neighbours, and they will as soon ask my 'vize for any thing as rich men. So thick I will agree. You shall have her with my very good will, because we hear a very good commendation of you in every place, therefore besides thick, I will give you twenty marks and a weaning calf that's a year old, and when I and my wife die then you shall have the revolution of our goods."

Jack, however, gave the old man twenty pounds and other things. The book ends with Jack's death, and an imaginary epitaph.

Thomas Deloney wrote a novel called "The Pleasant History of John Winchcomb, in his younger yeares called Jack of Newberie, the famous and worthy clothier of England," which was licensed to three several persons in 1595 and 1596 ; but the earliest known edition is the eighth, published in 1619.

THE

Life and Death

OF

FAIR ROSAMOND

CONCUBINE TO

King Henry the Second

SHEWING HER BEING POISONED BY
QUEEN ELEANOR.

PRINTED AND SOLD IN ALDERMARY CHURCH YARD, LONDON

PERHAPS the earliest book about this frail beauty is " The
Life and Death of Fair Rosamond, King Henry the Seconds
Concubine, and how she was Poysoned to death by Queen
Elenor. Printed for F. Coles" (circa 1640); but afterwards
her story became very popular, and numerous editions were
published. She has more than once been made the subject of
a drama. There is one, however, by John Bancroft, which is
replete with historical recollections. It is called " Henry the
Second, King of England; with the death of Rosamond. A
Tragedy Acted at the Theatre Royal, by their Majesties Ser-
vants. Printed for Jacob Tonson, at the Judges Head in
Chancery Lane near Fleet Street 1693." Thackeray's " poor
Will Mountfort" wrote the " epistle dedicatory;" Dryden wrote
the epilogue. Betterton played King Henry II. ; Doggett
took the part of Bertrand, a priest ; whilst Queen Eleanor and
Rosamond were respectively represented by Mrs. Barry and
Mrs. Bracegirdle !

Respecting Rosamond's tomb, there is no doubt she was
buried at Godstow, for her father, Walter de Clifford,* granted
the nuns there certain property at Frampton-on-Severn (which
tradition says was the birthplace of the fair one), " pro salute
animæ meæ, et pro animabus uxoris meæ Margaretæ et filiæ
nostræ Rosamundæ." And in another document (same page)
Osbertus, son of Hugh, gave to the convent a certain saltpit
at Wich, at the instance of the said Walter de Clifford, " pro
salute animæ uxoris suæ Margaretæ et animæ filiæ suæ Rosamundæ *quarum corpora ibidem requiescunt.*"

The history of the " Rosa Mundi " is not told to advantage in
this Chap-book, but its facts are mainly in accordance with the
popular tradition ; and probably the stratagem used by Queen
Eleanor to effect an entrance into her rival's bower, *i.e.* by
sending a sham postman, may be as correct as the generally
received notion of the ball of silk being dropped and unrolled,
thus betraying the place of her seclusion.

The bowl and dagger scene so vividly given in the frontispiece, is in accordance with tradition, although among nearly

* Monasticon, vol. ii. p. 884, ed. orig.

contemporary writers there is no mention of her dying a violent death, nor was such suggested till long afterwards. In fact, we have no evidence at all in support of Eleanor's jealous violence. As before mentioned, Rosamond was buried at Godstow, a convent near Oxford, of which a very ruined portion still exists ; but her remains were not suffered to remain undisturbed, for Hugh, Bishop of Lincoln, coming to Godstow in 1191, asked whose tomb that was, and was told it was the tomb of Rosamond, " some time Lemman to Henry II." Then said the stern bishop, " Take out of this place the Harlot, and bury her without the Church." Tradition says her poor bones were then laid in the nun's chapter-house, but at the Reformation they were taken up and her tomb destroyed. Hearne * says, " After this Removal, it continu'd at rest 'till about the time of the Reformation, when 'twas taken up, as Mr. Leland himself acquaints us, and at the same time a Stone was found with it, on which was this Inscription ' Tumba Rosamvnda ' which is a different Inscription from this common one : †

> ' Hic jacet in Tumba Rosa Mundi, non Rosa Munda
> Non redolet, sed olet, quæ redolere solet.'

But the latter possibly is the Epitaph that was fix'd in the Quire of the Church before the Body was remov'd. Mr. Leland, I think, saw the Stone himself, and he tells us that when her Coffin was open'd they found her Bones in it, and a very sweet smell came from it.."

---

* Leland's " Itinerary " (2nd edit.), p. 101.

† In Corio's " History of Milan " (vol. i. p. 47) this epitaph is stated to have been placed on the tomb of Rosamunda, queen of the Lombards, who died by poison, in the sixth century.

THE

STORY OF KING EDWARD III

AND THE

COUNTESS OF SALISBURY

" Know this plain Truth (enough for Man to know)
" Virtue alone is Happiness below."

PRINTED BY J. BRISCOE, IN THE
MARKET PLACE WHITEHAVEN.

THIS Chap-book seems the only edition extant. It is no great loss in a literary point of view, for the supposed history is pure fiction. The countess is represented as the daughter of Earl Varuccio, and the whole novelette is about the endeavours of the king to seduce her. He tries when her husband is alive, and when she is a widow he still presses her to be his mistress, and is firmly but respectfully repulsed. He makes her father and mother sue to her, without success; and finally, being overcome by the sight of such immaculate virtue, marries her amid the plaudits of the people. The episode of the garter only occupies a paragraph at the end of the book.

THE CONQUEST OF FRANCE

With the Life and Glorious Actions of

𝕰𝖉𝖜𝖆𝖗𝖉 𝖙𝖍𝖊 𝕭𝖑𝖆𝖈𝖐 𝕻𝖗𝖎𝖓𝖈𝖊

Son to Edward the Third King of England, his Victory, with about Twelve thousand Archers and Men at Arms, over Philip of France, and an hundred thousand Frenchmen ; his Vanquishing King John of France, and taking him and his Son Prisoners ; his Love to the Earl of Kent's fair Daughter, and Marriage with her ; Being a History full of great and noble Actions in Love and Arms, to the Honour of the English Nation.

LONDON : PRINTED AND SOLD BY C. DICEY, IN BOW CHURCH YARD ;
SOLD ALSO AT HIS WAREHOUSE IN NORTHAMPTON.

THE

HISTORY

OF

JANE SHORE,

Concubine to King Edward IV.

GIVING

An account of her Birth, Parentage, her Marriage with Mr. Matthew Shore, a Goldsmith in Lombard Street, London. How she left her Husband's bed to live with King Edward IV. And of the miserable End she made at her Death.

Newcastle: Printed in this present year.

ACCORDING to this Chap-book version (and it is as reliable as any other), this lovely, but erring, woman was the daughter of Mr. Thomas Wainsted, a mercer in Cheapside, whose business lay among the ladies of the Court, whither his daughter frequently accompanied him.   Her conduct seems to have been of extreme levity, and her father rejoiced when she was married to Matthew Shore, a rich goldsmith in Lombard Street.   Lord Hastings, having in vain tried to seduce her, and being forbidden the house by her husband, told the king, Edward IV., of her; who went to Shore's house, disguised as a merchant, and saw her.   By the contrivance of Hastings and a go-between named Mrs. Blague, Jane was enticed to a Court ball, where the king discovered himself and told her of his affection for her.   This was too much for the weak woman, and next day she left her husband's home.   Shore, finding where she had gone, was heartbroken, and went abroad; returned in poverty, took to evil ways, and was executed for clipping coin in the reign of Henry VIII.   Jane lived in great splendour until the death of Edward, and then Lord Hastings took her; but at his death she was apprehended, and had to do penance in a white sheet, with a cross and wax taper in her hand, walking barefoot and bare-headed through Cheapside. The Chap-book gives a graphic account of her sad fate : "Richard, not content with this, put out a severe proclamation to this effect; That on pain of death, and confiscation of goods, no one should harbour her in their houses or relieve her with food and raiment.   So that she went wandering up and down to find her food upon the bushes and on the dung-hills, where some friends she had raised would throw bones with more meat than ordinary, and crusts of stale bread in the places where she generally haunted.   And a baker who had been condemned to die for a riot in King Edward's reign and saved by her means, as he saw her pass along in gratitude for her kindness would trundle a penny loaf after her, which she thankfully took up and blest him with tears in her eyes.   But some malicious neighbour informing against him : he was taken up and hanged for disobeying King Richard's proclamation ;

which so terrified others, that they durst not relieve her with anything, so that in miserable rags, almost naked, she went about a most shocking spectacle, wringing her hands, and bemoaning her unhappy circumstances." After Bosworth Field and Richard's death, she hoped for help from Henry VII.; but receiving only fresh persecution, " she wandered up and down in as poor and miserable condition as before, till growing old, and utterly friendless, she finished her life in a ditch, which is from thence called Shore Ditch adjoining to Bishopgate St." *

There is a very lugubrious and classical poem of nearly two hundred verses, or twelve hundred lines, called " Beawtie dishonoured written vnder the title of Shore's wife" (London, 1593).

---

* It is needless to say that this derivation is utterly erroneous. It was probably called so because the ditch was a shore or sewer, or from Sir John de Soerdich, lord of the manor, *temp.* Edward III.

THE

HISTORY

Of the most Renowned

QUEEN ELIZABETH

And her great Favourite

THE EARL OF ESSEX.

ELIZABETHA REGINA

NEWCASTLE: PRINTED BY J. WHITE.

MORE than half this book is taken up with an elaborate confession by Elizabeth, to the Countess of Nottingham, of her love for the unfortunate Earl of Essex ; and, historically speaking, it has many blunders, such as making him privately marry the Countess of Rutland, instead of Sir Philip Sidney's widow, etc. It is mainly taken from " The Secret History of the most renowned Queen Elizabeth and the Earl of Essex. By a Person of Quality London 1695 ; " and, like that book, was sometimes published in two parts.

THE
HISTORY

OF THE

ROYAL MARTYR

King Charles the First

WITH THE

EFFIGIES of those *WORTHY PERSONS* that Suffered; and the Time and Places where they lost their Lives in his Majesty's Cause, during the Usurpation of *OLIVER CROMWELL*

SOLD IN BOW CHURCH YARD, LONDON.

Of this book there are two parts, and it is interesting, as it gives portraits of the celebrated men in Charles I.'s reign, with brief biographical notices of each, out of Clarendon. Space will only admit of the portraits out of the first part.

WILLIAM LAUD, ARCHBISHOP OF CANTERBURY.
BEHEADED 10TH JANUARY, 1644.

DR. HEWIT.
BEHEADED 8TH JUNE, 1658.

EARL OF LITCHFIELD.

EARL OF KINGSTON.

EARL OF NORTHAMPTON.

EARL OF STRAFFORD.

EARL OF CARNARVON.

EARL OF LINDSEY.

England's Black Tribunal;

BEING THE

Characters of King *CHARLES* the Firſt, and
the Nobility that Suffer'd for him.

*Ecce Spectaculum dignum ad quod reſpiciat Deus operi ſuo
intentus, Vir fortis cum mala fortuna compoſitus.*
Sen. de Prov. c. 2.

LONDON : Printed for *E. M.* near *White-Hall.*

THIS Chap-book is extremely like the "History of the Royal Martyr," as it simply consists of portraits and short biographies of

Sir Bevil Granville.
Viscount Falkland.
Earl of Lichfield.
Sir Ralph Hopton.
Earl of Carnarvon.
Earl of Holland.
Marquis of Montrose.
Earl of Kingston.
Archbishop Laud.
Earl of Lindsey.

Dr. Hewit.
Earl of Northampton.
Lord Capel.
Sir Henry Slingsby.
Earl of Strafford.
Duke of Hamilton.
Colonel Penruddock.
Sir Charles Lucas.
Sir George Lisle.
Earl of Derby.

The Foreign Travels of

SIR JOHN MANDEVILLE

CONTAINING

An Account of remote Kingdoms, Countries, Rivers, Castles, &c. Together with a Description of Giants, Pigmies, and various other People of odd Deformities; as also their Laws, Customs, and Manners. Likewise, enchanted Wildernesses, Dragons, Griffins, and many more wonderful Beasts of Prey, &c. &c. &c.

PRINTED AND SOLD IN ALDERMARY CHURCH YARD LONDON

THE earliest printed English edition seems to be that by Wynkyn de Worde: "Here Begynneth a lytell treatyse or booke named Johan Mandeuyll Knyght born in Englonde in the towne of saynt Albone, and speketh of the wayes of the holy londe towards Iherrusalem, and of marueyles of Ynde and of other dyuerse coūtrees;" colophon: "Here endeth the boke of Johan Maūdeuyll Knyght, of the wayes towarde Jerusalem and of the meruayles of Ynde and of other diverse coūtries. Emprynted at Westmynster by Wynkyn de Worde. Anno dñi 1499." But the British Museum possesses earlier editions in other languages—for instance, in French, 1478; Dutch, 1470; and Italian, 1488; which goes to show how universally his work was read.

The original of this book was intended as a guide for pilgrims for Jerusalem. Of Sir John Maundeville, Knight, very little is known but what he tells us—that he set out on his travels in 1323, and returned and wrote the account in 1356. He afterwards went to Liége, and is said to have died there, according to one authority in 1371, and to another in 1382. He either was extremely credulous, and believed everything told him, or he drew very largely upon his imagination for his facts. Anyhow, in the fourteenth and fifteenth centuries his work was most popular; and even the marvels contained in the condensed form of a Chap-book are sufficient to satisfy the most rabid craving for literary stimulants. As this history is not well known, it is given in its entirety.

CHAP. I.

SIR JOHN'S TRAVELS TO THE HOLY LAND; AND OF THE ENCHANTED HAWKE.

I, SIR John Mandeville Kn^t born in the Old town of St Albans set forward to travel on Michaelmas Day 1322,* to the Holy Land; and shall give an account of all the remarkable things in the countries thro' which I passed, as follows;

* The Chap-book says 1372, but that is a misprint.

First, In my way to Jerusalem, I passed through Almain, Hungary, and so to Constantinople where before St Stephen's Church is the image of Justinian the Emperor, sitting on horseback crowned, holding an apple in his hand. From thence I passed thro' Turkey, Nika, and several islands, where I beheld men hunting with pampeons like leopards, catching wild beasts quicker than hounds. From thence I passed to Hierusalem and went on a pilgrimage to the Church where is the holy grave; in the middle of the Church is a tabernacle, on the right side of which is the Sepulchre of our Lord Jesus Christ; and the Cross on which he was crucified standing in a Mortis by it. In this mortis, it is said Adam's head was found after the Flood.

Travelling on further I came to a country whereon stands the Castle of Cyprus; where I beheld a curious hawk sitting on a porch, and a beautiful Lady of Fairy Land keeping it; and it is said, he that will watch seven days and seven nights, without company or sleep, this lady will come and grant him the richest of worldly things he shall crave; and the truth of which hath been proved often by experience.

The men here are proper and of fine complection, their cloaths richly beset with rubies and gold; but the women are short, hard favoured, and go for the most part barefooted, their garments poor and short, that it comes but to the middle of their thighs, yet their sleeves, so extraordinary long that they hang down to their toes. Their hair long and lank.

CHAP. 2.

DESCRIPTION OF AN ODD SORT OF PEOPLE, OF INDIA'S EXTRA-ORDINARY EELS; AND OF OTHER REMARKABLE WONDERS.

FROM thence I came to the land of Ethiope, where I beheld many strange things. Here is a well, whose water is so cold in the day, as no man dare drink it, and so hot in the night as you cannot bear your finger in it. There is still one thing remarkable in this place, for there is a sort of men who have one foot, yet so swift as to exceed the deer in running. This foot is so large in compass, as when they are minded to rest, lying on their backs it shelters the body from the heat of the sun or showers of rain—When their Children come first into the world they are of a russet complection; but as they grow up they turn perfect black.—One of the wise men who sought for Our Lord in Bethlehem, was King of this Country.

From thence I went thro' many Islands into India, where there are eels thirty feet in length, and the men who commonly fish there are of different colours, such as green, yellow, blue, &c. In the heat of the day the men and women lay themselves under water, and the women are not ashamed to appear naked before the men.

In the island of Lombe they worship images according to their own imaginations; and here there are wonderful rats, exceeding the tallest hounds; and they hunt these rats with mastiff dogs, who can scarce conquer them.

From thence I passed thro' the forest of Tombar, where grows abundance of Spices, and came to a city called Polomes, where there is a well, whose waters are variable every hour of the day, taking of changeable spices and rich odors; and whoever drinks of this water three times is cured of all diseases: They call it, The Well of Youth. I drank thereof myself, and believe I am the better for it ever since.

Here they worship an Ox for his simplicity, whose dung and urine they preserve in vessels of gold, and present it to the King, who puts his hand into it, and anoints his breast and forehead, saying, " I am anointed with the virtue of the Ox." And after him the Nobles do the like, as long as any is left. The idols they constantly worship are half men and half oxen, before whom they often slay their Children by way of sacrifice. And when any man dies they burn him, in token of penance ; and if he leaves no children, they burn his wife with him, saying she ought to bear him company in the next world, as she did in this.

CHAP. 3.

OF THE COUNTRY OF LEMORY. OF THE KING OF JAVA'S GOLDEN PALACE. AND OF THE KINGDOM OF TELONOCK.

FROM thence I came to Lemory, where the men and women go naked, and glory in it, saying God made Adam and Eve both naked, and why should they be ashamed of what God made? Here is no marriages, but all are common one with another. Their riches is as common to each other as themselves; and though they have plenty of corn and other dainties yet their chief food is Man's flesh.—Children from other Countries are brought hither as Merchandise to be sold; and those that are fat and plump are killed like pigs for stately banquetting; and those that are lean they fatten and kill also. Near this isle is another, where the nobility, as a mark of distinction are burned in the face with a red hot iron. These people hold a perpetual war with the aforesaid naked men and women.

From thence I travelled to Java, a place abounding with all manner of Spices; the King thereof has seven Kings under him, and so wealthy is he, that the stairs and floors of his palace are covered with massy gold and silver; and the walls with the same. On which are written ancient stories of renowned Knights and valiant men at arms.

Travelling from thence by sea, I came to the land of Telonoch; the King of which has as many wives as he pleases, and never lies but once with each woman. Here is a miraculous wonder, for the various sorts of fishes that breed in the sea, come once a year to land, and lie there three days, in which time the inhabitants take what they please, and the rest return. Then comes another sort and does the like, till all have taken their turns; and no one knoweth the reason, except it be, as they say, that they come to worship their King; who is a mighty Prince, and has at his command forty thousand elephants, upon whose back, when he goeth to fight he placeth mighty Castles, whereby he conquers his enemies.

CHAP. 4.

OF A BLOODY KIND OF PEOPLE; AND OF PEOPLE THAT HAVE HEADS LIKE HOUNDS.

NOT far from the last mentioned place is an island called Tarkonet, inhabited by a wicked kind of people, whose delight is in the slaughter of mankind, whose blood they drink with as much pleasure as if it was the richest wine in the world. Moreover, he is accounted most famous who commits most murders; and if two are at variance they must drink of each other's blood before they can be reconciled.

Departing from thence, I came to the isle of Macumerac, where the men and women have heads like hounds, and worship the Ox. They fight well, and send the prisoners to their King; who is a peaceable and virtuous man, hindering nobody from passing through his country. About his neck he wears three hundred pearls, with which he says three hundred prayers every morning before breakfast. Here are wild beasts, serpents, &c.

CHAP. 5.

OF THE SAVAGE PEOPLE DWELLING IN THE ISLE OF DODYN.

AFTER three days journey I came to Dodyn, where the Child eats its parents, and its parents the child; the husband his wife, and the wife her husband. If a parent lies sick, the son goes to enquire of the Oracle whether they are for life or death? if for death, he returns with the priest and immediately stops the breath of the parent; which done, the body is strait cut in pieces, and the relations invited to come and feast upon it; having eat the flesh, they bury the bones with joy and musick.

The King of this place has twelve isles under his government, viz. in the first are men that eat fish and flesh raw, having but one eye, and that in the middle of their foreheads —In the second are men whose eyes are in their shoulders, and their mouths in their breasts, having no heads.—In the third are men with plain faces, without noses or eyes, but have two holes instead of eyes, and flat mouths—In the fourth are men with plain faces, without nose, mouth or eyes; but they are on their back and shoulders.—In the fifth are men with lips so large that they cover their faces while asleep.—In the sixth are men very small, being but two feet high.—In the seventh are men hanging below their shoulders—In the eighth are men that have feet like horses, and run as swift—In the ninth are men that run upon all fours; their skins are as rough as bears—In the tenth are men going upon their knees, with eight toes on each foot—In the eleventh are men with fingers and toes a yard long—And in the twelfth are people that are both men and women.

Chap. 6.

Of the Kingdom of Mancia. Of Pigmies. Of the Province of Cathay, and the Grandeur of its Emperor.

Departing from Dodyn, I came to Mancia, in which is the City of Cassa, having ten thousand bridges, and on each bridge a stately tower. Here married women wear crowns on their heads by way of distinction. The fowl are six times as large as in England—Hens instead of feathers wear wool like sheep —Men have beards like Cats, yet are rational, and of good and sound understanding.

From thence I passed along the river that leads to the Line of Pigmies, where the men and women are but three spans long, and marry when but half a year old; for as they are but of small stature, so their days are short; for he is looked on to be old who lives eight years. They are very ingenious at working silk and cotton, which is their employ. Large men that live among them till the land, because they are not strong enough to perform such hard labour.

From thence I travelled to the province Catha, where are two Cities, the Old and the New. The New has twelve gates, each a mile asunder. In these cities the palace of the great Caan is; in the hall are thirteen pillars of fine gold, the walls covered with red skins of beasts. In the center is a lofty seat for the great Caan, adorned with rubbies, pearls, and diamonds ; and underneath are fountains flowing with liquor for the supply of his court. At the left hand are three seats for his three wives who sit in a degree below each other ; and on his right hand sits his son and heir. In this hall is an artificial vine which extends its branches over every part of the hall, on which appears fine clusters of grapes.

Here the Emperor informed me of the origin of his title, which was as follows ; Under his government are seven Lineages, and it is not long since a poor man, named Chanius, sleeping on his bed, was visited by an apparition in the likeness of a Nobleman, saying unto him, Arise, for God hath sent me unto thee to say unto thee, Go unto the seven Lineages, and tell them, that thou shalt be their mighty Emperor to deliver them from their enemies. The old man went, and having delivered his message, they not only laughed at the old man, but called him an hundred fools.—Soon after this, he appeared to the Seven Lineages, telling them it was the will of God it should be so for their deliverance ; whereupon they took the old man, and made him Emperor, calling him Great Caan, which continues to this day. To try the loyalty of his nobility, he summoned them together and ordered them to smite off the heads of their eldest sons with their own hands ; which they accordingly did. After this convincing proof he sent them forth, and conquered all the countries around him ; together with the land of Catha, and then died, leaving his eldest son Chico Emperor whose grandeur made him the greatest Emperor in the World.

This Caan is great, and may expend forty millions yearly ; but his money is made of leather, for he builds his palaces of silver : in his presence chamber is a gold pillar, in which is fixed a carbuncle that gives continual light in the dark ; his subjects have as many wives as they please : some have forty, fifty, an hundred, or more ; and they marry their relations, except mothers, sisters, and daughters. Men and women go all in one sort of apparel. When the Emperor dies he is put in a cart, and placed in the midst of a tent, and they set before him a table furnished with meat and mare's milk and close by it a horse saddled and bridled, loaded with gold and silver; and having dug a deep pit, they lay him in it, with all the stuff about him, and also the horse, mare and colt, that he may not want for horses in another world, and one of his Chamberlains is buried alive with him, that he may do him service in another world.

CHAP. 7.

OF THE LANDS OF GORGY AND BACTRINE.

TRAVELLING from thence I came to the land of Gorgy, where dwell many Christians. A great part of this Country is hid with perpetual darkness; nevertheless they have often heard the crowing of cocks, the cries of men, the trampling of horse, and clashing of arms, though none know what sort of people they are; but it is said, a bloody minded Emperor who pursued the Christians to put them to death, and was opposed by the hand of heaven, and the land covered with darkness, so that he could pursue them no longer; but remains with his host in continual darkness.

Then I travelled to the land of Bactrine, where are many marvels. Trees bearing wool, with which they make Cloth. Likewise creatures that are half horses, living sometimes in water, and sometimes on land, and they devour men when they meet with them. There I have seen griffins, and the fore part like an eagle, and the hinder parts like a lion. There is likewise another kind of griffin much larger and stronger than the former; also a great number of wild animals of all kinds.

CHAP. 8.

OF THE LAND OF PRESTOR JOHN, AND PARTS ADJACENT; AND SIR JOHN MANDEVILLE'S HAPPY RETURN TO ENGLAND, &C.

FROM thence I went to the Country of Prestor John, who is a noble Lord and wedded the only daughter of the Great Caan.

Such plenty of rich stones and diamonds there is in this country that they make them into Cups and dishes. In this land is a gravelly sea, which ebbs and flows like the ocean, yet not one drop of water is to be seen therein, yet never the less men catch fishes in it. A sand runs in three days in a week, among which are found many rubbies. Trees grow from sun rising to mid day, bearing apples that are harder than iron, which fall into the earth at noon successfully each day. Here are wild men, who are very hairy, with horns on their heads, they speak not but roar like swine.

At Pitan, a place in this Kingdom, are men very small, but not so small as the Pigmies. They live on the smell of Apples. On another island are men overgrown with feathers, like the fowls of the air. Near the river Poison there is an enchanted valley between two hills; here are tempests and storms like shrieks and cries so that they call it the Valley of Devils; both day and night the sound of musick and much feasting is heard in it; it also contains great store of gold and silver, for the lucre of which, many have gone into it but never came back again. Beyond this valley is the isle of Girty, where men are 40 feet high, and sheep bigger than oxen.

The Emperor Prestor John when he goes to battle hath three golden Crosses carried before him, set with precious stones, and each cross guarded by One Thousand fighting men. He has a most superb palace, and seven Kings, seventy two Dukes, three hundred Earls, and thirty two bishops to wait upon him every day.

Beyond this place is a large wilderness, in which grow speaking Trees, called The Trees of the Sun and Moon; and whoever eats of the fruit thereof live four or five hundred years; and some never die. These trees foretold Alexander his death. I would willingly have gone to see them, but was prevented by lions, dragons, etc.

The reason of this Emperor's being called Prestor John was as follows; He happened in his progress to go into a Christian Church in Egypt, on the Saturday after Whitsunday, when the Bishop gave Orders; and he asked who they were that stood before the Bishop? the answer was, They are priests. Then said he, I will no longer be called Emperor, but according to the name of the first that comes forth, whose name was John. Therefore the Emperors of that country ever since have been called Prestor John.

Towards the East of this place is an island wherein is a mountain of gold dust, kept by pismires, whose industerous labours is to part the fine from the coarse. They are larger than the English hounds, and it is difficult for any one to gain the treasure, through fear of them, for they sting to death.

Near this place is a dark Wilderness, full of mountains and craggy rocks, no manner of light appearing to distinguish the day from night. Beyond this is the Paradise where Adam and Eve were, whose ground is the highest in the world. The Flood was not so high as this mountain.—No man can come to the Paradise by land for huge rocks and mountains, nor by sea for restless waves and dangerous waters ; some that have attempted it have been struck dead, others blind.

This Prester John and his people are baptized, hold with Three Persons in the Trinity, and are very devout in what they profess. They have plenty of Cattle ; and the land is divided into twenty two provinces, every one of which hath a king. In this Country also is a gravelly sea containing the like wonders in that before mentioned.

Towards the east side of Prester John lies the Island of Taprabone, being a very pleasant and spacious place, abounding with unspeakable plenty, and all manner of rich fruits and spice. The king of this Country pays obedience and is subject to Prester John ; to whom he pays a very large revenue. This king is always made by election. To our wonderful admiration here are two summers and two winters every year ; they have two harvests, and as for their herbs and flowers they always flourish. The people are of a kind and loving disposition, being for the most part of them Christian professors ; whose laws, customs, manners, and actions are as reasonable as their profession ; to which they adhere very strictly.

Between Prester John's Country and this island is a small

river that men wade over from country to Country, without danger of being drowned.

These islands and kingdoms of Prester John are directly under the earth, from England. We are foot to foot I can assure the reader, from the great experience of my long travels ; of which I at last grew weary, and being desirous once more to see the land of my nativity, and accordingly I set sail for England, and after a very favourable passage, arrived safe on my native shore, to the great joy and satisfaction of all my friends. And since my arrival, have been employed by the help of my journals, in compiling this book, which gives an account of what I have seen in my travels, some of which for their strangeness may seem incredible ; but those that will not believe the truth of these things, let them but read the book of Mappa Mundi, and they will find a great part of it there continued ; and great many stranger things than are here recited.

FINIS.

The Surprizing

LIFE

and most Strange

ADVENTURES

OF

ROBINSON CRUSOE

Of the City of York, Mariner.

GIVING

An Account how he was cast on Shore by Ship-wreck (none escaping but himself) on an un-inhabited Island, on the Coast of America near the mouth of the great River Oroonoque, where he lived twenty eight Years, till at length he was strangely delivered by Pirates, and brought Home to his native Country.

PRINTED IN THIS PRESENT YEAR.

FROM Defoe's original edition of three volumes in 1719, to the
12mo Chap-book, is a great drop, and, naturally, the story is
much condensed. As it is so well known, only the illustrations

are given, which in this edition are quainter than in the earlier one published at Aldermary Churchyard.

ROBINSON AND XURY ESCAPING FROM THE MOORS.

HE SETS SAIL ON HIS EVENTFUL VOYAGE.

THE WRECK.

HE KEEPS A RECORD OF TIME AND EVENTS.

ADVENT OF FRIDAY.

ARRIVAL OF SAVAGES WITH CHRISTIAN PRISONER.

LANDING OF MUTINOUS CREW ON ISLAND.

A Brief Relation of the

ADVENTURES

OF

𝕸. 𝕭amfyeld 𝕸oore 𝕮arew

For more than forty Years past the

KING OF THE BEGGARS.

PRINTED AND SOLD IN LONDON.

THIS Chap-book gives a very fair account of the adventures of this misguided man, who so wasted his fair natural abilities. It is hardly worth giving *in extenso*, but, as generally, his eventful life is not much known, it may be interesting to give the story, and some extracts.

Bamfylde Moore (so named from his two godfathers) Carew was the son of a clergyman near Tiverton, and was born in 1693. While at Tiverton School, he and some of his school-mates got into serious trouble for hunting a deer, and, rather than face the certain chastisement, they ran away, and joined a company of gipsies, with whom Carew abode. He swindled a lady out of twenty guineas by pretending to tell her where a treasure was buried, and generally followed the bad example of his companions, until the fancy took him to return home. He did so; but the fascination of his wild life was too great, and he once more ran away and joined his beloved gipsies. His disguises were innumerable, and he even feigned madness successfully, at all events in a monetary point of view. Once, when disguised as a rat-catcher (see frontispiece), he was recognized, and a gentleman present, one Mr. Pleydell, said he had often wished to see him, but never had. "Yes, you have, replied Carew, and given me a suit of cloaths; do you not remember meeting a poor wretch one day at your stable door, with a stocking round his head, an old mantle over his shoulders, without shirt, stocking or scarce any shoes, who told you he was a poor unfortunate man cast away upon the coast with six-teen more of the crew, who were all drowned; you believing this story, generously relieved me with a guinea and a good suit of cloaths. Mr. Pleydell said he well remembered it, but on his discovery it is impossible to deceive him so again, come in whatever shape you will—The company blamed him for thus boasting, and secretly prevailed upon Carew to put his art in practice to convince him of the fallacy thereof; to which he agreed, and in a few days after, appointing the company present to be at Pleydell's house, he put the following scheme into execution. He shaved himself closely, and cloathed himself in an old woman's apparel, with a high crowned hat, and a large dowde under his chin; then taking three children from among his fraternity, he tied two to his back, and one in his arms; thus accoutred he comes to Mr. Pleydell's door, and pinching one of the brats, set it a roaring; this gave the alarm to the dogs who came out with open mouths and the whole family was soon alarmed; out came the maid, saying, Carry away the children, good woman, they disturb the ladies.—God bless their ladyships, I am the poor unfortunate grandmother of these helpless infants, whose mother and all they had, was burnt at the dreadful fire at Kirton, and hope the good ladies, for God's sake, will bestow something on the poor famishing starving infants. In goes the maid with this affecting story to the ladies, while our grandmother keeps pinching the children to make them cry, and the maid returned with half a crown and some good broth, which he thankfully received, and went into the court yard to sit down to eat it, as perceiving the gentlemen were not at home. He had not been long there before they came, when one of them accosted him thus—Where do you come from, old woman?—From Kirton, please your honours, where the poor unhappy mother of these helpless infants was burnt in the flames, and all they had, consumed.—Damn you said one of them, here has been more money collected for Kirton than ever Kirton was worth; however, they each gave the old grandmother a shilling, commiserating the hard case of her and the helpless infants; which he thankfully receiving, pretended to go away; but the gentlemen were hardly got into the house before their ears were saluted with a Tantivee, Tantivee, and a Holloo to the dogs, on which they turned about, supposing it to be some other sportsmen, but seeing nobody, they directly suspected it to be Carew, in the disguise of the old Kirton Grandmother; so, bidding the servants fetch her back, she was brought into the parlour among them all, and confessed herself to be the famous Mr. Bamfylde Moore Carew, to the astonishment and mirth of them all; who well rewarded him for the diversion he had afforded them."

This is a fair specimen of his tricks, and he was very successful in duping the not-over-acute country gentlemen of his time. On the death of Clause Patch, the king of the gipsies, he was elected to succeed him ; and there the Chap-book leaves him.

His after career was very chequered. Soon after his accession to regal dignity, he was apprehended as an idle vagrant, tried at the quarter sessions at Exeter, and transported to Maryland, where on his arrival he ran away. He, however, gave himself up, and was severely punished with a cat-o'-nine-tails, and had a heavy iron collar fastened round his neck. He excited the pity of some ships' captains, who helped him to fly, by giving him some biscuits, cheese, and rum ; he travelled some time until he fell in with some friendly Indians, who relieved him of his iron collar. He gave them the slip, and stealing one of their canoes, landed near Newcastle, in Pennsylvania. Here he plied his old trade of deception, pretending to be a Quaker, and made it pay very well. Thence he got to New York, and set sail for England, where he rejoined his beloved gipsies. His ultimate fate is unknown, but he is said to have died in 1770, aged 77.

There seem to have been at least two books written about him during his lifetime—" Accomplish'd Vagabond, or compleat Mumper, exemplify'd in the bold and artful Enterprizes, and merry Pranks of Bamfylde Carew " (Oxon., 1745); and "An Apology for the Life of Bamfylde Moore Carew (by Robert Goadby) " (London, 1749).

The Fortunes and Misfortunes of

𝔐𝔬𝔩𝔩 𝔉𝔩𝔞𝔫𝔡𝔢𝔯𝔰

Who was Born in Newgate.

And during a life of Continued Variety for Sixty Years was 17 times a W—— 5 Times a Wife, whereof once to her own Brother, 12 Years a Thief, 11 Times in Bridewell, 9 Times in New Prison, 11 Times in Woodstreet Compter, 6 Times in the Poultry Compter, 14 Times in the Gate house, 25 Times in Newgate, 15 Times Whipt at the Carts tail, 4 Times Burnt in the Hand, once Condemned for Life, and 8 Years a Transport in Virginia. At last grew rich, lived honest, and died penitent.

Printed and Sold in Aldermary Church Yard. Bow Lane London.

DEFOE wrote "Moll Flanders" in 1721, and his book is chiefly remarkable for the graphic account of the plantations in Virginia. This Chap-book is a condensed version, and is not very edifying reading. Its contents may be imagined by the titlepage, which is far fuller than Defoe's.

YOUTH'S WARNING-PIECE

OR, THE TRAGICAL

HISTORY

OF

GEORGE BARNWELL

WHO WAS

UNDONE BY A STRUMPET

THAT CAUSED HIM

TO ROB HIS MASTER, AND MURDER HIS UNCLE.

By other's harm learn to be wise
And ye shall do full well.

STOCKTON
PRINTED AND SOLD BY R. CHRISTOPHER.

GEORGE BARNWELL.

And behold there met him an Harlot, subtle of heart; and
she kissed him, and said unto him, I have decked my bed
with fine linen, come let us take our fill of love until the
Morning.

SARAH MILLWOOD.

The lips of a strange Woman drop as an honeycomb, and her mouth is sweeter than oil ; but her end is bitter as wormwood, sharp as a two-edged sword.

EDITIONS of this popular story were published in several towns, and the present one has been chosen as having the most curious illustrations, there being none specially illustrated to exemplify the text, any female head doing duty for Sarah Milwood. The story of George Barnwell, of his lapse from virtue, and his rapid declension from theft to murder, together with his penitence and execution, is so well known that it needs no repetition. It is a very old story, dating back, it is said, to Queen Elizabeth's time. The earliest ballad on the subject in the British Museum is,* "An excellent ballad of George Barnwell, an apprentice in the City of London, who was undone by a strumpet, who caused him thrice to rob his master and murder his uncle in Ludlow" (London, 1670). Lillo dramatized it in 1731, and within very few years since it was always acted at the minor theatres on Boxing night, previous to the pantomime, as a warning to apprentices.

* 643, m. 10
109.

THE
Merry Life and Mad Exploits

OF

Capt James Hind

The great Robber of England.

> The true Portraiture of Captain *JAMES HIND*, the Robber, who died for Treaſon.

NEWCASTLE: PRINTED IN THIS PRESENT YEAR.

THE history of the famous highwayman Captain Hind, is evidently taken from a little black-letter book, published 1651, Old Style (or 1652 of our calendar), called "Wit for Money;" and in that also is found the original of this frontispiece, even more roughly executed.   In place of "The true portraiture," etc., is

> "I rob'd men neatly
>   as is here exprest.
> Coyne I ne'r tooke
>   unlesse I gave a Jest."

Indeed, most of the accounts of Hind are full of his "merry pranks," as, for instance, "We have brought our Hogs to a fair Market; or Strange Newes from New-Gate," etc. (London, 1652), a book which was of such importance, that two pages of "The Faithful Scout" for January $\frac{9}{16}$, 1651–2, are taken up with extracts from it.   In this book are two portraits of Hind, which, from their resemblance to each other, are probably authentic. In one he is represented as "Unparallel'd Hind," in full armour on horseback; the other is similar to that given on next page, which is taken from "The Declaration of Captain James Hind (close Prisoner in Newgate)," etc.

In "The True and perfect Relation of the taking of Captain James Hind" (London, 1651), it says that "A Gentleman or two, desired so much favour of him [the keeper], as to aske Mr. Hind a civil question; which was granted.   So pulling two books out of his pocket, the one entituled, Hind's Ramble, The other Hind's Exploits, asked him whether he had ever seen them or not : He answered, yes ; And said upon the word of a Christian, they were fictions : But some merry Pranks and Revels I have plaid, that I deny not."   Nay, his exploits were even dramatized in "An excellent Comedy called the Prince of Priggs Revels or The Practises of that grand Thief Captain James Hind," etc. (London, 1651).   A play in five acts.

Hind was born at Chipping Norton, in Oxfordshire, and, according to one account, his father was a saddler.   He was sent to school, but being too fond of play, he was apprenticed

The true
Portraicture

of Captain
James Hind.

London, Printed for *G. HORTON,* 1651.

to a butcher, from whom he ran away, and came to London, where he fell in with "a Company of idle, roaring young Blades," and he became a highwayman. The Chap-book is full of his robberies, and introduces "How Hind was enchanted by an old Hagg, for the space of Three Years," a performance which seems to have provided for his personal safety during that time. Finding England too hot for him, he went to Holland; but "Hind finding that this country was not fit for his purpose, resolved to retire as soon as an opportunity offered," and he went to Scotland to join Charles I. The king put him under the command of the Duke of Buckingham, "because his own life guards were full," and he was present at the engagements at Warrington and Worcester. He escaped from the latter, and came to London, where he was apprehended on November 6, 1651, in a barber's shop in Fleet Street.

He was examined at Whitehall on the charge of rebellion, and committed to Newgate.   On December 12, 1651, he was tried at the Old Bailey, and remanded to Newgate, where he lay till March 1, 1652, when he was sent to Reading to take his trial for killing a companion at a village called Knowl. It was, however, proved to have been only a case of manslaughter, and he was pardoned through an Act of Oblivion ; only, however, to suffer death for treason against the State, being hanged, drawn, and quartered, at Worcester, on September 24, 1652.

THE HISTORY

OF

JOHN GREGG

AND HIS FAMILY

OF

ROBBERS AND MURDERERS

Who took up their Abode in a Cave near to the Sea Side, in Clovaley in Devonshire, where they liv'd Twenty five Years without so much as once going to visit any City or Town.

How they Robbed above One Thousand Persons, and murdered, and eat all whom they robbed.

How at last they were happily discover'd by a pack of Blood hounds; and how John Gregg, his Wife, Eight Sons, Six Daughters, Eighteen Grand Sons and Fourteen Grand daughters were all seized and executed, by being Cast alive into three Fires, and were burnt.

LICENSED AND ENTERED ACCORDING TO ORDER.

THIS Chap-book is precisely similar to the History of Sawney Beane, who lived *temp.* James I., only the names and locality have been changed. The lovers of horrors can be fully gratified by reading Sawney Beane's life, either in Captain Charles Johnson's " History of the Lives and Actions of the most famous Highwaymen, Street Robbers," etc., 8vo (Edinburgh, 1813), pp. 33–37, or vol. i. p. 161 of " The Terrific Registers."

THE

BLOODY TRAGEDY

OR

A Dreadful Warning

TO

DISOBEDIENT CHILDREN

GIVING

A sad and dreadful Account of one John Gill in the Town of Oborn [Woburn] in Bedfordshire, who lived a Wicked Life.

How, coming home drunk one Night, he asked his Father for Money to carry on his Debaucheries, who putting him off till next Morning, he grew so impatient and desparately wicked, that he arose in the Dead of the Night, and cut his Father, and Mother's Throats in their Beds.

How afterwards binding and ravishing the Maid Servant he murdered her also, and then robbed the House of Plate and Money, and set it on Fire, burning the dead Bodies to Ashes.

With the Manner of the Discovery, and being apprehended, what Confession he made before the Magistrates.

How the Ghosts of the dead Bodies appeared to him in Jail.

Together with his Dying Speech at the Place of Execution.

With several other Things, worthy the Observation of Young People.

London, Printed in Aldermary Church Yard. Bow Lane.

THE UNFORTUNATE FAMILY:

In Four Parts.

Part 1. How one John Roper, through want of Grace, broke the Heart of his Mother, and strangled his Father, taking what Money was in the House, and fled to a Wood.

Part 2. How the Spirit of his Mother appeared to him in a Wood, in an Angry manner; and how Conscience drove him into the hands of Justice.

Part 3. His Lamentation in Dorchester Gaol.

Part 4. His last dying Speech desiring all Young Men to take Warning by him.

To which is added, A Notable Poem upon the uncertainty of Man's Life.

Licensed according to Order.

PRINTED FOR E. BLARE ON LONDON BRIDGE.

THE

𝕳𝖔𝖗𝖗𝖔𝖗𝖘 𝖔𝖋 𝕵𝖊𝖆𝖑𝖔𝖚𝖘𝖎𝖊

OR

THE FATAL MISTAKE

Being a Terrible and Dreadful Relation of one Jonathan Williams, a Gentleman of a Considerable Fortune near Sitting-burn in Kent, who had a Beautiful and Virtuous young Lady to his Wife, who disgusting a light Huswife, her Chamber Maid, she vowed a Bloody Revenge upon her Mistress; then forged a Letter to make her Master Jealous: When one Day, as the Plot was laid, sending up the Butler into her Bed Chamber when she was in Bed, and sent her Master after him; who immediately killed him with his Sword, and afterward did the like by his Wife, protesting her Innocency with her dying Breath; upon which horrible Tragedy the Chamber Maid confessed her Treachery, shewing her Lady's Innocency; upon this he killed her, and after fell upon his own Sword and died.

TOGETHER WITH

The Copy of the LETTER, and all the Circumstances attending so Tragical an End; and how upon the sight of this Bloody Tragedy their only Son and Heir run Distracted and Died Raving Mad.

LICENSED ACCORDING TO ORDER.

LONDON: PRINTED FOR T. WILLIAMS NEAR WOOD STREET 1707.

The Constant, but Unhappy

LOVERS

Being a full and true Relation

OF ONE

𝕸𝖆𝖉𝖆𝖒 𝕭𝖚𝖙𝖑𝖊𝖗

A young Gentlewoman, and a great Heiress at Hackney Boarding School, who being by her Father forced to Marry Mr. Harvey, a Rich Merchants Son near Fan-church Street, against her Will; one Mr. Perpoint, a young Gentleman of Considerable Estate, who had courted her above two Years, grew so Discontented that he went a Volunteer to the wars in Spain, where being Mortally Wounded at the late Battle of Almanza he writ a Letter with his own Blood, therein putting a Bracelet of Madam Butler's Hair, and then ordering his Servant to bake his Heart to a Powder after his death, he charg'd him to deliver them in a Box to the above-said Gentlewoman. His Man came to England, and went on 6th June to deliver the Present to Madam Butler, but it was took away by her Husband, who gave her the Powder in a Dish of Tea; which when she knew what she had Drank, and saw the bloody Letter and Bracelet, she said it was the last she would ever Eat and Drink, and accordingly going to Bed, she was found dead in the Morning, with a copy of *VERSES* lying by her on a Table, written in her own Blood.

LONDON : PRINTED BY E. B. NEAR LUDGATE 1707.

A Looking Glass for Swearers, Drunkards, Blasphemers, Sabbath Breakers, Rash Wishers, and Murderers.

Being a True Relation of one Elizabeth Hale, in Scotch Yard in White Cross Street; who having Sold herself to the Devil to be reveng'd on her Neighbours, did on Sunday last, in a wicked manner, put a quantity of Poyson into a Pot where a Piece of Beef was a boyling for several Poor Women and Children, Two of which dropt down dead, and Twelve more are dangerously Ill; the Truth of which will be Attested by several in the Neighbourhood. Her Examination upon the Crowners Inquest and her Commitment to Newgate.

A Full and True Account of a horrid, barbarous and bloody Murder, committed on the Body of one Jane Greenway and Four of her Children, by Robert Greenway her Husband, on Sunday last being the 2nd of this instant January, near Beaconsfield in Buckinghamshire. His Examination before the Worshipful Justice Lewis Esqre of Beaconsfield, and his commitment to Ailsbury Gaol. Note the Truth of this will be Attested by the Beaconsfield Carriers that comes to the Bell in Warwick Lane.

Likewise an Account of several Damages and other Accidents that have happen'd in Town and Country, by the present great Frost and Snow. First Four Men that were lost in a Boat going from Gravesend to the Buoy of the Nore. 2dly. Two Boys that were drown'd by sliding on the River of Thames. 3rdly. Two men drown'd at Battersea. 4thly. A Farrier that dropt down dead off his Horse near Paddington, as he was going Home. 5thly. A Gentleman in Surry that was found dead on Horseback at his own Door. 6thly. A Carrier that was lost on the North Road with two of his Horses.

TOGETHER WITH

An Account of a dreadful Fire that happen'd on Sunday Morning at the Cock Pit near Grays Inn; where one of the Feeders was burnt, and the other missing.

TO WHICH IS ADDED.

A True and Amazing Relation of one Mr. B——l an Eminent Butcher in White Chapple; who having made a Vow never to kill any Cattel on a Sabbath Day, and on Sunday Night last, as he was opening the Bowels of a Calf, there issued out of its Paunch a dreadful flash of Fire and Brimstone; which burnt his Wigg, and His Apprentice's Face and Eye Brows in a sad and dismal manner.

LONDON: PRINTED BY W. WISE AND M. HOLT IN FLEET STREET 1708.

Farther, and more Terrible Warnings from God.

Being a sad and dismal Account of a dreadful Earthquake or Marvelous Judgments of God.

That happen'd between Newcastle and Durham on Tuesday the 24th day of August last; which burst open the Earth with such Violence, that near an Hundred Souls, Men, Women and Children were Kill'd and Destroy'd; being Buried Alive in the sad and dreadful Ruins thereof. Besides great Damage to many Houses and Persons for several Miles round. With the Names of some of the Persons Destroy'd thereby. With a Sermon Preach'd on that deplorable Occasion, and of the late dreadful Thunder and Lightning.

BY THE REVEREND MR. SALTER MINISTER OF THE GOSPEL AT HARETIN NEAR NEWCASTLE.

LONDON, PRINTED BY J. NOON. NEAR FLEET STREET 1708.

The Constant Couple.

OR THE

TRAGEDY OF LOVE

Being a True and Mournful Relation of one Mrs. Sophia Elford, a Young Lady near St. James's, that Poyson'd herself for love of a Captain in Flanders ; who hearing that her Lover was kill'd, and not having any Account from him since the Campaign, on Monday last being the 21st of this Instant, she took a strong Dose of Poyson that ended her Life.

ALSO,

How the same Night she was Buried, there came a Letter from her Lover, giving an Account of his being now a Prisoner in France ; which her Parents receiv'd and having read the same, they fell into a greater Agony of Grief than before.

WITH

The Melancholly Answer they return'd him back, and the Copies of several Endearing Letters that have pass'd between these Unfortunate Lovers this Campaign.

LONDON : PRINTED FOR J. D. NEAR FLEET STREET 1709.

The Distressed Child in the Wood;

OR, THE CRUEL UNKLE

BEING A

True and dismal Relation of one Esq : Solmes of Beverly in Yorkshire ; who dying left an only Infant Daughter, of the Age of two Years, to the care of his own Brother ; who with many Oaths, Vows, and Protestations promised to be Loving to her ; but the Father was no sooner Dead, but out of a wicked Covetousness of the Child's Estate of three hundred Pounds a Year, carry'd it into a Wood, and there put it into a Hollow Tree to Starve it to Death ; Where a Gentleman and his Man being a Hunting two days after, found it half Famish'd, having gnawed its own Flesh and Fingers end in a dreadful manner.

With an Account how the Cruel Unkle to hide his Villany, had caused the Child's Effigies to be buried in Wax, and made a great Funeral, as if it had been really Dead ; with the manner of the whole Discovery by a Dream, and taking the Wax Child out of the Grave ; with the Unkle's Apprehension, Examination, Confession before Justice Stubbs, and his Commitment to Gaol, in order to be Try'd the next Assizes, for that Barbarous Action. To which is added a Copy of Verses on the said Relation.

LONDON, PRINTED BY J. READ, BEHIND THE GREEN DRAGON TAVERN IN FLEET STREET.

THE LAWYERS DOOM.

Being an Account of the Birth, Parentage, Education, Life and Conversation of Mr. Edward Jefferies, who was Executed at Tyburn on Friday the 21st of December 1705, for the Murther of Mr. Robert Woodcock the Lawyer. With an Account of his being Clerk to a Lawyer in Clifford's Inn; the many Pranks he has play'd after he came out of his time; his Marriage; and spending an Estate of One Hundred a year, on Leud Women; with the manner of Murthering Mr. Woodcock; his being Apprehended, Committed to Newgate; his Tryal, Examination, Condemnation, with a true Copy of his Reprieve, and last Dying Speech and Confession at the Place of Execution.

LONDON: PRINTED FOR W. PATEM BY FLEET STREET

THE WHOLE

LIFE AND ADVENTURES

OF

𝕸𝖎𝖘𝖘 𝕯𝖆𝖛𝖎𝖘

COMMONLY CALLED

THE BEAUTY IN DISGUISE

With a full, true and particular Account of her robbing Mr. W. of Gosfield in Essex of Eleven Hundred Pounds in Cash and Bank Notes for which she now lays to take her Trial at Chelmsford Assizes.

PRINTED IN THE YEAR 1785.

THE Chap-book version and the *Annual Register* agree as to Frances Davis's story, but, as the latter is more concise and truthful, it is here given:

"Sep. 3, 1785. An extraordinary robbery was committed last Saturday morning at Mrs. Bennet's the sign of the Three Rabbits on the Rumford Road. Mr. W—— of Gosfield in Essex, who is agent for the Scots and Lincolnshire salesmen, came to the above house on the evening before, in order to proceed to Smithfield market, with upwards of eleven hundred pounds, in drafts and bank notes, besides a purse containing 162 guineas and a half in his pocket. He went to bed early that night, and placed the above property in his breeches beneath his head. A youth, genteelly dressed, lay in the same room, and found means to convey the notes and money from under Mr. W——'s pillow, and departed with the whole, before break of day.—At seven o'clock, Mr. W—— discovered the theft; and sent immediately to all the different public offices in London. After a long search, a woman was taken into custody yesterday morning, at an obscure lodging in the Mint, Southwark, who, upon examination, was discovered to be the identical person who had taken up her quarters at Mrs. Bennet's on Friday night. Eight Hundred pounds in Notes and Cash were found concealed in her cloaths. She was soon after carried to the public office in Bow Street, where the Notes were sworn to by Mr. W—— and her person ascertained by the chambermaid of the inn. Her boy's apparel was also produced. She denied any knowledge of the transaction with great composure, and was committed to Tothill fields Bridewell. It appeared in course of the evidence, that on her coming to town she had changed some of the notes at different shops, and had on Saturday last visited a female convict in Newgate, to whom she had made a present of a pair of silver buckles and other trifling articles. The name of the above offender is Davis; she is extremely handsome, and not more than eighteen years of age. It is said she is connected with a numerous gang, and has long been employed in robberies similar to the above."

Neither the Chap-book nor the *Annual Register* give her

ultimate fate, but there can be little doubt that it was that so vividly portrayed in the frontispiece. A portrait is given as hers. It may be : but the practice of using any blocks that came handy renders it doubtful ; besides, the costume is too early for the period.

THE LIFE AND DEATH OF

CHRISTIAN BOWMAN, ALIAS MURPHY;

Who was burnt at a Stake, in the Old Bailey, on Wednesday the 18th of March 1789 for High Treason, in feloniously and traitorously counterfeiting the Silver Coin of the Realm.

Containing her Birth and Parentage, youthful Adventures, Love Amours, fatal Marriage, unhappy Connections, and untimely Death.

ARREST OF HUGH MURPHY AND CHRISTIAN BOWMAN.

THIS book is specially interesting, as being an account of the last execution by burning in England.

There is nothing uncommon in her story. Originally a servant, she married, but was deserted by her husband ; she then lived with a man named Murphy, a coiner. Of course they were found out, tried, and condemned to death. The man was hanged, and the woman, according to the then law, was burned. Blackstone gives the following curious reason for this punishment :—" In treasons of every kind the punishment of the woman is the same, and different from that of men. For as the decency due to the sex forbids the exposing and public mangling their bodies, the sentence is, to be drawn to the gallows, and there to be burned alive." The law was altered by 30 George III. c. 48 (1790), which provided that after June 5, 1790, women under this sentence should be hanged.

It must be borne in mind that the culprits were strangled before burning (Christian Bowman was hanging forty minutes) ; although, by the carelessness of the executioner, one woman, Katherine Hayes, was actually burned alive at Tyburn, November 3, 1726.

THE

DRUNKARD'S LEGACY.

IN FOUR PARTS.

Giving an Account

First, Of a Gentleman having a wild Son, and foreseeing he would come to poverty, had a cottage built with one door to it, always kept fast. His father on his Dying bed, charged him not to open it 'till he was poor and slighted, which the young man promised he would perform. Secondly, Of this young man's pawning his estate to a Vintner, who when poor, kicked him out of doors. Thinking it time to see his Legacy, he broke open the door, when instead of money, found a Gibbet and Halter, which he put round his Neck, and jumping off the Stool, the Gibbet broke, and a Thousand Pounds came down upon his head, which lay hid in the Ceiling. Thirdly of his redeeming the Estate; and fooling the Vintner out of Two Hundred Pounds, who for being jeered by his neighbours, cut his own throat. And lastly, Of the young Man's Reformation.

Very proper to be read by all who are given to Drunkenness.

PRINTED BY DICEY AND CO. IN ALDERMARY CHURCH YARD.

As the title is so voluminous and exhaustive, it is unnecessary to reproduce any of the text, and the three following illustrations tell their own story very well.

Good News for

ENGLAND

BEING

A strange and remarkable *ACCOUNT* how a stranger in bright Raiment appeared to one Farmer Edwards near Lancaster, on the 12th of last Month, at night; containing the discourse that past between the said Farmer and the Stranger, who foretold what a wonderful Year of Plenty this will be, and how wheat will be sold for four shillings a bushel, and barley for two shillings this Year; all which was confirmed to the Farmer by four wonderful signs.

PRINTED IN THE YEAR 1772.

A

DIALOGUE

BETWEEN

A Blind Man and Death

TO WHICH IS ADDED

A HEAVENLY DISCOURSE BETWEEN
A DIVINE AND A BEGGAR.

PRINTED AND SOLD IN ALDERMARY CHURCH YARD
BOW LANE LONDON,

THE argument of this metrical dialogue is that Death comes to a blind man, who asks him his name and business, and on hearing it, tries to escape from him. Death, however, explains matters to him, and brings him into such a seraphic state of mind that he exclaims—

"Now welcome Death upon my Saviour's score
Who would not die to live for ever more.

DEATH.

Sir, I perceive you speak not without reason,
I'll leave you now and call some other season.

BLIND MAN.

Call when you please, I will await that call,
And while I can make ready for my fall ;
In the mean time my constant prayers shall be,
From sudden and from endless Death, good Lord deliver me."

THE

DEVIL upon two STICKS

OR THE

TOWN UNTIL'D

With the Comical Humours of Don Stulto and Siegnior
Jingo ; As it is acted in Pinkeman's Booth in May Fair.

LONDON, PRINTED BY J. R. NEAR FLEET STREET. 1708.

THIS is a condensed version of a portion of Le Sage's famous " Diable Boiteux," only substituting Don Stulto for Don Cleofas, and Siegnor Jingo for Asmodeus. There is nothing about Pinkeman (details of whose life would be interesting) in the book. This worthy seems first to have acted at the Theatre Royal in 1692, in the play of " Volunteers, or the Stock Jobbers," where he had the part of Taylor (six lines only). He afterwards was a useful member of Drury Lane Company, and had booths, as had also Dogget, in Bartholomew and May fairs; in fact, he notices his ill success at the latter in the epilogue to the " Bath" (Drury Lane, 1701). He there said that he had made grimaces to empty benches, while Lady Mary, the rope-dancer, had carried all before her at May fair—

" Gadzooks—what signified my face ? "

His value as an actor may be taken from a play presumably by Gildon, " Comparison between the Two Stages," printed 1702 :

" *Sullen.* But Pinkethman the flower of——

Critick. Bartholomew Fair, and the idol of the rabble ; a fellow that overdoes everything, and spoils many a part by his own stuff."

He died 1740.

ÆSOP'S FABLES.

Fable 1.

A Fox and a Sick Lion.

A Lion falling sick, all the beasts went to see him except the Fox, upon which the Lion sent for him, telling him he wanted to see him, and his presence would be acceptable. Moreover he desired the messenger to assure the Fox that for several reasons he had no occasion to be afraid of him, since the Lion loved the Fox very well, and therefore desired to see him; besides he lay so sick, he could not stir to do the Fox any harm. The Fox returned an obliging answer, desiring the messenger to acquaint the Lion, he was very desirous of his recovery, and he would pray to the Gods for it; but desired to be excused for his not coming to see him as the other beasts had done; for truly, says he, the traces of their feet frighten me, all of them going towards the palace but none coming back.

Fable 2.

The Stag and the Vine.

A Stag, who was hard pursued, ran into a Vineyard, and took shelter under a Vine; when he thought his enemies were gone, and the danger over, he fell to, browsing on the leaves; the

rustling of the boughs gave a suspicion to the huntsmen, and on search he was discovered and Shot, and as he was dying he said, How justly am I punished for offering to destroy my shade.

FABLE 3.

THE CRANE AND GEESE.

As some Geese and Cranes were feeding in a Countrymans Corn field, he heard their noise, and came presently out upon them. The Cranes seeing the man fled for it, but the Geese staid and were caught.

FABLE 4.

A Trumpeter taken Prisoner.

WHEN an army had been routed, a trumpeter was taken prisoner, and as the soldiers were going to kill him, Gentlemen, says he, why should you kill a man that hurts nobody? You shall die the rather for that, says one of the company, when like a rascal you don't fight yourself, you set other people by the ears.

FABLE 5.

The Husbandman and Stork.

A POOR innocent Stork happened to be taken in a net that was laid for geese and cranes. The Storks plea was simplicity and the love of mankind, together with the service she did in picking up venemous creatures—It is all true says the husbandman, but they that keep ill company, if they are catched with them, must suffer with them.

FABLE 6.

THE WASP AND THE PARTRIDGES.

A FLIGHT of Wasps and a covey of Partridges being hard put to it for water, went to a farmer to beg some. The partridges offered to dig his vineyard for it, and the Wasps to secure it from thieves. Pray hold your peace says the farmer, I have oxen and dogs to perform those offices already, and I am resolved to provide for them first.

FABLE 7.

A DAW AND PIGEONS.

A DAW took particular notice that the Pigeons in the Dove House were well provided for, so went and painted himself of a dove colour and fed among the Pigeons. So long as he kept silence, it passed very well, but forgetting himself he fell a

chattering—On which discovery they beat him out of the house, and on his returning to his own companions, they also rejected him.

FABLE 8.

THE FOX AND SNAKE.

A Fox and Snake meeting, she began to entertain the Fox with a long story concerning the beauties and colours of her skin. The Fox, weary of the discourse, interrupted her, and said, The beauties of the mind were better than those of a painted outside.

FABLE 9.

THE CHOUGH AND SWALLOW.

THE Chough and the Swallow fell into a warm dispute about beauty, and the Swallow insisted mightily on hers, and claimed the advantage. Nay says the Chough, you forget that your beauty decays with the Spring, whereas mine lasts all the year.

FABLE 10.

A FATHER AND HIS SONS.

AN honest man who had the misfortune to have contentious children, endeavoured to reconcile them ; and one day having them before him, he bought a bundle of sticks, then desired each of them to break it, which they strove to do, but could not. Well, said he, unbind it, and take every one a single stick, and try what you can do that way. They did so, and with ease they snapped all the sticks. The father said to them, Children, your condition is exactly like unto that bundle of sticks; for if you hold together you are safe, but if you divide you are undone.

FABLE 11.

THE FOX AND HUNTSMEN.

A Fox that had been run hard, begged of a countryman, whom he saw hard at work in a wood, to help him to a hiding place. The man directed him to a cottage, and thither he went. He was no sooner got in, but the Huntsmen were at his heels, and asked the cottager, If he did not see the Fox that way? No, said he, I saw none; but pointed with his finger to the place. Though the Huntsmen did not understand, yet the Fox saw him; and after they were gone, out steals the Fox; How now, said the countryman, have you not the manners to take leave of your host? Yes, said the Fox, if you had been as honest with your fingers, as with your tongue, I should not have gone without bidding you farewell.

Fable 12.

The Fox and Bramble.

A Fox being closely pursued, took to a hedge, the bushes gave way and in catching hold of a Bramble to break his fall, he laid himself down, and fell to licking his paws, making great complaint against the Bramble. Good words, Reynard, said the Bramble, you should never expect any kindness from an enemy.

A CHOICE

COLLECTION

OF

COOKERY RECEIPTS

New Castle: Printed in this present year.

THIS is really a useful book of recipes, although some of them are scarcely in use now. A few examples may be acceptable.

" To Broil Pidgeons whole.

Cut off the Wings and Neck close, leave the Skin at the Neck to tie close, then having some grated Bread, two Pidgeons Livers, one Anchovy, a Quarter of a Pound of Butter, half a Nutmeg grated, a little Pepper and Salt, a very little Thyme and Sweet Marjoram shred; mix all together, put a piece as big as a Walnut into each Pidgeon, sew up their Rumps and Necks, strew a little Pepper Salt and Nutmeg on the Out side, broil them on a very slow Charcoal Fire on the Hearth; baste and turn them very often. Sauce is melted Butter; or rich Gravy, if you like it higher tasted.

A pretty Sauce for Woodcocks or any wild Fowl.

Take a Quarter of a Pint of Claret, and as much Water, some grated Bread, two or three heads of Rocumbile, or a Shallot, a little whole Pepper, Mace, sliced Nutmeg, and Salt; Let this stew very well over the Fire, then beat it up with butter, and pour it under the Wild Fowl, which being under roasted, will afford Gravy to mix with this Sauce.

A whipt Sillibub extraordinary.

Take a Quart of Cream and boil it, let it stand till it is cold; then take a Pint of White Wine, pare a Lemon thin, and steep the peel in the Wine two Hours before you use it; to this add the Juice of a Lemon, and as much Sugar as will make it very sweet: Put all this together into a Bason, and whisk it all one way till it is pretty thick. Fill your Glasses, and keep it a Day before you use it; it will keep three or four Days. Let your Cream be full Measure, and your Wine rather less. If you like it perfumed, put in a Grain or two of Amber-grease.

Egg Minced Pies.

Take six Eggs, boil them very hard, and shred them small; shred double the Quantity of good Suet very fine; put Currants neatly wash'd and pick'd, one Pound or more, if your Eggs were large; the Peel of one Lemon very fine shred, half the juice, and five or six Spoonfuls of Sack, Mace, Nutmeg, Sugar, and a little Salt; and candied Citron or Orange peel, if you would have them rich."

There are recipes for making " Raisin Elder wine; Sage wine, *very good ;* Raspberry wine, *very good ;* Cowslip or Mari-gold, Gooseberry and Elder-flower wines"; besides strong Mead and Cinnamon Water, as well as a curious compound—

" Birch Wine, as made in Sussex.

Take the Sap of Birch fresh drawn, boil it as long as any Scum arises; to every Gallon of Liquor put two Pounds of good Sugar; boil it Half an Hour, and scum it very clean; when 'tis almost cold, set it with a little Yeast spread on a Toast; let it stand five or six days in an open Vessel, stirring it often : then take such a Cask as the Liquor will be sure to fill, and fire a large Match dipt in Brimstone, and put it into the Cask, and stop in the Smoak till the Match is extinguished, always keeping it shook ; then shake out the Ashes, and, as quick as possible, pour in a Pint of Sack or Rhenish wine, which Taste you like best, for the Liquor retains it; rainge the Cask well with this, and pour it out ; pour in your Wine, and stop it close for Six Months, then, if it is perfectly fine, you may boil it."

The Pleasant History of *TAFFY'S* Progress to London; with the *WELSHMAN'S* Catechism.

Behold in *WHEEL BARROW* I come to Town
With Wife and Child to pull the Taffies down
For sweet *St. DAVID* shall not be Abus'd
And by the Rabble yearly thus Misus'd

LONDON PRINTED FOR F. THORN NEAR FLEET STREET.

THIS octavo is principally taken up with "Taffy's Catechism," which is in a kind of Welsh *patois*, and is not very interesting. The frontispiece is explained as under.

"TAFFY'S PROGRESS TO LONDON."

"The much renowned Taffy William Morgan having receiv'd a Letter sent by word of Mouth from London, which gave him an Account how Despiseable the poor Welshmen alias Britains were made in England on Saint Tafy's day, by the Rabbles hanging out of a Bundle of Rags in representation of a Welshman mounted on a red Herring with a Leek in his Hat, truly poor Morgan's Blood was up, he Fretted and Fum'd till he Foam'd at Mouth agen, and being exasperated as much as the French King was Joyful when he first heard of the great Victory obtain'd by Marshal Tallard over the Duke of Marlborough at Hochstet, he in a great Passion Swore by the Glory and Renown of all his Ancestors, famous in the Books of Rates for their being ever chargeable to the Parish, that he wou'd be Reveng'd on those that thus presum'd to affront Goatlandshire, and in order thereto he prepar'd for his Journey, taking Coach in a Wheel Barrow, Drove along by his Wife, who with a Child at her Back went Barefooted all the way, and by Taffy were compell'd to take this tedious Journey that they might be Witnesses to his Prowess and Valour; in case it was questioned by any after his return to Wales; so accordingly poor William Morgan ap Renald et Cetera, for his Name would take an hour to tell it at length, set out for his great Adventures about One in the Morning, it being the 33th of January last in the year 1890 after the Welsh Account, making it Six days before he Arriv'd in the abovesaid Pomp to Leominster, where he and his Wife and Children were charitably entertain'd in a Barn ; the next Day he came to Worcester, where begging Charity to bear their Charges forwards, poor Taffy and his Wife were Whipt out of Town ; but however this harsh Usage daunted not his Heart, which all Wales knew for certain to be bigger than a Pea, for resolv'd he was to be reveng'd still on those that Affronted his Countrey, and by Cruising all the way he

came, he at length reacht London, just the Eve before the
Welshmen's great Festival of Saint David, which is Solemnis'd
with so much Devotion, as to get every Welshman Drunk by
Night, now being Arriv'd in this great City, he fortunately lit
upon some of his Acquaintance who in Commiseration of his
and his Wifes great Poverty made him pretty Boosie, and
being Pot valiant he fell like Fury to breaking of Windows
where a Taffy was hung out, but being first well Beaten by
the Mob, he was then sent to Bridewell for an idle drunken
Vagabond, and being well Flaug'd and put to hard Labour for
a while, he and his tatter'd Family were pass'd down to their
Countrey, to his great Grief in that he could not Vindicate
Saint Taffy; and Swearing hur would never see England again."

The Whole Life

Character and Conversation
of that Foolish Creature called
GRANNY

Being a true Account of one Mr. Wilson an Eminent Lawyer of the Temple, who above all things, doated to Distraction on this Simple Creature ; and how he had two children by her, and the means he us'd to decoy her, and keep the thing secret.

Likewise That by his last Will and Testament which you may find in Doctors Commons, he has left her six hundred pounds in ready Money, five hundred pounds a Year in Land, for her and her Heirs for ever, she being at this time, with Child by him.

And lastly you have a Copy of Verses made on Granny's good Fortune.

Licensed according to Order.

Printed by A. Hinde in Fleet Street 1711.

A

YORK DIALOGUE

BETWEEN

𝕹𝖊𝖉 𝖆𝖓𝖉 𝕳𝖆𝖗𝖗𝖞

OR

*Ned giving Harry an Account of his Courtship
and Marriage State*

TO WHICH IS ADDED—

TWO EXCELLENT NEW SONGS.

A VERY mild description of the particularly uninteresting courtship and marriage of a small tradesman and a chambermaid, with the details of the subsequent hen-pecking the husband underwent, and of his wife's taste for gossiping, ending up with advice from Ned, and a determination of Harry's never to marry a chambermaid.

THE FRENCH KING'S WEDDING

OR THE

ROYAL FROLICK

Being a Pleasant Account

Of the Amorous Intrigues, Comical Courtship, Catterwauling and Surprizing Marriage Ceremonies of Lewis the XIVth with Madam Maintenon, His late Hackney of State.

With a List of the Names of those that threw the Stocking on the Wedding Night and Madam Maintenon's Speech to the King.

As also, a Comical Wedding Song Sung to his Majesty, by the famous Monsieur La Grice to the Tune of The Dame of Honour.

LONDON
PRINTED FOR J. SMITH NEAR FLEET STREET 1708.

APPENDIX.

List of Chap-Books published in Aldermary and Bow Churchyards.

Academy of Courtship.

Arimathea, The History of that Holy Disciple Joseph of.

Argalus and Parthenia, The History of, being a Choice Flower gathered out of Sir Phillip Sidney's Rare Garden.

Art of Courtship.

Armstrong, History of Johnny (of Westmoreland).

Bacon, History of the Learned Friar.

Barleycorn, The Arraigning and Indicting of Sir John.

Barnwell, The Tragical History of George.

Bateman's Tragedy.

Bellianis, Don, of Greece, The History of.

Bethnal Green, The History of the Blind Beggar of.

Bevis, Sir, of Southampton, The History of the Life and Death of that most Noble Knight.

Bloody Tragedy, The, or a Dreadful Warning to Disobedient Children.

Bowman, Life and Death of Christian.

Bunch : Mother B.'s Closet newly broke open.

Bunch : The History of Mother B. of the West (Part II.).

Cabinet, The Golden.

Cambridge Jests, being Wit's Recreation.

Canterbury Tales, by J. Chaucer, Junr.

Card Fortune-Book.

Champions, The History of the Seven (Parts I. and II.).

Charles XII., The History of the Remarkable Life of the Brave and Renowned.

Chevy Chase, The Famous and Memorable History of.

Children in the Wood, The History of.

Coachman and Footman's Catechism, The.

Countries, A Brief Character of the Low.

Courtier : The History of the Frolicksome C. and the Jovial Tinker.

Crusoe, The Life of Robinson.

Cupboard Door opened, The, or Joyful News for Apprentices and Servant-Maids.

Cupid's Decoy, The Lover's Magazine, or.

Delights for Young Men and Maids.

Dialogue, A, between a Blind Man and Death.

Dialogue, A Choice and Diverting, between Hughson the Cobler and Margery his Wife.

Dialogue between John and Loving Kate (Parts I. and II.).

Dialogue, A New and Diverting, between a Shoemaker and his Wife.

Divine Songs.

Dorastus and Faunia.

Drake, Voyages and Travels of that Renowned Captain Sir Francis.

Dreams and Moles, with their Interpretation and Signification.

Drunkard's Legacy, The.

Edward the Black Prince, The History of.

Egyptian Fortune-Teller's Legacy, The Old.

Elizabeth, History of Queen, and her Great Favourite the Earl of Essex (Parts I. and II.).

England, Antient History of, from the Invasion of Julius Cæsar to the Roman Conquest.

England, The History of, from the Norman Conquest to the Union of the Houses of York and Lancaster.

England, The Present State of; to which is added an Account of the New Style.

Erra Pater.

Fairy Stories (Blue Bird and Florinda and the King of the Peacocks).

Faustus, History of Dr. John.

Figure of Seven, The.

Flanders, Fortunes and Misfortunes of Moll.

Fortunatus, History of.

Fortune-Book, Partridge and Flamsted's New and Well-experienced.

Fortune-Teller, The High German.

Franks, Birth, Life, and Death of John.

Friar and Boy, The (Parts I. and II.).

George, The Life and Death of Saint.

Ghost, The Portsmouth.

Gotham, Merry Tales, or the Wise Men of.

Grissel, History of the Marquis of Salus and Patient.

Gulliver, The Travels and Adventures of Captain Lemuel.

Guy, Earl of Warwick, History of.

Hector, Prince of Troy, History of.

Hercules of Greece, History of the Life and Glorious Actions of the Mighty.
Hero and Leander, Famous History of.
Hero's Garland, The.
Hickathrift, History of Thomas (Parts I. and II.).
Hind, Merry Life and Mad Exploits of Captain James.
Hippolito and Dorinda, Loves of.
Hocus Pocus, or a New Book of Legerdemain.
Hood, A True Tale of Robin.
Horner, History of Jack.
Jack and the Giants, History of (Parts I. and II.).
Jack of Newbury, History of.
Jew, The Wandering, or the Shoemaker of Jerusalem.
Joak upon Joaks.
Joseph and his Brethren, History of.
Kings, History of Four, their Queens and Daughters.
Lady, The Whimsical.
Laurence, Lazy, The History of.
Legerdemain, The Whole Art of.
Long Meg of Westminster, Whole Life and Death of.
Long, History of Tom, the Carrier.
Maiden's Prize, The, or Bachelor's Puzzle.
Mandeville, The Foreign Travels of Sir John.
Martyr, History of the Royal, King Charles the First.
Matrimony, The Whole Pleasures of.
Merryman, Doctor, or Nothing but Mirth.
Montellion, The History of.
Mournful Tragedy, The.
Nimble and Quick.
Nixon's Cheshire Prophecy.
Parismus, Prince of Bohemia, The History of.
Poets' Jests, or Mirth in Abundance.
Prentice, The Famous History of the Valiant London.
Puss in Boots.
Rarities of Richmond.
Reading, Directions for, with Elegance and Propriety.
Reading, History of Thomas of.
Reynard the Fox, History of.
Rich Man's Warning-Piece, The, or the Oppressed Infants in Glory.
Rome, The Famous History of the Seven Wise Masters of.
Rome, The Famous and Renowned History of the Seven Wise Mistresses of.
Rosamond, Life and Death of Fair.
Shipton, History of Mother.
Shoemaker's Glory, The, or the Princely History of the Gentle Craft.
Shore, Life and Death of Mrs. Jane.

Simple Simon's Misfortunes.

Sleeping Beauty in the Wood.

Swalpo, Merry Frolics, or the Comical Cheats of.

Tom Thumb, The Famous History of (Parts I., II., and III.).

Tomb Thumb, The Mad Pranks of (Parts I., II., and III.).

Unfortunate Son, The, or a Kind Wife is worth Gold.

Valentine and Orson, History of.

Wanton Tom, or the Merry History of Tom Stitch the Taylor (Parts I. and II.).

Wat Tyler and Jack Straw, History of.

Welsh Traveller, The, or the Unfortunate Welshman.

West Country Garland, The New.

Whetstone for Dull Wits.

Whittington, History of Sir Richard.

Wit, a Groat's worth for a Penny, or the Interpretation of Dreams.

Witch of the Woodlands, or the Cobler's New Translation.

Witches, The Famous History of the Lancashire.

World turned Upside Down, The.